AND WEST IS WEST

AND WEST IS WEST

----

a novel by

RON CHILDRESS

Algonquin Books of Chapel Hill   2015

Published by
Algonquin Books of Chapel Hill
Post Office Box 2225
Chapel Hill, North Carolina 27515-2225

a division of
Workman Publishing
225 Varick Street
New York, New York 10014

Printed in the United States of America.
Published simultaneously in Canada by Thomas Allen & Son Limited.
Design by April Leidig.

This is a work of fiction. While, as in all fiction, the literary perceptions and
insights are based on experience, all names, characters, places, and incidents
either are products of the author's imagination or are used fictitiously.

Library of Congress Cataloging-In-Publication Data
Childress, Ron, [date]
And West is West : a novel / by Ron Childress. — First edition.
pages cm
ISBN 978-1-61620-523-2
1. Terrorism—Prevention—Fiction. 2. Special operations (Military science)—
United States—Fiction. 3. Drone aircraft—Fiction. I. Title.
PS3603.H5565A64 2015
813'.6—dc23   2015015872

10 9 8 7 6 5 4 3 2 1
First Edition

for Sondra

East is East, and West is West, and never the two shall meet.

—Rudyard Kipling

AND WEST IS WEST

PROLOGUE

July 2012
Nevada, Somalia, Florida

They are twined, all but, she and Voigt. He is leaning over her shoulder, his forearm atop her chairback. His lips are so close to her ear that each breath he exhales roars like a gale. This is all she hears inside the dim trailer. The glowing screens before her keep them immobile. They are frozen except for the motion of her hand as she centers the camera. The moment is near. This time he is going to let *her* do it.

"Aldridge. Are you ready for your first?"

"Yes, sir," Jessica tells Colonel Voigt. They are inches apart. But Sergeant Jessica Aldridge is also eight thousand miles away, ten thousand feet in the air, and she feels so near to the figures on the ground below her that she might reach down and pick them up like dolls.

They are five, outlined by their jalabiyas and the scarves that circle the glow of their faces. Jessica's squadron has been tracking them, a band of brothers, for the past two weeks as they acquired the rudiments of a device they are constructing in a desert hut miles from the nearest village and forty from Mogadishu. Tonight they must imagine themselves protected by a moonless darkness that even a hawk's eyes could not penetrate. Yet they are visible to Jessica. Irradiated by their own heat, each man appears to her as a distinct if ghostly blur.

A buzz returns Jessica to the trailer. Her eyes flick toward the noise, talk from Voigt's earpiece.

"That's it. We have a confirm. Go the angel," her commander says, releasing her to arm the "angel," their unit's euphemism for a missile.

As Jessica watches from the desert sky, the men cluster below her. Her partner, Airman Bob Sanders, at his parallel station, locks the men's coordinates. A touch of Jessica's hand will give them twenty seconds to live. They are beyond mercy.

"Fire at will, Sergeant," Voigt, standing behind Jessica, says. And then he waits for her to show him what she, the first enlisted airman to pilot a drone strike, will do.

But Jessica takes Voigt's "at will" seriously as *her* will and she hesitates. She senses something in the positioning of the men. That they are all, for once, traditionally dressed signifies the impending culmination of their mission. But that they have not dispersed to various tasks in or around the hut, that they stand near to each other at some informal attention—as if huddling themselves to be most effectively blasted to bits—this gives Jessica pause. Is their mission to be martyrs to anti-American propaganda?

"They're waiting, Colonel," Jessica says.

"Right," Voigt replies. "It's like they're waiting for *someone*."

And so in the trailer they also wait . . . hovering another half hour until a three-car train of SUVs stops alongside the battered pickup that had carried their initial targets to the hut.

"It's Yarisi," Voigt says. Through his earpiece he's been receiving and relaying information to which Jessica is not privy. But she knows Jabir al-Yarisi. He is a person of interest, a Yemeni suspected of bombing the British embassy in Addis Ababa. Lately he is believed to be recruiting rebels in Somalia, where Jessica's drone is. "This is the big time, Aldridge," Voigt says. "You up for this?"

"I am one hundred percent up for this, sir," Jessica answers.

"Good. We'll wait for a visual ID. Yarisi'll be the tall one."

Men with guns exit the front and rear SUVs. After searching in and around the hut they lead the men in jalabiyas to the central vehicle. Airman Sanders relocks the coordinates. A minute passes.

"Yarisi's not dismounting," Voigt says, his Carolina accent resonant. He leans closer to the screens and the glow of the monitors paints his crew cut blue. "Okay. We have a passive ID on the caravan," he says quietly. "Take the shot."

Just as his command comes, a side door opens in the target SUV. Jessica's trigger hand lets two seconds pass and she sees someone hop out of the vehicle, a slight figure who is followed by her twin. Their heat outlines show them to be dressed in burkas. Jessica can even determine that the pair are also wearing niqabs, leaving only a slit for the eyes. Al-Yarisi is known to travel with his wives, some being girls not of high school age.

"They're kids!" Jessica hears herself say.

"Screw my eyes," Voigt responds, and then he presses his earpiece against a shout even Jessica can make out. "Fire," Voigt says, almost whispering. "That's the goddamn order out of Langley."

Jessica's stomach turns. She feels a "But, sir!" rising to her lips.

"Fire," Voigt repeats.

Jessica's hand squeezes the launch switch and the screen hiccoughs as the angel takes wing. In the moment before the camera refocuses she imagines one of the young men in jalabiyas looking up at a shooting star that cuts through the night sky at a strange angle. He will shout a warning in the twenty seconds that remain. Everyone will scatter. Even the invisible man in the SUV will dive out and roll to safety. In her fantasy all this occurs.

But in life it does not.

After a dozen seconds Voigt quietly begins to count down from eight, as if the three of them in the trailer are all supposed to shout "Surprise!" at zero. When Voigt reaches "one," the silence is anticlimactic. The SUVs, the armed men, the boys in jalabiyas, and the two figures in burkas are engulfed by a soft, impenetrable halo. The heat of the explosion has blinded the drone's thermal eye. Not until dawn will anyone completely see what Jessica has done. She never will. Strike analysis is above her security classification.

Dear Jessica,

Your last letter puts me beside you at your command station. And even up with you in the desert night. But where do I start about all you have written except to say that ANGEL is a strange name for a missile.

Do you remember when I used to call you Angel? You might. You were six the last time your mother and I tried to reconcile. From your letters I do not think you have changed much. You could not stand to see me squash an ant. So about you wishing that those men would have seen your angel. Your shooting star. I say that was no misguided dream. It was only your natural impulse not to harm other living creatures. You must keep those feelings alive.

Beyond that I cannot judge what you have done. You accuse yourself of taking two innocent lives. But I can only tell you to think of the people you have stopped who would murder a hundred innocents for their cause. Above all you must remember it is not you alone who fires those angels. It is all of us. This whole country. But we are hiding behind you. You take the heat and we do not get burned. There is plenty of guilt to go around so dont take it all on yourself.

And do not worry about me either. I am heartened by the truth that though I have done many bad things in my life they are not the crime that convicted me. I am no first degree murderer so my appeal and some other possibilities are progressing. In the meantime I read and exercise and work. The lye from my job in the laundry has burned off my cuticles but soon I hope to be shelving books in the library. In the meantime the days here in Seminole City tick by quicker than the nights. And the nights come too fast. Already I see I have just a minute before lights out to finish this letter.

Bless you for coming back into my life. And thank you for the cigarette cash as you call it. But I hope this old habit of mine is not yours as well. My one wish is for you to travel a long and happy road.

Your loving father,
Don

PART ONE

FAMILY

September 2011–August 2012

CHAPTER 1

New York City

"Yes!" Zoe says.

It is a minute into the new year and a significant event of Ethan Winter's adulthood has just occurred. Spontaneously he has asked his girlfriend to move in with him. Immediately he begins to register misgivings.

How much does his twelfth-floor, glass-walled apartment and a nearby subway line convenient to the UN, where Zoe is applying for a postgrad internship, have to do with her *yes*? Is he just her steppingstone into adult city life, another course for her to take and pass before she moves on?

He analyzes the raw data—her appearance against his. Height-wise they are compatible. Zoe is five-ten to his six-one. But from here they diverge. Zoe has large emerald eyes, thick blonde hair that fans girlishly over her shoulders, a fine nose with a tiny aristocratic bump that gives her distinction. She is not thin enough to be a model but would be after a week of lettuce dinners. And she has excellent posture—unlike Ethan's. He could add another inch to his stature if he did not hunch. But he cannot break the habit even though posture is more easily correctible than his other shortcomings. His head he believes is too small for his height, his eyes too close set. His nose he fears resembles an unshelled peanut. And adolescent acne has left his complexion the texture of a Persian melon. Yet, at other times, from certain angles in a certain light, and usually when he is in the company of Zoe, who says he looks like a man should, he feels "almost handsome"—just like the Peter O'Toole character said he did in the sixties comedy he and Zoe watched the other night.

Of course there is more to attractiveness than appearance, and Ethan works for UIB, United Imperial Bank, a Wall Street behemoth. This is impressive. However, Ethan's job parsing numbers, aside from the paycheck, is hardly charismatic. And his social network of financially fixated co-workers with whom he shares Friday beers is no plus either. Ethan leads a downtown life, but not the cool one he had dreamed of as a teenager in New Jersey. Basically he works all the time. This leaves him with one asset by which to attract a woman as captivating as Zoe—the stuff he owns. Most notably, his corner-unit condo on the Hudson.

But Ethan does have another selling point: his interest in culture, art in particular. Though they are not the Picassos and Basquiats that the hedge fund billionaires collect, canvases fill his minimally furnished apartment. They make it and his life seem fuller than they are.

"That's great," Ethan finally replies to Zoe's "Yes! Yes I'll move in with you." She kisses him again. Then, with her head resting on his shoulder, they return their gazes to the starbursts over the harbor—the New Year's fireworks, which are conveniently visible from his living room couch. Now, his and Zoe's living room couch.

"HERE SHE IS," Alex had said.

It was a sunny September weekend and many young women crowded the city campus, but Ethan instantly knew whom Alex meant—the young woman crossing against the signal at Houston and Mercer, head down, hands at half mast, thumbs tapping a device. She was oblivious to the cab bearing down on the green light, and Ethan's heart raced at her peril. But it was too late to shout a warning. Too late to save her.

With the light beckoning, the cab neither beeped nor swerved. Its tires though, at the last millisecond, bit pavement, and Zoe Leston, in high-heeled clogs, clomped safely past. Noticing the commotion she'd caused, she lifted her sunglasses at the turbaned cabbie and flashed a goofy smile that had melted Ethan's heart.

Their introductions were brief. Alex and Zoe were going to the Angelika for a film. Zoe invited Ethan along.

"It's supposed to be really freaky," she said. "Or is that the name of it?"

"It's *Freaks*," said Alex. "A classic. Double billed with *Svengali*."

"Uh," Ethan hesitated before pointing his eyes farther downtown. "I need to catch up at the office."

"You work Sundays?" Zoe said. "*That* sucks."

"Ethan's always working." Alex said. "And it's always on something top secret. You'd think he was CIA planning a hit on the next Osama bin Laden. But he just crunches data for one of those too-big-to-fail banks. What do you call yourselves? Quacks?"

"Quants," Ethan replied, not to Alex but to Zoe. "Maybe next time," he added dismally.

The pair, holding hands, left Ethan, who crossed the street into a glare reflected from the windows above a Jamba Juice. He was melting inside, hollowing out, going empty. He was already desperate to see Zoe again.

The next day, Alex, Ethan's friend since college and seven years on still the struggling painter, started describing his evening with Zoe. Ethan told him to shut it, not jokily but with a fury he had never before felt toward Alex.

Alex had smiled. "Is that jealousy?"

Ethan felt his left eye twitch—the same tic his mother displayed when she was seriously irritated.

"That's beautiful, man. Pure unadulterated postadolescent desire. I was beginning to take you for a cyborg lately. How about I get you two together? Zoe's more your type anyway. Pure in her own corrupt way. She's just finishing a poli-sci degree. What a match you two'd make. The banker and the politician. Your kids'll definitely grow up to be our overlords."

"Right," Ethan said, feigning indifference to this imagined scenario.

"So, want to go for it?"

Alex was always trying to fix Ethan up, but he had never gone so far as to set him up with someone he was currently dating. "Sure," said Ethan offhandedly because Alex must have been joking. His heart, though, surged with hope.

"Done. Now check this, bro."

They were standing in Alex's tiny Rivington Street studio, in front of a paint-stained sheet that hid something propped on an easel.

"Voilà!" said Alex as he uncovered the canvas—a tic-tac-toe of black lines and mysterious scribbled ciphers, a painting of the kind that Ethan was likely to wander into and get lost in. If Alex was pandering to his predilection for art that resembled algorithms, Ethan did not care. He was high on his dreams of a future with Zoe and he took out his checkbook.

THREE MONTHS AND thirty-two sleepovers with Zoe later, Zoe moves in. Though both of them are busy—Zoe finishing her degree, Ethan programming for his bank—the winter passes happily for him. There in his bed every night is someone warm, someone he can sense beside him in the dark even when he is too exhausted to make love, which is more often than not.

And then spring break arrives and Zoe has more time.

"We need to go out more," she says one morning, tousled in bed, while Ethan is dressing for work.

"Don't worry, things will slow down at the bank in summer."

"The summer," she says. "That's months."

"I know. But I've been under a lot of pressure lately."

And then, surprisingly for Ethan, it is summer and Independence Day arrives. The evening is not too humid and he and Zoe are seated at a sidewalk table in Little Italy. Later they intend to wander back to Ethan's condo and from the building's roof deck watch the fireworks—fireworks that, Ethan imagines, might become a tradition for them.

Alex has met them at the restaurant with his latest girlfriend, blackbanged Lola, a performance artist who claims to have studied magic.

"Observe," Lola says and holds her finger, steadily and impassively, over the candle on their table.

They all watch as Lola's finger turns black. Excruciating seconds pass and when the smell of singeing flesh rises, Alex grabs away Lola's hand.

"Excuse us," says Alex and escorts Lola toward the bathroom.

Ethan admires Alex's coolness in such situations, even if his friend's confidence is founded on his movie-star looks.

"Wow!" says Zoe.

Ethan shakes his head. "There're some crazies out there. Makes me glad I'm no longer dating."

Zoe gives Ethan a blank look. Is it because they never fight? Because they share cooperatively in the housework? Because they stay out of the other's way when work calls? Because they have comfortable sex two or three times a week? Is Zoe's empty stare, in other words, accusing Ethan of making her one-half of a dull couple?

He hopes not. They have been living together a bright six months in Ethan's glass-walled Battery Park condo and lately he has been imagining his sun-swept days with her repeating endlessly into the future.

Their mornings usually begin with a cup of Nespresso near the corner window—through which can be seen growing the upper skeleton of the Freedom Tower, only a few blocks away. Being slightly myopic, Ethan generally limits his focus to the steam rising from his cup. The blinkering enables him to speak about their life together in a way he cannot when he looks at her lovely face—a face that he still cannot believe rests next to his every night.

This morning, after mentioning that Alex wanted to introduce them to his newest "friend," Ethan tried to turn the conversation back to themselves. Looking into his latte he'd said: "I've calculated the tower's solar transit. When the top floors go up we're going to lose thirty minutes of afternoon sun. But only in January and February." When Ethan looked up at Zoe she *was* looking at the tower, but her gaze was empty. It was as if she had not understood what he was implying—that they would still be a couple at the building's completion, that by then, in a year or two, he would be ready to suggest a permanent commitment. *Marriage.* Perhaps even *children.*

Alex and Lola return to the sidewalk table where Ethan and Zoe have been silently waiting. Lola's finger, swaddled in beige gauze except for the tip, resembles a miniature papoose.

"The cook shared his first-aid kit," Alex says.

"So, you're okay?" Zoe asks Lola.

"It's all magic," Lola says. "Nothing can hurt you if you don't let it."

"Uh-huh," says Zoe.

"The manager took one look at Lola's finger and comped our meal," Alex says. "*That's* magic."

"Ha-ha," says Lola and goes petulantly silent. With her uninjured hand she fiddles with an odd little spike pushed through the top of her left ear.

Alex turns his attention to Ethan. "So, given any thought to the loft?"

"What loft?" Zoe asks.

"A floor in an old paint warehouse off Canal," says Alex.

"Right. I'll just go write a check," Ethan says sarcastically, even though he could do exactly that.

"Sell the condo," Alex says. "River Terrace is so close to New Jersey you might as well still be living with your parents." This is Alex's standard joke about Ethan's apartment, usually made when he visits to hang a new painting of his that Ethan has bought. "Plus," he adds wryly, "you're running out of wall space there." Alex turns to Zoe. "If Ethan puts up the money I can do the renovation. Build out a studio for myself and an apartment for Ethan. He'll have twice the square footage."

"That would be *so* great," Zoe says. "Ethan, why haven't you told me about this?"

Ethan would like to say to Zoe, "Because Alex wants to build a bachelor pad and I'm no longer single." Instead, he says, "The neighborhood's still pretty rough."

Alex comes back at him. "It'll turn. Then your investment triples." He winks at Zoe. "That's how you talk to bankers."

"Fine," Ethan says, employing his voice of reason—his Gregory Peck cadence. "But in the meantime we'll have to live there. And I just don't think it's safe." His voice, which is higher than Gregory's, makes the sentiment sound more wimpy than wise.

"Jesus, man, for once in your life take a chance," Alex says. "Be a real New Yorker."

"It does sound cool," Zoe says.

Now even Lola joins in. She crinkles her face and looks at Ethan like the decision is a no-brainer. "If I had the loot I would jump on that like it was Chris Hemsworth."

Ethan's three dinner companions aim their eyes at him as if their gathering has become an intervention.

Ethan is getting angry. "You saw those needles in the alley. There're probably addicts squatting in the building," he tells Alex.

"Who's going to mess with you? You're nearly six-three when you stand up straight."

"Okay. I'd be worried about Zoe then."

Now something goes wrong. Both Alex and Zoe look away as if conspiratorially embarrassed.

Lola breaks the silence. "I've lived in some pretty crappy hoods. You just have to watch your back."

Ignoring Lola, Ethan looks from Alex to Zoe. "What? What is it?"

"Ethan," Zoe says quietly. "I've told you that I've been looking for work in Washington."

Ethan tries to swallow. His mouth is dry. "Oh?"

"Come *on*!" she says, annoyed that his out-of-itness might be real.

Actually, it is. Lately Ethan has become ultrafocused on his algorithms. Certain new possibilities are emerging. He has been preoccupied. He allows that Zoe must have mentioned her job search—how could she not have since her two-month UNIFEM internship is almost over. This is logical. Ethan clenches his hand. His face turns to stone.

"There's the *mask*," Zoe says—her word for Ethan's brooding expression, which he displays regularly enough for her to have named it. "Now I've gotten your dandruff up," she adds sympathetically. She puts a forgiving hand on his.

"Dander," Ethan corrects, noticing some flecks on his sleeve that most likely come from his scalp. He had put on a black shirt for tonight because he wanted to feel cool. Now all he feels is humiliation.

THE WEEK FOLLOWING the Fourth of July Ethan puts in eighteen-hour days working on his own version of fireworks—a modification to UIB's currency trading algorithm, which currently monitors volatility in relation to news reports of terrorist activity. His new concept focuses on antiterrorist activity and has been okayed by his manager. This is what makes him useful to UIB: his combination of technical skill and real-world imagination, his ability to see connections that neither the pure programmer nor the pure trader is likely to see. He binges on coffee and Provigil to keep alert.

By the start of his second week on his project Ethan has added Ritalin to his brain cocktail in order to stay in the zone—that place where code pours from the fingertips in impulses directly from the brainstem with no detours up to the cerebral cortex or higher consciousness. Those parts of his frontal lobe have begun to suspect Zoe of more than a job search, for whenever he does make it back to River Terrace to crash, he more often than not finds notes and not her.

Out of town till Thursday on the great job hunt. Pizza in fridge. Don't eat cold. Microwave! read the first of these, left on the kitchen counter.

The latest: *Making a quick day trip. Don't wait up if you're home.*

He resists texting her for details because he knows how to play the game of hurt silence. Also he has a fantasy that by ignoring her absences he can stop them. But his suspicions about what she is really up to are growing. They have not had sex since Alex broke up with Lola—which happened the day after Lola torched her finger and then set his bed on fire while smoking. Whenever Ethan considers this time sequence his apartment begins to sway under him as though a hurricane is rocking the building.

His suspicion gives him license to go through Zoe's handbag whenever she is home. Late at night after she has gone to sleep, all Ethan finds are receipts for the Dragon Deluxe Chinatown bus to Washington. Then, a week later, a ticket stub for the Acela appears and he realizes what is happening. She must have a lover, a politician she met at the UN, and he has upgraded her travel arrangements to DC. Ethan imagines that he can outwait this stranger's play for Zoe. He is probably married anyway. Zoe will quickly see her mistake. At least it doesn't look like Alex is her lover.

It is three o'clock in the morning. Zoe is asleep in bed. Ethan is sitting with Zoe's purse in the living room. He swallows a Ritalin and opens his laptop to write code.

"HAVE YOU BEEN up all night?" Zoe asks. Already dressed for work, she locates her hobo bag and energetically rummages among the tissues, gum wrappers, and lip balm, all the contents that Ethan had carefully put back in their places. "Crap. Where'd it go?"

Innocently Ethan dips his nose into his espresso cup and averts his eyes. What he blurrily perceives—through the corner window, around a curvilinear glass monolith and over the canyon of West Street—is his fragment of the Freedom Tower, which is beginning to oppress. Passing by it lately during his morning commute, he looks up and the tower becomes, with its twitching rooftop cranes, a monstrous mechanism with a skeletal head topped by antennae—an autobot from the Transformers movies ready to wreak havoc on lower Manhattan and then the world.

He worries that the psychostimulants are overfertilizing his imagination.

"Have you seen my Amtrak receipt?" Zoe asks.

"What receipt?" he replies.

"My train ticket. I need it for reimbursement. A hundred seventy bucks."

Ethan puts a hand in his pocket and touches the ticket stub.

"Oh, well," she says, giving up. "Good thing I'll be cashing a real paycheck soon."

"A what?" Ethan says.

Zoe shrugs. "I didn't want to tell you until it was a sure thing. I got a job in Washington."

"Cool," Ethan says, though his face is locking up.

"I start next week."

"Cool," Ethan repeats through his teeth.

Zoe gives him a look, the one that always melts him—it is both a frown and a smile. "Ethan, you know that being with you has meant a lot to me."

"Sure," Ethan says. Unable to breathe he manages to keep looking at Zoe's lovely face. He may as well be looking up at the undercarriage of a subway car that is running him over.

"*Oh*, Ethan," Zoe says. "For a second I thought you *were* okay with it."

"I am okay with it," Ethan lies.

"God, I have such a hard time reading you."

After Zoe finishes readying herself for her penultimate day at the UN, she interrupts Ethan at his laptop. He is tracing an error in the code he wrote earlier that morning, a bug in a loop statement that is causing his program to repeat endlessly. His brain is stuck in a similar pattern, telling him over and over that he has lost Zoe forever, forever, forever.

"Hey," Zoe says. "Can I ask a huge favor?"

"Sure," Ethan says, staring at the laptop screen.

"My parents are back home. They're having a dinner tomorrow night and want to meet you."

Dr. and Mrs. Leston, now retired, have been on back-to-back world cruises, tours of the Northern and Southern Hemispheres that coincided with Ethan's life with Zoe.

What's the point? Ethan wants to say. *Aren't you moving to Washington? Aren't we done?* "Sure," he says, managing not to stutter. He keeps his eyes on his coding to hold himself together.

"Thanks. You're a pal," Zoe says and leans over to hug him. He inhales her hair. "By the way, I borrowed some of your Ritalin to keep me going. Busy times," she says and is out the door.

For the rest of the day, just as he might obsess over an algorithm, Ethan fixates on Zoe. On whether they are done or *not* done. On the possibility of a long-distance relationship. On the fear that they might never have had a true relationship but only a variation on a hookup. Yet if this were the case, if they had only been live-in fuck buddies, *why* had she invited him to meet her parents?

CHAPTER 2

Upstate New York

"Dr. Leston, I presume," Ethan says nervously. Extending a hand, he tries to grin away the lame joke.

Zoe's father regards him perhaps the way he regarded the tumors he once excised for a living. After a hesitation, he takes Ethan's hand and crushes it. Like many surgeons he makes his presence known. His height, an inch over Ethan's, his crystalline eyes akin to his daughter's, and his nose, arched and bony in a long face, give him a severe authority. Zoe had been a late child so he calculates that Leston must be at least seventy, but he still possesses a thick mane. "I presume you're referring to Dr. Livingstone, a great humanitarian," Leston says before releasing Ethan's hand and walking to the other side of his den.

"Dad, don't be such an old grouch!" Zoe says. In a black dress and a string of pearls, Zoe has regressed in appearance and manner to an era when people embraced adulthood earlier, a show of maturity obviously intended for her parents.

"What's your poison, Winter?" Leston asks. He opens the liquor cabinet.

"I, uh, don't," Ethan replies feebly. Leston's steady gaze forces him to explain. "It's a long drive back to the city."

"Stop drinking before we eat and you'll be fine," Leston says dismissively.

"Just sparkling water," Ethan says, feeling like a boy drawing a line in the sand. He moves toward the fireplace, which is burning with a decorative gas flame. Zoe comes up behind him.

"Thanks for this," she whispers and nips Ethan's ear. Then she wipes from the lobe what he guesses is her lipstick.

"Sure," he says, her proximity soothing, the side of her breast pressing his arm.

"Zoe, go check up on your mother," Leston interrupts. "Make sure her dress is on right side out."

"Stop it, Daddy!" Zoe shoots back. Then she whispers to Ethan, "Hold the fort."

"Huh?" he says before grasping her words. After she's gone he freezes as though he has stumbled into a cobra's nest. Leston's den is male, heavy with dark wood and leather upholstery. The volumes on the bookcases stand tidy and matching—the complete Dickens, Wells' *History*, Gibbon's *Fall of the Roman Empire*—with most of the spines creased. There is scrimshaw on a varnished plank table that looks like a boat hatch. On the wall above the bar hang black-and-white photographs of a schooner, once the doctor's, Ethan presumes. But he does not ask.

"So, Winter, my daughter tells me you're one of the masters of the universe," Leston says.

Ethan feels almost flattered, as if they might, in retro fifties fashion, be talking man-to-man. But he doesn't want to build himself up as something he's not—not yet. "Really, I just work for—"

Leston's mouth wrinkles into a sneer. "It wasn't a compliment." He approaches, tinkling, with iced drinks in whisky glasses. "You just enable them then?"

"Them?" Ethan takes the proffered glass.

"Those banking sons-a-bitches that wrecked my portfolio, the economy, a hundred million Americans' retirement, what have you."

Ethan's bank, United Imperial Bank, had contributed its share of shaky credit default swaps and collateralized debt obligations, but all this was outside his division. Leston is blaming him for steering the *Titanic* into an iceberg when he was only manning the ship's telegraph. His work as a quant, Ethan believes, actually hedged some of the damage by providing liquidity to the markets—his algorithms increased the number of daily trades and prevented the currency market from falling, albeit fractionally, farther than it might have. But try to explain this to anyone. Ethan gulps the drink that the doctor has put into his hand and it sluices down his throat like broken glass. Some of it comes back up.

"Slow down. That's good gin. Don't waste it," Leston says.

Through his coughing Ethan responds. "I'm just . . . an analyst."

The doctor, smacking Ethan's back, almost tips him into the fireplace. "Don't be modest, man. I know what a quant is. I might have become something similar if I'd grown up on the banks of the Orinoco."

"Really," Ethan says, not quite remembering where the Orinoco is.

"Yes. I'd have been a witch doctor."

"Columbia," Ethan says, offering his college in defense.

"They teach voodoo there? That's a shame."

The conversation is less male bonding than mano a mano combat. Silently Ethan watches the fire. He takes a moment to form his words and puts his drink on the mantel. "Dr. Leston. You do know that Zoe is leaving me to work in Washington?"

"Oh?" Anticipatory, the doctor's eyes gleam with malice. He swirls his glass and studies the rattling ice.

"That means we're not engaged. Or going to get engaged."

The assertion makes Leston smile large. His teeth are so even and so white that Ethan decides they must be false. "God forbid that," the doctor says with a laugh.

Ethan swallows the insult. "And that means you don't have to worry about me. Or prove your dominance. In a matter of days I'll be out of your daughter's life and you can forget we ever met. You do know that?"

"Yes." Leston nods agreeably.

"Then why are you knocking me?"

A burst of laughter sprays Ethan and again Leston slaps his back in macho, comradely fashion. "Why? You ass, you've been sleeping with her. People like you, the advantage takers, disgust me. You take up with some bright-eyed young girl and get rid of her after you've had your fun."

Ethan feels like he's stepped through a time warp. Does he really need to explain to the doctor how relationships work these days? If anything, Zoe is more casual about what they are doing together than he. After all, *she* is the one who is leaving.

"Having a nice chat, boys?" a throaty voice calls through the double doorway separating Leston's den from the living room. "Bring yourselves on in here."

Solid but elegant, Elizabeth Leston stands as tall as her daughter and also wears black. But this is all they have in common—Elizabeth is a much softer woman: her face round not oval, her nose snub not aquiline. Around the high neck of her gown glistens a spray of diamonds. If real, they must be a better investment than her husband's stock portfolio. Being numeric, and now morally freed by Leston's verbal assault, Ethan begins to appraise the couple's possessions. Elizabeth's necklace—fifteen thousand. The renovated country farmhouse—six hundred thousand. The five-year-old Mercedes in the driveway—thirty thousand. The Inuit scrimshaw and other unseen household valuables—one hundred thousand, roughly. Leston's damaged retirement portfolio—one million, two maybe. In total Leston is worth, generously, three million. While Ethan, if he can last as a quant for another five years and make VP, hopes to earn twenty percent of that amount per annum. He steps over a leather footstool in the shape of a bull and exits the doctor's study. "Mrs. Leston," he says brightly when he reaches her.

"You've lovely eyes, Mr. Winter. So pleased to meet you." Mrs. Leston's clutching hand feels cold to Ethan, or perhaps his is warm from baking in front of the doctor's unseasonable blaze. In the living room, between floral wingchairs, glows another gas fireplace. This is where Mrs. Leston is leading him, very slowly. Or is he leading her? He grips her arm, suddenly fearful she might trip over one of the many tapestry footstools. "Suzie, dear, you didn't tell me your young man was such a charmer. So clingy."

Passing out of his study, Dr. Leston jerks to a halt. "That's Zoe, Liz," he says tersely.

Zoe, standing behind one of the wing chairs, examines her mother and then shoots a worried look at her father.

"I lied," he says quietly to Zoe. "Your mother puts on a good front, but she's not any better. Tonight I hoped she would be all right for you."

Mrs. Leston smiles, oblivious to the discussion about her. "We were so worried about our Suzie," she says to Ethan. "I'm glad it was only a fever. Walter thought it was meningitis, but what does he know. He's a surgeon. What did you say your name was, Doctor?"

"Ethan. But I don't have a PhD. Still working on it."

"*Ethan*? Ethan who?"

"Winter."

"No. I'm afraid I don't know any Winters who are physicians."

In the car coming up from the city, Zoe had explained to Ethan that her parents' extended cruise had been therapeutic. Her mother was recovering from a stroke. Ethan has no medical background, but to his mind Elizabeth does not display the paralysis or slurred speech he'd imagine that affliction would cause. Rather she appears to be suffering from dementia.

"Daddy. Who's Suzie?" Zoe asks.

Her father approaches the chair that Zoe is standing behind and he sits down. He has shrunken considerably. "Just a name."

It is becoming clear to Ethan that the Lestons' recent travels were not for recuperation but a last hurrah.

Suddenly, Mrs. Leston begins to speak loudly. "Now wait a minute. I believe we did know an Archbishop Winter. But that was in Hartford. You're not from the Hartford diocese, are you, Father?" Even in her confusion Mrs. Leston still manages to play the hostess.

"My family is from New Jersey," Ethan says.

"No. I'm afraid that's not right. I believe it was a Bishop Snow."

Ethan gently shakes his head.

"Lessard," Dr. Leston says to his wife, rescuing Ethan from her imprecise gaze. "You're thinking of a blizzard, Liz. It was Bishop Lessard."

"Yes. Bishop Blizzard. That's it," Elizabeth says, grasping Ethan's hands. "Welcome, Bishop." The poor woman, Ethan sees, is trying to keep herself together through pretense.

"Oh, Mom," Zoe says and goes to her by the fireplace. "You've spilled your drink. Come upstairs with me. We'll get you cleaned up."

Mrs. Leston lowers her gaze, as does Ethan, to the liquid accumulating around her high heels and the back of her dress. "Oh dear," she says. She releases Ethan's arm and looks at her daughter. Her voice goes small. "Please, Suzie, help me."

As Zoe leads her mother from the room, Ethan's face feels scalded. He fears he might appear eager to bolt from the house, a coward.

"Oh hell," says Dr. Leston. Then he refocuses the distress on his face into a coldness aimed at Ethan. "Stay, would you? You're our only guest tonight. We won't embarrass you in front of company."

ETHAN'S EXPERTISE IS the Monte Carlo simulation, a mathematical model that tries to account for all likely outcomes of a given scenario. His bank, UIB, has been using the Monte Carlo to exploit currency movements during particular events: a merger, a national disaster, and the more exotic events on which he works. For the past two years his specialty has been algorithms based on terrorist incidents. When word of the bomb blasts in Stockholm hit the newswires a year and a half before, his programming triggered UIB's high-frequency trading mainframes to sell what kronas it owned or managed for clients. As the market caught up, his algo measured the krona's volatility and, microsecond by microsecond, began to repurchase and sell that currency with the dollar, renminbi, or euro—whatever was momentarily most favorable—as the currency seesawed down to a lower valuation. And then when the algorithm sensed the krona's bottom, it pulled out of it completely. Ethan was glowing by the end of that day, and not just because of the bonus he would earn. His work has kept him enthralled ever since.

His latest algorithms have shown such good results that yesterday, after the Pentagon announced that Jabir al-Yarisi had been eliminated, UIB's director of liquidity, Dwayne Hoke, rushed to Ethan's office to watch the currency prices gyrate. Now Dwayne is hot over Ethan's new concept, the subprogram that focuses on antiterrorism—in particular, on drone strikes against Al Qaeda leaders. Lately the military has been touting the strikes as a means of keeping America safe, boasting of successful kills as if the Middle East weren't its next Vietnam. Following each strike, Ethan had noted a volatility in South Asian currencies against the dollar and he began to see what should have been obvious, that antiterrorism to one country was terrorism to another—say, an American drone strike on a Pakistani madrassa. As such, with minor tweaks, his current terrorist-incident algo spawned an antiterrorist algo.

"Beautiful," Hoke had said. "We'll not only kill the bastards but make money from them twice over."

The comment made Ethan blink, until he recalled that one of UIB's vast array of investments included military drone technology.

Ethan knows that his work is not the work of a genius, though it can give him this impression when he watches UIB's arbitrage profits mount.

What he does—thanks to the speed of the bank's globally located main-frames and the short transmission routes through which they place orders—is a little like scalping tickets for a Lady Gaga concert. The show's going to be a sellout so the real trick is to buy as many tickets as you can before the true concert-goers have a chance. Dwayne, however, has assured him that what they do is useful and good: it is helping a currency establish its true value.

Zoe, however, operates outside his technology. Having used the Monte Carlo on her he has concluded that their relationship can have several likely outcomes: that they will marry, that they will live together a number of years before marrying, that she will leave him for another man, that he will leave her for another woman, and most recently added, that she will leave him for an out-of-town job. What his mathematics cannot account for is what is happening now.

"Stop," Zoe says as their Mini Cooper glides through the misty Ulster County countryside.

"What?" Ethan asks. "Here?"

"Just pull over. I need to think."

Two minutes earlier they had said their goodnights to her parents. Mrs. Leston had managed to complete the dinner without further incident except for a few name slips, calling Ethan "Bishop," and Zoe "Suzie." She had, apparently, completely forgotten wetting her dress and changing into fresh clothes. There are aspects of dementia that are not cruel.

Ethan pulls onto the gravel shoulder.

"My mother doesn't know me," Zoe says to the windshield. "She kept calling me Suzie."

Ethan studies the side of Zoe's face, her forward stare. He fears that she will break down and sob. But what can he say to make her feel better? Perhaps that Suzie and Zoe are names easily confused. "Your mother just slipped up," he says. "It's nothing serious."

"Alzheimer's is not serious?"

Ethan sees that he has been dismissive. He keeps quiet.

"It's bigger than that," Zoe says. "My mother thinks I'm someone else."

"This *Suzie*?" Ethan is on firmer ground here. As a mathematician he is quick in logical deduction. "Your mother must have known a Suzie. Isn't that how memory works? Your older experiences are the last to fade. You must resemble her Suzie."

Now Zoe looks at him. The car's headlights, reflected by the mist, light the vehicle's interior and reveal Zoe's glistening eyes. "Someone I resemble? That wouldn't be anyone on her side of the family. I look more like my father."

"Then what about, I don't know . . . another daughter maybe?"

"Another daughter my parents never told me about?"

Such family discipline in the Lestons would not shock Ethan, not after his encounter with the doctor. "Something bad might have happened to her. Something they wanted to forget," he says, realizing too late that his words were thoughtless.

"Take me home," Zoe says.

"Okay," says Ethan, relieved. He puts the car in drive.

"No," Zoe says before they have gone twenty feet. "I mean *my* home. My parents'."

Ethan drops her off without going inside. Then he sits in the dark car watching Zoe and her father through a kitchen window. Dr. Leston, his sleeves rolled up, is at the sink. He has his back to his daughter as he speaks.

CHAPTER 3

New York City

Ethan,

Well, here's your key so I guess this makes it final. Sorry about standing you up for lunch. For me it's better we part like this—with a lonely legal pad note left on your Jellystone countertop. Hey Yogi, did I get the name right this time? Never mind, I know it's Giallo granite. Really I'm not putting you down for having nice things, for having a job that allows you to buy them, but it's all too seductive for a little bear like me. I won't respect myself if I get sucked into a materialistic life so soon after college. This could be naive but I still dream the world might be a better place if I help.

Anyway, hope you don't think I've been using you for the past six months just for a place to live in the city. Joke! That's the problem with pen and paper. You can't really backspace out the thoughts you put down. But what I guess I'm avoiding saying is that I really am fond of you even if we are so different. So different I don't think we'd have gotten together if not for Alex. He really does love you. With him it's always Ethan this or Ethan that. Your friendship is deeper than anything we ever developed. But, I mean, how could we, with you always at work and me finishing my degree and then being crazy busy at the UN. About all that stays with me of our time together are the glum espresso breakfasts when we stared at the Freedom Tower going up.

So I've packed up my last things from your apartment and will be on the train to DC before you read this. (Wow! I'm on page 2 of your legal pad already. Fergive the lack of sppelchek but doing this by text or email would have been sucky.) Anyway, don't you think my simply disappearing will be the easiest goodbye? Except for a few loose ends maybe. If we'd have had our lunch today and I was brave enough, here's what I might have tied up.

About that dinner at my parents, I apologize for taking you. It wasn't right. The thing is I'd been getting madder and madder at you for a while, maybe to make my leaving easier. Now I see that I'd decided to torture you a little. I knew my dad would go after the man who "defiled" his little girl. Sorry. But at least your coming wasn't for nothing. He might not have told me about his other daughter. Not that he told me much more than Suzie died in a car crash around when I was born. It's all very strange. He couldn't even show me a picture of her. As stony as he acts I know it's still traumatic to him. It's frustrating that he won't tell me more.

Not that this makes any better of an excuse for standing you up today. You're probably waiting in the Blue Planet right now if the text chime in my bag is you. But learning that I had a sister I never knew has been too much. So it's not just from you I'm breaking clean. I'm starting a new life. I need to think about just me for a while.

Damn, Ethan. You confuse me because we did have nice moments. And the night you came to my parents you were at your best. You held your ground with my dad without getting mean. Best of all you were kind to my mom. A kiss for that. Many kisses. But please don't call me. Don't text. Don't email. Especially don't write. I couldn't take reading a messy letter like this. Everything has changed for me now and hearing from you would only hold me back. I've got so much to do.

Goodbye,
Zoe

CHAPTER 4

Nevada

Pancho's—a cinderblock warehouse with a bar and three pool tables on a dirt road off Route 95 between Indian Springs and Vegas. Inside Pancho's, Jessica stares into a vending machine mirror. Then she remembers what she is doing.

She pulls a pinball-style lever and a hard pack of Marlboros drops down the chute like she's won a prize. She could have bought a Twix from the adjoining machine, but start that and soon she'd be an elephant, sitting for work as she does. The term *chair force* is becoming truer every day.

Nearby, a spinning slot machine makes the airman attached to it moan. For the past hour Jessica has been watching him, a sensor operator from her squadron. His eyes are glassy but she's not seen him being served, so drink is not the cause. The likely culprit is a drone monitor stared at for too many hours. There aren't enough drivers or sensors for all the flights being guided out of Reeger and crashes are on the rise. But with unmanned aerial vehicles—UAVs, RPAs, drones, eyes in the sky—whatever you want to call them, no one gets hurt but the taxpayers at twelve million a pop. So up they keep going.

"Your shot, von Richthofen," Bob Sanders calls from a pool table. She puts the Marlboros on the rail and takes a cue.

"Don't call me that," Jessica says. Bob has left her a split with the eight ball. She makes it. Game over.

"Technical Sergeant Aldridge," Bob salutes.

Recently Jessica took a promotion. Pilot shortages have compelled the Air Force to experiment with using enlisted personnel to fly UAVs. Three months ago she was a sensor operator, like Bob, feeding flight and target data to the ex-F-16 commander beside her. Then her commander, Colonel Voigt, sent her to UAV pilot school. When she was done she had both stripes and wings. The next thing she knew, she was firing a missile at al-Yarisi—and those girls.

She taps up a Marlboro for Bob that he declines.

"Killing yourself," he says.

"Like you're not," she says. Bob's gut hangs over his belt and is holding up his promotion, though it's not as if he'd have to squeeze into a cockpit to fly a drone. Jessica changes the subject by nodding toward the airman feeding nickels into the one-armed bandit. "Last thing I'd want to do after a shift is bond with another machine," she says to Bob. The man at the slot is intense, committed, addicted. At least he's only losing nickels.

The war on terror, what was once known as Operation Enduring Freedom, has lost its official name. On the base they call it Operation Expanding Waistline, partly because covert snacking is the main pastime during shifts at a drone monitor. What she and the members of her squadron do, all day and night, is a high-tech version of a detective stakeout. They watch. They wait. They don't sit in unmarked cars or vans but in single-wide trailers. Yet unlike a stakeout, there is no scenery, only images on monitors. The same desert or mountain for hours. At first being an eye in the sky thrills. But a cop gets to pound on a door and make a bust. For UAV drivers, the rare instance of firing a missile, what Jessica's squadron calls an angel, makes the adrenaline flow to no purpose. She's just pulling a switch. And this is why Colonel Voigt has pinned sergeant stripes and his hopes on her: he's decided that women are more adaptable to this type of mission. He thinks they have patience. He thinks they will be the ones to save the drone program because they won't go nickel-slot-machine crazy like the men.

"Hey, killer," a familiar voice calls to Jessica. Lieutenant Dunbar, entering with his crew, is dark, handsome, cocky—a real top-gun wannabe. He had logged two hundred hours in his father's Piper before enlisting to be a jet pilot and astigmatism shot him down. But you don't need much depth perception to drive a drone.

Jessica absorbs Dunbar's mandatory rib. Word is spreading about the al-Yarisi kill because someone in Washington decided to let the world know another terrorist has died in a drone strike. If the triggers on these operations were not anonymous, Jessica might have become famous for taking out Al Qaeda's number three. This makes her Dunbar's competition. The lieutenant has let it be known, discreetly since what they do is even internally classified, that he has been the trigger in a dozen operations where angels flew or demons dropped—a demon being a laser-guided five-hundred-pound bomb. Dunbar is the base's unofficial drone ace, if there can be such a thing.

"Don't call her that," Bob says to Dunbar.

"I know he's your man, but I didn't know you two were married," Dunbar says to Jessica, and Bob's face goes red. Bob *is* her partner, her sensor operator, but that's as far as it goes.

"The fuck we're married, sir," she tells the lieutenant.

Now Dunbar really notices her. Jessica imagines what he is studying and to her it is not impressive—a pale face, wispy brown hair trimmed short, insubstantial nose, eyes naively large. In warning, Dunbar points a finger at her. Then he snatches back his hand and heads for the bar.

"You're going to lose those new stripes," Bob says.

Jessica shrugs.

Pancho's serves Pabst, peanuts, pretzels—apparently whatever starts with a *p*. The owner is actually not a Pancho but a Phyllis, the ex-wife of an ex-airman named Frank who ran off to Cuernavaca in the eighties. Phyl could serve as a standing advertisement for the American Cancer Society. Her voice is an infrequent rasp and her skin a roadmap folded too many times. She is huffing through what might be anywhere from her forty-seventh to her seventy-seventh year. But everyone knows not to suggest she give up her Lucky Strikes—that would lead to immediate ejection.

Dunbar's mouth is curved in a way that Jessica likes. In fact, she likes his whole silhouette. She is watching Phyl fix a shot glass for him from a bottle of wormy tequila kept under the bar. She stares as Dunbar knocks it back. Then he speaks some quiet words to his buddies, a pair of second lieutenants, who snort at his comment. Jessica thinks Dunbar is mocking her. But none of the trio gives her a glance. When finally Dunbar looks her way he may as well be looking through Pancho's walls and into the desert beyond. She lowers her eyes, noticing as she does how her uniform makes her chest seem even flatter than it is.

"You okay?" Bob asks.

She lights a cigarette and exhales the smoke away from his face. "Let's get out of here before you catch cancer," she says.

What is it about overconfident jerks that makes them attractive? Dunbar should not be on her sexual radar. But damn the Force's fraternization policies, he is. Jessica doesn't look toward the bar again but heads for the front door, passing the airman at the nickel slot. A dead cigarette sits between his knuckles where a burn blister has emerged.

"Are you all right, Airman?" Jessica asks. As a new NCO this is her first official act over a subordinate.

The airman drops a nickel into the machine. He cranks the lever and Jessica waits until the reels stop: two cherries and a bell. Coins rattle down the machine's throat, but this doesn't stop the airman from playing.

"Why don't we drive you back to base?" Jessica suggests. At his lack of response she puts a hand in front of the airman's eyes. But he knows how to play the machine by feel and he does so again.

"There a problem here, Sergeant?" Unseen, Dunbar has come upon them.

"No problem, sir," Jessica responds, protective of her fellow enlistee. She does not want whatever is up with him to go on his record. Despite manpower shortages, and perhaps the cause of them, it is easy for an ordinary airman to get bounced from drone duty if his psychological profile slips. The Air Force has the lowest accidental civilian kill ratio of all the services and wants to keep it that way.

"How much have you been drinking, Airman?" Dunbar asks the man, but there's not a bottle around and the airman's breath smells dry.

His eyes are blank from screen fatigue not alcohol, Jessica wants to say. What is more, off-duty bingeing is not what pilots and navigators, even stationary ones, do. The steadying vice is nicotine, taken via gum when indoors on base or through the standard cancer sticks while enjoying a break under the desert sky. One might imagine there is no battlefield stress an ocean away from the front, but this is the problem: lack of physical danger in operations that take lives—even enemy lives—never feels quite right. Jessica knows how the silent guilt builds. You learn to deal with it or crack. In other words, you smoke. Maybe, she thinks, risking their lungs is some atonement for being beyond the line of fire. God bless Philip Morris. She and Bob leave Pancho's without the airman.

A week later the airman is booted from the drone program. His next stop will be guard duty at a Kyrgyzstan airbase. Though this is Dunbar's doing, Jessica feels rotten for not adequately watching the man's tail, like any good wingman would. But she cannot discuss her unhappiness, not even with Bob. She would be putting her own psych profile out there to be picked over. The only person safe enough to talk to, to write to, about this is two thousand miles away. Is it common DNA that makes a father understand his daughter so well? What else could it be; Jessica has not seen Don in fourteen years. Yet from his letters she feels that he understands what she is going through like no one else could. Maybe because he's a prisoner.

CHAPTER 5

Florida

Dear Jessica,

What a surprise. I was not expecting your monthly letter for two weeks. And I was not expecting you to send more cigarette cash. Since you keep calling it that I am guessing you have the habit. When I was young I could burn up three packs a day easy. Hope you are going lighter. I am. Last year the state banned us from smoking. Too many fires and sick prisoners. But the warden here is okay. He has allowed us music players to make up for the smokes. So on music is how I will spend your dough.

Anyway I have a little good news. That library job I mentioned in my last letter. I got it. There was a shakeup over some smuggled DVDs and now I am a book stacker. No more hands blistered from laundry lye. I bet I feel as good as you did when you got your stripes. But I am sorry you are a little down about your promotion now. Remember you are new at the job so dont kick yourself too much over your lost airman. You probably could have done nothing more to help him than what you did. Probably you assumed his worries were like yours and he could handle them. But maybe the lieutenant you mention had him pegged right as a crackup. Who knows? Anyway you should keep for yourself a little of the forgiveness and understanding that you give to others. That includes me.

When I think back on how I wronged you and your mother. Leaving you cold. Not sending you anything to live on. Then all this time later to have gotten that first letter from you. Did you know your last one adds up to twelve? Nearly a full year of letters. Your kindness brings tears to my eyes. Which are not something I can afford in a place like

this. Like you I am forced to show the world a face that dont crack.
When I cry I do it after lights out. Or just before like I am now.

 So goodnight Daughter. I blow a fatherly kiss to you across the miles
and over the waters and deserts and through the walls that separate
us. Even if I am never to hear from you again it will be the mystery and
miracle of my life that for a while you came back to me. You are more
than I deserve and I expect every letter that comes from you to be the
last. But never feel badly if you must stop writing. I will understand.
And I will cherish till my last breath what I have received.

Your loving father,
Don

PART TWO

SEPARATION

September–November 2012

CHAPTER 6

New York City

It is the day before Labor Day but nevertheless it is a *school* night for Ethan, as was last night. A holiday weekend at work is why he has arrived late at (Le) Poisson Rouge on Bleecker, where Alex is eating nachos at a side table below the musicians. Alex's latest is the avant-garde cellist onstage above them.

"It's serious this time," Alex says and stuffs his mouth as if the waitress, who serves in mime, is about to snatch his plate. Silently Ethan admires his friend—how he devours meals, alcohol, women, and life. Ethan's approach to living is less exuberant—he catches himself, constantly if metaphorically, patting his lips with a napkin after each bite, sip, or kiss.

As he looks up at the instrument between the cellist's legs and at her strong, bare calves, Alex spits something wet into his ear. "I don't get what she's doing with the bow, but she plays hell with me in bed. A real Paganini of the sheets."

"Paganini was a violinist," Ethan says. "And a man."

"Whatever," Alex replies.

They watch Eva saw. Her cello screeches like a yowling cat. Ethan assumes this is deliberate.

"Listen to that. Pure sex," says Alex, chewing. He swallows hard and for an instant he appears to choke. Then the bump descends through his esophagus and he is breathing again. Ethan thumps him between the shoulder blades anyway. "*So.* What do you think?" Alex asks in a particular tone with which Ethan is very familiar.

After Zoe left, Ethan told Alex to lay off trying get him laid. But Alex is an inveterate matchmaker. A *goyim* Yente Ethan often calls him, priding himself on the cultural reference since he has focused his life on mathematics. But Ethan does know *Fiddler on the Roof* because in high school he lost his virginity to the pretty girl who played Grandma Tzeitel. He thinks of her sometimes but not as much as he continues to think about Zoe. And so for the past month, through the dog days of August, Ethan has said No, No, and No to Alex's various requests that they double date, or that Ethan take a friend's number, or that he meet him at a SoHo bar where he has just run into a pair of beautiful sisters. "You and your wallet are hot property, amigo. Take advantage of it," Alex says. "Look what I have to do to get by. Be a genius."

Being intelligent but a non-genius and somewhat human, Ethan relented at last. His blind date is not one of the musicians tonight but the cellist's page-turner, and he sits on tenterhooks watching her. The performance is agitato and muscular and his date must slap the read sheets out of the way. He keeps expecting the music stand to fly across the room and the music to crash to an embarrassing halt as if a wrench has been shoved into the gears of a screaming engine. He worries that his date's long dark hair, which swings whenever she dives forward to flip, will snag Eva's cello. Whenever the page-turner catches his eye and winks, his stomach pitches because she might miss her next cue and the audience, voracious in their love of extreme performance, will hiss her shamefully off the stage.

Through all this tumult Ethan considers Alex's *What do you think?* What Alex really wants to know is whether he likes the page-turner enough to try to take her to bed.

The music, now at an earsplitting pitch, prevents him from responding to Alex with his own question— *Why would Yahvi want to sleep with me so soon anyway?* What Yahvi and he are on, if it is a date, is a first date. Ethan is aware that his restraint may be old fashioned, but Yahvi, or her family, is from India, where a public kiss can earn an admonishment. This gives him some relief, expecting that she will not behave like some of the other blind dates. Yet India is also the birthplace of the Kama Sutra.

What will he do if she wants to come home with him? Considering her enthusiasm as a page-flipper, the prospect terrifies. Or is it scary because she would be the first person in his bed since Zoe? It has now been fifty-one days since Zoe slept next to him and forty-four since they communicated—which means that he has, to date, spent about one percent of his adult life in post-Zoe limbo. He does this calculation every day.

Then the cacophony of music-like sound implodes. The abrupt cessation of noise creates an aural vacuum in the club, an emptiness so sudden that even the dim lighting seems darker. The audience stands to deliver its applause.

All the women on stage are taking bows. It is a little strange, Ethan thinks, that Yahvi, the page-turner, should be among the applauded and not be one of the applauders. Is this what we have become in an era of universal reward—spoiled children who receive gold stars for mere participation?

"She's the composer, dimwit," Alex says after Ethan makes his observation verbal. This information scares him even more. For what if this supremely competent woman, this woman capable of forging sound into a brain-piercing rapier, does come home with him?

"You were amazing," Alex says leaping to embrace Eva as she comes down to their table.

"Hope it wasn't too harsh," Yahvi says as Ethan pulls back a chair for her to sit.

"It was . . . beautiful," he responds and wishes to swallow his hesitating tongue.

"Yes. It *was* beautiful. If you have the right ears. Do you have such ears, Ethan?" Yahvi's eyes, large and dark, laughing and forgiving, embrace him.

THROUGH A SLIVER of morning sky Ethan sees a boom moving across his fragment of the Freedom Tower. He is saddened that his apartment will not have a clean view of the spire that will lift the structure to its symbolic height of 1,776 feet. *Que sera.* He should have bought an apartment on a higher floor. But how was he to know that the Goldman Sachs monolith on West Street would block most of his view of Ground Zero? This is the hazard of living in a mobile city, a sleepless city that also never lies still.

A contradiction, the French for a building, *immeuble*, comes to him— in high school he was much better at programming languages. And then comes the word for furniture. *Meubles.* The *immovable* and *movable* to an old-world culture. But here, in this city, change is the status quo. A building is implicitly a process, a gerund, a *building*. And a piece of furniture is not necessarily a *movable*—to which the weekly sidewalk piles of discarded chairs, tables, mattresses, lamps, and bookcases attest.

He prepares espresso over these thoughts, waits for Yahvi to smell the coffee and arise. It has been six weeks since their first date and she has spent the past three consecutive nights in his apartment. On this happy, crisis-free Wednesday he decides he will do something remarkable, unprecedented, amazing. He will call in late to the bank.

He spies Yahvi tangled in the sheets, a dervish come to rest. Parts of her—an ear, a breast, a knee, a cascade of dark hair—spill from the Egyptian cotton. Watching her, recalling how his fingers stroked her skin and the way last night she pulled him into her, he wants this again. Should he go to her or clatter about in the kitchen scrambling eggs to awaken her? They are now more than hookups but not quite in a relationship. Or are they? If he slips into bed, will she think he's a lech? If he makes her breakfast, will he come off as the mathematical nerd that he is?

"I see you," she says from inside the mouth of her sheet cave. Her hand, like a genie's bejeweled with silver rings, spiders out and beckons. He puts his coffee cup on the dresser and gets a knee on the bed before a chittering stops him. He's in an updated fable. His choice: *the Lady* or *the BlackBerry*.

He retreats to the dresser where the device vibrates. Since no one ever calls this early it must be important. Perhaps disastrous. Has there been another financial meltdown? The caller ID is unknown. He does not even recognize the area code.

"Hello?" he says.

"Ethan Winter?"

The voice, deep, harsh, hovers on the edge of recall. Instinct tells Ethan to ignore it, to shut the phone, to go to Yahvi. The bangles she has worn to bed rattle as she beckons—a petulant child demanding gratification, her full lips pout. Stupidly he turns his back to her. "This is Winter," he says.

IN A CHAIN cafe around the block from his building, Ethan locates at a window table Dr. Leston eating eggs with a plastic fork.

"You and my daughter lived in an interesting neighborhood," the doctor says.

Ethan corrects him, "I still live here."

"I'm aware of that." Leston beckons him to a chair.

Ethan wants to speed up this encounter, whatever its purpose, so he can return to Yahvi. But he sits. Dr. Leston appears less solid under daylight than he had in the fireplace glow of his study. He is eating hunched over and a bit of egg has caught on his angular chin. Ethan notices that the doctor has shaved poorly and that his coat seems big. In the three months since their introduction the doctor must have lost weight.

"Can I help you with something?" Ethan says.

Leston presents a leathery smile and puts down his fork. With a finger he wipes a bit of egg from his lip. His eyes, deep in their sockets, drill Ethan's. "I don't doubt you're the one person I know who can help me with this problem."

Ethan almost cuts him off. "If you need a broker, I'm not one. And any work I do for UIB is confidential. I couldn't tell you what to invest in."

The doctor erases Ethan's words with a contemptuous wave. "You think I would trust your bank again? What I am talking about now is Zoe."

Ethan feels a stab under the ribs. He'd thought he was over Zoe, or close to it. "We haven't talked since she left for Washington."

Leston's unruly eyebrows rise. "She's doing well," he says.

"Well good for her," Ethan answers but fails to feel sarcastic. Though Yahvi is waiting twelve stories above, his post-Zoe reality begins to slip.

"She works for an organization that assists rural women in developing countries. Microloans. Legal aid. That type of thing."

Ethan nods. He sees Zoe bustling through an office run by bureaucrats who measure personal success by their proximity to power. He imagines the politics, both office and international, slowly corroding her shiny enthusiasm. "I'm happy for her," he lies.

"Yes, everything is good for her. For the moment."

"Mind if I get coffee?" Ethan says.

When he's at the register he watches Leston pour out and swallow pills. The doctor's hands shake. He is ill, Ethan determines, quite ill. Or else why this meeting? Ethan deduces that this could be just the beginning of the bad news.

"How's your wife?" Ethan asks, returning with his coffee.

Leston smiles as if at an unspoken joke. "Elizabeth, as I imagine you could guess, is worse than when you met her. She has grown to be too much for me to handle at this point."

Despite his dislike of the doctor, Ethan allows that Leston is not as hard a man as he tries to appear. "Well, I guess you of all people would know of the best places to take care of her."

"Facilities where she can sit around in diapers with no memories and stare at wallpaper?"

Ethan holds Leston's gaze. "How sick are you?"

"Pancreatic cancer," Leston says. "And when I am deceased I'll need a favor from you. Not for me. For Zoe."

"But you know we're not even friends anymore. As I've said, I haven't spoken with her in months."

"Yet Zoe has mentioned you to me *more* than once."

Ethan feels his spine straighten. "What?"

"The strongest relationships are based on respect. I see that Zoe may have this for you and that my judgment of your character may have been hasty. It's your line of work, you see. But listen to me now. Today Zoe wants her own life. Give her time. Be patient. Keep an open heart."

Open heart. Ethan would expect the doctor to use the phrase medically, not metaphorically. From the briefcase by his chair, Leston lifts out a bulging manila folder bound with rubber bands. He grimaces with the effort of handing it to Ethan. "This will explain all," he says. Shakily he leans hard on the table to stand. "Zoe knows very little of her true background. I'm counting on you to look after her when she discovers the whole truth. I cannot tell it to her. I've kept her in the dark for too long and now I've run out of time." Leston starts shuffling toward the door. He would be running if he were not infirm.

Ethan tucks the manila folder under an arm and picks up the doctor's abandoned briefcase. Leston is supporting himself on each table that he passes and Ethan hurries to offer him his free arm. Leston accepts the aid without comment. This sudden capitulation seems caused by the doctor's illness or a debilitating medical treatment. But perhaps it has to do with what the doctor, in all practical terms, has just bequeathed—his daughter and her "background." Ethan guides Leston out into the sunny fall day, normally a most perfect kind of day.

"My car is just there. I found parking on the street. Lucky me," Leston says.

"Christ. You drove down to the city?"

Leston has enough strength now to push Ethan away. He has parked his Mercedes in a loading zone but has no ticket. Ethan stands by the driver's door to protect the old man from traffic and waits as he lowers himself into the seat and gets a leg inside. With a gnarled hand the doctor lifts in the other leg and its pants cuff comes up to expose a fallen sock garter. The doctor's shoe is dangling on a foot melted by illness. When Leston is settled Ethan passes him his briefcase and watches as he struggles to place his key in the ignition.

"I'll drive you home," Ethan says.

Leston shakes his head. "The nausea has passed. I will be fine for a bit." He races the engine, which makes the fan belt screech, then reaches to close the door Ethan is still holding. "Come on," the doctor says, mildly amused at his reluctance.

"How long do you have?" Ethan asks.

Leston's smile seems relieved, as if he is glad to get a last detail out of the way. "Three months." He shrugs. "A week." Leston is still smiling. "In my condition, who can tell? *God*?"

Ethan closes the car door and Leston puts the Mercedes in drive. "Call her," he reads on the doctor's lips through the closed window.

"WHAT'S THIS? WORK crap?" Alex asks, nudging the banded bundle on Ethan's kitchen pass-through. Leston's folder has sat there for a week.

"That's what I told Yahvi," Ethan says, sliding Alex a can of Pabst. For himself he fills a glass from a bottle of ale with a winged dog on its label. "But it's from Zoe's old man. Family secrets."

"What were they?" Alex asks.

"Haven't looked. Not my prob."

"That's chilly," Alex says but doesn't dig further. He's preoccupied by a group show at an eighth-floor Chelsea gallery. And he's just broken up with the cellist, Eva—which is why he's stopped by. "It's going to be awkward if you're still hooking up with her friend," he tells Ethan as if they were symbiotic dating twins.

"I'm not hooking up with Yahvi anymore," Ethan says.

"No! Say it's not so, bro." Alex's boyish, grinning face reminds Ethan of James Franco. But Alex is a few inches shorter than Franco and handsomer.

"We're doing sleepovers now."

"You serious?" Alex's grin leaks away. "Well, if you start hearing gossip about me, stay cool."

"How am I going to hear any gossip about you? It's earnings week so I'm at the bank all the time."

"Big deal, you're always at the bank. And by gossip, I mean girlfriend talk."

"What?" Ethan says. Then he realizes that Alex means Yahvi, that Alex is worried about Yahvi speaking with Eva. Now it's Ethan's turn to grin. "So, what's she going to tell me?"

"Fuck, dude. Nothing."

"Better I hear it from you first." It's not often that Ethan gets a chance to tease Alex. Normally he is on the receiving end of any comedy.

Alex, as though he's breaking sweat, wipes his brow with the side of a hand. "Christ."

"Fess up."

"All right." Alex guzzles the Pabst and then mashes the aluminum can flat on the granite countertop. Ethan opens another beer for him and waits.

Being with Alex is often as nostalgia inducing for Ethan as a stroll down the street where he grew up. But Alex, nearing thirty, and despite producing hundreds of canvases, has not made a mark on his profession. Ethan suspects that the paintings he purchases from him are his primary means of support. He has vowed to himself that his friend will not starve, that he'll financially support Alex into old age if it comes to that. And why not? He'll have the bucks. With his bonus this year alone, Ethan could pay off a good chunk of his condo. Of course, he can never let Alex know about his plan. It would wreck their friendship.

"What happened was . . . ," Alex starts, hesitant, his second Pabst gone, and partly down his chin. He backhands his mouth dry. "I was trying to talk Eva into a threesome, all right?"

Ethan shakes his head. "Dude! No you didn't!" Beer buzzed, he feels quite jolly; Alex always recovers quickly from his dating debacles. With his mug empty, Ethan is considering a refill, the beginning of a full night of frat boy commiseration with his dumped best friend. Then he remembers that it's earnings week and he needs to be sharp for tomorrow. But he *is* overdue for a binge. Really, it's been years—the last was on Alex's twenty-sixth birthday.

Now Alex is looking at Ethan with a pained expression. "You're not getting it, are you?" He leans an elbow on Leston's folder. "Well, since you're collecting family secrets. I wanted Eva to sleep with me and another guy."

"But," Ethan says, his jaw loose, "you're not gay." He looks down at the fresh Flying Dog he is pouring himself—it is foaming onto the counter. Alex pulls Leston's package away from the puddle.

"Bi, dude," Alex says and pitches his empty Pabst toward the recycle bin. Basket. "Been that way forever. I'm gonna go now. Let things sync up with you."

Trailing Alex to the door, Ethan feels as whimpery as a dog being left behind in an empty house.

"It's cool you never saw it," Alex says. "It's not like I ever wanted to do you. At least not since freshman year. So about my opening next week. Bring Yahvi if you want. We're good then, right?" He is gone before Ethan can answer the question.

TOE-TO-TOE, ETHAN AND Yahvi rise in a crowded elevator. She is smiling up at him and he has the desire to give the tip of her nose a little peck, just as if they've become one of those publicly cute couples. The hoop Yahvi wears through her left nostril makes her unpretentiously exotic—nose rings are traditionally Indian. In her green leggings and platform sandals she is presenting herself as what she is. *Bicultural.* Anxious about Alex, he immediately corrects this label to *human.*

"Penny for your thoughts," Yahvi says. "No. *Inflation.* One dollar." She taps his arm playfully. "Now you've gotten even *me* talking like a banker."

Ethan's eyes wander over Yahvi. "Forgive me," he whispers and touches his lips to the spot on her brow where occasionally, though not tonight, she places a stylish bindi. Until her mention of banking, he had almost erased his day's other anxiety—earlier his new algorithm had logged an unusual return, trading in Pakistani rupees. This would have been a good thing except that some of Yahvi's extended family lives in Pakistan. When he looked up on the wire what had triggered the profit, he read of a drone strike on the Afghanistan border—it was just the raw, quickly telegraphed text that his algorithm, in microseconds, had processed to gain an arbitrage advantage. However, twenty minutes later, Dwayne Hoke was in his office showing Ethan images already posted to Al Jazeera's Arabic news site—an incinerated pickup truck and beside it a large piece of something burnt that shouldn't have been but was likely human. "Good work," Hoke had said as if Ethan had fired the missile himself. "We cashed in some more evildoers."

No. I will not think of this, Ethan tells himself as the elevator door slides away. He and Yahvi and the other art partygoers disperse into the hall.

Alex's group show is opposite the elevator, in a wide gallery space with partitions. Ethan sees phosphorescent seascapes and high-finish, classically rendered portraits of Mr. Magoo, Elmer Fudd, Scooby-Doo. But he spots nothing by Alex. He takes a flyer from a stack near the entrance and recognizing one of Alex's images reads its caption to Yahvi.

"'A metaphysical union of Franz Kline and Cy Twombly filled with postmortem irony.' Isn't it supposed to be *postmodern*?"

Yahvi squeezes his arm. "Then it wouldn't be ironic."

"I am so uncool," he says.

He has been brooding about Alex for a week, about the person he thought was his best friend but who, for a decade, has withheld part of his identity from him. Alex's revelation makes Ethan admire his friend. But it also distances him. The embrace of all experience is an ideal he could never emulate.

He and Yahvi now walk around a partition. Two of Alex's paintings, large ones with atypical slashes of color, fill a corner of the gallery. Alex, dressed smartly—or is it ironically?—in vest and cravat, stands beside his work. He is listening closely to an angular woman of indeterminate age. Then Alex turns to him and opens his arms. Ethan exhales and steps forward.

CHAPTER 7

Nevada

Colonel Voigt heard of the security breach during a call from Washington. Sergeant Jessica Aldridge had been relating sensitive information about the al-Yarisi strike in letters to her father, one Donald Alan Aldridge, a convict in Florida. It has led to this, her final briefing.

At attention Jessica keeps her eyes high, mostly over the colonel's head, on his wall filled with certificates of merit and photos of jets plowing contrails. When her lips stop moving, after she has told Voigt everything and there is nothing more to say and he is satisfied, he pushes toward Jessica a document he has signed and looks away.

"All packed up?" Voigt asks.

"This is the last of my stuff, sir," Jessica says, showing him the backpack she is wearing.

"Dismissed."

"Thank you, sir," she says and salutes. Voigt does not return it.

Two beret-wearing security forces escort her to a jeep and, with the sun baking their necks, they drive her out of the base gate. At the highway bus stop one of her escorts, behind shaded lenses, gives her a hand flick before the jeep kicks up dust and leaves her there. A last salute. Somehow Voigt has gotten her a general discharge. The way she feels is that she deserves an other than honorable.

Jessica does not blame her father for what has happened. *She* wrote to him about the al-Yarisi incident knowing the details were secret. But she expected them to be kept between Don and her, between father and daughter. She believed that letters sealed in envelopes were the final way one could keep a distant conversation private. And she expected that corresponding in handwritten words to someone cut off from the outside world would be even more private. She feels stupid. Her job was spying on locations half a world away. Why would she have assumed that anything can be hidden anymore?

A rig speeding by sends hot sand into her face. Then a car leaving the base pulls up beside her.

"Ride, Sergeant?" the driver asks, using her old title without irony. It does not surprise her that the pair haven't heard of her discharge. Voigt, for morale's sake, and also, she suspects, out of personal disappointment, has likely been keeping her failure quiet.

"You going to Pancho's?" she asks the airmen. But where else would they be going since they're not pointed toward Vegas.

"Fuck yeah. Hop in," says the passenger. His fatigues bear no insignia. Because he is not young Jessica assumes that he has been busted down several ranks, probably for insubordination. She bristles at his tone before swallowing the fact that she no longer owns the rank on her own fatigues.

Jessica climbs into the backseat and gravel rattles in the car's wheel wells before the vehicle aligns itself on the road. She feels strange, outside of herself, almost out of control like she is skittering down a water park slide and allowing what may come to come. If this letting go can be called a decision, she decides to apply no resistance. It is the path of least resistance.

At Pancho's, after she downs four quick beers, Phyl offers her some special attention.

"Hard day?" Phyl's two words, in one so laconic, are equivalent to a State of the Union address.

In answer Jessica requests another beer and Phyl pours it smoothly, does not press her question. Phyl, Jessica knows, will take care of her just as she has done with other airman. If she falls off her stool, Phyl will lay her down on a backroom cot to sleep off the drunk. No fuss.

Jessica only notices that hours have gone by when she sees that the ashtray where she has been mashing out her cigarettes resembles a forest of miniature stumps. Her throat feels raw. She has not peed since arriving, though now she senses the dull urge. At least she has eaten, if only from the peanut bowl before her. She seems to have created for herself a little world here, a smoky bubble reality filled with clacking billiards and juke box country. Swaying, she decides that she must stay here forever, must

ask Phyl for a job, must become heir to this desert pit stop. She sees herself
in a body as crusted and wizened as Phyl's. Saved.

"Sergeant Aldridge," a voice says pleasantly. It isn't Phyl, who has moved
out of Jessica's bubble. It's Dunbar.

Bastard, she thinks, and her sideways tongue tries to uncurl the word
against him. Now that she has nothing to lose she is ready to avenge the
gambling airman he'd banished to Kyrgyzstan.

"Button it!" Dunbar says over her mumbling as she tries to stand.

She is putty and Dunbar is helping her off the stool, picking up her
backpack and leading her. After they step outside the stars filling the sky
surprise her. It is as if she is seeing the desert night for the first time.

"Where we going?" her lips manage to say as Dunbar guides her into
a car.

He sits behind the steering wheel before answering. "To where you
sent your things, Sergeant. Amargosa?"

Her memory of packing her on-base dorm room, like the past few
weeks, is blurry.

"Quieter than Vegas, I guess," Dunbar says conversationally.

"Better hiking," she slurs.

"That so?"

"Death Valley."

She sees Dunbar frown. Right now she thinks it funny that *death* is in
the name of her next destination. She hadn't thought so far ahead, only
that she wanted solitude. Amargosa, on the unpopulated edge of the Funeral Mountains, seemed the place to go. It was a nowhere town where
she knew nobody.

"Buckle up," Dunbar says, and she manages to. Despite his warning
he pulls out of Pancho's dirt lot slow and easy with the brights on. Is he
a cautious man under the bluster? Jessica thinks she might have misread
him from the start.

They tunnel through the night for half an hour before she asks Dunbar
to pull over. Jessica walks onto the roadside and goes behind a bush that
she can tell from its pleasant odor is sagebrush. Pulling down her fatigue
pants, she looks up and traces the stars. But there are too many dots to
connect and she is unable to identify a single constellation. It's all white

noise up there, pressing down on her the way the overabundance of information from a drone's cameras sometimes did. But she had known how to read through the garbage. She had been a damn good sensor operator. She might have become an even better pilot. Better than Dunbar, she bets, with his corrected astigmatism. But not anymore. Not anymore. *Fuck it.* "Fuck it," she shouts.

"You good, Sergeant?" Dunbar calls. Jessica remains quiet. "Sergeant," he calls again.

"Yes sir." She stands and buttons up. After lighting a cigarette she finds her way back via the glow of the taillights. "You're really going out of your way," she tells the lieutenant, who is leaning against the idling car. "You live in Vegas, don't you?"

"Boulder City."

"Quieter than Vegas, I guess."

"Less smog."

"Right," Jessica says and flicks the cigarette into the sand. She is sobering and headachy.

JESSICA UNLOCKS THE door and pushes it in. A burnt dust odor mingles with the smell of fresh cardboard. She finds the light switch and illuminates a few boxes piled in the center of the room by the movers. She regrets the expense a little. She doesn't own much and could have left it behind.

"Well, that's it then," Dunbar says from the walkway. "You good to go?"

"You mean *to stay*," she says. She notices a coffeemaker atop the dresser. "Come in. I'll make you a brew for the ride home." She is studying him out there, his shadowed face handsome as a sculpting. She would have him come inside and take her to bed without sentiment until she is blotted out. But this sudden fantasy is hers alone. Such thoughts seem to be nowhere near Dunbar's. Aside from the reality that he is physically out of her class, Jessica understands that she is a security risk. In all ways she has become an untouchable to her former colleagues.

"Thanks, but I'll be going. Just wanted to be sure you landed safely," says Dunbar.

"I'm still up in the air."

"You'll be all right," he says without conviction. Even though these could have been his goodnight words, he pauses for three fast heartbeats and Jessica expects him to walk into the room and take them in another direction. "Ssoo," he says, the hiss of the word a prying screwdriver, "you aren't going to be hiking the Valley alone?"

Dunbar, she decides, isn't a bad guy, not at all. And that he isn't extinguishes her wish for his touch. Sure, he has an ego and likes it stroked. But underneath he is a responsible type. What he has just asked is whether she is equipped for a desert hike, not so much gearwise as psychologically.

If she knew she might say.

She untwists some bills out of her fatigue pocket, change from the hundred she had broken at Pancho's, and holds them out. "For the gas," she tells Dunbar.

"The ride's on me, Sergeant."

"No. It's not." She lets the bills float down to the walkway, to Dunbar's feet, and then she shuts the door between them.

AWAKENING IN A strange, overly soft bed Jessica feels achy and disoriented. Then her boxes of packed belongings bring her back to who she is. Who she was.

Snapping out of bed from habit, she goes straight to the curtain and draws it aside. Below, out the window, glints the motel's elaborate pool. It is shaped like a lagoon. Beyond this artificial oasis a bleak scrubland unfolds. And at the edge of this lowland, distant enough to be shadows in their predawn gloom, loom the hogback peaks of the Funeral Mountains.

Jessica does not believe that humans are the toys of destiny; she believes that people can choose their fate. But if they stop choosing, that's when destiny arrives. The Funeral Mountains seem like a good place to be after a debacle. A place where you can bury the past. This is all she knows for the moment. For with nothing before her and with as much time for herself as she used to lack, her wheels are spinning waiting to catch. But there is no traction. What she was is over, has been reduced to two sensations: thirst and hunger. She gets dressed in yesterday's fatigues.

Downstairs, the breakfast bar has opened. She eats reconstituted eggs, rubbery pancakes. A young boy with his parents stares at her through a skeleton mask. She stares back. Then she remembers it's the thirty-first. Halloween. Since she is wearing fatigues maybe the boy thinks that she, too, is in costume. And she is, kind of; being in uniform makes her an impostor now. She's not a protector anymore, a self-conception on which her self-esteem has depended. When she looks at the boy again his mother is lifting the mask to the top of his head so he can eat. Jessica polices her table and passes near the family.

"Morning, Sergeant," the father cheerily says. Though he's not in uniform, he has the presence of an officer of some service.

"Good morning, sir," she says rigidly. Shamed by her deception, her wrinkled uniform, her very being, she drops her eyes to the floor.

By the casino entrance—for what would a Nevada motel be without slots, roulette, and blackjack—a sundries shop beckons. From a cooler Jessica removes a bottle of water and pays a coot who stares at the AL-DRIDGE US AIR FORCE across her chest. His crusted eyes seem not to be reading but reconnoitering past the letters and the camouflage pattern of her shirt as to whether or not she has breasts. What she does have are plastered flat by a sports bra.

"One dollar. Sold," the coot says like an auctioneer.

Outside in the sun Jessica adjusts her cap and begins walking. She crosses a footbridge over the fake lagoon and passes through a tarmac parking lot where RVs float on heat waves. When her boots crunch gravel she calculates the distance ahead. The ripples of distorted air only allow her to guess that the first mountain might be five or ten or fifteen miles off. She swigs from the water bottle and then marches militarily into the emptiness. Every now and then she veers to avoid a creosote bush, the kind of scrub that becomes tumbleweed in a storm. There is no breeze except for the heat rising from the ground.

What am I trying to prove? she thinks.

Nothing, she answers.

The mountain grows. A palm of water she slaps onto her forehead leaves streaks of momentary coolness, but the air is so dry nothing drips from her chin. She has not brought enough liquid for an hour's excursion. Yet she keeps walking and does not look back.

Somewhere she crosses a border and each step gets harder, but not because she is tiring—she will not admit to that. It is because she is walking up a grade toward the foothills. She finds shade beneath a rock eroded into the shape of a mushroom. After smoothing the ground with a boot, she sits. Then she lies back, lethargic with heat and fatigue. When she awakes and starts walking again, it is into the shadow of the mountain. The sun has come around into its decline.

Second by second twilight encroaches. Before darkness arrives Jessica chooses a place on the slope to camp. There is an inch of water left in her bottle. For dinner she allows herself a capful to dampen the grit in her throat. She coughs and spits, instantly regretting the lost moisture. Her training in this tells her that she is in a yellow zone where her electrolytes might crash and her brain will short circuit. She almost wishes this would happen so she could stop remembering her dismissal and those girls in that other desert. Curling up on the slope, she offers her bones to the ground.

Streaks of light cross the black sky. Shooting stars or dreams? She cannot tell how long she keeps her eyes open, or even if they are open. She is shivering.

When dawn strikes the mountain it is like an anvil on her skull. The weight comes not from the atmosphere but her dehydration. She squints at her water bottle and notes that during the night she had emptied it. She does not feel upset. There is no panic in her. She gets up and starts trudging back the way she came and into the sun. It would be too easy to go up the slope and get lost forever, but she is not suicidal. That is not why she is here. She knows this now. But whatever has called her out here is not finished with her yet.

Reaching the flats she kicks through a dune and her reason for being here announces itself.

"No," she says as a voice tells her what to do. She sits down on the hot sand and pushes her fingers through its surface. "Just let me go," she says.

But they aren't going anywhere, she and the sun. Reasoning, she determines that she is not delirious because the sun's voice is a whisper. But it will rise into a shriek if she does not have water soon—sooner than the four hours it will take her to walk out of the desert.

"All right," she says, relenting to the voice. "But I keep the pants and boots."

The sun does not argue.

Jessica claws out a foxhole deep enough to crawl into and she lets fall into it her camouflage cap and military ID. Then she removes her shirt and after folding it neatly, honorably, lays it in the hole so that the identification tags ALDRIDGE and US AIR FORCE are visible to the sky. She is nameless now. As she buries her past, the sun licks her bared skin.

CHAPTER 8

Florida

Dear Jessica,

As you sent no response to my last letter I have been reluctant to write again. But as I am where I am today because of bad judgment here goes. I especially hope writing you is no mistake after what happened here a few weeks ago.

    The guards went through my cell and took all my old papers away. Everything I wrote about and everything you wrote to me about is gone. I thought it was punishment for a contraband pack of cigarettes I got caught with. But afterward a guard told me that your letters contained secret military information.

    Nothing you wrote seemed that secret. Even the part about the wives of that terrorist guy. Though what does a fool like me sitting in a cell know? I hear the country out there has gone crazy. That you cannot climb into a plane without getting a naked x-ray now. That the police have cameras watching every street corner. Are steel bars the only difference anymore between being in a prison and being on the outside? The length of a leash though certainly does count so I hope those letters they took from me have not shortened yours. I wish I could turn back the clock and warn you about what not to write. But then my keepers would have read the warning. No matter how I turn it around this was going to be a lose-lose situation. And now I have lost you.

    My child I guess I dont have anything else to write. You know where I am if you ever want to drop a line. If not bless you for the letters sent. That they were taken from me proves they were more than I deserve. Good thing I read them over a thousand times. I can remember every word.

Your loving father,
Don

CHAPTER 9

Nevada

"What the devil is willful defiance?" Voigt, at his desk behind closed doors, asks his wife. Linda rarely disturbs him at work. It's about their son Luke, suspended for two days.

"Some catch-all the schools use now," Linda says.

Voigt hears a horn beep. Linda's on her way to pick up their son at Canyon High.

"Apparently he was defending you to his homeroom teacher. It got heated."

"The teacher bring up the subject?" Voigt asks. Recently there'd been drone protests outside the base. People arrested for lying down in the road and blocking traffic. It's not a mass movement yet, just an indicator of dissatisfaction. Is Luke's suspension another? If it weren't for that, he might admire the teacher for taking up the pacifist side in a school with a good percentage of students from military families. Isn't this, theoretically, what he's fighting for? Freedom.

"I don't know," Linda says. "Luke threw a book at the blackboard and they have zero tolerance for any hint of violence."

"Hell," Voigt says. "I'll speak with him tonight. At least it's only two days."

Linda pauses a moment. "Everything good there?"

This is the Voigts' code. "Yeah, we're good." What Voigt means is that there were no strikes today. That he won't come home brooding. For other than this, he cannot go into details about what he does. "Just some paperwork from DC today."

"Good. See you tonight then."

"You bet," he says and rings off.

He turns to the letter again—a copy of Don Aldridge's latest correspondence to Jessica. A Janet Sloan from Homeland Security has enlisted him in the effort to monitor any future breaches related to Sergeant Aldridge's old duties.

Sloan, in her call to him, had explained how an observant correctional officer at Seminole City, reviewing prisoner letters for contraband and illegal communications, noticed that Don was writing to an Air Force sergeant about the recent al-Yarisi strike and seemed to have information that wasn't in the news reports. New at his job and ex-military, the guard went beyond his primary duty of enforcing prison regulations and passed the letter up to an assistant warden, who then raided Don's cache of correspondence from his daughter. One of those letters contained other information not publicly released, about the two dead girls, but it had been let through by a less scrupulous screener. The assistant warden brought the letter cache to the warden, who made a call to Homeland Security in DC. It was a see-something, say-something situation.

Voigt considers that it might have been better if Jessica's violation had never been seen. Clearly her intention wasn't to go public about the Yarisi strike not being a clean kill. And Don, sitting in Seminole City Correctional, wasn't likely to spread the word. But to hell with the what-ifs.

Reviewing the latest letter, Voigt makes a note that Don has mentioned al-Yarisi's wives. This observation does not require his special familiarity with the situation. Everyone involved knows those deaths are to be kept quiet. It's just a busybody's work, this task.

Yet through the correspondence, Voigt is gaining more insight into his ex-sergeant, more than he had gotten from her security screening or her record as a drone operator and then pilot. And her father, all things taken, seems a somewhat decent man. Voigt hates to think this, but he is curious about Jessica's next letter to him. About how she is taking her dismissal. It will be good to keep track of things, and not just for the sake of security. He files the letter, a secured PDF copy, on his hard drive.

CHAPTER 10

New York City and Upstate

"Ethan?" Zoe's voice is trembling. "Ethan?"

Caller ID on his BlackBerry had revealed Zoe's number to him. For the past five seconds, after standing up from his desk in his office at the bank, he has been faking a bad connection, waiting for Zoe to disconnect. He'll need to change his number.

"My father said I should speak to you . . . Ethan?"

Zoe, a catch in her voice, sounds ragged. He has been remiss. It is two weeks since Leston gave Ethan his documents and gradually he has moved them from his kitchen pass-through, to a shelf under the counter, to the recycle bin. The latter was an act of bravado. He was only pretending to throw them out, just as he is only pretending now that he will not speak to Zoe.

"Hello," he says.

"Oh, you're there."

"I'm here."

The ache of her absence returns. It is what he has been avoiding by not opening the folder that Walter Leston gave him.

Zoe takes a quick breath. The sigh she releases quavers.

"Are you okay?" Ethan asks.

There is dead air. "Of course, you don't know anything. You couldn't, could you?"

"Know anything?"

"I mean, even though you were in touch with my father."

"Just once. He came into town to see me."

"And what did he want?"

"He gave me some documents . . . I've been meaning to mail them back. He wanted me to look them over, but I haven't."

"Why not?"

"He said they were about your . . . family. Not any of my business."

"Then why did he give them to you?"

"I . . ." Ethan hesitates. He does not wish to say that her father was try-ing to manipulate him. That the doctor believes that Ethan's possession of the papers might bring Zoe and him back together. An unwell man, a dying man who likes control, he wants Ethan to take care of his daughter when he is gone. Despite their headbutting, Ethan gives himself credit for being the best option Leston had found for his Zoe. Less agreeably, per-haps Leston sees in him the stiff, analytic dourness by which the doctor governs his family. Or is it *governed* his family? "Has your father . . . has he . . . *already*?" Ethan says.

Zoe's fury is sudden. "*You* knew? You knew what he was planning?" Zoe's wail pierces. Ethan leans a hand on his desk to stay steady. "You fucking heartless bastard. Why didn't you tell me? I could have stopped him."

Her reaction makes Ethan leap to the worst conclusion—not that Leston is simply dead but that he has taken the easy way out. "Oh, Zoe," he says. "I'm so—"

"How could you *not* do anything, Ethan?"

Suddenly it's clear. Leston had come to him as part of his final prepa-rations. Looking back the signs were there: the ironic demeanor, the coy prognosis about how much time he had left. Facing a terminal illness, he wanted to die in his own way. Suicide under such conditions was logical. Ethan could easily construct a quality of life algorithm that would make the same decision. But he cannot tell Zoe this. "Your father only told me he was sick," he says pathetically trying to excuse himself.

"But if you had read what he gave you, it might have changed things," Zoe says, pleading against the facts, as do all who are in the early stages of grief. Ethan pulls himself back into detachment. He knows that he can only help Zoe right now by taking some of the blame. Zoe goes on with a sob. "At least it might have changed things for my mother."

"Your mother?" Ethan absorbs Zoe's words until their meaning burns through. Irreligious as he is, "Jesus," he blurts. He takes a gulp of air. "I'm sorry, Zoe."

Ethan's breathlessness must be proof of innocence. Now Zoe's the one detached. "Somehow he arranged for an EMS to arrive after it was over."

"How did they? . . ."

"Nembutal and wine. They were in their bed. I was told they went peacefully. I don't even think my mom knew what was happening."

"AREN'T YOU EVEN curious?" Alex asks.

"No," Ethan says. It has been four days since Zoe's call. He has still not looked at the documents her father gave him. Whatever Dr. Leston was up to, he will not be drawn into his web. "My life has moved on from Zoe."

"That's icy, man." Buckled in the passenger's seat, his head turned away, Alex seems to be gazing out his window. Through breaks in the tree line Ethan sees flashes of the Hudson below. He has rented a black BMW and he and Alex are on the Palisades gliding north to the Lestons' funeral.

"Could you do it?" Alex asks.

"Do what?"

"Off yourself like her old man."

"Who knows," Ethan says.

Alex has pulled his hair into a neat ponytail. He has evened out his movie star's stubble and put on unscathed black jeans and a clean black shirt. He is wearing work boots though, originally black but now flecked with the pigments he's not been able to scrape off. The dark sports coat that Ethan has loaned him lies draped across the backseat. Its arms are too long, but Alex has folded the sleeve ends into cuffs. He is handsome enough to make any clothing look deliberate, as if they are a new and edgy style.

"Barbiturates and booze. Those are the sane man's choice," Alex says.

"You've been thinking about this, have you?"

"Why not. At our age dying is still a game. You can choose to or not. When you're old your choice is basically to die slow or to die fast."

"And if you choose fast? What about the people you leave behind?"

"At least they won't have to watch you fall apart."

Ethan has heard this argument before, if not so overtly. He'd heard it in Leston's study when the doctor described his wife's future with dementia.

"So you think Zoe is better off?"

"Are you high?" Alex says. "She's suffering. I don't know why you didn't go up there already to help her through this."

"We are not together anymore. Maybe her new boyfriend is handling those duties."

"Does she even have one? I spoke to her and she's up in the country alone."

"Then why didn't *you* go?"

Alex shakes his head. "Because I never lived with her."

"Zoe's life is not my responsibility," Ethan says.

Alex comes back at him hard. "We're not animals. We're all each other's responsibility."

"Sort of like . . . ," Ethan starts. He was about to say *sort of like buying someone's paintings so they don't starve.* Instead he gnaws his inner cheek.

Alex reaches into the backseat and pulls Leston's manila folder onto his lap.

"Put it back," Ethan says.

"You can't *give* this to her without reading it." Alex undoes the clasping rubber band.

"Put it back," Ethan says.

"What are you afraid of?" Alex opens the folder. "Dude, it's just old newspaper clippings," he says. And then he begins to read aloud.

LOCAL TEEN MISSING NEARLY A MONTH

Monroe, Conn., Jan. 20, 1989—The Monroe Police Department is asking for help in locating a missing 16-year-old girl. Susan Leston, who goes by the nickname Zee, was last seen on December 26th in her home at 28 Oak Court. She is believed to be unaccompanied. Leston is described as a white female with blonde hair and a fair complexion. She is approximately 5 feet 7 inches tall and weighs 105 pounds. She was wearing a leather coat when she disappeared. Anyone with information should contact Sgt. Murak of the Monroe Police.

CONNECTICUT RUNAWAY FOUND IN MIAMI BEACH

Miami, Fla., Feb. 10, 1989—A 16-year-old missing for almost two months was detained by Dade County police after using a false ID to enter a popular Miami Beach nightclub. Parents of the girl flew to Miami where she was held in juvenile detention. The girl's father credited both the Miami and Connecticut police for locating his daughter, commenting, "They worked together in exemplary fashion." Interviewed by phone, Sgt. Ray Murak of the Monroe Police said he had met the family at the airport. "When a teen crosses the state line it really becomes a needle-in-a-haystack situation," said Murak. "We got lucky. The girl is back home, tanned and healthy. She must have spent lots of time at the beach."

CRASH KILLS TEEN

Trumbull, Conn., Mar. 7, 1990—A late-night crash killed 17-year-old Susan Leston of Monroe. Leston was speeding on the Merritt Parkway when her vehicle hit a bridge abutment. According to EMS officials the teen died instantly on the scene. Ray Murak, a sergeant with the Monroe Police, says the crash remains under investigation by the Connecticut State Police. A former student of the Ethel Walker School, Susan is survived by an infant daughter and her parents, Walter and Elizabeth.

Ethan's molars clench the inside of his cheek. "Read that part again."

"You mean the 'Susan is survived by an infant daughter' part?" Alex says.

"It's Zoe."

"Seems so. Here's the court documents. Her grandparents adopted her after the crash."

"Christ."

"This is too fucking much," Alex says. "Why didn't they tell her?"

"I don't know, but now I'm the messenger."

"Yo, Eth. You can't let her know any of this today, not on the day she's burying her parents. I mean, her grandparents."

And maybe I shouldn't ever tell her, Ethan thinks, running a mental Monte Carlo simulation on Zoe's future—the two paths she might follow.

In the one where she remains ignorant, the past recedes from her. In the other, the past alters her, becomes the focus of her energy, the source of regret, sorrow, and anger. Another response in this Monte Carlo would be to grab Leston's folder from Alex and fling it out the window of the car. With all her family dead, does Zoe need to know that she's lived her whole life without knowing who her parents were? Ethan punches the wheel with his palm as if it's the doctor's grinning face. "Why did the old man put this on *me*?"

"Because he was too weak to do it himself," Alex says.

"Or because he was a son of a bitch."

"Man, I'll bet that was all a front. I mean, look at you. People who don't know you might mistake you for . . ."

Ethan is half listening. He has just taken out his buzzing BlackBerry. "For what?"

"For kind of a dick?"

"Thanks. And fuck you, too."

"But you're not. Not underneath. I'll bet the old man identified with you."

"So you're saying I resemble him."

"Just guessing. I never met him. But if he was a surgeon he had to be as focused on his work as you. Ethan! Look at the road!" he yells. "This is a day of mourning. I don't want there to be another one next week for us."

"Sorry," Ethan says. He had been reviewing the spate of text alerts on his BlackBerry. Palestinian rockets have just hit Eilat on the Gulf of Aqaba and he's sweating over his terrorism-response subprogram. Four months after he'd conceived it, it went live this week. Detached from the mainframe he is powerless to apply fixes. If Israel responds immediately, his absence from work could diminish the bank's profits and affect his year-end bonus. Wars don't happen every day and he's responsible for capitalizing on them.

THE OBERLUND FUNERAL Home is a gabled house with a parking lot full of older Mercedes, vehicles similar to Leston's. Alex enters first.

"Be prepared," he whispers. Then Ethan sees what his friend has seen.

At the far side of a great room stand two biers holding the Lestons' coffins. Both lids are raised.

"Is that necessary?" Ethan whispers, partly to Alex but mostly to himself. He doesn't think Zoe would have asked for such a display. The open caskets must be by Leston's request. Yet his daughter or, rather, his *granddaughter*—Ethan is still absorbing this new data—has chosen not to override that decision. While Alex hovers in the back, Ethan is drawn forward and finds himself in the short line to the biers. Bouquets of white, red, and yellow flowers hide the closed bottoms of the coffins.

Dr. Leston is looking distinguished in a gray suit. His full head of hair is immaculately coifed and brushed back from his forehead. Ethan lets his eyes wander down to Walter's chest, which seems immense, artificially inflated. He wonders if the mortician hasn't stuffed a Sunday *Times* under Walter's shirt. And strangely, or so it seems to Ethan, a handkerchief sits folded in the dead man's breast pocket. It's as if Walter might take it out later to wipe his brow. Perhaps he will, for the doctor's complexion is florid, full of the heat he showed when he'd tested Ethan by the fireplace in his study. Unnerved, Ethan sidles to the next coffin.

Elizabeth, poor Elizabeth, is wearing the elegant gown she'd ruined on the night she'd met Ethan. Ethan comprehends that it must have been a favorite outfit. Then he is distracted by weird and pointless thoughts about the success of the gown's dry cleaning, about whether Elizabeth will be wearing a soiled gown through eternity. But since he can't see into the lower half of the coffin he focuses on Elizabeth's disturbingly blank expression. Even in death she cannot escape the disease that was shutting down her brain. And Ethan cannot help but think that her husband did the right thing, served as her god of life and death. Beyond this, however, it is a little perverse for her murderer to be laid out in the same room. Then he remembers that human laws do not apply to the dead.

A gap opens in the crowd and Ethan spies Zoe arm in arm with Alex almost as if this is a wedding ceremony and he is giving her away. Taller than Alex, Zoe seems elongated in her mourning dress, her calves look thin in their dark hose, her feet attenuated in black heels. It is as if he is looking at a painting of Zoe rendered with expressionistic exaggeration. Ethan thinks she resembles one of those generically anorexic but facially distinctive runway models that fashion designers prefer—the hollowness of her cheeks and the bumped ridge of her nose more pronounced than ever. Ethan does not think he has ever seen her so clearly. She is an actor spotlighted on a darkened stage.

She smiles at him during the last instant of her approach and Ethan feels her cool cheek pressing his. It is not a kiss. "Hey," she whispers into his ear as if he is the one needing comfort. And he does. Their faces are touching but all he can feel is the void of their separation. "I shouldn't have yelled at you on the phone," she says. "What my father did was his doing alone."

"But . . . maybe I could have done somethi—"

Zoe cuts him off. "No." She stands back and grasps his arms while looking into his eyes. He can feel her nails through his jacket. "No. You didn't know him. I'm sorry he got you involved."

Then she turns away, called by an older couple who, in practiced routine, hug her tightly as if they are overaccustomed to attending the funerals of acquaintances. Ethan drifts backward and other mourners fill the space between Zoe and him. He finds it hard to breathe.

"You look peaked, old man," says Alex approaching Ethan from the side. "Zoe's really handling this nightmare. She must be doing some good meds."

"What if she is? How else could she get through this?"

"Hey, I'm not criticizing her," says Alex. "I'm admiring her being chemically responsible. Me, if my old man pulled a trick like this, I'd be getting myself seriously fucked up on anything I could smoke, swallow, sniff, or shoot. By the way," Alex whispers, jabbing an elbow into Ethan's side, "Don't gramps look pissed off as hell being stuck in that box?"

"Yeah. Wouldn't you?" Ethan says flatly. This is as much humor as he can muster.

Half an hour later the coffins are taken away and Ethan and Alex are in their BMW a few cars behind the hearse. There will be no church service. Because of the crowd Ethan and Alex must stand behind a mound of dirt covered by a blue tarp. Next to the coffins, floating on motorized straps over their respective graves, stands Zoe, head bowed and tearless. One of Leston's former colleagues recites a final, secular sentiment, and then a thunderclap and raindrops send everyone back to their cars.

By the time Ethan and Alex arrive at the Lestons' home for the reception, they have driven through an eastward-moving downpour. The sky
is clearing and the air is fresh with electrical charge. Beyond fields over
which the farmhouse watches, a rainbow shimmers and mourners pause
on the porch before going inside. There is talk by some that the rainbow
is a sign that what has happened has been forgiven. Walter could not have
planned a better moment.

STANDING NEAR THE mantel of the Lestons' dark fireplace, Ethan recalls Elizabeth Leston's sad attempt to entertain him the previous July,
not quite four months before. Alex's discussion with Zoe, however, is
within earshot and it pulls him into the present.

"It's ten by sixteen. The biggest I've attempted so far . . ."

Alex is deliberately talking about things other than the funeral, reminding Zoe about all the tomorrows that remain to the living. It is time,
he is saying, to begin to turn away from the dead.

"That's great, Alex," Zoe says, but seems unreceptive. She holds her
arms tightly against herself.

Then the man standing at the other end of the fireplace addresses
Ethan. The man offers him his hand. "Hi, Hal Stanhope. And you must
be a friend of Zoe's."

"Ethan Winter," Ethan says, grasping the man's humid flesh. "Zoe and
I used to live together," he corrects.

"Oh?" Stanhope sounds disappointed. A peer of the Leston's, he had
probably come of age in the fifties. But his disapproval of premarital cohabitation seems as much based on snobbishness as antique morality.
That Stanhope, like Leston, boasts a luxuriant head of hair gives Ethan
another reason to dislike him. Ethan, at least, has an advantage in height.
"Perhaps you and Zoe will be getting back together now," Stanhope says
ingenuously.

Why would you say that? Ethan wants to ask. But Stanhope's dull eyes
indicate his annoyance would be wasted. *Witless old turd*, Ethan thinks.
And then an older woman with an unnaturally taut face and bouffant
hair comes to his side. She's carrying an hors d'oeuvres plate and from it

Stanhope picks up a cracker spread with liverwurst. "My wife and wait-ress," Stanhope says. "Tracy, Ethan, and vice versa."

"Then you're a friend of Zoe's," Mrs. Stanhope says. She offers Ethan her hand, which unlike her husband's is a dry bundle of twigs.

"I was just telling your husband I once lived with Zoe."

"The Zoe I know is a delicate child," Hal says.

"We've known her since she was three," Tracy adds.

Ethan's brain engages. "That must have been when the Lestons moved here."

"Weren't they from Hartford?" Stanhope asks his wife.

"No. It was Danbury. Or Waterbury. Or was that just where Walter practiced surgery? Anyway they lived or he worked in some 'bury' out west."

"Don't you mean *east*, in Connecticut?" Hal says.

The Stanhopes impress Ethan as fonts of misinformation. Despite this, he keeps steering the discussion toward Zoe's past. "Why do you say Zoe's delicate?" The Zoe Ethan knows is independent and unsentimental, at least about him.

"Zoe had emotional troubles as a kid," Stanhope says. "They got her straightened out though."

"Valium. Lithium," Tracy Stanhope lists before reconsidering. Her in-discretion flusters her. "Elizabeth and I used to talk."

"Our kids never went on the stuff," Stanhope says.

"Children weren't prescribed those drugs so much when ours were growing up," Tracy says. "Plus we were lucky. We had boys. It's all in the cards."

"And your astrological sign," adds Stanhope.

"Oh please, *Hal*," says Tracy, though she seems happy for the opening. "Don't start making fun of my hobby again." Tracy looks at Ethan. "Still, Zoe *is* a Libra and it really shows. She puts on a good front but really keeps her cards close."

"Guess Ethan's sign," Stanhope tells his wife. "No, let me."

"Hal is actually quite good at this," Tracy says. "But he doesn't take his ability seriously. Imagine, he even refuses to use the stars for stock tips."

"After the past few years I may start," says Stanhope. "I can't do any worse." Then, eyeing Ethan, he bursts out, "I'll bet a hundred dollars you're a Virgo." Ethan finds this judgment vaguely insulting. "Wouldn't you say Ethan's a Virgo, dear?" he asks his wife.

"He *is* rather quiet," says Tracy.

Ethan sips down his vodka and licks his lips, which are going numb. "Pisces," he says, although he is a Virgo.

"I *knew* it," says Tracy. "I was thinking Pisces."

Ethan fixates on his empty glass. "Refill time," he tells the Stanhopes and lurches away.

TRACY STANHOPE, WASHING the few dirty plates the caterers missed, talks about Salvador Dalí with a solicitous Alex, who is unloading the Leston's dishwasher from its last run. Ethan has been rearranging the salvaged party food to fit the refrigerator. Zoe has been attending to the departing mourners as if each needs the brand of her personal farewell. Perhaps this is justified. Many of these aged people, her grandparents' friends, she will likely never see again.

Finally, the rest of the house goes quiet. Ethan goes to find Zoe, and through the living room windows he sees movement on the porch and glimpses her from behind, her back long and slender. She is standing beside a swaying glider, on which Hal Stanhope sits. Both are facing the descending sun. A white puff blooms around Zoe and Ethan is astonished to see that she is smoking a cigarette. They have been apart for only four months, yet she is utterly strange to him.

Has he never before paid her such close attention? Had he only seen in her what he expected to see? Sometimes her kisses tasted metallic; he thought it was her diet but now determines that this might have been the aftereffects of secret cigarettes. Or a mood stabilizer. *Lithium?* How much had she kept from him? Or was it that he had never allowed her the space to open up?

"Hey," she says, turning as he squeaks through the porch's screen door. "Thanks for cleaning up." Smoke exits her nostrils in plumes. Her eyes seem heavily made up. Then he realizes they are shadowed from weariness.

"That a new habit?" Ethan inquires of the cigarette, unable to stop himself.

She flicks the butt into the driveway and sparks skitter. Dusk is arriving. "You heading back to the city soon?" she asks, and Ethan is duly reprimanded. She is shooing him home like the rest of the mourners.

"Will you be all right? Alone up here."

"We're next door," says Stanhope. "If Zoe needs anything she just has to cross the yard."

"That's good," Ethan says, annoyed by the squeaking of the glider chain.

"Thank you both," Zoe says. "I'll be fine. I won't have time to brood on things if that's your worry. I've plenty to do. Cleaning up. Putting the house on the market. Financial stuff. My father left neat piles in his study. His lawyer is coming tomorrow to go through them with me.

"Speaking of which," Zoe says to Ethan, "those documents my father brought you, did you bring them up?"

Ethan thinks. He could give Zoe the folder without discussing its contents. After which he can go back to his financial modeling, his relationship with Yahvi. He will have abandoned Zoe decisively and perhaps this will kill his longing for the life he might have had with her.

"I forgot them," Ethan says.

Zoe nods. Does she think this is his ploy to see her again?

"Why don't I just send them to you?" he says.

CHAPTER 11

Nevada

DISORIENTED HIKER FOUND NEAR HIGHWAY

Pahrump, Nev., Nov. 2, 2012—A truck driver taking a rest stop on Route 373 rescued a hiker who had been wandering the Amargosa Desert for two days. Jessica Aldridge, a 24-year-old former Air Force technical sergeant, stated that she became disoriented after running out of water in the Funeral Mountains. Aldridge, found partially disrobed, was initially thought to be the victim of an assault. Investigators now speculate Aldridge removed some of her clothing after suffering heat stroke. She is recovering from dehydration and sunburn at the Pettis Memorial VA Medical Center in Loma Linda, California.

CHAPTER 12

- -

California

The man working the counter has a braided beard and baggy eyes. When Jessica comes into his shop he is leaning over a newspaper spread on a display case of piercing jewelry—tongue rings, studs, ear gauges. After a friendly glance he returns to his perusing and Jessica heads to the wall to examine samples of roses and butterflies and dragons and tribal marks, none of which interest her. But there are also photographs—of elaborately scarified arms, of a man's back imprinted with action cartoon panels, of a bald woman inked from head to toe in jungle flora. Through a beaded curtain at the back comes a mechanical buzz mingled with mumbles that sound like a dental patient attempting speech.

"Oh, keep quiet," a woman's voice orders from the other side of the beads. The man's mumbling declines to a whimper.

"Ain't usually that bad," the man at the counter says. "She's doing a mouth." He pushes up from the newspaper and rises to his full, sad-eyed height, which is over six feet. He is wearing jeans and an armless leather vest—the better to advertise his tattoos, many of which resemble oversized Asian calligraphy. He settles onto a walker and shuffles out from behind the counter. "Considering a tat?"

"Maybe," says Jessica.

"You over eighteen?"

She is wearing camouflage pants, a tank top, and no shoes—basically what she snatched from her hospital room's closet before she got on the bus that dropped her in San Bernardino. She glances into the shopkeeper's eyes and gets that she must look to him like an underage runaway. "I have ID," she says.

"Yeah, well. Might need to see some alternate verification, too. We got in trouble once for putting angel wings on a sixteen-year-old."

Jessica then notices that she is still wearing her hospital bracelet. In the back pocket of her pants she feels the wad stuffed in there and takes it out. "How about my Air Force discharge papers?"

He lifts an eyebrow. "Those'll do."

Jessica turns to show him her right shoulder blade. "I want this covered up."

"May I?" he asks and with a delicate touch stretches her skin. "Good inks," he says. "Miss Shelly could make something pretty out of this. Guess you want to start with the initials, seeing as you're no longer USAF property."

"Right."

"And the bird?"

"I don't feel gung ho enough to wear an eagle."

"See anything on the wall you like?"

"Not really."

He looks down at her, perhaps at her hospital bracelet, and pulls at one of his chin braids. "There's a doctor I know who lasers tats. Might take quite a few sessions to blast it out though."

"I'm leaving town tomorrow."

"All right."

"But I can't have this on my back anymore."

"Well, let's wait and see if Miss Shelly can help."

WHEN MISS SHELLY emerges through the beaded curtain Jessica recognizes her. She is the shaved, tattooed woman in the wall photo, which must be fifteen years old. Miss Shelly is tinier than Jessica imagined she would be from her picture and she has grown her hair, which stands in sparse gray punky spikes. All her fingers to the first joint display bands of rings. Her smile reveals a gold incisor and causes her face to crinkle deeply. Jessica sees then that what she first took for wrinkles is a tattoo of a spider's web and a black widow, identifiable by its red mark, which is centered on Shelly's forehead. Only after Jessica takes all this in does she notice that Miss Shelly wears a tube clipped into her nostrils and is wheeling behind her a tank of oxygen.

"Hey. Be with you in a minute," Miss Shelly says to Jessica in an accent that is not West Coast. And then she turns her attention to the clicking curtain. "*Harvey*, get your hairy butt on out here."

A hulk parts the curtain. He is covering his mouth.

"I swear, you big ones are the wussiest. Now show us what you got."

The man lowers the covering hand and Jessica is surprised to see that his mouth, chin, and cheeks display no art. Then Harvey pulls his lower lip inside out and a tattooed ROSALYNN appears right side up. His upper lip is grinning.

"Harvey, know what you ought to have did before you came to me?" Miss Shelly asks. "Shacked up with a girl named Sue."

LEANING FORWARD IN a masseur's chair, Jessica cannot see Miss Shelly at work.

"Skin fresh peeled from a sunburn makes a good canvas," Shelly comments. "The ink goes deep. But it don't tickle."

They are behind the beaded curtain, in a back room more the size of a closet. Jessica's top is down and a rotating table fan intermittently chills her. Miss Shelly's vibrating needle pricks over the bone of her shoulder blade and she clenches a fist.

"There's not much meat on you so it's gonna hurt extra," Miss Shelly says. "I'd pour you a tequila if I could, but we ain't allowed to serve drinks or drunks. Let me know when you want a break."

"I'm good," Jessica says. "As long as we can finish today."

"This'll take a couple few hours. Never done one of these. A lot of phoenixes. Never a sphinx."

Jessica has picked the image from a book on Greek urns in Miss Shelly's limited but odd library—which includes volumes on Disney cartoons, Maori sculpture, Balinese ceremonial masks, fractal geometry, Chinese astrological symbols, scarification in Ghana, ancient Egyptian writing, whatever might inspire a customer. The sphinx will incorporate her eagle's wings and turn the claw-clutched USAF banner into hieroglyphs. "Ever heard of a palimpsest?" Miss Shelly asks her. "That's writing on top of writing. We fix a lot of tats that way. Keeps a part of your history while changing it."

"Fine," Jessica says and drifts.

Jessica had always charted out her long-term future like a psychic predicting happiness: a disciplined twenty years that would culminate in a military pension and return her to her beachside hometown in Florida. There she would invest her savings in a small apartment building, which she would paint pink and manage alone. Sure, she would meet a few men . . . yet she would not marry—her marriage to the Air Force having been sufficient. This life to come had appeared as solid as a monument cast in bronze.

Attuned to the vibrating needle, Jessica comprehends that her new philosophy is to be adrift. She will keep on the move for the same reason she is undoing her tattoo, and for the same reason she had slipped away from the hospital: to be no longer what she was. In order to start again, she must now not do *anything* with military deliberation. She must drift and even in this drifting she must let herself drift.

Under the music of Miss Shelly's needle, time passes. Is it moving forward or jumping backward? Through the curtain seeps a smell that Jessica recognizes. She had avoided proximity to this odor after her enlistment.

Miss Shelly quiets the needle. "How about that break?"

"Okay," Jessica says and, rising stiffly, rolls her shoulders. A mirror displays Shelly's work in progress. Jessica's USAF has been transformed into hieroglyphs representing a woman, a serpent, a hill, a lamp wick—because those ancient symbols have shapes similar to the letters Miss Shelly is burying. Above them, Jessica's American eagle is but half metamorphosed into the stony female sphinx it will become and Jessica does not know if she likes it. Carefully she pulls up her tank top, and then Miss Shelly holds the curtain for her to exit the work space. The odor gets stronger, but strangely there is none of the usual smoke.

"Cannabis for Newt's back," explains Miss Shelly. "It's legal. Though in the old illegal days it was easier to get. Now you got to go to LA to fill a prescription. Unless you grow your own." She and Shelly watch as Newt inhales through one end of a long flexible tube—the other end of which he is pressing into some device with a power cord.

"Yep," Newt says. "City council has banned dispensaries here." He puts the tube down onto the display case. "I'm getting some air."

Using his walker Newt clomps out the front door. A fuming truck charges past and diesel mingles with the cannabis odor in the shop. And then Miss Shelly and Jessica are alone. Shelly is scratching at a crust of blood on the inside of her arm, which Jessica notices is badly scarred.

"It may look like I shoot up, but this is from dialysis. Ain't half as much fun."

"I didn't . . ."

"Oh hell, I'm no innocent." Shelly shuts off the oxygen tank and unclips her breather. "For example, it ain't exactly legal to share 'scripts and I don't currently have one myself." Shelly picks up the tube near the silver device and does what Newt had done. After exhaling she smiles at Jessica. "Likewise it would be real dumb of me to offer a customer a hit off this even if she was sore from my needlework. But that ain't compassionate. Ever vape? Believe you me, it's easier on the lungs than toking."

THE NEEDLE'S HUM goes quiet, but the tingle in Jessica's scapula goes on, thanks to Newt's cannabis.

"*Finito*," Miss Shelly says and aims a mirror so that Jessica can view her work.

"S'good," Jessica responds. The sphinx, fiercely protecting her flank, looks livelier than it had an hour earlier as a crippled eagle. But, according to Miss Shelly's book on classical urns, the question it asks is not the usual one a sphinx asks: *What walks from morning to night first on four legs, then two, then three?*—with the answer being *man*.

No, the riddle Jessica's sphinx presents is a woman, a serpent, a hill, a wick. But if the riddle is gibberish then won't the answer be whatever she gives it? And if it's whatever she says, then doesn't *she* become the answer?

"Whoa!" Jessica's thoughts say loudly. Or maybe she has spoken aloud. The next thing she'll be doing is talking about the atoms in the thumbnail of some cosmic giant who is himself an atom in the thumbnail of a giant. She notices that her cheeks ache from grinning.

"Stuff's pretty potent. Hybrid. Plus the vape," Miss Shelly says. "You okay?"

It's hard, but Jessica manages to form some words. "Sorry. Never really got high. Just a few times in high school. What do I owe?" Jessica yanks a pocket inside out and watches bills flutter into the air like comic, clumsy birds. Trying to catch them she starts to laugh.

"Newt," Miss Shelly calls. "I do believe our friend here is having a reaction to your kush."

IN THE DESERT, after burying her uniform, Jessica had aimed herself toward the scrub plateau in the direction of her motel—or where she'd thought it was. But in a vise of dehydration that approached delirium she had wandered. And when under a three o'clock sun her boots touched blacktop, she could go no farther. She would have to wait until someone came to her. A trucker finally did.

The hospital room, the bus ride, the tattoo parlor—maybe they were all a wishful dream. She is still lost in the desert, huddled in a fetal curl against a hot wind. Then her crusted eyelids open to reveal a topless wall of mountain that resolves into brown weave. Behind her a panting warms her neck. A wolf? She turns and her nose bumps a snout. A sandpaper tongue intermittently licks.

"Hey," Jessica groggily tells the dog. After dragging her feet from couch to floor she huddles her arms and coughs into her hands until a catch in her throat clears. She looks around. What place is this?

Crepuscular light identifies it as a living room, off which opens a kitchen where she goes to wash her hands in a sink stacked with plates. The dog, a long-haired female shepherd, blonde as a desert coyote, pushes against her thigh. She scratches its ear and follows it to a door cracked open to reveal a bed bowed under a snoring mound. An ogre's gnarled foot pokes from the bed sheet. Jessica pushes the door wider and its groan alerts the ogre—a slight figure with a tube dangling from her nose. Miss Shelly, the smaller part of the mound, sits up in the bed and stretches.

"Sleep well?" Shelly asks her through a yawn.

"Very deeply," Jessica says, recalling now a ride sideways in the back of a pickup.

Miss Shelly, whom Jessica had thought was wearing tie-dye, is unabashedly sitting there only in her tattoos.

SEATED ON NEWT and Shelly's front stoop Jessica sees, between roof-
tops, a mountain range. Subtracting this horizon and the parched air, the
neighborhood feels to her like South Florida with the concrete homes and
chain-link fences.

She inhales on a scavenged cigarette, the first since her desert hike. But
the nicotine only reminds her of being on a drone duty break.

"Hey," Miss Shelly says before opening the screen door behind her. She
hands down a mug of coffee to Jessica. In the yard the shepherd, puppyish,
prances and yelps.

"Skittles," barks Miss Shelly. "Don't get us kicked out of the neighborhood."

The coffee's heat dissolves a knot in Jessica's forehead. Shelly drops a
newspaper section onto the stoop.

"You kinda weren't in any shape to get back to your VA hospital last
night," Miss Shelly says. "Don't imagine those military doctors approve
of certain medications anyway. But hell, no one ever overdosed on weed.
Prescription pills are a lot more likely to do you in." With a tattooed foot
Shelly nudges the newspaper toward Jessica. "Seen this? You got famous."

The newsprint coheres into a headline describing a disoriented hiker.

"Maybe you discharged yourself a little early," says Shelly.

"No. I'm better."

Miss Shelly looks out at the yard. "Got any family here?"

Jessica shakes her head and then flicks her cigarette onto the patchy
lawn. She feels trashy for doing this, but she has taken Miss Shelly's question as a hint that they, Shelly and Newt, have their lives and Jessica has
hers. She puts down the mug and starts for the gate.

"Thanks for letting me crash," she says.

Shelly follows and takes her arm. "Hey. I was gonna suggest you use
our couch for a week or two. You know, till you figure stuff out. Anyhow,
a couple of falling-apart old farts like us wouldn't mind the company."

AFTER NEWT AND Miss Shelly leave for work at Tattoo Heaven, Jessica
leashes Skittles and explores the neighborhood. Several nearby homes
stare vacantly with foreclosed eyes. Occasional children twirl behind the
fences of drought-struck yards. An older boy on an undersized bike pedals

toward her and Skittles, his front wheel in the air. He turns at the last instant and Skittles jerks against her collar while Jessica pulls her back.

"Tattoo freak daughter," the kid says.

At a corner store she scavenges groceries from the inadequately stocked shelves.

Late in the afternoon, she cleans up the kitchen sink and makes chicken thighs and okra. As the sun settles toward the rooflines Newt arrives. He is without Miss Shelly.

"Just dropped her at her CPA class," he explains.

"CPA?" Jessica says.

"The tattoo business isn't what it was. Not for us. Young people want to get tattoos from young people."

"You're not old," Jessica lies.

"We're old enough to not be cool, and that's ancient," says Newt. "Plus, when you're over fifty you got to start saving. Shelly figures her face tattoos might scare off clients so she's going to work online or over the phone. Anyway, she has a plan. She's the brains around here."

Newt and Jessica eat and after dinner Newt snaps a chicken bone and lets Skittles lick its marrow from his fingers. Behind him sits a side table heavy with framed photographs. They are mostly of people in black leather who might have been Newt and Miss Shelly's peers twenty or thirty years ago.

"Do you have any children?" Jessica asks.

"Nah, we never got around to having kids. But then we also never got around to getting legally married. I suppose we're common law by now, or would be if they had it out here. Back in the day you would have called us anarchists. Mainly we partied. I did anyway. But time caught up with us. You never think it's going to happen when you're young. Then one day the mirror starts scaring the crap out of you."

After they clear the dishes Newt spreads a newspaper over the plank table and drops onto it a gnarled clump of green-brown vegetation. "Mind if I clean this?" Then he extracts a sizable joint from his t-shirt pocket and puts it between his lips. "Old school," he says.

In communion Jessica takes out the pack of cigarettes she bought at the corner store. She taps one up. "You mind?" she asks in turn.

"I almost do," Newt says. "Those things'll kill you. They spray 'em with pesticide. But this"—and he shows Jessica the doobie—"is one hundred percent guaranteed organic."

Newt lights up and offers Jessica his flame. As they creak back in their chairs with their separate drugs, a thought strikes her. "Don't you have to pick up Miss Shelly?"

He smiles. "Oh, I'm never too stoned to drive. Anyway, a classmate is dropping her."

By the time Newt has deseeded the cannabis, Jessica is almost high from the aroma. Newt wraps the waste into the newspaper. That's when they both notice the lost-in-the-desert article Shelly had shown her that morning. Carefully Newt tears it free. "For my scrapbook. To remember you by after you've gone on your way."

"Can I have it?" she asks.

The next day Jessica returns to the corner store to buy an envelope and stamp. She mails the clipping to Florida. Only the clipping. It will be enough to let Don know that she is alive, that she is as well as can be expected, that she is thinking of him. But she dare not tell him where she is, which is off the grid—unless there happen to be transistors in her fillings.

She's not paranoid crazy enough yet to imagine she might be wired with transistors. But, after all, her business had been surveillance; she knows there are watchers watching out there and that the watchers can do bad things since she has done the worst of those things. Killed innocent people. If she wrote again of that event to Don, his watchers would learn of it and hers would not be happy. They might send people to make sure she keeps quiet. They might have done so already. She dares not risk including a return address.

CHAPTER 13

Florida

My Dearest Jessica,

Getting an envelope addressed in your hand sped my heart. But finding no letter inside almost stopped it. The prison authorities claim there was only the newspaper clipping. But why should I trust them after they took all your other letters? Now I must guess how you are doing from a scrap of newsprint and this is torture. For it seems I have brought upon you my own bad luck. Know that I would cut off my toes to get you back your Air Force job. For you not to be burned and laid up in a hospital. But what can I do?

Do you know a man called Voigt? An Air Force colonel. He wrote to say he would return your letters to me after they were redacted. I looked up the word and it means censored. Maybe I should tell him that I can recite from memory what you wrote and will keep quiet about it only if he rehires you. A man like me in a cage has his fantasies.

Anyway. I can only pray that your situation will improve. Except for losing your letters mine has. I got a new cellmate. An honest to God professor named Ramirez. He is a funny man who calls me Senor Aldridge no matter how many times I tell him first names are fine. His is Ector and Ector does not have the hygiene problems of my old cellmate. Like all born Cubans Ector wears pressed clothes and washes behind the ears. He plays a sweet guitar too. Nylon string. Kind of soothing to hear him strum. I am listening right now because the professor gets to practice in our cell. This is part of the warden's music program just like allowing CD players. I have one of those thanks to your cigarette money. But it seems your generosity is a one way road. For what can I give back? Only my best hopes. So here they are.

*With luck Jessica you will not get this letter because you are no
longer where I sent it. With luck you are healthy again and out of
the hospital and putting your new life together. With luck you will
be leaving the problems of your old life behind. I know you have lost
much. Your job. Your Air Force friends. Your future as you imagined it.
But do not let misfortune break you like it broke me.*

*Your loving father,
Don*

CHAPTER 14

New York City, Ulster County

"Who's the babe?" asks John Guan. A kleptomaniac when it comes to his co-workers' personal data, Guan has cracked Ethan's BlackBerry password. Sitting in Ethan's chair, heels propped on Ethan's desk, he is going through the photos on Ethan's phone. Ethan has just returned to his office—a windowless twelve-by-twelve shell next door to the UIB servers. The white noise of their spinning hard drives penetrates the walls. But, frankly, Ethan finds the buzz soothing. And this space is his alone, not a cubicle in a bullpen.

"Here's your coffee. Now get out of my Aeron, shithead," he tells Guan.

"Touchy." Guan stands up, a good foot shorter than Ethan, and hands over Ethan's BlackBerry.

Actually, more often than not, Ethan finds Guan likable. As with most of the workers in the analytics section of the UIB tower, Guan is socially inept. Guan's difference is that he embraces his awkwardness—an archeologically stained tie, for example, is his hipster beard; the saggy jeans and Keds, his concept of gangsta; his bedhead hairdo of cowlicks, a punk manifesto; the way he frequently probes an ear with a finger, his version of the "peace out" sign. But when you need good data fast, Guan's your go-to. He can add a column of twenty ten-digit numbers quicker than Ethan can click the sum button in a spreadsheet. But this is only a parlor trick. Though fourth-generation American, Guan knows Mandarin and the Mandarin mindset. He can tell you what to expect out of Beijing and Shanghai—and right now Ethan wants him for just that. He is adding scenarios to his drone-strike algorithm and needs variables and odds pertaining to potential Chinese reactions. China, after all, is heavily invested in natural resources in Africa, where US drone activity is increasing. Guan moves to the chair opposite Ethan's desk and slurps his coffee.

"Give me five," Ethan says, referring to the number of scenarios he hopes to plug into his model.

"I'll give you twenty-five."

"No, too much work."

"But you want to be accurate. You want to duplicate the potential reality of the situation."

"And you know that's impossible. I just need to model close enough to know if there'll be movement between euros and yuans in *most* situations."

"*Okay,* I get it," Guan says. "You wanna track yuans to tell if you're over the euro."

"Uh, yeah."

Guan looks intensely at Ethan's left ear—Guan never looks anyone in the eye; the ear is as close as he gets. "But you should also register if the renminbi is making the dollar duller and the peso passé."

"Fine," Ethan says and leans back in his chair. "Please, go ahead. Get it all out of your system."

"Thanks a zloty."

Ethan looks at his BlackBerry, at the image Guan has brought up. Zoe.

"I'd like to pound her," Guan says.

"What?" Ethan says. "Fuck you."

"Oh, sorry. She's your current see, huh?"

"My ex."

"Ex-*cellent,*" says Guan. "You need to give me her number right now."

"Don't think so."

"Ahh, I understand you well, white man." Guan twists the ends of a long, imaginary mustache. "Your winky is as tiny as you are tall. You fear that I bling your ex briss, do you not?"

"If you mean 'bring her bliss,' *no,*" Ethan says, trying to keep up with Guan's ADHD.

"You make fun of my race? The way I speak?" Guan pounds a fist on Ethan's desk. "There will be a person for you to see up in human resource!" Then Guan unknots his fake-angry face. "Seriously, guy, aren't you seeing another female now?"

At work Ethan does not discuss his relationships, and especially not with Guan. But Guan has broken into his phone and Ethan now sees that he has missed a text—a text that Guan has apparently read.

"Mangez avec moi?" says Guan just as Ethan scans the same words in Yahvi's message. Guan points a finger at him. "You guys with the schnozes get all the chicks. Big nose, big hose, am I right, bitch?"

Ethan only needs one hand to calculate his successes with women over the years. But as these dates were not with paid escorts or Russian mail-order brides, he appreciates Guan's point. He has been luckier than the average dedicated numbers worker. The clan of the quant does not devote much time to normal relationships. Whether it is their unwritten code of work-focused behavior or a weakness in the altruism allele of their genetic code, the lonely quant is more likely to settle for, as John Guan might say, cash and marry.

"Right," Ethan says.

ETHAN PASSES THROUGH UIB's light-flooded lobby and out into the relative dark. This time of year, mid-November, he walks a path of neon and brake lights from Exchange Plaza to Battery Park—a route he follows with postal dedication despite heat waves or blizzards or the gloom of night. It is the sole good thing he does for his heart.

A block into the walk, his thumbs retrieve Zoe's number from his BlackBerry. The thought of calling her has weighed on him all week.

"Sorry, you've got my voicemail," says Zoe's digitized voice. "And I've got your number. I'll get back to you soon."

"Hey, Zoe," Ethan starts, attempting to be casual. "Look, I've been meaning to call. About your dad's papers . . . Sorry I didn't mail them up there until Saturday. I, uh . . ." Ethan stops himself from going on, from re-canting his ignorance about the folder's contents. "Sorry about the delay. If you need anything you have my number. Take care of yourself."

And that is it. He is through. Ethan is worried that the papers tell only part of the story—possibly a grotesque story that he would not want to help Zoe uncover.

Having recently seen *Chinatown*, he speculates that Susan Leston might be both Zoe's mother *and* her sister. The doctor's euthanasia of his unaware wife legally made him a murderer and revealed his problematic morals. Incest may be a leap, but it is not a leap over a canyon. Yet if this were true, wouldn't Leston have destroyed the papers?

The other alternative is almost as complicated—that Zoe has a father she never knew. That she is kin to a whole family she doesn't know. Some apparently sad or pathetic family that Dr. Leston was trying to protect his granddaughter from.

Whatever the truth, the doctor's gambit to make Ethan responsible for Zoe will not work. He is moving on.

Ethan strides along Trinity Place, not as invigorated as usual by the walk. He shortens his stride past the construction bordering Church Street as he opens the photo album in his BlackBerry. Locating the Zoe folder, he begins to delete her images—the way he might delete virus-infected email. Zoe is not the only one who needs protection from her past. Erasing her from his life is the best thing that Ethan can imagine for the both of them.

Then he calls Yahvi.

"Hey you," Yahvi says, her breezy voice dispersing the Lestons' clouds. "I've just finished the second movement of my Ganesh suite. It poured out of me. Bollywood references and all."

"That's great," Ethan says.

"You don't think I'm a sellout? Making the India link so explicit."

"Come on. You're expressing your heritage."

"Yeah. Kind of. I'm almost guaranteed to get a grant or award if I write . . . *ethnic*."

"Artists do what they need to do to get by. I bet Alex wishes he was from somewhere cooler than Delaware."

"You mean like me? Ohio."

An incoming call bleeps. "Hold a sec," Ethan tells her and then looks at his phone. Zoe's picture smiles up from the screen. He lets the phone chime . . . and answers on the last ring before voicemail. "Hey."

Zoe sounds distracted. "You just called? I was finishing with the real estate agent."

"How'd it go?"

"The house goes on the market Sunday. She thought we could get a better price if we did some cleanup. But I'm going to dump it, contents and all."

"That's understandable." Crossing Vesey, Ethan dodges a veering Mister Softee truck—he doesn't ever recall seeing one in motion. They're usually lurking on side-street corners.

"God*dammit*, Ethan," Zoe says.

Hearing her sob, this is exactly what he had feared. Emotion. "Zoe—"

"Look, I don't care about the house, or that the lawyer said my father was broke when he died. I care that I didn't know who I was. And you read these papers, didn't you?"

"Wait, Zo, no. Not at first. But, then, uh, yeah, just before the funeral."

"So why didn't you give them to me *yourself*? You drop this on me through the mail?"

"Zo—"

"I don't even know what to think. Oh, hell!"

"Zoe. Are you okay?"

"Oh, I am just great, Ethan. Getting better every second." Zoe's voice sounds distant. As if she has put down the phone to free her hands.

"What's going on up there?"

Zoe doesn't say for a second. "What do you think? I'm filling a tumbler with my dad's Hendrick's. *Fuck* you, Ethan. Fuck you for not taking even the smallest responsibility on your own. Damn you. Damn him."

"Just a sec, Zoe. I was on another call." Ethan switches to Yahvi. "It's work. Call you back."

"Phooey!" Yahvi says and is gone heartbreakingly fast.

Ethan goes back to the other line. "Zoe?" he asks. But she is not there. "Shit," he says and redials, but to no result. And then he calls Alex. The phone rings and rings. Finally there's a pickup. "Alex!" Ethan says.

"*Non, c'est moi*," says Juliette, Alex's latest, whom he'd met at Alex's last opening.

"Let me speak to Alex," Ethan says. He has stopped on the sidewalk. Pedestrians are peeling around him in a stream like schooling fish.

"*Ami*, he is busy in the middle of work. You know, in the *zone*."

"Juliette—"

"And later, Ethan, we have an event tonight that will be very, very important, you understand. This is Alex's future. Okay. I will give him your message and tell him to call when he can."

But Ethan has not given Juliette a message. "It's about Zoe."

"Ah," Juliette says. "Poor girl. You are taking care of her, I hope. You know she is your responsibility." And then "*Quoi?*" Juliette says, but not to the phone. "*Ami*," she says to Ethan, "Alex needs me for something. You take care. I will pass on your message."

Ethan tries Zoe again. Again there is no answer. As the people on the street dodge around the obstacle he's become, he feels himself turning. Physically turning back toward UIB. He is calculating. If he puts in three hard hours tonight he can complete the programming he needs to do for work tomorrow. Coffee and a five-hour energy drink will get him through. He will keep trying to reach Zoe. Maybe he will even try to call her neighbors—but what was the couple's name? Really, though, why is he getting nervous? Is it because he *does* owe her a face-to-face? He has been an asshole about those papers. And there's still time, if not to correct the situation then to make him feel less crappy about it. If he gets a Zipcar after writing code tonight, he can get up to Accord by one. He'll sleep in the car outside the house until morning if he has to and that's okay. He needs to prove to Zoe, to himself, that he, unlike her father, is human, is *not* a monster.

"HEY," ETHAN SAYS to Zoe in her hospital bed.

She swallows, winces, blinks up at him, brings a hand toward her throat.

"Easy," he says taking the hand. "You've got an IV."

She lifts her eyelids higher, struggling as if they're held by elastic tape. "Eth?" Zoe says. "Oh God. My head."

"I came up last night," he says, leaning closer. "I knocked after I saw you on the couch. You weren't getting up so I broke in."

"Oh, Ethan," she says, looking at the tubes running toward her forearm, the monitor beeping by the bedside.

"It's okay, Zoe. They just pumped you out a little. I don't know. I may have overreacted bringing you here, but I couldn't wake you up."

"I just took a couple of pills, Ethan. And a drink. That's all."

"No. I know. It's cool. No one thinks you did this on purpose."

When the doctor comes, he eyes Ethan carefully and then charges him with making sure that he disposes of Dr. Leston's pill stash.

"This is not going to happen again," the doctor states firmly.

"No, sir," Zoe says to the man's deep-set eyes. She swallows, blinking with pain.

"Your esophagus will heal from the tube in a couple of days. Stick with soft foods."

"Yes, sir."

BY NOON ZOE has signed herself out of the hospital. She has not said much to Ethan so far—it hurts to speak. Nor has Ethan said much to her. The sun, however, is shining. It is a crisp, pleasant day. In the hospital parking lot Ethan opens the passenger's door for her.

Leaf-peeping season is over and a flickering background of bare foliage goes by as he drives. Ethan turns now and again to gaze at Zoe, who does not look at him. The hospital was not far and it takes only ten of these long looks before they are pulling up to her parents' house. *No*, he is still trying to get this right. Her *grandparents'* house.

"You may as well come in," she tells Ethan. "Wouldn't want you to get in trouble for not clearing out my dad's . . . my granddad's stash. Who knows what I'm liable to do next."

"*Zoe*," Ethan says.

She smiles at his scold. "Ethan, I would have been fine. I was brought up in a doctor's household. For God's sake, I *know* about pills. Come on in. I'll make us some eggs."

Seated at the Lestons' kitchen table, Zoe is flipping through the documents as if she has missed something from an earlier perusal. She takes a cigarette from the pack on the table and lights up. Inhaling she grimaces. "I wish dad had put a photo of my mother in here. *Jesus*, I mean granddddad."

"He was both, Walter was, wasn't he?" Ethan asks, waving a hand to disperse the smoke.

Zoe's eyes snap to Ethan's. "What do you mean?"

"Just that. He adopted you, didn't he? So that makes him both your father and your grandfather."

Zoe shakes her head at him. "That's insane." She goes back to one of the newspaper articles. "You read all of this, right?"

"Alex read them to me on the drive up. I didn't really look at anything in there after that."

"And . . . why not?"

"I don't know, Zoe."

"Apparently, I don't know Zoe either," she replies. "I thought I'd lost a sister, not a mother. After I left you the night of the dinner, Dad told me Susan was my sister. Could he have been *that* ashamed of having a pregnant, unwed daughter? Were people still like that in the eighties?"

"It wasn't like it is today. They condemned people for having AIDS," Ethan says.

She puts down the news clipping. "Anyway, what did he expect you to do with this information? Because you were right. It isn't any of your business." Zoe exhales smoke and then touches her throat.

Looking at her long neck, Ethan thinks of that famous bust of Nefertiti. He also likes the bump on the bridge of her nose, a family characteristic that comes from her grandfather's side of her family. Did her mother have a similar bump? Zoe is touching hers now, thoughtfully. Then she offers him the sympathy of her smile. "You must be tired, being up all night."

"I got a little rest in the hospital."

"Between the text, text, texting."

"Well, I ran out of battery and forgot my charger. So I got some z's."

"Still, I think you should sleep a little before you drive back. I don't want to be going to your funeral next."

"I'm good," Ethan says.

"Look," Zoe says, taking up their plates. "The workday will be over by the time you get back to New York. Just go upstairs and use my old room. Don't worry, you'll be safe. I'm not using it because it's too creepy—my . . . grandmother kept it just like it was when I was in high school. I'll go put on some fresh sheets."

While Zoe is upstairs, Ethan faces the folder on the kitchen table. It is open to one of Susan's report cards. Zoe's mother attended the Ethel Walker School and got straight A's, except for a C in phys ed. Beneath this Ethan sees a letter. It is addressed to Dr. Walter Leston from a Dr. Sarnoff.

Dear Walter,

Something awkward happened last Wednesday that I think you should hear about from me before there is any misinterpretation. Susan missed her session that afternoon, but when I was leaving my office I discovered her waiting in the parking lot by my car. As we had been getting nowhere in our sessions, I took this as an opportunity for an out-of-office interview that might be useful and drove Susan to your home, leaving her just down the street as she requested. During that drive, I had hoped that she might open up about the father of the child she is carrying, which she did not. I drove and we talked. Susan asked about my family and I told her a little but always circled back to her story, offering her tidbits about my life to try to draw her out about hers. By the time we had reached her street, I had learned nothing more about Susan while she had learned that I had married young, that my wife was schizophrenic, and that I had divorced her after she was institutionalized. The greatest shame of my life. This is all very embarrassing and unprofessional, so I felt compelled to make a clean breast of it. As such, I do not think it would be appropriate of me to see Susan again in a professional capacity. Be aware that she is a highly intelligent young woman. Should you decide to discuss this any further with me, I am willing. Also, I would like to recommend a substitute for my services so that Susan can continue her psychiatric treatment, which I believe is critical at this stage.

> *Yours sincerely,*
> *Carl Sarnoff, MD*

LATER THAT EVENING, curled asleep in Zoe's childhood bed, Ethan opens his eyes. The room, pink in the daylight, is purplish with the night's ambiance. Then the atmosphere changes. Is it the door opening behind him? Ethan keeps still.

No. There is no one there.

He thinks about what he has read in Leston's folder. Not just Sarnoff's letter but something included especially for Ethan to consider: the doctor's financial documents. Walter, deep in the stock market, had disastrously cashed out in '08. Even this house has no equity. He has bequeathed Zoe nothing but debt. It is the injury atop the insult of her inheritance.

The weight on the bed shifts. Ethan tightens, pushes his face into the pillow. He dares not breathe. He is convinced this is a dream. And then Zoe is pressing herself against his back.

"*Ethan?*" she whispers, pressing closer.

CHAPTER 15

- -

California

Dear Mr. Aldridge:

Enclosed is your letter to Jessica, which you will note is unopened. I am returning it myself because I hope you have since heard from her.

   Jessica was here in the hospital for a week, during which time I had two sessions with her concerning her hiking misadventure and recent separation from the military. What gives me concern is her lack of interest in therapy to help with her transition to civilian life. More troubling is her leaving the hospital without being discharged. As her consulting psychiatrist I urge you, if you do manage to contact her, to have Jessica seek support from any veterans' organization. Having recently been interviewed by investigators working with the Air Force, I know they, too, are concerned about your relative's disappearance.

Wishing you and your family the best,
Captain Shoshana Levy, PsyD
Jerry L. Pettis Memorial VA Medical Center
Loma Linda, CA

CHAPTER 16

Nevada

Voigt, taking calls, prefers to stand. Bluetooth in ear, he is looking through his blinds at a ground crew moving a Reaper out of a hangar. But he is speaking with a Captain Levy, who has called to inform him about Jessica's recent stay and disappearance from the Pettis med center. Voigt already knows that Jessica has sent Don a newspaper clipping about her hiking mishap. He has even read Don's return letter, which Dr. Levy is sending back to Don unread. The captain does not know that he, Voigt, is mentioned in the letter. And of course he cannot tell the doctor that soon, after it goes through the prison's censors, he will be reading *her* letter to Don.

"I've been in touch with Mr. Aldridge," he tells the doctor, which is as much as he can securely say. "But I'd like to hear your straight opinion of Jessica's condition. Why did she walk off into the desert like that? Did she really get lost? Or was it deliberate?"

Captain Levy's voice is pleasant but direct. "She's not suicidal. She's too strong for that. She's confused."

"All right," says Voigt, relieved and not relieved.

"I also think she could be fearful."

"Fearful?" Voigt turns away from the blinds. "Of what?"

"She'd told me why she was discharged. Not the specifics but that it had to do with a security breach. Now she's worried that she's a target. Paranoia might be a closer diagnosis. Although"—and here Levy pauses—"the paranoia might be justifiable and not delusional."

Voigt has no response to this. Levy goes on.

"During her stay, Jessica did have a visitor. Someone from DHS."

"Homeland Security?" This does not surprise Voigt.

"A Janet Sloan. More bureaucrat than agent. I believe she was trying to influence my diagnosis."

Voigt twists his jaw. "How so?" he asks.

"She thought Jessica might benefit from institutionalization."

"And what was your recommendation?" Voigt says.

"Oh, I told her Jessica would be fine in a day or so."

"And . . ."

"I think I was about to be removed from the case when Jessica disappeared from the hospital. Good instincts, I guess."

Voigt absorbs this. "Anything else?"

"Just one thing. Jessica mentioned you, Colonel. Said she'd trusted you."

CHAPTER 17

Ulster County, New York City

Ethan's right arm traverses a wilderness of twisted bedsheet. "Zoe?" he says. But the house remains still. Growing more awake, Ethan feels as though he is surfacing through quicksand. His body is sore, aching, torn. Gingerly he touches the back of a shoulder. Blood.

He and Zoe had never before made violent love, but last night they had collided as though she were trying to obliterate herself, as though she needed to erase her memory.

Could he have refused her then, when she joined him under the sheets and the familiarity of her body defeated him? Beyond this he'd wanted her to know that, whatever her heritage, she was a whole and pure being. Was this some kind of love he had for her?

But Zoe wanted something meaner, to be split in two. Perhaps she had used him. And that was fine. Except now she was gone.

"Zoe," Ethan calls more loudly.

Upright finally, he goes to a window and lifts the shade. Squinting, he tries to glimpse Zoe's fugitive form outside.

"Zoe!" he calls again, and then has a moment of panic. His BlackBerry, battery dead since yesterday, sits on one of Zoe's night tables, next to a digital clock decorated with stickers. There is a princess phone there, too. An antique landline. He dials a number and hears a voice that he sometimes finds amusing, sometimes obnoxious.

"Hashtag *mystery caller*—"

Ethan cuts John Guan off before he can start a riff. "It's Ethan. Everything cool? Did you cover for me?" He had left Guan a voicemail from the hospital room. UIB gives its employees five personal days a year, but nobody uses them. He'd already taken one for the funeral and two was bad form, indicating a lack of dedication. But this is not what's making him nervous. Being incommunicado for twenty-four hours is the big worry. Hopefully Guan has been watching his back.

"Yo, mofo. It be ten a.m. and tickin'. Where you at, homey?" Guan's attempt to sound ghetto is more exaggerated than usual. Not a good sign.

"Okay, John. What's wrong?" Ethan asks.

"Apocalypse now," Guan says. "We've shut down the currency mainframe. It started buying rupees at ten times their value. The bank took a major hit. Don't tell me you got no alerts—oh, right, your phone's down. Bummer. Rumor is one of your algos spazzed."

"One of *my* algos . . . bullshit."

Guan's voice for once sounds serious, like there's a real person beneath all the blather. "There was another Middle East thing. You know this stuff better than me. Pakistan. Car bomb. Dead American contractor. This yada-yada-whatever group claiming responsibility. Revenge for the al-Yarisi drone hit. That's all your territory, bro."

"Hold the fort. It'll take me two hours to get back to the city."

"Yo, but like we are talking Fort Apache, white man. You better watch your scalp."

Ethan hangs up and puts on clothes sour from the previous day and night. Tramping downstairs, he calls out again, "Zoe! *Zoe?*"

There is no reply, only a bang like the sound of a screen door. Following the noise Ethan comes to the kitchen. He stands a moment on the creaking linoleum. A cigarette smolders in a small dish filled with butts. A breeze wafts from the screened side door. Ethan pushes out onto a landing with steps that descend into the backyard. "Zoe!" he shouts from the railing. But there is no answer.

On the drive out of Ulster County, Ethan repositions his concerns. Zoe knows how to take care of herself. Again, he has been stupid about her. Again, she has taken what she has wanted and left him hanging. Meanwhile, he mentally backtracks through his last hours at work. Before he'd left to visit her, he had adjusted a formula that would signal the bank's computers to trade the rupee against the renminbi against the dollar, a triangular arbitrage, in the event of a terrorist incident, of which that Pakistan car bomb would qualify.

Through his mind's eye, Ethan reviews his code. He had made only simple tweaks, nothing that required testing or managerial verification, just no-brainer refinements. Of course, he had put in a fifteen-hour day and was jazzed on energy drinks toward the end. Could he have screwed up?

Nah.

Yet . . . what if he had shifted a decimal point the wrong way, keyed his algo to bid for rupees at ten times their worth? In the event of a terrorist attack, the bank would essentially be trading dollars at one-tenth their value. This would suck ass. This would cause a run on UIB's dollar holdings, costing tens, perhaps hundreds of thousands before the fail-safes shut the system down. *If* they shut it down. *Jesus*, he thinks. *The damage could be in the millions. Tens of millions.*

Dumping the Zipcar outside the UIB tower Ethan hustles inside to the elevator. On the twenty-seventh floor, rushing past cubicles as their occupants stare over the partitions, Dwayne Hoke rushes out and shoves him against a wall.

"What the fuck, Dwayne," Ethan says as Hoke breathes into his face. A former lacrosse captain at Duke, his boss outweighs him by thirty pounds.

"Where were you yesterday, asshole? Penthouse conference room. Five minutes," Dwayne says and walks off. Such public dramas are how Hoke maintains office discipline.

It might be easier to go back and jump down the elevator shaft. Nevertheless, Ethan continues his walk of shame past his co-workers to his office. It resembles Macy's after Black Friday. His desk drawers are upside down on the floor. His three computers are gone, leaving eviscerated cables. No doubt UIB data forensics is sifting every byte and scrap for evidence of something. Fraud, most likely. His bosses can be very suspicious: Barings in England had gone under because of one employee's unauthorized speculations. In France, Société Générale had needed governmental help to stay solvent after a trader went rogue. At J.P. Morgan, a bond trader called the London Whale hid billions in losses. Etcetera. Ethan wonders if he is soon to be mistakenly ranked among these villains, soon to be frog-marched to jail in handcuffs. Few things are salvageable in such a situation and a job is not one of them. One last time he settles into the caress of his thousand-dollar ergonomic programmer's chair.

Leaning back, Ethan notices a glint inside his desk where the center drawer used to be. Forensics has missed the penknife from the career fair where UIB recruited him, where they were poaching bachelor's of science students from the true sciences. Inscribed in gold on the black handle is the suggestion CUT THE BS. GET YOUR MFE. Ethan did and went after a master's in financial engineering, taking some serious financial aid from UIB in exchange for his future.

For the first time Ethan has a real use for the knife. He takes off his coat and, like an art thief, starts sawing Alex's *Demimonde in D Minor* out of its frame. It is his favorite of the three paintings of Alex's that Ethan has hung in his office. He won't risk losing it to UIB.

"Whoa, chief," a familiar voice says. "What you be doin'?" John Guan has snuck up behind him.

"This is *mine!*" Ethan says, sounding even to himself a little crazed. In his windowless office Alex's paintings had connected him to a world beyond his number-splitting work.

"My man, you know you're bleeding through your shirt back," Guan says. "The Hoke-man do that? There's talk of an incident in the bullpen."

Ethan has *Demimonde* almost free when a pair of UIB security men arrive and one of them twists Ethan's cutting arm and efficiently places him facedown onto the floor.

"Sir, you are no longer authorized to be in this office," his partner says.

Meanwhile the man who put Ethan onto the ground helps him to his feet. "Your bloody shirt is not on me, mate," he says in his Australian accent and then helps Ethan into his coat.

Upstairs, exiting the penthouse elevator, Ethan and his guards traverse a glassy foyer monitored by Cassandra, who could be a Victoria's Secret model. As Ethan passes she offers him a smile. And then his guards simultaneously open in front of him the double doors to a conference room that gleams with polished wood and smells of leather.

Like all executive conference rooms in lower Manhattan, this one contains a table the length of a pier. New Jersey is visible through the glass wall, along with Ellis Island. In Ethan's five years at the bank he has entered this space only twice and has always been one among dozens. This time he completes a group of three.

Hoke lunges at Ethan like a hungry hyena. "Didn't hurt you down-stairs, did I, buddy?" he asks and claps a hand on Ethan's damaged shoulder. Hoke pushes him the length of the table toward a man studying papers laid out on the reflective mahogany.

The stranger, who has high cheekbones and silver hair pulled into a ponytail, rises and offers Ethan his hand. "How are you, Mr. Winter. Ben Littletree from legal. We have documents awaiting your signature. After that, you can be on your way."

"On my way?" Ethan asks.

Littletree lifts his eyebrows at Hoke.

"You're fired," Hoke says, doing his best Trump imitation. "What did you think? The upside for you is that UIB's not going to take this to the feds."

Ethan's nape hairs bristle. Pride begs him not to go down easily. "The feds? For a decimal point mistake, if it was even that?"

"I'm just saying, buddy," Hoke says. "We can be really hard on you if you want. You should have seen the uproar around here when your program kicked in. Good thing the fail-safes worked. We're still looking into a conspiracy to manipulate."

"A conspiracy?"

"With currency traders at other banks."

Ethan shakes his head. Then he glances at the waiting paperwork. "Maybe my lawyer should see these first."

Littletree takes over. "Mr. Winter, these papers simply restate what's in your employment contract addendum."

"Meaning?" Ethan asks.

"Well, that you agree to indemnify UIB against any losses caused up to the amount of your secondary compensation."

"Meaning?" Ethan repeats.

"Well, buddy," Hoke says. Despite their weight difference, Ethan is ready to hit him. "That currency mainframe was down for twenty minutes before Guan got it back up. That's major dollars. It basically means you pay back your bonuses from the past few years. It's what we all had to agree to here, after the meltdown."

The *meltdown*. Ethan has not seriously considered the meltdown since the protesters exited Zuccotti Park. In the banking universe, the meltdown is Roman history. But apparently some artifacts remain. After Lehman blew up in '08 and the world nearly followed, UIB tossed a bone to the Fed by tying employee bonuses to long-term performance, claiming a claw-back clause would prevent shortsighted trading.

Of course UIB's executives and stars were exempt from the clause. They could still day trade as aggressively as any aspiring white-collar criminal. But employees at Ethan's level—the counters and geeks—would have their bonuses clawed back if their trading ultimately resulted in red ink.

And so, calculating his bonuses as three-fourths of his income, Ethan is about to lose . . . let's see, carry the decimal point . . . *everything.* His six-figure bank account. His retirement investments. His platinum credit limit. Perhaps even his condo.

In the previous century the sin of losing money was forgivable. Bankruptcy was lenient. The rich were neither so rich nor so greedy nor so paranoid. But with the American century shrinking in the rearview mirror, the country has given up on being the land of second chances, or even first. Basically, the new millennium sucks for latecomers.

Ethan swats Littletree's papers off the table and turns his back on Hoke. The security team grabs him up and escorts him down to the gum-splotched New York sidewalk. He feels like a hatchling ejected from the nest.

PART THREE

LEAVE-TAKING

December 2012–September 2013

CHAPTER 18

Washington, DC

A freeze harassed the city last week, but the bench they sit on is warm under a crisp December sun. Zoe and Mariatu Nowrojee are enjoying lunch on an unseasonably warm day that in a former age might have been called Indian. But use the term *Indian summer* in this town and you will get your hand slapped. At the same time you can root loudly for the Redskins.

Zoe's annoyance at such hypocrisies makes her impatient especially when there are more important things in her life. She is overwhelmed by her work at her NGO. Her organization, WIDO, Women's International Development Organization, assists impoverished women overseas—women at risk of being stoned for adultery or burned alive on their husbands' funeral pyres.

"Zoe, stop thinking so hard. Look at the blue sky," her friend Mariatu says.

Zoe looks up and feels ashamed. Certainly her personal woes are minor compared to Mariatu's, who once had been attacked by soldiers in the classroom where she taught, her cheek crushed by a blow. Her students were taken away to be drugged and instructed on how to fire AK-47s at their neighbors. Mariatu has lived through a hell that makes Dante's seem naive, because Dante only punished the guilty.

"I think he was just teasing you, Zoe," Mariatu says.

Zoe's cheeks warm. It was so irrelevant—her "Indian summer" comment and Porter, Dr. Coombs, scolding her for it.

"Oh, it was very, very funny when you then yelled at him for being a Redskins fan," Mariatu says. "Go, Zoe!"

Mariatu's laugh lightens the air and the knots inside Zoe relax. Her laughter comes and soon the two of them are laughing toward the blue sky. They make a small spectacle for passersby. Then Zoe's eyes fall again to the scar on Mariatu's cheek.

AT THE CENTRAL office of WIDO, Zoe is trying to micromanage a microloan situation. A contract they made with a collective of women farmers in Burundi has inspired the men of the village to imprison their wives in their huts. The village is to be the first stop on a tour of WIDO's Central Africa projects by one of their major donors—a technology entrepreneur turned philanthropist. Zoe's task is to settle the situation before WIDO's hired photographer heads into the Burundi countryside to take preliminary site shots. She phones her contact in Bujumbura, Jean-Pierre.

"You must give money to the husbands," Jean-Pierre says.

"But that's not okay," Zoe replies.

"Still, you must give money to the husbands. Five million francs."

Zoe relays this information to Dr. Coombs, her boss, and he calls it extortion. "They live in grass huts for God's sake. Can't the women escape?"

The solution is simple but not anything Dr. Coombs can discuss. So Zoe does. She has already calculated the exchange rate. "Five million Burundi francs are only a few hundred dollars," she says.

Coombs knits his graying eyebrows.

"Look," Zoe says. "I know that you can't"—and she raises her fingers to form air quotes—"*know* anything about this, but—"

"No," Coombs cuts her off. "If word leaked that we paid a bribe as official policy, our donations would dry up."

"But it wouldn't be official policy, not if *I* arranged the payment behind your back," Zoe answers. "If something goes wrong, the burden of blame is on me."

Coombs considers this. "You would make that sacrifice?" Respect glints in her boss's eyes. This is what Zoe is living for now, that glint. "Well, we *are* backed into a corner."

Zoe nods. She is not afraid of losing her job for the cause. Although at this point she is vague on what, exactly, their cause is. Are they trying to help the women in the village? Or are they trying to make sure WIDO's donors keep donating?

Zoe calls Jean-Pierre, but he does not pick up. Twenty minutes later, when Jean-Pierre finally answers, he tells her that now the village men want ten million francs to let the women go back to work. As there are no cell towers near the village Zoe knows that Jean-Pierre cannot have spoken directly with the husbands about the new demand. And if this much is a lie, what about the rest of Jean-Pierre's story? Perhaps everything is fine in the village. But even if Zoe were sure of this, she cannot refuse Jean-Pierre. If she did, he might go to the village and create the problem.

"Jean-Pierre," Zoe says, "We only have five hundred dollars in our African account," she lies. "Won't the men accept that? It's twice what we loaned their wives."

Jean-Pierre is silent and Zoe worries that she has insulted him. She worries that she has just ruined a photo op for WIDO's most important donor. But finally, Jean-Pierre speaks. "I will give you an account number for the wire transfer," he says in his cheery French accent.

THAT EVENING THE Burundi situation is causing Zoe's temples to pound. At lunch with Mariatu she had been five thousand miles distant. Now, here, ordering Ethiopian with Mariatu and her friends on Ninth Street, Zoe lags hours behind. Again and again she is reliving how Jean-Pierre cheated her until the menu she is studying displays not dinner choices but transcriptions of Jean-Pierre's persistent, "You *must* pay the husbands. You *must* pay the husbands." Their waiter is waiting on her.

"Per-plexed?" Johannes, Mariatu's friend, asks. Immaculate in his gray suit and yellow tie, perpetually smiling, he musically punctuates each of his syllables as if showing off his deep voice. "I would try the *kitfo tartare*."

"But you can't go wrong with the *shiro fit-fit*," interrupts Johannes' friend, Hajhi. He is slighter, less sure of himself, and habitually touches his sparse goatee as if to make sure it's there. "They serve it vegan here."

So far Zoe likes Hajhi better than the blustery Johannes. "*Shiro fit-fit*," Zoe says to the waiter, who nods and departs.

"I think you made the right choice," Johannes says and reaches across the table to pat Zoe's hand. He is not referring to Zoe's selection of a meal but to her bribe to Jean-Pierre. *She ought to have kept quiet about it.*

Now Johannes turns to Mariatu. "Do you remember Professor Kamara?" he asks.

"Oh yes," Mariatu says sadly.

Johannes, speaking well over the conversations of neighboring tables, explains to Zoe, "The professor was failing a student whose papa worked for De Beers. One day a small pouch of uncut diamonds appears on our teacher's desk." Johannes lifts his eyebrows as if the conclusion of the story is apparent.

"Well, what happened?" asks Hajhi.

"Oh, Dr. Kamara," Mariatu sighs.

Johannes turns to Mariatu. "Sorry for bringing up the old days."

Mariatu's eyes glisten. "It is fine. Go ahead, Jo."

Johannes begins. "During our civil war it was common for citizens to barter in rough diamonds, though this was very illegal. Dr. Kamara, of course, turned in the mysterious pouch. But this was not enough for him. He failed his failing student and made a stir about corruption at the university. He became the Socrates of Fourah Bay. It was inevitable that he would be arrested." Johannes stops talking, perhaps out of consideration for Mariatu. The story, though, must be finished.

Mariatu inhales and speaks. "Dr. Kamara was charged with possession of the contraband he *himself* turned in. Then he was accused of supporting the rebels. Even before the trial he lost his professorship. I started a petition."

"A dangerous thing," Johannes interrupts.

"Not so," says Mariatu.

"Yes," says Johannes. "And what good did it do for you to risk your future." This last statement hangs in the air.

Zoe cannot stop herself from asking. "What happened to your professor?"

"After receiving a sentence of fifteen years . . . Dr. Kamara hanged himself," Mariatu says.

There is silence until Hajhi snaps at Johannes. "But this has nothing to do with Zoe's problem."

Johannes slowly wipes his face with his napkin. "My good friend, it has everything to do." He turns to Zoe. "America operates differently from the world. Here you are not as desperate. You have the luxury of playing fair and you expect others will. So it is a shock when you go into another world and there are different rules. You think you are being cheated. But in some places a bribe is simple business. Not to ask for a bribe is a mark of stupidity. And not to offer one is bad form. When you are more experienced you will understand that a bribe is just a commission. As they say, 'The monkey works, the baboon eats.'"

"Johannes, you are not only corrupt but a complete idealist about America," says Hajhi. "Here bribery is called a political donation."

After Johannes finishes laughing, Mariatu asks him, "What is Freetown like now?"

Johannes considers the question. "Same-same."

Mariatu nods.

"When was the last time you were home?" Hajhi asks, and this makes Mariatu smile.

"Five years ago. And I'm afraid my country was still not ready to deal with this." Mariatu touches the dent in her cheek. To Zoe, her friend's injury seems more pronounced now, perhaps because of the restaurant's lighting.

"You could have it fixed," suggests Johannes.

"No," Mariatu says simply.

"Then I still do not think you could find a job in Freetown." Johannes turns his eyes to Zoe. "It has been more than ten years and everyone is still traumatized by the war. They want to pretend it had not been so terrible. But if you have a wound like Mariatu's, you remind them."

"You're drunk," Hajhi says to Johannes. "He had three beers before you arrived," he explains to Mariatu.

Johannes pours the contents of his current beer down his throat and sighs "ahh" as if to antagonize Hajhi. Zoe cannot tell if the two men are spatting lovers or simply friends irritated with each other. "I am celebrating my reunion with Mariatu," Johannes says. "And I will drink."

"Drink. Drink," says Mariatu. "So I can always count on you to tell me the truth."

"JOHANNES IS MY time machine," Mariatu tells Zoe. They have said goodnight to Mariatu's friends and are walking west on U Street. "That is why I enjoy seeing him. He reminds me of what I must try to be." Mariatu crosses her arms against the night's chill.

"Arrogant?" Zoe says.

Mariatu laughs. "*Honest*. In Freetown, Johannes was beaten up many times. He was brazen in presenting himself as a man who loves men. In Sierra Leone a man cannot be as apparent as one is here. There, for men to have sex together is a serious crime."

It is a Thursday night and on U Street's narrow sidewalks the privileged young mill about. Zoe and Mariatu pass through crowds of them outside nineteenth-century townhomes that have been converted into cafes and bistros, funky clothing stores and shops filled with trendy furnishings.

"Johannes inspired me to go into the countryside to teach," Mariatu says. "I was warned that it would be risky. My family forbade me to go. But if Johannes stood up for what he believed in, how could I not do what my conscience asked?"

They pass a check-cashing store that seems out of place.

"The rebels came to my school more than once," Mariatu says. "At first they were afraid of me because I showed them no fear. They did not know what this rich *uman* was doing in the village. They probably thought I knew Charles Taylor. They were ignorant men that you can sometimes stand up to. But, yes, it *was* arrogance to imagine I could send them away time and again. When you are young you believe that your ideals can save you and the world."

On an island in the intersection where they are about to part, Mariatu asks if Zoe has read Simone de Beauvoir. Guiltily Zoe shakes her head. Mariatu continues. "When she was young Simone was a ferocious hiker and traveled everywhere alone, hitching rides through the countryside whenever she grew exhausted. A colleague at the school where she taught warned her that this was dangerous. Simone, however, believed that the warning only reflected her colleague's spinsterish fantasy. Then one day Simone accepted a ride from two young men. Only after they made a wrong turn in the direction of a desolate valley did she understand their intention."

Zoe begins to imagine that this story has a lot to do with Mariatu's life—with how Mariatu turned around what would be for most people an insurmountable trauma. "Is it because of what the men did to her that she wrote *The Second Sex*?" Zoe asks. Though Zoe has not read Beauvoir she does know the title of her most famous book.

"No. No," Mariatu corrects. "As the men were driving her away Simone threatened to jump from their moving car. She intimidated them and they let her go. *Then* she went on to write *The Second Sex*."

"Because she was not raped?"

"Exactly," Mariatu says. "Simone said that her escape strengthened her delusion that she could always get herself out of any fix. It helped to make her audacious. If she had been abused by those men, perhaps she would not have become the writer we know. Perhaps she would have been broken. Our lives turn on such fortunes."

The walk light has now come and gone several times. Mariatu and Zoe hug goodbye. But after Zoe steps into the street she looks back at Mariatu. "Do you ever wonder? . . ." Zoe stops speaking.

But Mariatu is quick. "Do I wonder what the alternate me, the me who was not attacked, is doing now? I do not wonder this. I know," Mariatu says as if announcing a cosmic joke. "If she had been able to stop those soldiers, today she would be the president of her country and also satisfying the hunger of multitudes with a single loaf of bread. That is how arrogant and impossible I was then. That I might still be that way. The Mariatu you see before you, I am afraid, is not her."

DR. PORTER COOMBS lives six blocks from work on a street mixed with residences and embassies and art galleries. His row house, a brick federal three windows wide with black shutters and stone lintels, looks as formal as Porter behaves at the office. Zoe turns her key and steps inside. Strangely, she hears the television and smells popcorn. And before she can backtrack she is caught.

"Hey," Cassie Coombs says over the back of the living room couch as if Zoe's late appearance in her father's home is the most ordinary of things. Cassie, just four years younger than Zoe, is enrolled in prelaw at

Georgetown. She lives in the dorm and sometimes spends the weekends here. But she never stays overnight on school nights, so she has surprised Zoe.

"Hi, Cassie," Zoe replies awkwardly. Porter, even though his ex-wife is remarried, likes to keep his worlds separate. Or is it that he doesn't want his daughter to find out that his girlfriend is almost thirty years his junior?

"Dad's taking a bath," Cassie says.

"Okay," Zoe says, her smile locked.

"So you guys are dating," Cassie says, then offers Zoe popcorn from a steel bowl.

"Just ate," Zoe apologizes. On the television, investigators at a crime scene are standing over a corpse. Cassie settles back in the couch to watch.

Upstairs, Zoe hears water slosh. "It's me," she whispers through the closed door.

More water sloshes and then it goes still. "Zoe?" Porter whispers back.

"Sorry. Can I come in?"

Porter meditates a moment. "What the heck."

Later, when Porter goes downstairs to say goodnight to Cassie, Zoe gets in bed and checks her phone. There's an email from Alex castigating her about Ethan. For not communicating. She deletes it.

"You all right?" Porter asks when he returns.

She puts the phone on the nightstand and turns out the light. "It's nothing."

The bed creaks as Porter gets under the sheets with her. "*Shhh,*" Porter says. "You can hear a pin drop through these floors."

But Zoe hasn't moved. Now she runs a hand up the inside of Porter's thigh. "What do you think she thinks we're doing?" She sees Porter's eyes sparkle, darting in the ambiance filtering through the closed blinds. "Your daughter is grown up," Zoe says.

"And she seemed fine with us?"

"Like it was barely worth commenting about."

"Wait till her mother finds out."

"Finds out what?" Zoe asks even though she knows he means their age difference. For the hundredth time Zoe considers that their age gap might make her laughable. Within herself, however, she imagines herself to be his peer. Her hand touches Porter's penis, which is thickening. She clenches it as if squeezing a lemon.

"Ouch," he whispers. "I'm sorry."

Everyone is sorry for something tonight. "Sorry for what?" Zoe asks. Is he sorry for calling her out about her Indian summer comment? Is he sorry for letting her send extortion money to Jean-Pierre in Burundi? She squeezes Porter again.

Porter squirms and tries to restrain a giggle, but he does not push Zoe's hand away. They are equals now. They are both acting like naughty, gleeful children. But the moment passes. Zoe takes back her hand and listens to their breathing. In the dark, she hears Porter swallow.

"I'm sorry for not going with you to your parents' funeral. I should have been there for you," he says.

CHAPTER 19

New York City

"Red cadium," Ethan says, brushing the snow from his fleece top.

"You mean cad*m*ium," the clerk corrects.

"Cad*m*ium? Are you sure?" Ethan asks. He reviews Alex's list. It reads *cadium*.

Ethan is a double-checker. How he lost his job over a misplaced decimal point is a mystery. He was overtired, certainly. He had worked the previous night through, yes. But he had tested the algorithm twice with pseudo-data before making it live. Over the past three months he has mentally reconstructed his keystrokes countless times and has concluded that the decimal point shift was not his. That someone had sabotaged him.

"No such animal," states the clerk like an offended expert. He is close to a decade younger than Ethan, boasts fingernails encrusted with pigment.

"Do you know Alex Carr?" Ethan asks.

The put-upon clerk—put upon because he is wasting his genius on an art amateur like Ethan, put upon because he is probably only clerking here to steal the painting supplies he can't afford—says, "I've heard of Carr."

Things are happening fast. Alex's local fame is the new norm. His star began to rise—following a mention in *Time Out* and a sidebar review in the *Voice*—after Ethan's imploded. Ethan shows the clerk Alex's list. Taking dictation, Ethan had scrawled the supplies on the back of a Duane Reade receipt for Wellbutrin. "This is his handwriting," Ethan fibs, pointing to his own misspelling.

The clerk takes the list. "It's cadmium," he mumbles as he goes into the aisles, efficiently returning a few minutes later with the list items—the ten tubes of paint, the extrawide hog bristle brushes, the turpentine, the linseed oil. Scanning barcodes he asks Ethan, "Carr wouldn't need a *good* studio assistant?" Ethan says nothing and gives the clerk his credit card.

While the card is run Ethan asks himself if this is true—not whether he is a lousy studio assistant, but whether a studio assistant is what he now *is*.

He has spent much of the past three months assisting Alex—though it could be argued that Alex is assisting him. Picking up supplies, stretching canvas, helping Alex move to his new studio in Chelsea have been healthy distractions for Ethan while he takes on his old company. His lawyer's advice was to go on the offensive. This would be expensive, perhaps ruinously so. But UIB's clawback would have ruined him anyway. Why not fight?

Having never sued anyone, he is finding the process exhilarating. The strategy sessions, the briefs, the petitions, the counterclaims are, in fact, overstimulating. He cannot settle down to the drudgery of looking for a new job. And what work could he find anyway, with his professional reputation in shreds? For that matter, away from the influence of Dwayne Hoke, he's been reflecting on his old work beyond the math. "Think of it as creative destruction," Hoke had said whenever he'd expressed the slightest reservation about profiting from military violence, or sometimes just, "The world's going into the shitter, pussy. Man up and do your job."

Well, he had, and if he's to go after another job like his old one, he will have to hold his nose and man up again. Maybe this, he thinks, is what's caused him to delay his job search. Disgust.

But how can this be? Poker-wise he'd gone all-in on a banking career. He can't just fold. What else does he have?

Helping Alex set up his Tenth Avenue studio, running out for their lunches, stretching canvases, has proved an effective therapy against the anxiety of his indecision. It's even given him an occasional sense of joy—no doubt aided by the Wellbutrin. But drugs and Alex's friendship are stopgaps to his falling apart and not a sustainable career path.

It is late afternoon when Ethan exits the supply store and the weather has deteriorated. A sideways sleet gums his eyelashes. Flagging blindly with a bag in each hand, he is refused by one cab after another until their hissing tires send him to the subway. He surfaces at Chambers Street into a wet wind smashing up the Hudson. In his lobby's mirror, his gaze meets the stare of a teary-eyed, white-haired, red-faced old man. It is just himself—in forty years. He brushes the snow from his head.

THE NEXT DAY, traces of the blizzard imprint the sky like muddy boots. Today Yahvi has consented to see Ethan for the first time since their split, after he slept with Zoe.

As he crosses Canal Street a scrap of blue tantalizes at the horizon's vanishing point. Ethan continues north, trudging over arctic berms. At the agreed-upon coffee shop Yahvi kisses Ethan warmly on the cheek.

He orders up two espressos and they perch on stools at the counter-top in front of the window. When Ethan begins to speak she hushes him with a finger to her lips. "Listen," she says. Ethan opens his ears. The sound of an engine grows until finally a snowplow crunches past their window. Then the stillness settles back in. The lack of traffic, the muf-fling snow, the cloud-saturated sky, have transformed what should be a rush hour. For once on the streets it is not the sound of engines that takes precedence. He and Yahvi can hear nature's silence. Even inside the cafe the conversations are muted to match the outer calm. Yahvi had always pointed out street noises to Ethan when they were together—the sound of dueling car horns harmonizing, the oddly affecting drumming of a talented busker. He recalls telling her about the Fibonacci sequence and how Black Star used it in the song "Astronomy." Mathematicians and mu-sicians were not that far apart. He and Yahvi had once had real potential. Ethan blinks hard to dissipate a tear. Yahvi turns from the window to study him.

"You've lost weight?" she says.

"Have I?" Ethan prevaricates, unsure if her question is a criticism or a compliment. His ghost in the window does seem thin to him.

Yahvi clasps his arm. "You must eat. You *must*." Her sympathy soothes like a quilt tucked around him. *This* is why he wanted to see her. Also, he cannot bore Alex with any more of his problems.

To appease her concern Ethan buys a danish. "I'm not on a regular feeding schedule," he says. "Anyway, you look wonderful."

Yahvi's kohl mascara makes her eyes immense. When she was young her grandmother taught her to make up this way to scare off malign spirits. At times she keeps up the tradition. Ethan is glad she did this today—even if it means that she is putting up her guard against him.

"On dark days you must dress brightly," Yahvi says, referring to the layers of gold and orange silk that envelope her against the weather.

In his gray fleece top and faded jeans, Ethan is particularly drab and their mismatch makes him miss her even more.

"I heard your suite," Ethan manages. In January he'd taken the subway to Brooklyn College for the premiere of *Ganesh in America*, the composition she'd started when they were dating.

"Why didn't you say hello?" Yahvi asks.

His memory is of leaving the postperformance reception after spying her on the arm of the bearded lead violin, who played his instrument so violently he had to replace his bow. He and Yahvi seemed a matched pair and Ethan had felt punched in the stomach. "I waved to you over the heads of the crowd. You were the evening's superstar. I couldn't get close to you," he says.

"And what are you up to these days? Where do you work?"

"Remember that UIB thing? It's not quite done."

"Wait? Does this mean you don't have a new job yet?"

Ethan has no good answer to her amazement. Perhaps his overnighter with Zoe wasn't the only reason Yahvi and he broke up. What he is, a man with a limited focus, has disheartened her again.

"Ethan, it's time to move on and grow."

Ethan hems. "There's been some progress. My lawyer just forwarded UIB's proposal. They'll back off on the bonus clawback if I desist from my wrongful termination claim."

"That's great! Then you've won."

Ethan shakes his head. "Not yet. Someone sabotaged me and I'm going to prove it. All I need is a look at the mainframe backups from my last day at work. I know UIB kept them—legal would have insisted. What I need to show is that the program I was working on was resaved after I left the office."

"But there's a problem with this?" Yahvi asks.

"UIB won't release the backups. And my lawyer is having trouble with the subpoena."

"Then, Ethan! Just let it *go!*" Yahvi's cry turns heads in the cafe. She digs her pianist fingers into Ethan's wrist and whispers. "*Move* on with your life."

"KEEP MOVING," ETHAN tells himself. His sneakered feet are frozen, his fingers about to snap off in their gloves. On the clearer avenues, cabs slip over the packed snow as he marches in the streets with the other pedestrians.

Alex's new work space, found by Juliette, and temporary, is in a Chelsea warehouse that is soon to blossom into a boutique apartment building. Inside, Alex is leaning from a ladder to reach the edge of a twelve-by-twelve canvas, blank except for a horizontal black stripe. The ladder tilts and Ethan steadies it while Alex sweeps a fat curve through the stripe. They move the ladder and do another curve. Alex has created a sideways dollar sign that Franz Kline might have painted. "Got my cadium?" he asks.

"Cad*mium*," says Ethan.

But only after Alex stops painting does any conversation begin.

"Looks good," says Ethan about the red-framed dollar sign.

"Later it won't be obvious," Alex says. He builds his paintings in layers. "So, what up?"

Ethan shrugs. "Nada. Yahvi says hello."

Alex nods. "You two going out again?"

"Nah. Just had coffee. She's dating a violinist."

"Shall I cut his strings?"

"Would you?"

"Done. And what else? You're wearing your badass face."

"Am I?" Ethan says. He's been waiting to talk about this with Alex. "Flying Tiger," he says. "I'm committed now."

"Fuck," Alex says.

The Flying Tigers was Ethan's favorite movie as a boy after he saw one of the actual planes at an air museum. It was about a squad of American pilots in China prior to Pearl Harbor. In the final scene, John Wayne and a Clark Gable lookalike named John Carroll are on a mission to blow up a Japanese ammo train. But at the last second their plane is hit and Wayne bails thinking Carroll is right behind. Wounded, Carroll chooses to dive-bomb the plane into the train in best American kamikaze style. He's going to die anyway so why not make it worthwhile?

"Your lawyer. Does she recommend a suicide attack?" Alex asks.

"She says that this latest offer is the best I'm likely to get. That if I piss off UIB by not accepting they'll dig in their heels and outspend and out-last me."

"Sounds like a good read of the situation," Alex says. "They just want back your bonus from last year, right?"

"That's not the point anymore. And besides," Ethan says, jokey, "I've already changed my Gmail address. Flytiger3.1416."

Ethan's complaint, a lost career, he knows is minor compared to what others have lost to the banks: homes and families. But he feels a similar humiliation. It's insulting that despite the ruin they have inflicted, they still tread like giants. That Ethan is one of the few who can resist obligates him to try. "I'm going to nail UIB," he says.

"*Magnifique*, Ethan," says Juliette, who has just entered the studio.

CHAPTER 20

Florida

Dear Jessica,

Though your last letter is five months old and contained but a newspaper clipping and no return address I am still trying. Once a month I send a letter general delivery to the San Bernardino post office that postmarked your envelope. I would not be having to tell you this if every one of those letters did not come back to me stamped RETURN TO SENDER.

Why do I not stop writing? My faith in you tells me we will somehow connect again. When that happens I will offer these returned letters as proof that I am no longer the unreliable father who was not there to see you grow or be your mothers support. By the way you should not blame her for running off. She learned that trick from me. When I heard she had left I almost went to get you. But staying with an aunt and cousins was better for a twelve-year-old than being raised by the lost person I was then. I never visited you fearing I would spirit you away if I did. I HAD to let you go.

And now even though you are not receiving my letters I CANT let you go.

The selfish reason for this is that I have nothing better to do than scribble words on paper. The better reason is that I want to be your example of what not to be. My hope is to keep you from giving up on yourself the way I did when my life started going south. A cell I can pace with five steps is where that attitude brought me.

But enough of the pity party. You still have a life and so do I. And things are not so bad in here. My cellmate Ector Ramirez has begun to teach me some Spanish guitar. Have you ever heard Malagueña (thank

Ector the professor for the spelling)? I was never a real smooth picker but when I was young I could jangle a tune. This song though is a complicated animal. And as we only have one instrument and because of regulations only one hour a day to strum I practice on a neck made out of a paint stirrer. After lights out I take up my practice board until the sound of tapping makes the professor shush me.

One more piece of news that is neither good or bad. My Hail Mary appeal is dust. This is no tragedy because it was an unlikely hope that my public defender would admit to screwing up at my trial. Maybe though I was denied not for lack of evidence but because the warden thinks I am a loon for writing to myself. Time and again I mail off these letters to you only to get them back a few weeks later. But maybe this is not crazy. Even if you have not read them my minders have. I can tell from the taped envelope flaps. So I aint just talking to myself here. Be sure to keep this in mind if my letter gets through and you choose to write. I would sooner smash my fingers with a brick than do anything else to hurt you.

Your loving father,
Don

CHAPTER 21

California

"The house is a wreck and it's in a neighborhood from hell, but it's yours," Miss Shelly says, getting close to a topic Jessica refuses to discuss. "I spoke with Newt's brother and he don't want it. Says he has enough stuff to work on."

Jessica looks away from her friend.

"Honey," Shelly says, "There's a notary here and it would be better if we take care of the paperwork before I'm too weak."

Out under the jacaranda at the hospice, Jessica picks at blades of grass while a breeze waves the branches overhead. She had known that Shelly was not well on the day they had met. But she didn't know then that Newt's bad back was metastasizing cancer. He is gone. Soon Shelly will be. It's her choice.

"Come on, Jessie. I'd like to do this for you. I know Newt would have wanted to, too. Why you stayed with us through all this is a mystery. But I'm grateful. I've got to do something for you."

Looking up at Shelly, withered and yellow, her oxygen breather shut off and dangling from her neck while she sips from a shrinking, pencil-thin joint, Jessica wants to tell her there is no mystery. She has stayed because too many of the people in her life were not there when she needed them.

"What do you say?" Miss Shelly asks.

Jessica's only line of defense is reproach. "Why don't you go back on dialysis? Why don't you get in line for a kidney?"

"I'm not a good prospect, not with stage four hep C. My liver's tanking, too."

They had never talked about Shelly's decision to die. Shelly hadn't even told Jessica that she was going off dialysis. Jessica's cheeks are damp now and she wipes one with the side of a fist. She takes the joint from Shelly's lips, sucks at it, and coughs.

"You should give up those damn Marlboros," Miss Shelly says.

Jessica extinguishes the remainder of the joint, a roach now, by licking it. Then she swallows the roach, like Newt taught her. Also thanks to Newt she doesn't have to worry about getting weed. Shelly and she could never burn through all the cannabis hanging in the shed.

The two women get down to business. Shelly fills out checks for the bills Jessica has brought—bills for the house's electricity, water, telephone; bills for the private hospice charges. Even at this point Miss Shelly is meticulous with her figures, like the CPA she was studying to be. When she's done with her bookkeeping she gives Jessica a serious look.

"Jessie, you are the most goddamn responsible person I know. I want you to start taking care of all this stuff for me." She offers Jessica her checkbook. "There's not a lot a bread in the account but I signed a bunch of blanks. Guess I'd better kick soon or they'll be moving me to a public bed."

BACK AT THE house Jessica collects the day's mail and drops it on the dining room table. It's mostly bills, including past due notices from several of Newt's doctors. While Jessica contemplates the figures, his ghost watches her from his old chair. Then Skittles sits up and her golden eyes pose a question.

"What do you want, girl?" Jessica asks her.

Skittles makes a hum in the back of her throat.

"You don't really think I should write checks for these?" Jessica says. "If I do and Miss Shelly is still alive in three months, there won't be enough for her hospice. She'll be sent to a hospital that won't be half as nice as where she is. Is that what you want?" Lately Jessica has begun to have many one-sided conversations with Skittles.

Across the table, Newt's ghost smiles.

"What do I do?" she asks of the burly shadow. "You know I don't want anyone to find me yet. You know I don't care about the money. I'd tap my old bank account in a second to pay this pile of bills. But that would put me on the map, send me out of this safe place you made for me."

Newt's gentle eyes remind Jessica of what he had whispered in her ear toward the end—that with her around it was easier for him to let go, since he knew that Shelly would not be alone. He reminds her that she is responsible for Shelly.

"Okay," Jessica says, her relief palpable. "You're right. You're absolutely right, Newt."

At the sound of his name, Skittles lifts her head, confused at the attention Jessica is giving to an empty chair. But Jessica knows that Newt is there and what he wishes her to do.

THE NEXT MORNING Jessica drives to the Bank of America monolith in downtown San Bernardino. She gives up her name, account PIN, her social security number, her former address on a Nevada Air Force base, a current address that she lies about, and she is finally allowed access to her military savings. From a nervous teller she requests money orders for the doctor's bills she's brought along. Exiting, Jessica cuts between a pair of surprised businesswomen, who step back and gawk at her, she imagines, as they would at Bonnie Parker making a gunpoint withdrawal. Or do they just see some kind of street trash?

That's how Jessica lately has begun to feel under the gaze of middle-class eyes, dressing as she does in jeans and a tank top. She hasn't taken scissors to her hair since her Air Force discharge and it has grown wild down to her shoulders, almost Rastafarian. And, after Newt's death, she had let Miss Shelly ink her arms with a wild cosmology—the right with jungle flora, the left with Maori spirals. But does her appearance deserve those glances? Are they even real? Or is this silent tsking that follows her of her own doing—the result of her disciplined military side, the old Jessica, emerging.

Loudly, publicly, she introduces her two halves, "Jessie, this is Jessica. Jessica, Jessie," and makes a formal bow.

At the post office, a clerk sells her postage and points her toward a table with forms. Miss Shelly is having her mail in Newt's final taxes, and per her instructions, she is sending them certified.

She puts stamps on the doctor's bills and returns her certified slips to the mail clerk. He looks at the envelopes that she has addressed to the IRS and Sacramento.

"You know it's the sixteenth. You're a day late with taxes," he says, reviewing what she's given him.

"Not if you're dead."

"Just trying to help," he apologizes. And then his face brightens. "Your name is *Jessica Aldridge*?" he asks. "From *Florida*, maybe?"

The hairs on Jessica's arms bristle—ten minutes after putting her name back into the system at BoA and they have found her. And by *they*, she does not know who she means. But there *are* wanted posters on the nearby walls.

"Hey. Slow down," the clerk says as Jessica backs away. "It's an innocent question. For the past six months we've been getting general delivery letters here addressed to a Jessica Aldridge. She never picks them up and we keep returning them to the sender. We just got another. They're as regular as clockwork."

Jessica manages to halt her retreat—partly because she has not yet paid for the tax mailing. "There must be a lot of Jessica Aldridges."

"No doubt," the clerk says.

"So why would I be *that* Jessica Aldridge?"

The clerk, a middle-aged man with brown eyes and short curly brown hair, looks askance. "I'm just asking, ma'am. It's my job." Now his pupils dart across Jessica's tatted arms.

"That letter from a penitentiary?" she asks.

"Yes," the clerk answers. "So then, *you* are . . ."

"Yeah. Well, I guess I do look like a person a prisoner would write to."

"Nah," the clerk lies and goes back to business. He rings up the certified receipts. "Thirteen dollars and sixty-six cents," he tells Jessica. "Thirteen sixty-six. That's a good lottery pick. Now let me go find that letter of yours."

SKITTLES DANCES IN the yard while the concrete stoop pinches the skin under Jessica's rear. Over the past weeks she has lost even more padding on her butt. She doesn't care. Miss Shelly is not getting any weaker; maybe Jessica's fasting, like the cosmic balancing she would like to believe in, has something to do with it? Not likely.

At Jessica's feet Skittles drops a toy, a stuffed ape made limbless. Again Jessica tosses the rag into the yard, weedy and barren from drought. Skittles, instead of chasing, nuzzles Jessica's hand and Jessica wonders if she can scent Don on the letter.

Pieces of her memory quilt together a past she has tried, for ten years, not to acknowledge. Her aunt telling her about Don's conviction. Her pretense that he, having disappeared from her life, was meaningless to her. Her ache for her absentee mother. Her denial that she wanted a father. Her fury that he should be a drug dealer and had killed a man.

"Go away," she tells Skittles and pushes the dog's snout from her face. She studies Don's envelope. Its sealed flap is singed where she has tortured it with a cigarette, hoping to see it ignite. But it didn't. Now she puts a pinky into the burn hole and tears.

Skimming the letter, Don's words feel like the touch of a soft hand.

CHAPTER 22

Washington, DC; New York City

The summer has been hot, but Zoe is shivering. She is seated in the audience of a Broadway musical playing at the Kennedy Center and is chilled by more than air-conditioning. Beside her, Porter is rocking his rather large head to the left and right. She becomes aware that this might be disruptive to the people seated behind them. She becomes aware of how unaware Porter seems to be of anything but the singer on stage and her syrupy lyrics. And she begins to shift her attention from what is on the stage. She notices the ornate fixtures high above in the opera house, the elderly woman in the fox stole in front of her who is sitting next to an empty seat, the family beside her dressed in flip-flops and shorts. Seconds pass as slowly as minutes. And locked in her cold islet Zoe is mostly noticing that her hand is covered by Porter's—whose fingers twine through hers and pinch the skin around the diamond solitaire.

Its stone intermittently glints as Porter rocks her hand to the tempo of the song, something schmaltzy about lost love. The stone is neither too large nor too small. It is not schmaltzy. It is a stone as flawless as the pitch of the petite blonde on stage.

Because Porter is her boss, she has so far been able to avoid the spectacle of wearing this perfect ring to the office. In fact she has not worn it at all unless prompted by Porter. He may attribute this to discretion, to her concern for their careers. In truth, she has not yet gathered the will to give back the ring. This is unsurprising since she couldn't find the will to not accept it when—while they were preparing a lazy dinner of bruschetta and Chianti last Saturday—Porter got down on one knee.

"Shall I knight you or call your osteopath," she had joked as his knee cartilage popped on the terrazzo. Her comment dimmed the spark in his eyes. With Porter you cannot take certain things lightly—not sexism, not domestic violence, and as she was to learn, not the ritual of a marriage proposal. Is this generational? Porter's serious expression had left her seriously at a loss, until he'd unclasped his hands to show her a small velvet ring box. Upon his opening it, she could only respond, "*Excuse* me," as if someone on the Metro had indifferently stepped on her foot.

She let Porter slip the ring onto her finger. For him this proposal must have been the foregone conclusion to their cohabitation. For her it only made imminent the inevitability of her leaving him. Immediately she should have said, "*No*, Porter. I'm sorry. I can't." But a torpor sank her into a chair. And after this she'd overindulged in the Chianti, with Porter assuming that they were celebrating.

Zoe's funk has continued through the five days since, aided by Porter's wine closet and Xanax. So far he's made no comment about the empty bottles of grappa in the recycle bin or the pills disappearing from the bottle she found in his desk. He hasn't mentioned her beached dolphin passivity during sex or even her inability to complete the sub-Saharan donation report he'd asked her to turn in by Tuesday. Porter had been as clueless to these signs of her discouragement as he is to the sighs of the person sitting behind him at the Kennedy Center—a stranger who, just as Zoe does, finds Porter's oversized bobblehead annoying.

After centuries pass, and like a wildfire on a windy day, applause crackles up around her and blows toward the stage. Porter's sweaty hand releases Zoe's and he rises. He slaps his palms so furiously that Zoe fears they'll rupture and spatter her with blood. After he stops clapping, they slow-step with the crowd into intermission.

The August night is humid as they exit onto a terrace as vast and characterless as a parking lot. Porter goes to a parapet and stares at the lights across the Potomac. In the middle distance a dinner cruise putt-putting toward Georgetown transmits the clinks of glassware. How many more calm and tepid nights like this might there be if Porter and she marry? Zoe considers whether such a life might not be so bad after all.

Porter has charm. He is handsome and fit for his age. He is capable and loyal. He is able to laugh at himself and generous about the faults of others. He is intuitive in his decision making but analytic about the merit of his ideas. In other words, he is an easy person with whom to work. And this might not be a bad attribute in a husband.

"Porter," she says before her speechlessness returns.

"It's all right, Zoe," he says. "I understand."

But Zoe does not. How can he know what she needs to say? And if he does know, does such perceptiveness and sensitivity make him an even better prospect for a life partner?

"I guess I was kidding myself," he adds.

The whine of a jet descending toward Reagan allows her a moment for composition. "It's not about our ages," she says. "It's about . . . It's that . . . *You* are a fully formed person."

After many seconds he smiles. "So you think I've stopped growing?"

Porter is on the wrong track. Zoe tries to clarify aloud to him and to herself what she means. "*No*. It's that . . . you would always be taking the lead for us." In her stumbling she feels much less mature than he, like a student speaking to her professor, which confirms her argument against their marrying. And she realizes something curious then: she cannot recall their ever fighting. Their relationship has progressed so smoothly that it is as though she is being funneled into a cage. Still, she trusts Porter and she knows he is not toying with her. It is *her* feelings that are the trap. Her months with him have passed without incident, except for a growing affection and solidarity. Marriage does seem the logical conclusion. *This* is the trap.

"If you need time," he says.

"Perhaps a decade might help . . ."

"Put us on the same plane?"

Confusing the metaphor, she tracks another descending jet.

"A decade is a long time," Porter says. Then he sings a short bar. "'Will you still need me . . . when I'm sixty-four?'"

She doesn't answer the question.

"Ouch," Porter says lightly. "You're right. We shouldn't get married."

Apparently Porter has different rules for making a proposal than for rescinding it. In the latter case humor is a permissible Band-Aid. But now she's the serious one.

"I care for you," she says. "I'll always appreciate what you gave me. The time and space to grow up enough to be on my own." This may not be true. But they're words to toss into the vacuum she's creating.

Porter looks toward the black water and for an instant the night encloses them. The Kennedy Center's foyer lights have flashed, signaling the end of intermission.

"But didn't you live alone when you first moved to DC?" Porter asks, weakly contradictive.

"I was with you every day in the office, even before we were together."

Porter's leaning forearms pull back from the parapet rail. His lanky frame pivots toward the bright glass walls. He takes a step and nearly sinks. When he is upright he rests against a planter, then against Zoe. "Stunned there for a second," he says.

Somehow this cheers her—not that she is causing him pain but that she has made him alive again. This will be their first and last disagreement, she decides. But if they'd had more disharmony, if they'd been more immature, maybe then she would have accepted him. Arm in arm they enter the foyer as the more focused concertgoers shuffle up carpeted steps toward the auditorium.

"You finish the show," Zoe tells him. She hurries away before she can't. She doesn't glance back to see if he is following.

"COFFEE?" MARIATU ASKS as Zoe props her bag by her door. Though it is late Mariatu is curious. Or perhaps she is primarily offering a sympathetic ear—after all it is past midnight and tomorrow is a workday, though not for Zoe. In the goodbye note she'd left for Porter, she'd scribbled how it was best if she resigned. She'd weighted the note with his engagement ring.

"Coffee," Zoe confirms.

While Mariatu fills the brewer Zoe tells her about her night. Like a psychiatrist Mariatu asks no questions, merely *hmms* sympathetically at intervals to let Zoe know she is listening. She fills two mismatched mugs—swag, Zoe sees, from various work-related conferences. Is it cynical of Porter to assign Mariatu consistently to event duty? Her plaited hair and distinctive face make her a representative not easily forgotten.

"So you will not even return to the office?"

"I need to leave right away," Zoe explains.

She senses herself judged, as much by Mariatu as by the ritual masks on the wall, which with their high foreheads and small features represent a tribal Sierra Leone vision of female dignity and calm—traits the opposite of Zoe's for many weeks.

"But," Mariatu pleads, "won't you *miss* your work?"

My work, Zoe thinks. What has become of it anyway? Since April, when WIDO's accountant finally nosed out the bribe she had sent to Jean-Pierre in Burundi last December, Zoe has only been tasked with proofreading donor reports. So far the scandal has not leaked to the outside world, or even to the other staff, but she fears that Porter might be preparing to fall on his sword. Her leaving is the best, or at least the easiest, solution for everyone.

"I'll miss the people," Zoe says.

Mariatu strokes Zoe's cheek and she is overcome by the loss of what she is giving up—which is not simply Porter or her job or even her friendship with Mariatu. She is losing her future. She has failed, here in DC, to invent herself. The next morning, ignoring Porter's texts, deciding to get a new number, Zoe is on the train back to New York.

"I'VE ALWAYS DEPENDED on the kindness of strangers," Zoe tells Marla, her freshman-year NYU roommate.

"Me, too. Thanks for the house-sit." Marla has been waiting on the stoop of her Henry Street building. Zigzagged with fire escapes it might have been teleported from a 1950s Hollywood movie. And Marla, smoking and leaning back on her elbows, looks like she belongs in one—except with the sexes reversed. Her most famous role to date was as Stanley in a cross-gender production of *Streetcar* last year, and even now she is wearing a wife-beater.

"Man, it's hot. You up for some brewskis, Blanche?" Talking through her cigarette, Marla scratches her chin like a longshoreman.

Zoe feels lighter. "God, it's good to see you."

Marla flicks away her cigarette and gets up so she can squash Zoe into her with her man-arms.

"REMEMBER THAT GUY?" Marla asks. They are seated in Marla's favorite dive, the old Skinny on Orchard. "Ben what's-his-name? You know, from our modern poetry course. The lit major you thought was hot."

"I thought *you* thought he was hot."

"Come on. *You* stalked him to that gay cowboy disco in Hell's Kitchen. That's how much you liked him."

So far Zoe and Marla have consumed two plastic pitchers of ale.

"*That* was a rumor," Zoe says. "And, hey, it's not like I outed him or anything. He wasn't even gay."

"I know, I know," Marla says. "He went there to score some ecstasy."

"I heard it was Ritalin and that he needed it to cram for midterms."

"Maybe. But he got kicked out for selling Ambien to that divinity student."

"The Nigerian who woke up sleepwalking naked in Washington Square."

"So, I have a confession," Marla says. "I hooked up with him once."

"With the Nigerian?"

"No. With Ben. I was experimenting. Are you angry?"

Zoe is laughing, perhaps too hard. "He was a good-looking boy, but I never stalked him to Hell's Kitchen. "But . . . but"—and here, laughing, emphasizing, she jabs an index finger at the air—"I did run into him one night up in Times Square."

"What the hell were you doing up there?"

"My parents came into town to see *Phantom*." And as if she's run into a wall, Zoe's laughter stops. "I mean . . . my grandparents."

"Get the alibi straight, girl. Was it your parents *or* your grandparents? . . . Zoe? . . . What's wrong?"

Zoe's eyes are welling.

THE TAVERN'S TOILET has a door with a broken latch that only gives Zoe a moment's privacy to stare into her bloodshot eyes. She doesn't want Marla worrying that she has invited a train wreck to crash in her apartment. It's burden enough for her to have come to Marla because of a breakup. She can't also dump onto her friend the horror of her grand-parents' passing, the issue of her revised parentage.

Some people like to live as if there is no tomorrow; Zoe is trying to pretend there is no yesterday. But, now and again, the things she has bur-ied rise like vampires to bite. Zoe rinses her face in the tavern bathroom's filthy sink, then heads out to the bar.

"HARRY, THIS IS Zoe. Zoe, Harry," Marla says the next morning. She's leaning over a terrarium on the kitchen counter. "Harry's total contra-band. Something about salmonella poisoning and kids kissing their shells. So no kissing."

"Sorry, Harry," Zoe cheeps, hung over, as she looks through the side of the turtle's glass lagoon.

"I owe everything to Harry. Harry's the guy who got me off off-off-Broadway and on off-Broadway. He never gets tired of hearing me run lines. Do you, handsome?"

Marla, in a swirl from packing, informs Zoe that Harry is a connois-seur of raspberries, the riper the better. "Thanks for watching the place. See you in September," she says, hugging Zoe.

"Break a leg," Zoe says with forced joy and snares Marla's cheek with a kiss.

After the door closes behind Marla, Zoe dissolves back into the futon. She feels like a salted slug.

CHAPTER 23

New York City

Because Ethan prefers to sulk alone he begs off whenever Alex invites him to dine with him and Juliette. He is a little jealous of her. She has taken over Alex's life, has even gotten him a solo at Medusa, a first-floor gallery in Chelsea. Ethan ends up at Sixth and Thirty-First, in a Starbucks where he orders a caramel Frappuccino and sticky rolls, sugar being his latest stimulant of choice.

"Eleven twenty-eight," says the barista, a pretty woman in a head scarf.

Ethan looks at her, contemplating how their religious differences might affect their potential future together and why she has just given him the time of night. Then Ethan snaps awake. "Oh, sorry," he says and gives her his Visa. Shockingly it's not rejected. He's been getting warning letters for not keeping up with his minimum credit payments. He'd intended to pay back his incipient debts after the check for his condo sale cleared, but he'd leveraged the mortgage and what he's getting won't even cover his lawsuit fees.

At a counter before a window Ethan sits a few stools down from another lone diner and imagines they are posing for a contemporary *Nighthawks*; the man is studying his smartphone like it's a naked woman and Ethan is connecting his laptop to the free Wi-Fi.

Ethan navigates to his own kind of porn—the calculation of what UIB is gaining by using his algorithms. Imagining dominance over the markets is his version of fantasy sex—his lustful scenario involves erratic exchange rates among the dollar, euro, renminbi, rupee. He runs his numbers at least once a day. More often on lonely days.

But it is finally just a fantasy; without UIB's mainframe computing power he can't react in real-time to international events. His laptop can only slog through retroactive analyses of what might have been. Masturbation by another name. Yet he can't stop this self-abuse. Every day he opens his browser to hunt for headlines that would have engaged his algorithm.

Today's news cycle has been light. But not for Ethan's algorithm. The big event is a botched drone strike: a terrorist supposedly blown up a year ago has resurfaced. Now he's inflaming the Arab street with a web video. Mullahs are inciting protests outside US embassies.

Ethan's fingers, on autopilot, input the day's Forex data and he learns that the Pentagon's announcement of its failure caused the dollar to drop by three-quarters of a cent. This was followed by an immediate two-thirds recovery. The movement is not huge, but that the gyration went on longer than the usual two-hour decay *is*. And based on the funds UIB allotted to his program on the day before he was fired, Ethan's algorithm has just turned a fantasy profit of almost two million dollars, of which a fifth of one percent would have been added to his annual commission. Ethan slumps over his laptop as if they, he and the machine, have just had sex.

"Some bullhockey, huh? This al-Yerassi stuff," says Ethan's companion at the counter. The man is wearing a uniform, a blue windbreaker with matching pants. "'We're knocking 'em out one by one,' they tell us. Then thirteen months later they come back with an, 'Oops, sorry. We blasted a convoy but missed the target.'" The man shows Ethan his phone as if he can read its screen text across five feet of space.

"I hear you," Ethan says, abashed that his current fantasy is to make money from what pisses people off. At UIB, when he actually *was* profiting from military destruction and screw-ups and had felt a twinge of shame, he'd told himself that if he wasn't writing the programs someone else would. "Doing God's work," John Guan used to kid. But Guan was dissing an even worse justification by many of their co-workers—that their work was if not exactly divinely mandated, then close to it. But the true justification, for everyone, was the bonuses. The revelation of the al-Yarisi miss might have netted him four thousand dollars. For a midlevel quant that's more than a decent day's pay.

"So now this guy, Yerassi, he's back from the dead, pledging death to America from his spider hole," says Ethan's companion. "Some muck-up, huh? Fog of war for a whole darn year? *Sure*. How dumb does Washington think we are?"

"Plenty fucking dumb," Ethan says overloud. Maybe it's his oversug-ared blood. Maybe it's about being screwed out of his imaginary bonus. And who might be getting it now. *Hoke?*

Ethan's interlocutor lifts his hands in arrest. "Whoa, pal. You lose a brother in the towers or something?"

The man's comment is rhetorical and exempts Ethan from responding. Yet, in fact, Ethan *is* pondering a loss, not familial but financial. *Fucking Hoke*, he thinks. *It was him!* Ethan has an impulse to call John Guan and pry facts out of the man, ask if it wasn't Hoke that set him up, had moved that decimal point. But Guan probably wouldn't say. More likely Guan wouldn't even answer his call. Because of Ethan's lawsuit, the bank has forbidden his former co-workers from communicating with him.

Ethan packs up his laptop and goes out into the humid, rancorous odor of taxi exhaust. He is midtown on Avenue of the Americas, yet flashing inside the dark of his brain an explosion launches his ex-boss through the glass of the UIB tower. A burning Dwayne Hoke, framed against a starless sky, is scrambling in midair . . . and then, sickeningly, is falling. What Ethan is left with is what Hoke himself had planted in his head. It is almost always before him now, blocking his path. A horror of charred flesh that appears to be half a man.

CHAPTER 24

Florida

Dear Jessica,

Ever heard that Elvis song Return to Sender? I did every time San Bernardino General Delivery sent back my mail. I was ready to give up on these longshot letters just for the quiet. But then a miracle happened. My March letter did not boomerang and I figured your reply was on the way.

One month and the next passed and I waited. Then three. Then five months. And now my patience has paid. I am holding your package. Though it has no return address I know it is yours by how you loop the D in Don.

So I want to play a little game. When and if you read this letter I want you to imagine that you are handing your package to me in person. For as I open it now on this fifteenth day of August I am pretending you are here in front of me. Maybe by imagining hard enough we can come together across space and time. It is worth a try since today in my time is my birthday. And hearing from you is the best gift I could have got.

Jessica. I have opened your package and I kiss your cheek for the CD. But I will not blame the prison authorities for confiscating your letter because I dont think you included one. After all that has happened because of our writing I know you cant risk sending me words. Sometimes anyway music is a better way to talk. I am putting in earphones now to hear what you sent.

WOW. The Malagueña my cellmate strums flows steady as a river, but your Roy Buchanan version is real Hendrix at Woodstock. A wild

ocean of sound. You can bet I will be celebrating today by playing your
disc until the grooves wear out.

   Guess what. Ector reading this over my shoulder says CDs have no
grooves. I guess he should know since he is educated. He also tells me
that he spells his name with an H as in Hector.

Your loving father,
Don

P.S. Hector has finally gone back to his guitar so now I can quick finish
this letter. Dont worry about not giving me your address. I am guessing
you are not wanting to be found. Is it the VA chasing you for walking
out of their hospital? If so I expect you wont be checking in again at
San Bernardino General Delivery anytime soon. Which means for me
another serenade from old Elvis. And for you this letter to read in some
maybe time to come.

CHAPTER 25

Nevada, Pakistan

Two weeks ago the Pentagon announced what Voigt has known for over a month: al-Yarisi is alive, has been in hiding for a year after the drone strike thought to kill him. As the local commander in charge, Voigt has been getting an earful. But recordings of what went on in the operations trailer have pretty much cleared his actions. The order to fire had come straight from Langley and only *through* him. Jessica, he knows, without that command, and after seeing those girls hop from the SUV, would not have pulled the trigger. He'd been right to make her a pilot.

Clearly she's in hiding. For what else can it be when these days you leave no trace of your whereabouts, for a good ten months. More power to her if DC wanted her shut up in a psych ward; after the al-Yarisi revelation, Washington would have buried the key.

The situation is such a live grenade that the FBI agent assigned to find her doesn't even know the full story. Voigt was directed to tell Tom Daugherty as little as possible and nothing about the collateral damage. Talk about government dysfunction. But, then, Voigt doesn't really want Jessica found, certainly not to be a victim of some Beltway bureaucrat's damage-control campaign.

His aide in the outer office buzzes. "Colonel?"

"Here," Voigt says, taking the phone. Reading Don's last letter to Jessica, he's thinking about picking up that Roy Buchanan CD the convict mentioned. But then again, he might be getting too close to the Aldridge situation.

"We've got a Pred down in Waziristan," the aide says.

Voigt would like to curse but he doesn't. "Who's crew?"

"Shadow." They go by code names even here.

"Black box still transmitting?"

"Yes, sir. We've got coordinates."

"This was a recon flight?"

"Yes sir, no payload."

"Well, that's something anyway. Who else is in the area?"

"Newport, trailer ten. A Reaper east of Kandahar."

"Full payload?"

"Paveway and Hellfires."

"All right. Retask Newport to the crash. Get Shadow over to ten. I'll be there in sixty seconds." Voigt secures Don's letter and is out the door.

They've gathered tightly in trailer 10, behind the crew at the monitors. Newport is Lieutenant Dunbar, one of the good younger pilots, if a little rich for himself, Voigt thinks. His tag, Newport, or Nieuport, is the biplane World War I ace Eddie Rickenbacker flew. But Dunbar's air of pride about drone duty is generally good for morale and Voigt would not deflate it.

"What failed?" Voigt asks Shadow, aka Major Hollis, an Air Force lifer who came up with Voigt during the first Iraq invasion, flying F-16s out of Dhahran.

"Unknown. Power out over Sikaram."

"That where you brought it down?"

"Glided it onto a ridge."

"How accessible?"

"By air, probably. By ground, yes. It's just above the tree line."

"Dunbar, ETA?" Voigt says.

"We're six hundred klicks out. Seventy minutes at red line."

"Let's go get it," Voigt says. They're on another search-and-destroy mission, but for one of their own machines.

Twenty minutes later, at sunrise there, the drone has a view of the peak. Sikaram. A crag on the border of Pakistan and Afghanistan. It's barren, seemingly inaccessible, three miles high, but near the pass where bin Laden likely escaped in '01 after Tora Bora. Forty minutes later the Reaper is close enough to sight where the Predator's black box is signaling. There is smoke. And on the ground, a half mile from the crash, at the periphery of the drone's camera, ants navigating the side of an anthill.

"You see those?" Voigt asks. Dunbar's sensor does and zooms. The ants are men. "Can we beat them to it?"

"If not, no problem, sir," Dunbar says.

"Unless they're shepherds?"

"Then they wouldn't be above the tree line, sir."

"That was a joke, son," Voigt says. Still, he doesn't want to be blasting blindly at unknown targets. And the men, or their fathers, might actually have been shepherds once.

Fifteen minutes later, the line of men and the Reaper are converging at their ground zero.

"I've got it," Dunbar's sensor says and zooms onto the dull metal tube that was the drone. One of the wings is gone. "I can have a laser on it in two minutes." The laser will guide the five-hundred-pound Paveway to its target, incinerating just about all evidence, melting it into Sikaram's rocky face. At least then it won't be carried down the mountain and trumpeted as an American atrocity among the tribespeople.

"Zoom out, operator," Voigt says. For all their sophistication, UAVs have a clumsy field of vision. Voigt's experience is that their cameras take in only about ten percent of what an airborne pilot can observe from a cockpit.

And there they are, coming around the ridge. The shepherds. Or militants. They don't carry staffs. Their slung rifles are clearly visible. A show of weapons like this is all that's needed to justify an engagement.

"Shall I get a go on this from Langley?" asks Dunbar's mission intelligence coordinator. She's on speaker, not in the trailer, but monitoring the situation before her own screen. She can see the Paveway won't be launched before the men arrive at the drone. She's ready to compress the kill chain.

"Wait," Voigt says. He's studying the men. "Zoom to the two in back," he says to the sensor.

"Shit," says Dunbar.

The two are smaller than the other men. Boys. Perhaps ten or eleven. No doubt, following after their fathers and uncles.

"We're in launch range," the sensor says as the men and boys on the ground hurry across a boulder and come in sight of the wrecked drone. In twenty seconds, the time it would take for the Paveway to hit, they will be on it.

"Negative," Voigt says. He is looking at the men on the screen. They are excited. Victorious. Firing their rifles in the air. "Let them take the damn thing."

CHAPTER 26

New York City

"I'm thinking about buying that," Sergei Sokolov says of a large Picasso, a curtain the artist had done for the Ballets Russes. He leads Ethan and Juliette through the atrium on Fifty-Second Street and into an art deco dining room, where they are seated.

Ethan doesn't know what to think about Sergei. Juliette has arranged the meeting. Sergei is one of her clients. She has been helping him find art for his dacha in Sevastopol. Alex, after his opening next week, is going to fly over there to do a mural.

"Juliette tells me you are at war with UIB," Sergei says to him.

The Russian is neat, trim, alert eyed, pleasant. He looks nothing like the oligarchs of Ethan's fancy—stocky men with red faces in askew business suits. He doesn't even resemble the billionaires Ethan had glimpsed at UIB—men who dressed down in hoodies and sneakers if they were young; attempted business casual with shirts deeply unbuttoned Richard Branson–style if they were midlife; and blossomed with the full camouflage of bespoke suits and Windsor-knotted ties if they were seniors. Sergei is wearing a windbreaker that might have been bought at Target. Not that Ethan is dressed any better. The maître d' had slipped him into a wrinkled blazer.

"They're trying to claw back my bonuses. But that's not what's motivating me now," Ethan says.

"Ah, revenge," says Sergei and picks up his menu.

"Our friend is using all his money to fight them," says Juliette, touching Ethan's arm. "But it may be a losing battle."

Ethan looks at Juliette. Alex has been telling her more than he would have expected. But, then, they are a couple now.

"I hear you have been working on very sophisticated algorithms, currency related," Sergei says.

Now Ethan looks at Sergei. This is not something he could have learned from Alex. Even through all this, *especially* through all this, he has kept his UIB confidentiality agreement. Ethan then becomes aware of a fourth place setting at their table that the waiter has not removed. "It's not work that I'm proud of" is all he says to describe what he did.

"I hear you were accused of a decimal point error," Sergei says. "But that your fundamental knowledge is deep."

The flattery is succor. "If I made the error, that's bad. But what I mean about not being proud is something else." He knows that he can't get into the specifics of his work in currency-volatility exploitation; UIB would really have a right to sue him then.

A commotion turns Ethan's head. Someone who's entered the dining hall has crashed into a table. Silverware clatters. "John?" Ethan says.

"Ah, here's Mr. Guan," says Sergei, rising and extending his hand.

"Yes, sir. Yes, sir," says Guan, looking nervously about. He stares a moment at Sergei's hand before taking it. "Hope no one from work recognizes me," he says.

Yeah, that's real likely, Ethan wants to say; if anyone else from UIB was here, they'd be executive level management or beyond. Such a person noticing Guan would be like a pharaoh identifying one of the thousand stonecutters building his pyramid. "What's going on?" he asks Guan sharply.

"Don't be angry with your friend," says Sergei. He takes some documents from his windbreaker and asks a waiter for pens. "I'll explain everything. But, first, if you will kindly sign these nondisclosures . . . just in case, you know, you decide not to accept my job offer."

CHAPTER 27

New York City

Outside Medusa Gallery a queue, held back by a doorman with a clipboard, snakes down the sidewalk. The crowd, Zoe is guessing, is lined up for some art star's opening. She takes out her phone to recheck Alex's e-vite.

She had holed up in Marla's apartment for almost all of August—turtle-sitting Harry, ignoring Porter's emails. She was ready to break her solitude, and not in the least because Alex's invitation signaled the end of a general communications embargo. After her grandparents' funeral, after she had slept with Ethan and then raced back to Washington, after the reprimanding email from Alex, she'd become a persona non grata to both of her ex-lovers.

The address in the e-vite, she sees, *does* say the Chelsea Medusa. The subject line had even been personalized with a "Please come, Zoe." Her address hadn't just been swooped up by mistake from one of Alex's old email lists. Still, she is wary as she approaches the doorman.

"Leston . . . Zoe," she says quietly.

"Uh-huh," the doorman says, but he checks his list.

Medusa's glass maw parts for her. Zoe's mouth opens nearly as wide. She sees people whom she recognizes from movies and music videos. Then her eyes rise to the pretext of this vanity fair—the art. The walls are hung high with monumental paintings—some collision between Matta and Twombly if she is accurately recalling her freshman art history. But what she sees next just cannot possibly be. And then she is grinning in pleased amazement. She has not slipped down a rabbit hole. The exhibition's title, in foot-tall letters, proclaims ALEX CARR—NEW WORK. Alex has *made it*.

Zoe had always taken Alex to be three-quarters the hustler leavened with one-eighth the charmer. She had granted a mere eighth-part of him, a mere patina over the pretense, as having anything to do with artistic ability. But here he is, not in his person for she has not yet glimpsed his corporeal self. Zoe means, here *he* is, alive and transcendent in his work.

"Champagne?" a man asks, and suddenly Zoe is holding a flute while experiencing a deeper thirst for the line and color of Alex's painting. Her eyes drink and drink, like camels watering after a trek. And then she feels shaken.

Why had she not seen Alex's potential before this? Was her vision deficient, her brain ossified, her heart unreceptive? Or was what her art professor had argued true—that "it is the occasion of true art to make its need felt most desperately only after repeated encounters." Those paintings that hung in Ethan's apartment must have been preparing her for this moment of aesthetic hydration.

"I just bought that," the man says, pleased with her attention to the canvas. It is not one of the biggest in the show, but it might be the most seductive. The man and Zoe part the crowd before the painting and it alters. Zoe can no longer see the large *S* or dollar sign that centers the image from afar. This close up she sees glistening shards of impasto licking up from an elsewhere flat surface. The brushstrokes, rising in small bloody wavelets, seem a critique on the commodification of this painting, of art in general. Then she pushes aside all this interpretation—the influence of her professor's astute but distracting theorizing—to soak up the image as image. She is even able to ignore the painting's title, *Money Shot*, which she hates. She inhales the smells of turpentine and oil paint and worries that the image is already hardening, mutating away from the wet, liquid perfection of its birth.

"What he's done with the red impasta is something," says her drinking companion. He moves nearer to the canvas and raises a hand toward it as if to push through a door. Zoe notices he has a long lacquered thumbnail and for a moment she fears he will dig it into the paint.

"Impas*to*," she says sharply, noticing his overlarge but handsome face, his broad shoulders and chest. Her mouth twists into a half smile as she realizes that he is famous and she doesn't recall his name.

"Dean Cato," he says and offers her the hand with the strange nail.

Zoe stares but doesn't otherwise react. Her expression might be a frown.

"Sorry. The nail's for a role I'm playing," Cato says. "Some kind of war-lock. But a good one." He holds out the thumb like an artist sizing up a tree for a landscape. "Creepy, isn't it?" Cato looks about thirty, both boy-ish and manly, and she wonders how much of an act he is putting on—the pretense of being a regular guy.

"If you're Dean Cato, where's your entourage?" she asks.

Cato's grin grows. "I'm here alone."

"So you're here to hook up."

He tilts his head. "I love art lovers," he admits.

Zoe's eyes drift from Cato's, passing through and over the noisy crowd, which has left the two of them a circle of space as if they are a pair of street fighters being wagered on. But this crowd is not betting on Dean Cato's attempt to score. Why would they be? They are the famous and celebrated and are engaged in their own small duels—all except one who is famous only to Zoe. Her heart speeds a bit upon seeing him.

"Eth," she calls, though he has already disengaged from the man with whom he was speaking, a man in a windbreaker. Her ex seems ready to dissolve backward into the crowd.

Ethan is not smiling. He never did when it did not come naturally. Clearly he still has no concept of how important dissimulation is for mak-ing others give a damn about you. What's more, he's no longer following the UIB dress code—he'd kept the manual on their dresser. Now with his uncut hair camouflaging his ears, the stretched-out Izod pullover, the ill-fitting jeans and scuffed dress shoes, he radiates an unfamiliar shabbiness. He holds himself apologetically stooped and then lurches forward. She rises onto her toes and Ethan awkwardly accepts her kiss on his cheek.

"You came," he says, less in gladness than like a man relieved of a burden.

"I was surprised Alex invited me. Isn't he supposed to be your best friend?" Zoe says through a smile. But she is being too glib. Ethan has a tendency to extract meaning from small talk.

"Alex doesn't really hate you," he says, confirming to Zoe that Alex probably *kind of* hates her. But this is not really news.

Zoe keeps her smile. "Anyway, it's nice, not being *really* hated enough to get an invitation."

Ethan looks away. "I'm the one who undeleted you from his list."

Her smile fades. "Why?" she asks. If anyone has a right to hate her, Ethan does.

"Maybe for the same reason you came tonight?" he says with a faint upturn of his mouth.

"I was in town," Zoe says, afraid Ethan will imagine that her presence here has a hidden meaning.

In the silence that follows, Dean Cato pops back into Zoe's periphery. "So, like, you two were an item of yore. Or still are?" he asks.

"*Of yore?*" Zoe says meanly.

"Did I say yore? I'm still half in character. It's difficult to turn off," says Dean, marking his territory as a somebody, probably for Ethan's sake.

"Acting must really be hard. Dean, this is Ethan. He's in finance," she says even as she realizes that Ethan's derelict appearance is embarrassing her.

Now the two men face off—Cato grinning upward self-confidently, Ethan looking down like a pilot circling in a fog and unable to land. Zoe can't help but compare the two men to Ethan's disfavor.

"*Bonsoir*, Dean!"

Cato does an about face into an open pair of toned forearms. "Juliette!" he responds.

Zoe sees a glittering face, a face as taut as a Greek mask depicting ecstasy, above Cato's shoulder. "You have bought *Money Shot*! Congratulations."

Cato lifts the woman, spins about and lands her.

Juliette is older but obviously flogged daily by the whip of a personal trainer. Her dress is a brief costume—a silver halter that exposes the wings of her back and, below, reveals a tanned thigh through a slit. Gladiator platforms augment her height, show off her sculpted calves. This is a woman Zoe would hate to confront in any arena—especially dressed down as she is in the waistless black dress and thong sandals she'd found in Marla's closet.

Nearby a camera fires and Zoe and Ethan, bit players, retreat from the photo op. For a flash, Zoe regrets that she won't be finding out how spectacular Dean Cato's apartment might be.

"You're up from DC?" Ethan asks her, the scruff on his face shadowing his cheeks. This or they are hollow from lost weight.

"No. Washington is over for me."

Ethan leans forward, just short of pressing his folded arms into her breasts. Or is someone pushing him from behind? The art crowd, closing in on them, makes him glare to the left and right as if fearing a stampede. "Let's get out of here," he tells her.

AROUND THE BLOCK in a diner booth, Zoe forks disinterestedly through a plate-size waffle. Meanwhile Ethan pours sugar into his third refill of black coffee. Zoe checks his shaking hand to stop the cup from overflowing.

"Still the sweet tooth," she says and Ethan eyes her as if they had never lived together and she should not know this detail. Yet he has already updated her about losing his job, his UIB lawsuit, his money woes, the days he spends helping Alex, and Juliette, who is supplanting him in his friend's life.

"She's even trying to get me a job to get me out of Alex's studio. That guy I was with when I saw you wants to hire me. *Sergei.* He's been courting me for months."

"But that's great," Zoe says.

"I don't want to work on Long Island. I've got things to do here."

"And what if you don't get a judgment against UIB? You'll have sold your apartment for nothing and not even have work?"

"At least I'll have fought."

The obvious stays behind her lips—that Ethan should stop tilting at windmills and take the offered job. Zoe stares down at Ethan's hands, which are strangling his coffee cup. His fingernails are stained and grimy.

"Paint," he says apologetically and relaxes his grip on the ceramic. "From cleaning Alex's brushes."

"That's nice of you," Zoe says, thinking that Alex should do his own dirty work.

He reads her disapproval. "I don't mind. Repetitive tasks are like Zen. *Ommm,*" he hums briefly then coughs. "Still working on the circular breathing." His humor, poor though it is, reveals a seed of sanity. Zoe feels herself relaxing.

Zoe understands that Ethan's state is a mirror of hers, that though apart they have been traveling similar downward paths. She tallies her obvious wrong turns—sleeping with her boss, moving in with her boss, denying that this course was unsustainable, losing her career because of the bribery mess. The loneliness of where she has arrived is killing.

"Don't," she tells Ethan, whose eyes emit a compassion she had never received from them before. Maybe he wasn't joking about the Zen and has begun working on his karma.

"Zoe," Ethan breathes, and she feels herself choking up.

"I've completely screwed up my life," she blurts.

Zoe's tears are not quite welling but it won't take much—silence or the touch of Ethan's hand across the table.

Unexpectedly Ethan's face lights up. "You need a reboot," he says. "That's what I'm doing. What my lawyers are helping me do. Wipe the slate so I can start over. Prove that my supervisor moved that decimal point, not me."

Zoe cannot completely follow Ethan's burst of talk. Nonetheless the idea that, just like a machine, all she needs is a reboot, douses her in ice water. The old reductive Ethan has returned and he has broken her mood.

"Start over from the very beginning? You mean like *reincarnation*?" she is able to quip.

WHEN ZOE ARRIVES in front of Marla's building, Sun Wah grocery is closing its sidewalk produce stand for the night.

"Half price," Mr. Wah tells her. He offers a box of raspberries that look overripe.

Ms. Wah, toting a crate of peaches, speaks sharply in Cantonese at her husband or brother. Shrinking, Mr. Wah turns a tea-stained grin on Zoe. "Free for neighbor," he says, bowing in apology. Zoe bows back.

Upstairs she finds Harry awake on his terrarium's island and she places a mushy raspberry in front of him. He pulls his head into his shell.

"Hey, mister, it's the way you like them." Zoe stares at the turtle's patterned back, but Harry refuses to come out. "Do you want to hear more stories?" Her grandfather's folder is by Harry's tank. She's read aloud to him the news clippings about her mother. "Well, maybe this will get your interest," she says and pulls off her dress. Then she uncovers the nearby bathtub, an old tenement tub, opens its hot tap and plugs the drain.

While the water rises, Zoe burrows into Marla's liquor cabinet, comes out with a fifth of raspberry vodka, a wood box stamped PROSECCO DI VALDOBBIADENE, a Dewar's miniature, a sticky bottle of amaretto. She opens the miniature and swallows. The liquor burns her throat like arctic air. She inspects the Prosecco box. Two bottles remain and she removes one.

From higher cabinets, she takes down a tall tumbler and a coffee can of candles and incense sticks. She pops open the Prosecco, fills the tumbler, and immediately half drains it. With matches from Balthazar, a restaurant where once she ate ceviche with Ethan, she lights a candle and drips wax on the rounded rim of the tub, getting a few candles to stand on the rim. She surrounds the tub with incense, mounting the sticks in the seams of the wood floor. She lights the candles and incense and turns off the kitchen lights. She gazes at her handiwork, which has some similarity to an altar. But she is not quite ready yet.

In the weeks that she's been living at Marla's she's resisted digging through the medicine cabinet. But now she starts to rummage among the sulfur salves and sleeping pills, the antihistamine tablets and acid-reflux chewables, the creams for wart control and yeast infection. At last she locates Marla's Vicodin and Soma. In college Marla used them to manage her scoliosis spasms, though sometimes she and Zoe abused them recreationally. The dusty labels have expiration dates from early in the Obama era, which possibly indicate that the yoga Marla practices has helped her spine. Zoe gathers up the old drug booty and, taking along a fresh bath towel, returns to the kitchen.

There she sees that Harry has come out and is looking at her as she stands naked in the hazy, incense-darkened candlelight. Zoe almost regrets the filthy kitchen window. She is just a blur to any voyeur on the fire escape or across the street peeping through a blind. Somehow she wants an audience. It's as if by living in Marla's space she has channeled an actor's desire to perform.

Unfortunately, no one is on the iron-barred escape. They are alone, she and Harry. And the solitude Zoe feels serves as a reminder. She playfully constructs a small pyramid of raspberries on Harry's little islet. Harry won't starve on her account if this goes on for a few days.

What? She's indulging in a little ritual of self-pity. A reboot is what Ethan suggested. And *this* is close. Getting completely wasted. Touching bottom so you can push back to the surface.

She refills her tumbler with Prosecco and then follows it with a cocktail of Soma and Vicodin, no doubt half strength at their age. She's allowed to self-prescribe, no? After all, she is a physician's granddaughter—and his daughter as well. But she'll think about that later.

Lifting a foot over the tub rim, Zoe dips a toe in scalding water and hops back on her grounded heel—causing Harry a tsunami when she bumps his terrarium. "Sorry," Zoe says, but Harry's already ducked into his shell. She opens the cold tap for a minute before stepping in. Going down she seems not to displace much water, she sinks like bones due to her diet of late—lentils scavenged from Marla's pantry or a brown banana courtesy of Ms. Wah. Even tonight's Belgian waffle with Ethan brought no inspiration. She'd simply hacked at it.

She settles against the curved back of the tub, her mouth at the waterline. Now the water has become too cool. With her toes she turns the hot tap to a trickle and, through fluttering eyelids, watches the candlelight rippling over the bathwater's surface.

CHAPTER 28

New York City

To: zoeleston2@nyu.edu
From: flytiger3.1416@gmail.com
Subject: Last night

Zoe,

I know I'm breaking our radio silence. I've given you space this past year just as you wanted when you moved to DC. No calls, no emails, no texts. But maybe now, after last night, we can start again. Let me explain.

I will not say that I had no hopes for us after last November, after that last night together. For days afterward I waited to hear from you, for you to tell me our night meant something more than your reaching out for comfort. But now I know this is all it was. And I can accept that.

I guess what I'm stumbling to say is that I'd like us to be friends. I can do this now and I think you too are ready, maybe more than you know. By coming to the opening you took your first step home. And by home I mean a place where people care about you.

As for me, after our talk last night I decided to look into Sergei's job. Tomorrow I'm off to Long Island for a couple of days to check things out. Can we talk when I'm back? Hope we're past all the bad stuff.

E

CHAPTER 29

Sagaponack

The Town Car, which had picked Ethan up in front of the Popeye's below his walk-up on Lexington, now deposits him in a driveway off Hedges Lane in Sagaponack. Ethan can smell the ocean as he stands below a multileveled, Gehry-influenced structure that towers over him in glass, steel, and cedar. One story too high for local regulations, the village has levied the building a ten-thousand-dollar-a-week fine—a cheap bribe compared to Russia, Sergei had told Ethan when they'd arranged his visit. He is being courted and it is flattering.

Expected by the staff, Ethan is escorted to his room, which has a private bath and windows that overlook not the dunes but a field of high grass. He is here at Sergei Sokolov's Long Island home, or is it a base of operations? Ethan sits on the bed and shuts his eyes.

"Mr. Winter," a voice calls from the open door. It's a young woman wearing a jacket bearing Sergei's SAS logo—the *A* for Aleksandrovich—which is monogrammed everywhere here. "Mr. Sokolov will see you now. He is on a very tight schedule."

In an elevator his escort holds a finger to a touchscreen panel. "Biometrics," she explains as the doors close. Ethan's stomach rises, but he cannot tell how far down they are going. The ride becomes motionlessly smooth. There's not even a bounce at the end before the doors are sliding away. And here is Sergei.

"Mr. Winter. At last," he says.

Sokolov is wearing one of his SAS windbreakers, as if transmitting to everyone who works for him that he, too, is just part of the team. He grips Ethan's hand and Ethan almost expects a bear hug to follow. But it doesn't. "This way," says the Russian. Though a head shorter than Ethan and almost as slim, Sergei fills the space with his dynamism. This is a type

Ethan recognizes, a force of nature, a person who, tornado-like, sweeps others up into his enthusiasms.

Lengthening his stride Ethan chases Sergei down a corridor that, from its halogen lighting, glows warmly like the interior of a Hollywood-imagined spacecraft. Ahead Sergei steps through a portal resembling an airlock door found in a submarine. "This is the vault," he says from the other side. "Secure against everything from ocean surges to Chinese hacker attacks."

After ducking under the door header Ethan finds himself in a low, wide, depthless room that is lit just as delicately as the corridor. The next thing he is aware of is the hum, the familiar-to-him hum of a serious mainframe. Its subtle vibration takes Ethan back to UIB, to his old office which adjoined the server room. In that space he had felt much as he is beginning to feel here, like he is at the center of a beehive. But unlike Ethan's solitary chamber at UIB, Sergei's operations center is a bullpen that doesn't offer even the privacy of cubicles. The arrangement suggests that Sergei, as if in a nod to old communist Russia, expects everyone to work for the benefit of the whole, that employees should expect fewer of the superficial inducements of capitalistic prestige prominent on Wall Street—the fancy job title, the corner office, the toy-box swag of watches, electronics, golf clubs. There are in this common room perhaps a dozen workstations, which are mounted on several conference tables as opposed to separated desks. And bent over these dozen or so stations, clicking away at keyboards, are workers who seem as focused on their jobs as drones in a hive. None have even glanced up at Ethan and Sergei's entrance. But Ethan knows why. These young men, for they are all young men, are coders fixated in their solipsistic coding universes, which nonetheless can alter societies. "Cozy, isn't it," Sergei says. "This is where you will be programming."

Ethan just smiles. For although he has signed a confidentiality agreement, he has not yet signed an employment contract—even if Sergei's offer is not one he can imagine refusing. Coding is what holds him together, his deepest pleasure, his essence. But now, standing in this chilly space, something twists in Ethan's stomach. It is not a distaste over the communality—he will not have to rub elbows as there is plenty of room between the workstations. It is something deeper, rawer.

As Ethan's stomach gurgles he notices that Sergei is studying him and guesses that the Russian is waiting for a response, a positive statement that will counter the stony face Zoe had often criticized him for, and which he can sense overcoming him once again. He should try to smile and talk admirably about what Sergei has built here. But he decides to ask another question. "Mr. Sokolov—" he says.

"Please, it's Sergei."

"Sergei. Why did you set up out here, so far from Wall Street and Weehawken?" Weehawken is where much high-speed trading occurs.

Sergei, beaming, leans forward so that his face and then his black irises and pupils are all that Ethan sees. "You are one of us now so I may tell you," Sergei says. "We are just doing the speed tests today . . ."

"Tests?" Ethan says.

"There is a transatlantic cable nearby." Sergei grins. "It's fiber. Very low latency. We are *tapped* into it."

Ethan feels his jaw relax. With the tap the Russian's computers will be getting data from London milliseconds sooner than the mainframes operating on Wall Street a hundred miles west. The difference in practical terms is gold, for a millisecond in speed-trading is comparable to the time saved using a telegraph over flag signals in the nineteenth century. *This* is impressive.

But then Ethan's stomach cramps again. He manages to stand straight, inconspicuously pressing a thumb into his solar plexus. "Wow," he says.

"Yeah," says Sergei. "You know, I like people like you. Motivated. Ambitious. And, in your way, *passionate*. It was dumb of you, but I liked that you took on UIB. And maybe I was a little unsure about your programming talent after I heard how you lost your job. There was that decimal point contretemps you were accused of, no?"

"Yes," Ethan says feeling disparaged. For though he has long since concluded that the error was not his, the world still thinks otherwise.

"But then," Sergei says, the skin orbiting his eyes crinkling, "I did a little more investigation. You do know that Dwayne Hoke, your own boss, set you up, yes?"

Ethan presses his thumb deeper into his solar plexus but even this cannot control the deepening cramp. He bends over and grasps his knees. What Sergei has just told him should give him relief. But it does not.

A sympathetic hand touches the small of his back.

"I know. I know, son. It is unbelievable." Sergei helps Ethan toward a chair, a mesh programmer's chair. He snaps his fingers and gestures at somebody, and this unseen person rushes off. "More important, do you know why you were betrayed?"

Ethan, looking down, can only shake his head.

"Think about it. Oh, but maybe you don't know where Mr. Hoke is working now. He is gone from UIB. Look for him in Stamford, at a nice hedge fund job. I am pretty sure that Mr. Hoke was the one who moved your algorithm's decimal point so that somebody at this fund could bet against your bank's trades. It is the case of one good turn deserving another, *no*? This Dwayne Hoke, I'd say, is making much from your *mistake*. Plus bonus."

Sergei offers Ethan an open bottle of Perrier that has magically appeared. "Thanks," Ethan murmurs, more for the liquid than for the information about Hoke. He sips from the bottle and its liquid bubbles down toward his stomach.

"And now you will have your retribution," Sergei says. "For getting rich is the best revenge, don't you think?" The Russian leans against the edge of the table by the chair Ethan is using.

Ethan tries another sip of water. He has identified what is wrong with himself. In his ideal reality, he wouldn't be coding for revenge, to screw people over.

"Well," Sergei says, squeezing his prospect's shoulder as if their deal is done. "I will leave you to it. You will find a familiar face here who can brief you on your tasks. Because, of course, you do intend to take this job, yes? Welcome aboard, my friend." And then Sergei is gone.

Hoke's treachery doesn't surprise Ethan. He had speculated on it but could gather no proof. Yet Ethan doesn't feel greatly angry with Dwayne, not now that someone else knows the truth about the misplaced decimal point. It is a vindication that should be emotionally, psychologically, physically satisfying. Yet it is not. It has not, for example, provided Ethan with relief from the spasms wrenching his gut. When he looks up, the familiar face that the Russian had mentioned is there. It's John Guan.

CHAPTER 30

Florida

Dear Jessica,

I know it is not the usual month since I last wrote. But I have been stirred up by some terrible news. It is not news that needs trouble you but it is why I am sending one last letter. A letter I expect you will never see. For what all my returned letters have made clear is that you have not gone back to the post office to where I mailed them. And why would that be? After many sleepless nights I have figured it out. Including why you dont and cant write to me anymore. It is because you have enemies and they are looking for you. What I say here then is not to you but to them. So if you ever read this Jessica I hope you understand. I had to do something to help you.

To Whom It May Concern. To YOU Who Are Hunting My Daughter and Reading Her Letters in Secret,

I know you are out there and I know what you are doing. As much as you are watching me I am watching you. Dont forget we still have newspapers and TV in prison so I know what you want. You want to keep your robot planes flying. You want to keep pressing those buttons to make your problems disappear. You want your wars to go on until all your enemies are dead or in Guantanamo. You will let nothing get in your way. And that includes my daughter. But you can stop looking for her because here is what I have done.

I have written up everything about her drone missions that I remember from those letters she sent me and which you confiscated too late. I have written about how she thought she was blowing up Yarisi and not just his wives. About how she was ordered to pull the trigger even though she knew something was off.

By now my lawyer has given these facts to the Miami Herald. Plus I have added a few details of my own. Like how you might have got Yarisi by now if you had listened to Jessica. Like how you go after honorably discharged soldiers like her to make sure they keep quiet.

What this means is that your secrets are out and my daughter can do you no more harm than I have already done you. So leave her be. Damn you. Leave her be.

A True American,
Donald Alan Aldridge

CHAPTER 31

California

Miss Shelly wanted to be outdoors for her birthday, but the wind has shifted and it's blowing now from the drought-brown foothills. Though the fires are not close enough to endanger the six gathered on the hospice lawn, a haze cuts short their celebration. The last time these six were gathered was a sadder occasion—Newt's funeral.

There are Peter and Pete, two men with shaved heads who consistently wear leather—though now more from nostalgia than conviction. Their arms, like Jessica's, are mapped with Shelly's visions. Peter, whom Jessica differentiates from Pete by his closely trimmed mutton chops and frailty, is leaning on Miss Shelly's wheelchair. Meanwhile Kane, Newt's brother, kneels to adjust the chair's dragging brake.

"That'll do 'er," Kane says proudly, his long tangled hair pushed behind his ears. Like Newt, Kane has heavily lidded eyes and a sleepy look that matches his easygoing manner.

"Okay then. Let's get out of the smoke," says Wanda, Kane's wife, the more assertive of the pair. Wanda favors tiered peasant skirts, dyes her hair midnight black and adorns her wrists with amethyst healing bracelets. She takes Kane's arm as if to subdue his inclination to tinker with any ailing mechanism at hand.

But before they move off Miss Shelly tries to speak and Jessica leans in, nodding after she comprehends Shelly's whisper.

"Never thought I'd live to see another goddamn fire season," Jessica repeats verbatim to the group.

There is silence until Kane blurts brightly, "Fires are early this year so you haven't made it yet." Rethinking his words, Kane's face reddens.

By the time the six cross the picnic area to the residence—a distance the width of a football field—Miss Shelly is asleep, or at least she has closed her eyes. Peter, hanging on to the wheelchair while Kane pushes it, seems equally exhausted.

"That was a dumb thing you said back there," Peter tells Kane weakly. "Don't you understand that she is *trying* to die."

"Come on now, Peter," says Pete.

Kane, reprimanded, stares down at his boots.

"Time to get you home, Mr. Grouch," Pete tells his partner. Then he turns to Jessica. "You'll have dinner with us next Saturday? Maybe you'll bake us one of your special desserts."

"I'd like that." Jessica kisses Pete on the cheek and offers him the weed brownies that she had made for today's aborted celebration. "Enjoy," she says.

Jessica and Wanda roll Shelly to her room and help her into her bed. They settle her and kiss her goodbye, but Shelly is too soundly resting to notice. After a few minutes of communion the two women tiptoe from the room. In the hall Jessica sees Reggie, a nurse's aide with a teardrop tattoo and a gentle touch. He works an all-night shift because of his parole curfew, which starts at sundown. He may as well, he has joked, spend the dark hours making money instead of trouble. Reggie practically lives at the hospice.

"Call me, please, right away . . . *if* . . ." Jessica says to him.

"If there's any change, I will, Miss Jessie. And I'll check on her extra tonight," Reggie says and squeezes her shoulder.

Out in the parking lot, Jessica and Wanda discover Kane tinkering again. This time he's working under the hood of Jessica's ride.

"Just checking the carb," he tells Wanda and wipes his hands on his jeans. "You heard it backfiring coming up the hill. You don't want Jessie to end up walking."

But Wanda's squint is directed beyond Kane. Out in the street two men wearing dark suits and sunglasses are getting into a black SUV.

"Kane," Wanda says, her voice inflected with concern. "Those guys were parked out there when we drove in. Now they're getting ready to leave when we do?"

Kane turns to study the men. "Feds if anybody. But I doubt they're after me for six plants."

"You haven't been sharing again?"

"No, babe. I learned my lesson good the last time."

While Wanda shades her eyes to stare at the intruders, Kane lowers the pickup's hood. Jessica sees his shoulders slump. Kane wipes his face with the side of his hand. His eyes glisten with held back tears.

"Hey, Kane?" she says softly, touching his arm.

He turns to Jessica. "Just memories," he says. "Newt's goddamn cancer saved me from doing time in Chino."

This is not a story that Jessica knows.

"A few years back," Kane goes on, "you could semi-legally grow here. But then the county started cracking down on private use and I had a few too many plants. Newt wanted to help so my lawyer sent him to a doctor. We'd be able to give the judge a medical excuse that some of those extra plants were for my brother's bad back. And that's when they found Newt's tumor. Judge gave me . . . what did he call it, Wand? It's like the Golden Gate Bridge."

"A suspended sentence," Wanda says.

Jessica absorbs the story while watching the SUV. Moisture drips from its tailpipe. The occupants are shadows behind tinted windows.

"So what do they want?" Wanda asks.

Jessica can't avoid a suspicion, but she keeps it to herself. Instead she says, "Hey, you guys mind coming back to the house? Keep me company for a while?"

AT NEWT AND Shelly's, Jessica and Wanda dig up the makings for a late lunch. When Jessica brings the platter of tuna sandwiches into the dining room Kane is studying the photographs on the side table. Wanda follows behind Jessica with plates and paper napkins.

"Wand, remember this. Shell's fortieth. That was a trip."

"You mean *you* were tripping." Wanda turns to Jessica and shakes her head. "A garbage truck nearly compacted him after he fell asleep in a Dumpster."

"I was trashed and nearly got trashed. Good times," says Kane.

"If you say," says Wanda. "Come and eat."

Kane hugs Wanda from behind and kisses her ear as she sets the table. "Hey!" Wanda says.

Kane winks at Jessica and then sits and fills his plate with sandwich quarters.

"They're not going to run off," says Wanda.

"I'm starving."

"You always are."

Kane's eyes smile at Jessica as she sits. "I used to see that as criticism. Now I know it's *pure* love."

"Don't be sentimental," Wanda says, and then, "Baby, go wash your hands."

Jessica sees that the white bread quarters Kane has piled on his plate are fingerprinted with grease from Newt's truck.

"A little roughage for the digestion," Kane counters but goes to the kitchen anyway. From the dining room Jessica hears the sink tap open and Kane humming. Skittles passes under the table and brushes her leg before settling on a flank. "Here, girl," Jessica says and drops a bit of tuna that Skittles noses but refuses.

It's strange for her to entertain guests at Newt and Shelly's without Shelly. She feels like an interloper. She feels as though she is somehow hastening Shelly's death. And in her awareness of that approaching event, things grow vivid. The glint of her water glass. The wood grain of the table top. Her pink thumbnail gnawed to the root. She tries a bite from a sandwich quarter, but her stomach recoils and she napkins the mush. Tomorrow, and each day that follows, will bring her less of anything to do that pertains to her friend's life—or death. Last week Jessica had helped Shelly finalize her funeral arrangements. When Newt died the emptiness hadn't gripped her so badly because he was still alive in Shelly. But now, all at once, both of her friends seem gone.

"Baby," Wanda calls, but not to Jessica. When the splash of running water stops, Kane's sobbing comes through.

THE THREE SAY their goodnights outside the hurricane fence. Kane is speaking to Jessica over the roof of his old El Camino.

"Bring that truck in next week. I'll rebuild the carb before you fry a piston."

"Thanks."

As he unlocks his driver's door, Wanda crushes Jessica against the chunky layers of her necklace.

"What you've done for Newt and Shelly is stellar," she says. "I want you to know that we're okay about your getting the house." Wanda pauses to study the low cinderblock structure. "After all, it's not like Shelly's giving away the Taj Mahal here."

That's true. Newt and Shelly's, for that's how Jessica will always think of it, is a single-story one bedroom with one bath and an enclosed back porch. The roof leaks. The neighbors are scary. And jets take off nearby. But that Wanda even mentions the gift tells Jessica that the situation, for her if not for Kane, is complicated.

"I haven't thought much about it yet," Jessica says.

"Well, if you don't turn in Shelly's paperwork, the place will be going to Kane. I just wanted you to know that. So it's all up to you."

There's implication in Wanda's words and Jessica is about to ease her concern, tell her that she won't be claiming Kane's inheritance. But then Wanda's gaze shifts. To something beyond Jessica's face.

"There's that damn car again," Wanda says.

Jessica turns to see the black SUV from the nursing home. Or perhaps an identical vehicle is coincidentally sitting at the far end of the block. In this light its tinted windows don't reveal if anyone is inside. Jessica trots back toward the house.

"Hey, Kane," she calls as she jogs. "Why don't you take Newt's truck right now and I'll pick it up tomorrow?" Jessica returns with the keys.

"Whoa, I didn't mean to scare you about those pistons," he says. "You can still drive a few miles before—"

"It'll be the first thing he works on tomorrow," Wanda says.

"Whoa, whoa," Kane says. "I've got an engine to put together in the a.m."

Wanda takes the keys from Jessica and tosses them to her husband. "But you'll get on Jessie's truck first. And make sure it's ready for a long trip."

Kane, clueless, cocks his head like a curious dog—and Jessica is curious too as to how Wanda has read her mind. "Sure, babe," Kane says and tromps over to Newt's pickup. Meanwhile, Jessica opens the gate so he can back it from the yard. When Kane's got the pickup in the street he pulls up beside the El Camino and Wanda.

"I'll meet you at home," Wanda tells him.

Kane, trustful of his wife's mysterious ways, shrugs. "Later," he says and idles up the street. He passes the SUV, but the parked vehicle stays put.

"Well, that answers that," Wanda says. "They're not after Kane, though he must have two dozen plants in his grow house."

"I thought he learned his lesson?" Jessica says.

"He likes me to think so, so I won't worry. Now I just have to worry about you. Shelly told me of your Air Force troubles."

"How much do you know?" Jessica asks humbly, like an abashed impostor.

"Just what you let on to her and Newt."

This wasn't much. Jessica had only told her friends that she'd been discharged because some classified information had gotten out and that, after her trek in the desert, she'd likely been reassessed as a security risk. "I just don't want to be locked away in some psych ward," she says.

"Shelly said you'd gone underground." Wanda looks at the SUV and then back at Jessica. "What do we do now that they've found you?"

"We?" Jessica smiles at this token of friendship.

"Before he died Newt made us promise to look out for you. So how can we help? I mean other than by getting the truck ready."

Guilt stabs Jessica. "Can you tell Shelly I had to go? Take care of things at the hospice?"

"Of course." Then Wanda takes Jessica at arm's length and squeezes her biceps, making her wince. "Look, Shelly will understand if you leave. She'll just want to know that you're okay wherever you end up."

"I'll keep in touch."

"If you just disappear, it'll hurt her."

"I wouldn't do that."

"What I mean is, *you* have become the daughter she never had."

SKITTLES' BARKING CALLS Jessica from the uneaten tuna sandwiches
that she's mummified in plastic wrap and put in the can outside the
kitchen door. She's trying to keep the uneaten food from stinking up the
trash after she's gone. Now, coming around from the side of the house,
she sees Skittles doing a frantic back-and-forth behind the front yard's
chain-link fence.

They have come already. But they have not yet noticed Jessica, behind
the overgrown bridal broom at the corner of the house. Men like these,
however, are persistent types. Ignoring them, Jessica knows, will not
make them disappear for more than an hour or two.

"Skittles!" she calls, though she doesn't really want the dog to stop her
guard dog act.

The men's heads shift. The four lenses of their sunglasses reflect Jessica
in quadruplicate as she approaches. The men's expressions do not change.
They appear neither happy nor angry, neither relieved nor annoyed to
see Jessica. They fix on her as if she is merely an expected object that has
come into their line of sight.

"Miss Aldridge," the shorter of the men says. He is not asking if she
is Miss Aldridge but stating that she is. Still, the man seems not to be an
arrogantly confident type. Jessica can see that he only wishes to believe
that this person standing before him is Jessica Aldridge, the same Jessica
Aldridge that she was a year ago—before she trekked into the desert,
recuperated in a VA hospital, and then vanished. Jessica, playing Jessie,
crosses her arms to show her tattoos. The photos this man must have of
her are no doubt from when she wore an Air Force uniform, displayed
no ink and weighed thirty pounds more. "You *are* Jessica Aldridge? For-
merly Technical Sergeant Aldridge of the United States Air Force?" the
man asks.

"And you are?" Jessica asks. She is holding Skittles by the collar to keep
the dog between herself and the fence, whose perimeter the men have not
yet violated. The other man, the taller of the two, has bent his legs slightly
as if he is preparing to vault into the yard.

Skittles begins to growl quietly. Quickly, its vibration intensifies into
that ominous type of growl that announces the devolution of a domesti-
cated creature into a beast.

The shorter man's face breaks into a grin as false as the sentiment it tries to express, which is that all is well between Jessica and him. "Federal Bureau of Investigation, miss." The man opens his wallet and tries to show her a badge. But Jessica doesn't shift her eyes from her reflection in his sunglasses. And then the man takes the lenses off. His eyes are brown and, even asquint, surprisingly warm—dangerously warm enough to make Jessica want to trust him. "I'm Agent Daugherty and this is Agent Pyle," the man says. From the corner of her eye Jessica sees the taller man touch a hand to his hip just inside his coat.

At the gesture Skittles bursts out barking and Jessica tugs hard at the dog's collar until Skittles' paws are clawing the air. She lets Skittles pull and froth until the verbal man signals his partner to back off. Then Jessica makes an offer. "I can get a message to Jessica," she says.

Daugherty's eyes flicker. "That would be helpful. And you are?"

"A friend," Jessica says. "A close one."

Daugherty nods. "Then you wouldn't mind chaining up your dog and inviting us in for a friendly talk. Miss, excuse me, I didn't get your name."

"I said I could take your message to Jessica."

Daugherty is not flustered. He points his soft chin at the house. "Is Miss Aldridge inside?" When Jessica doesn't answer he takes out a business card that he pinches into a fence link. The card, with its insignias, resembles a small stiff flag. "Tell Miss Aldridge that her old friends in the Air Force are worried about her. Tell her there are people at the VA waiting to help. Tell her that it would be best for everyone if she came in on her own for an evaluation. All she needs to do is to check in and get checked out. Simple." Daugherty's smile is that of a used-car salesman.

TONIGHT JESSICA DRAWS the curtains early and, fully dressed, settles atop the couch—this after packing a backpack and dragging Skittles' pallet beside her. Skittles' regular sleeping spot is beneath Newt's dining room chair and so this night is proving restive for both of them. Every few minutes Jessica checks the flickering numerals of a clock to see if morning's come yet.

At midnight she gives in to her insomnia. Peering from a curtain, she sees nothing outside but the night's usual shadows. Yet she doesn't believe the agents have given up. They might be staked out up the street. She goes to the front door, then jerks her fingers back from the knob. Maybe her watchers are even nearer, right outside, just behind the flowering bridal broom.

"Let's get some rest," Jessica's voice tells her fuzzy thoughts.

But for the next hours, her eyes do not stay closed. She watches the slow red counting of the clock face. At zero four hundred, she pulls herself to attention.

"Skittles," she whispers and hears the jingle of the dog's collar, feels the bristle of fur under her reaching hand. With the other she takes the backpack and then they are moving through the dark back porch to its door. Skittles gambols into the yard, stops, looks back. As there's nothing out there that's made her bark, Jessica slips out into the starlight. "Come on, girl," she whispers, and when Skittles comes she takes the dog's collar and they skulk past Newt's grow shack. Then Jessica is struggling to lift the shepherd's sixty pounds over the rear fence. The dog tumbles over upside down but intelligently gives no yelp. With a heave Jessica joins her and they stalk low through the weeds.

It is a hike to the warehouse, down in Redlands, out of which Kane runs his mechanic's shop. Dawn is stretching their shadows before they arrive and Jessica finds a spigot to water Skittles. Then she bathes her face and neck and sips water from her cupped palm. Sitting on the tarmac with her back against Kane's garage door, she suddenly cannot keep her eyelids apart. Sleep, or something close, brings her visions of being able to throw herself high in the air, though with ever diminishing leaps that finally leave her earthbound. Her dreaming shifts to a dream that she knows is a dream—she is on the road with Newt, her ears filled with the familiar tick of his truck's valve train. Where Newt is taking her she does not care. She is just simply glad to see him alive again, even in a dream that she knows is a dream.

Then the dream crumbles. Groggy in the afterglow of Newt's memory, Jessica squints at a fan blade spinning through a truck grill. It's Newt's pickup. And through its windshield Kane stares down at her.

"Morning, Kane," Jessica says cheerily. Brushing the dust off her backside, she goes around to the driver's door and opens it. Inside, Kane is collecting items from the passenger's seat.

"Just picked up your carb kit, Jess," he says. "Gonna take an hour or so to install. Wanda told me you're leaving." Arms loaded, Kane eases out of the vehicle.

Jessica snaps her fingers at Skittles and like a sterling recruit the dog squirts past Kane and leaps into the cab. Her blue eyes gaze at Jessica with anticipation.

"Sorry. Gotta hit the road," she tells Kane casually. The less he knows the better. Jessica reaches for the coffee container he's holding. "Smells good," she says. "Fresh?"

Kane releases the cup and steps sideways so Jessica can slide into the truck. "Where you headed?"

"It's a distance," she says. "Call you when I get there."

Kane shuts her door. "Drive easy," he says.

As she engages reverse, the popping engine warns her as well. But she has to go. Already the men in black, Daugherty and Pyle, are knocking at Newt and Shelly's front door. Of course Jessica is only imagining this—seeing the men in her mind's eye as if she is aiming a drone camera at them. Yet she knows they will be *here* soon, for this is how they will operate, not like kidnappers under the cover of night but as bureaucrats in the full light of day. They will gather her up for a psych, which she is pre-doomed to fail. Then, officially, her government will own her again, own her because she is the ex-airman who knows too much—knows about the flaws in their drones' ballistic sighting that can cause collateral damage, knows about the cover-ups of mistakenly targeted schoolyards and hospitals and wedding parties, knows about CIA-directed assassinations in neutral countries, knows all the details of the al-Yarisi miss. She just knows too many damn things. She's a risk to the security of the security state, to the state of things as they are, to the status quo of war.

And so her country will take care of her as efficiently as it did the catatonic, nickel-slot-playing airman at Pancho's. But as Jessica is a civilian now, she cannot simply be deported to some remote Kyrgyzstan airbase. Rather, she will be deposited "for her own safety" in some quiet, walled place for rest and medication. She will be allowed to play checkers with the other inmates until she is as dazed and defeated as any lost soul. All this will happen as surely as the next sunset—unless she goes and goes and keeps going.

She grinds the gearshift into first and offers Kane an apologetic glance. He raises his hand in farewell, and then his Jessie is gone.

CHAPTER 32

New York City

To: zoeleston2@nyu.edu
From: flytiger3.1416@gmail.com
Subject: An invitation

Hey, Zoe,

I promised myself that if you didn't answer my last email I would respect your silence. And for four days I have. Tonight there's a send-off dinner for Alex at Red Cat, 8 p.m., so I'm trying you again.

Where is Alex going all of a sudden? The Black Sea. To paint a mural. It's for Sergei, the guy who wants to hire me. Alex, being anti-self-celebrity, says he's happy to skip town while his show is up at Medusa. The trip, like my job offer, is Juliette's doing. With Alex away she can be sure he won't sabotage his new reputation, which is all you need to know about Juliette. Well, you saw her at the opening—fawning over a Hollywood actor while ignoring us two, the nobodies. Or maybe I'm just jealous. Ethaniago, that's me.

But Juliette is good at what she does, which is to make opportunities. So about my trip to Sagaponack. It's a nice village. I could live there. The base of operations is a short walk to the beach. In theory the job looks great. But I don't know.

See you tonight at Red Cat. I hope.
E

To: zoeleston2@nyu.edu
From: flytiger3.1416@gmail.com
Subject: Red Cat update

The dinner has been pushed back to 8:30. See you there. No problem though if you can't make it.

To: zoeleston2@nyu.edu
From: flytiger3.1416@gmail.com
Subject: We're here

In case you're out there looking for us, we're dining in the private room. Just
tell the hostess you're with the Giroux party. And don't worry about arriving
late—the festivities should be going on here for quite a while. I'd be texting
you this if your old number worked. See you soon.

To: zoeleston2@nyu.edu
From: flytiger3.1416@gmail.com
Subject: Fuckin RSVP please

Zo,

So where you? farewell party over. Everybod gone but me. Wish you'd been
here. Had a merry time after splling a Campari down Juliette's blouse. Told
Alex to fuckoff after three scotches at the bar. I'm up to numero six and
bartender says go home. Fine. Need a clear head tmorrow to drive Alex to JFK.
Juliette, strangle her, booked him on a Aeroflot to Kiev. Since dying always a
good career move for n artist and with Aeroflots crashing one a week laetly,
I raised a toast to Julie's manager skills. That's when I got bar exiled. No wait.
It was after I called Sergei an *oil*agarch. Thought that was good since he's
a petrochemical squillionaire. Hung around here hoping you would show
eventulaly so I could test it on you. Least you coulda told me yu wern't come.
What? NYU sundenly cut off your studnet email? Or u fall out a widow or
somethig?

Love,
Enth
your X
remember me??

To: zoeleston2@nyu.edu
From: flytiger3.1416@gmail.com
Subject: Last night's email

Zoe,

I apologize for being a jerk. Obviously I need a Breathalyzer app that stops me from drunkmailing. Not that I get wasted often. If it's any consolation my head feels the size of a pumpkin. What's funnier though is that after I emailed you Sergei joined me at the bar to tell me I was all right. My new job is on.

Anyway, right now I'm pulled over on a JFK access road. I just dropped off Alex and am watching his plane take off. I don't know why I'm doing this. What is this fear? Have I gone delusional? Tell me. Tell me anything because I'm worried as much about you as I am about Alex.

Zoe, if we ever meant anything to each other stop torturing me with your silence. I know you have your own problems and don't need mine on top. But you know how I fixate on things. So just let me know you're okay. With Alex gone, I've got nothing else to do but go over and over the reasons for your silence. If only I could shove my obsessions in a sack and drown them and be out of my misery. But I can't. Damn it, Zoe, help me out a little here. Answer me.

E

To: flytiger3.1416@gmail.com
From: zoeleston2@nyu.edu
Subject: Tonight

8 p.m. 169 E. Broadway.

To: zoeleston2@nyu.edu
From: flytiger3.1416@gmail.com
Subject: RE: Tonight

I'll be there.

PART FOUR

PURSUIT

September 2013

CHAPTER 33

New York City

After rereading Flytiger's emails, Sarah Chen puts away the victim's cell phone so she doesn't twist an ankle clomping along East Broadway on her three-inch pumps. And there's Eddie now, outside the 169 Bar where she'd set up the meet. Ridiculously, Banco opens the door for her.

"Nice shoes. Louboutins?" he says and grins like they're on a date.

"Zappos," Chen answers.

Tall and slim, Eddie Banco is a handsome young guy pretending to be a metrosexual. But he's gay and fooling no one at work. As Sarah passes through the door she gives him a soft punch and the side of her fist bounces off Eddie's lean trampoline gut.

"The thanks I get," he says, falling back on his habit of talking rougher than he looks. They both overcompensate.

At a two-top near the bar Chen orders a cranberry seltzer. Banco asks the waitress for a pickle martini, which is advertised colorfully on a chalkboard. After she leaves he says to Chen's stare, "What? I'm off-duty doing you a favor here."

"We're early, Banco. Just don't get wrecked on me."

"Chen the Merciless," he says—her office nickname. Despite its racism it's somewhat empowering so she leverages it.

"Detective Chen to you," Chen replies, instantly regretting pulling rank on Eddie. "Or just Chen. Or just Merciless. Or how about *Sarah*. Take your pick."

At the precinct house Sarah and Eddie—because they don't fit the stocky, balding mold of detective and plainclothes officer—have to grin through every challenge to stay in the club. The jokes, the sexism, the nonironic racism. But complain once, Sarah knows, and you'll never have backup when you need it.

After their drinks arrive, Eddie raises a toast, "To expense reports."

With the departmental budget cuts—which have thinned their ranks so that Sarah can't even keep a regular partner—she wasn't supposed to take the Leston investigation this far. "Wrap it up," the captain had said. But after the computer forensics lab cracked the victim's cell password— and this took days—some loose ends turned up.

The bar hasn't drawn a crowd yet—just a seeding of hipsters and grad students ignoring a few Wall Street types who are trolling for coeds.

"You think this guy'll show?" Eddie asks. "I wouldn't pick him from a lineup of anyone here."

"He's coming because he's desperate."

"So, if he's desperate, he's guilty then?"

"Maybe. I'll get it out of him."

"Is that why the clothes?"

Instead of her usual oxford walkers and pantsuit, Sarah is wearing those painful pumps, a skirt and eye makeup. It's almost like the days when she baited the johns exiting the Cross-Bronx Expressway in their minivans. But Eddie's looking at her funny. "Do I still read as a cop or something?" Sarah asks.

Eddie leans toward her and straightens her collar, rests his fingertips on her shoulder. "You look fine," he says.

A man enters through the street door. Sarah checks her watch. It's seven forty.

Eddie's eyes follow Sarah's. "Is that him?" he asks.

The man is lanky and would stand six-two or more if he didn't stoop. His clothes are a mismatch of cheap and threadbare expensive—there's the designer cardigan shiny at the elbows, the five-hundred-dollar shoes that need resoling. In contrast, the baggy jeans are bargain bin—the man's ass sits in them as flat as the bottom of an iron. The pale back of his shaved neck betrays a twenty-dollar haircut. The man must be thirty to thirty-five, Sarah decides—though his eyes are those of a lost eight-year-old searching for his mom in a department store. He's not her killer. He's a sheep.

. . .

IT'S EIGHT THIRTY and Sarah has just abandoned her fourth former suspect at the bar—a man wearing a herringbone fedora and a shadow beard who as she walked away recommended she "chill."

"It's fine," Sarah tells Eddie, fanning her diminishing hopes. "The captain will let me trace Flytiger's email address now that I have evidence of guilt."

"Just because he didn't show tonight doesn't mean he's guilty."

"Wrong." This is not a subject on which she's going to agree to let Eddie disagree. "I've got Flytiger on the run now. He played the email alibi card in a panic. I called his bluff and he folded. I've got him now, or soon will."

Eddie shakes his head. He's starting his third pickle martini. "Truth or dare me," he says.

"Truth," Sarah says.

"You're desperate for a real case here, Detective. This one's a sow's ear."

"Sow's ear? You turning into a farm boy, Banco?" Sarah waves at the waitress and aims her gun hand at Eddie's martini glass. "One of those," Sarah mouths so the server can read her lips over the backbeat of reggae. She gets a nod back.

"Look," Eddie says. "You have the girl's phone. Send Flytiger another email as Leston. Ask him why he's not here?"

Sarah takes Zoe Leston's phone out of her clutch and examines the dark screen. Then she shrugs at Eddie. "I sent the first email unauthorized. Another one will cinch a wiretap violation."

"Shit," Banco says.

"Yeah. I could end up like Rupert Murdoch."

"If you do, buy me a yacht."

"I'M FINISHED HERE," Sarah says. Two pickle martinis have done their job. The world of this red-tinted bar is glowing with a pleasant, womblike crimson. "Where's the crapper?" she asks Eddie.

He points his chin. "That way, Detective."

The bathroom locks with a hook latch and Sarah hikes her skirt and balances over the splashed toilet, then she wipes the seat dry. After all, it is her job to clean up after the citizens. Or maybe she does it out of respect for immigrants like her grandmother, who spent her first years in America on Madison Avenue, mopping out women's lavatories in a corporate tower. She washes her hands, wipes the lipstick from her teeth, and unlatches the door.

"'Scuse," she says shouldering into the man waiting outside. She'll never get used to unisex bathrooms.

"Sorry," he says.

Sarah recognizes him from earlier, the guy with the saggy shoulders and scuffed loafers. He looks miserable and as if he's gone one drink over his limit, like her.

Seen close up—with his make-do clothing, nostril hair, and faintly pocked complexion—he is in no sense a lady killer. He's lost out completely on the trifecta of looks, attitude, and money, with his once nice shoes suggesting a former job that paid well. Sarah's nonjudgmental term for such types is *survivor*, and she fully dismisses him as a person of interest. He *can't* be Flytiger, her only suspect. For a second she considers bringing him in for questioning but then realizes Eddie is right: she *is* desperate. Desperate to make the Leston case a *murder* case.

"Hey," she says to the man as he steps around her. Half in the toilet, the man turns about and the closing door knocks into him. The man is drunker than Sarah thought—unstably drunk. This will make her work easier. "Looks like someone stood you up tonight. Maybe I know her. Maybe she sent me to tell you she couldn't make it."

Sarah's *survivor* looks down at her and his eyes almost focus. His face, soaked with little-lost-boy desperation, starts to brighten. "She sent you?" he asks. "Zoe?"

Sarah deflates: Flytiger.

"MR. WINTER. OVER here please," Sarah says, directing him to the chair beside her desk in the bullpen—which is empty but for two other detectives distantly pecking out reports. "I'll need your statement before I can answer your questions." So far, Sarah has told him nothing about Zoe Leston.

Back at the tavern, hoping the night air would clear her head, she had shown Winter her badge and asked him to take a walk. He'd agreed and all along the way, as if to bolster his alibi, drunkenly pestered her for information about the victim—"Where's Zoe? She in the hospital? Was she assaulted?" And at the precinct house, Winter began to chew a cuticle. Now, seated in Sarah's guest chair/witness chair/perp chair, Winter is as jumpy as a squirrel in an alley. He straightens his pants, crosses and uncrosses his legs, shifts onto one haunch and then the other as though the metal seat is a hot plate. In other words, he's overplaying the upset friend role and acting more and more as though he's guilty of something. Maybe Eddie is wrong, maybe the Leston case is a silk purse and she's not been torturing a friend of the victim by keeping the truth from him. This guy's the perp.

"Please, can't you just tell me if Zoe is all right?" Winter asks.

Sarah's conviction wavers.

She ignores the question and brings up the standard witness form on her computer, filling in the name and address fields from Winter's driver's license. Then she proceeds with her interrogation.

"The last time you saw Zoe Leston was six nights ago Thursday, correct?" she asks, going over what he'd told her back at the tavern.

"Isn't that what I said?" Winter snaps.

Sarah gives him a look and moves on. "Where did you last see Ms. Leston?"

Winter can barely contain his impatience. "At a mutual friend's opening. Medusa Gallery. Chelsea. Afterward we went to a diner. Moonstruck. Like I said, I paid with a credit card if you want to check. Then I walked Zoe to the Twenty-Third Street subway and went home. Except for her email this morning, I haven't heard from her since. So what's going on? Is she in trouble?"

"You didn't get on the subway with her that night?"

"No. Why would I?"

"Because you live downtown. In fact, you live almost exactly across town from where Ms. Leston was staying on Henry Street."

Winter appears bewildered. Then his eyes focus. "Oh, sorry. The license is wrong. I'm not on River Terrace anymore. I'm up at 75 Lexington now, across from the old armory."

"Uh-huh," Sarah says and clicks her cursor back into the address box of the witness screen. "I know the neighborhood," she adds to jab at his pride. When interrogating solo you're forced to play both good cop and bad cop. "You must be in the Popeye's building. I can smell the fried chicken on your clothes. You should file a complaint about their ventilator. Apartment number?" she asks.

"3B," Winter says, beaten down. And then his eyes narrow. "Wait a minute, you don't think I had something to do with . . ." Winter's question trails off.

"To do with what?"

"I don't know," he snaps. "You won't tell me. All I know, and it's all from you, is that Zoe is in some kind of trouble. She's missing, isn't she? I mean, how did you even know we were meeting tonight?"

Not wishing to mention tapping into the victim's email, Sarah refocuses her suspect. "Was Ms. Leston distraught when you left her at the subway?"

"Distraught? No. She recently quit her job in DC. I think she broke up with someone there. But I don't think she was unstable, if that's what you mean. She wasn't crying. She might have been upset, but she wasn't distraught."

Winter's fine distinctions bode badly for her theory that he might know more than he's saying. He is trying too hard not to imagine the worst.

"You say *she* broke up with someone?" Sarah asks. "Did you ever meet the person she was seeing?"

"No. Did he do something to her?"

Sarah is earning her Chen the Merciless nickname. But rule one: keep your witness in the dark for as long as possible. Memory is evidence best left uncontaminated.

"Have you ever known Ms. Leston to do drugs?"

"Drugs?" echoes Winter. "You mean medication?"

"I mean, say, recreational."

"No. So she's under arrest? Look, if it's a matter of bail—"

"And what about yourself? Are you on any medication?"

"What? I don't understand."

"If Ms. Leston was upset, you might have offered her some of your meds last Thursday. You know, to help her through."

Winter looks hard at her. "Jesus! What is this?" Coming to his feet he knocks over his chair and the crash echoes through the big room. *This* is no act.

"Yo! Everything good down there?" calls Lieutenant Ellison, the larger of the two officers typing reports tonight.

"We're good," Sarah tells him.

She returns to her witness, her *ex*-suspect. He is an open wound. "Please sit down, Mr. Winter," Sarah says gently. "May I get you a cup of coffee?"

"DROWNED?" WINTER SAYS, absorbing the information.

"The autopsy report isn't finalized, but that is likely the primary cause. I'm sorry." Sarah touches Winter's arm though she resists any deep sympathy. In her job she can't afford such emotions. The man is slouching now more than ever, crumpling over to stare between his shoes. "Let me refer you to a grief counselor." Sarah digs through her desk for a business card and places it in front of Winter. "Goodnight, sir. Thank you for your time."

Over the past hour Sarah has extracted all she is going to get out of her witness—which was basically next to nothing—so she is done with him. What she knows about Zoe Leston she knows mostly from her cell phone and a manila folder of family documents and news clippings found near the body. She knows that Zoe was a graduate of NYU and that her family history is as tortured as the Kennedy's. Zoe's grandparents became her adopted parents, both are deceased in a murder/suicide/euthanasia event. Her mother killed in an auto wreck more than two decades ago. Sarah could find no living next of kin—except for a maternal aunt with dementia in an East Setauket nursing home—until she contacted one Detective Ray Murak, mentioned in a clipping. Retired and now a volunteer who answers phones for the Monroe Police, Murak gave her the name of the victim's biological father, Donald Alan Aldridge, whom Sarah located in a South

Florida prison. Three days ago, Sarah had arranged a phone interview with the inmate, who had not seen his daughter since she was an infant.

All this research was what Eddie likes to call her *undue* diligence. For example, the interview with Aldridge was an investigative dead end that turned out doubly useless since there was no legal or practical way for an imprisoned father to claim his daughter's body.

The best option remaining is that Zoe Leston's ex-fiancé will bury her. Dr. Porter Coombs had sent Leston more than a few emails over the past weeks, but having been in Brussels on the night Leston died, he's no suspect; Sarah had finally reached him at a conference in San Francisco. Coombs will be arriving on a morning red-eye to officially identify the body.

Sarah Chen would ask Winter to do the ID if he weren't so high maintenance. Right now, ignoring her unsubtle goodnight, Winter remains firmly seated before her.

"But," Winter says, letting the word hang. *"How* could she have drowned in a bathtub?"

As Sarah knows from many years of this, Winter is attempting to refute the unlikely aspects of the death in order to deny the death. It would be more convincing if she just showed him the body. Yet even she is not that *merciless.*

"The toxicology report isn't in, but we found Ms. Leston's fingerprints on several pill bottles—pain meds that belonged to someone else."

"Oh," Winter says—with a bit of realization, Sarah notes, as if pill borrowing was in the victim's character. "She went to sleep."

"And sank down."

"Who . . . Who found her?"

"The next-door neighbor. Her tub overflowed."

"Don't you mean the downstairs neighbor?" Winter says, trying to catch Sarah out on a detail that will bring his friend back to life.

"The water leaked under the hallway door. This was an old railroad flat. It has a kitchen bathtub."

"Oh," Winter says. "This was in Zoe's new place?"

"Not hers. She was apartment-sitting for a friend—the friend with the back pills. She's out of the country. Had nothing to do with it."

Winter looks away from Sarah, though not at anything. If eyes were lasers, his stare would burn through the three city blocks of brick and concrete that separate them from where Leston died. "That tub shouldn't have overflowed," Winter says.

This is an intelligent observation. Sarah senses that Winter must be thinking that she's done a cursory investigation into the death. She represses her irritation and responds. "There was a rag stuffed in the overflow drain."

"Uh-huh. Is there anything else I should know?"

Sarah maintains her patience, barely. "Incense sticks and candles."

"Incense and candles?" Winter's eyes return to Sarah's. "You mean she did a . . . *ceremony*?"

"Or she just wanted to relax in a bath."

"Detective Chen, I'm asking you if Zoe committed suicide."

She was afraid Winter's reasoning would end here. The survivors of an untimely death always agonize over what might have prevented it, over their last minutes with the deceased and what understanding phrase or kind gesture might have changed things. Their guilt becomes an apology for their failure to stop their friend from dying. As Chen knows well, all of this second guessing is inevitable. None of it does any good.

And so it would behoove Winter not to torture himself with this possibility. In this the survivor's and the detective's interests are aligned; Sarah does not wish to consider Zoe Leston a suicide either. Frankly, if the death was not a murder, an accidental drowning makes for an easier report than an uncertain suicide. Either way the woman is deceased, and since she has no family there is less of a need to go after absolute answers. But Sarah has hesitated too long in answering Winter's question.

"So you can't tell me if she took her own life," Winters says, almost triumphant. "You don't really know if she did it on purpose?"

"She left no note," Sarah tells him.

Winter's gaze scolds her for not increasing his survivor's guilt. She knows what he wants—to feel not helpless, to feel as if, even though the situation is hopeless now, he *might* have been able to change his friend's destiny.

Then Winter's face loses its tension. His pupils dilate. "Before we said goodnight . . . Zoe mentioned reincarnation. I'd told her she needed to start over." Winter's eyes refocus. "I may have—"

"Mr. Winter," Sarah interrupts, "we can only accurately speculate from the *physical* evidence. Ms. Leston left no note and she drowned after taking a cocktail of drugs that are abused recreationally. Often we imagine that we have more influence over others than we do, but you were simply old friends who discussed random topics. Do not read too much into them. A grief counselor can explain this better." Sarah pushes the psychologist's business card toward Winter. "But there is one more thing I can tell you. There was a clean, folded bath towel by the tub."

"A towel?" Winter does not comprehend Sarah's point.

"Well, if Ms. Leston had planned to stay in the tub, *why* the fresh towel?"

For Sarah the towel was the most important detail. Her observation, however, leaves no impression on her witness. As he walks out, he leaves behind the psychologist's card. Clearly, Winter wants his guilt.

CHAPTER 34

Texas

Daugherty, behind mirrored lenses, brakes hard to follow the patrol car ahead to a stop on the shoulder.

Pyle, in the passenger's seat, perks up. "Sure been wondering where the ass end of nowhere began."

The agents step out of their rented Taurus and stand on a desert blacktop nine miles west of Cairo, Texas. The landscape is a scrubland rimmed by distant mountains, uninteresting except for a few pyramid-like hillocks in the middle distance. After a few seconds the hot breeze blasts the car's air-conditioning out of their suits. The county deputy who led them here is sauntering toward the agents. He removes his Stetson and dries the sweat on his brow with a shirtsleeve before pointing the hat at a pickup tilting on a rocky berm well off the road shoulder.

"There she is," he drawls.

Pyle grins nastily at the deputy. "Yep, thar she is, Sheriff," he says. Pyle's sunglasses reflect the deputy's into mirrored infinity.

"The FBI appreciates the assistance, Officer," Daugherty says neutrally, breaking up the stare-down.

"It's deputy," the deputy says to Pyle. Then he returns his hat to his head and looks at the desolate road, which travels to the horizon in both directions. "You all have fun out here," he says and goes back to his vehicle, U-turns up a swirl of dust that overtakes Daugherty and Pyle as they walk toward the truck.

"Maybe you should ease up on the caffeine?" Daugherty says. Pyle has been chugging Red Bulls since they got on a 6 a.m. at LAX.

"Maybe you should have let me take her at the house. We wouldn't be chasing her skanky ass across the country," Pyle says. They've both been up half the night, ever since word reached them about the abandoned pickup on Texas Route 90.

"We weren't sure that was her," Daugherty reminds him. "Besides, her dog would have chewed *your* ass."

"I would have handled the bitch," Pyle says.

"Not without stitches." Daugherty's seniority gives him the final word.

The pickup is unlocked and inside the cab Daugherty smells something sweet—burnt antifreeze. "She must have blown a head gasket," he says.

"Yeah, well she can blow me," Pyle says. He starts tweezing hair samples from the headrest. "It's her," he says holding a strand to the daylight, as if he's able to sight-read DNA.

"That could be dog hair," Daugherty says, noticing the mats of blonde fur on the passenger's-seat upholstery. "This is all we're going to get here. You done?"

"I am now," Pyle says, slipping an old Rand McNally from the driver's-door pocket. He shows Daugherty. The atlas is folded to page 121, Louisiana.

IN THE DUSTY heart of Cairo, Pyle, as he always does at roadside cafes, orders a chicken sandwich on toast without the chicken.

"Very funny, mister," the waitress says not blinking. She's about forty-five and with enough ultraviolet damage to make her face just this side of scary. "That would be toast in my universe."

"Sorry, ma'am," Daugherty says. "My partner's been out in the sun too long." He shows her his federal ID and a photo of Technical Sergeant Jessica Aldridge. "Face ring a bell? She's lost a little weight. Won't be in uniform. Travels with a dog."

The waitress places her hands backward on her hips. "What kind a dog?" she asks.

"The kind that huffs and puffs and will blow your fucking house down," Pyle says.

"Honey," the waitress says while placing the knuckles of one hand on the table and leaning toward Pyle's face, "that's what's known as a wolf."

"So you saw her," Pyle says, not asks.

"Didn't say."

"She was here first thing when you opened yesterday morning."

The waitress lifts a drawn eyebrow. "How would you know?"

"Go ahead," Daugherty says, not hiding his curiosity about Pyle's insight.

Pyle, kind of sadly, looks at his partner, the stolid hopeless investigator who, unless he collapses on the job, will be locked into field work until retirement. "It takes about twenty hours to drive here from California. We know Aldridge left the garage in Redlands in the morning. That means her truck broke down late at night. She wouldn't have walked an unlit desert highway. She would have waited until dawn." Pyle looks back at the waitress. "Right here is the first open shithole she would have reached."

Right, Daugherty thinks. He could have put all that together, given another few minutes and a distance calculator. But Pyle is the one who suggested they not stop at the other two restaurants they passed entering Cairo because neither served breakfast.

"She a deserter?" the waitress asks.

"She'll be the chicken in my chicken sandwich," says Pyle.

"Uh-huh. I get it. None of my damn business. So what're you boys eating for real? Or are we just going to chat?"

Pyle takes out his notepad and clicks a pen. This, Daugherty knows, is just for show because Pyle remembers everything. *"Rita,"* he says, stretching out the name. Though the woman wears no name tag, Pyle's leap isn't much of a mystery. The sign outside says RITA's and aside from her there's only a cook working the joint. Pyle, writing in his pad, points his chin at a lipstick-stained water glass on the table. "I don't think your dishwater's hot enough. And that ticking exhaust fan is probably dropping metal flakes onto your grill. There's a lot here an inspector might thumbs down, even in South Texas. Probably cost you ten grand to make it all right."

Rita keeps her defiant stance a few seconds more before she sighs and slides her knuckles off the table. "She came in yesterday. Not in uniform but carrying a knapsack. I gave her a bowl to water her dog and served her some eggs."

"Then what?"

"Asked about the post office." She nods to a clock behind the counter. "Closes in ten minutes. Up the street. Left at the Exxon."

Daugherty leaves a five-dollar tip for the water and follows Pyle out the door to the Taurus. "Was it necessary to crawl up her ass like that?" Daugherty says.

"That or I could have stuck my finger up yours and mine. I'm from Arkansas, but this is still my territory. These people hate feds in a way *you* don't want to imagine."

At the post office Daugherty and Pyle get no hassles from the local postmaster—being a government employee he's amenable to cooperation. They learn that after buying a postage-paid postcard, Aldridge had inquired about transportation out of town and that takes the agents next door to the Western Union, which serves as the bus depot. There Aldridge learned she couldn't buy a ticket for her dog on any bus line or even for the Amtrak that stops nearby in Alpine.

"She asked if there was a pet-friendly motel in town," the Western Union man says.

At the Thunderbird Inn, Aldridge with her dog had checked out seven hours before, at the same time as a couple with a Subaru Outback and a Labrador. But this is all the kid at the front desk is willing to reveal.

Pyle gestures the boy nearer and Daugherty can barely hear his partner's schoolmasterish warning. "Now, either we subpoena you as an uncooperative witness or you accidentally print a duplicate of Mr. and Mrs. Subaru's hotel bill and put it in the trash. Then go for a slow walk around the block. When you come back, we'll be gone and all will be forgiven."

The desk clerk begins stroking his fuzzy upper lip as if it's a pet mouse. Meanwhile Pyle and Daugherty exit to watch dust devils in the street. When the clerk walks by them, they go back to the unattended desk, which is monitored by a camera.

"Where'd he go?" Pyle asks loudly. After a little pretend waiting, he moves to the side of the desk and takes a wad of Kleenex from a box. "Fricking desert dust," he says and makes a show of blowing his nose and looking behind the desk for a place to dump the tissue. He tosses and misses the trash. But he's conscientious and cleans up the mess.

Out in the dust again, Pyle removes a crumpled sheet of paper from his jacket sleeve.

"HOW DID I get your cell number? Well, Mr. Clayton . . ."

Before being stonewalled Pyle had extracted from his call that Mr. T. Everett Clayton, recent guest at the Thunderbird Inn, was returning to San Antonio with his wife from the Marfa Lights Festival and a few days of hiking in Big Bend. Pyle relayed the information to Daugherty, still at the wheel, by rephrasing Clayton's statements as if they were especially fascinating. Then T. Everett drops his bombshell: he's a semi-retired attorney.

"Mr. Clayton, let me pass you on to my superior," Pyle says. He smirks while offering Daugherty his cell phone and Daugherty gives him the finger. Since they'd gotten Clayton's details from the Thunderbird via theft rather than warrant, Daugherty was leery about cold calling the man. But Pyle won the coin toss. Now they've hit the jackpot—a lawyer with too much time on his hands.

"Agent Daugherty here," he says to the phone.

"Ah, Agent Daugherty," says a self-satisfied, cross-examining voice. Daugherty pictures a fit man of seventy-one with flowing gray hair and a North Face jacket. "Why, exactly, is the FBI interested in my movements across South Texas."

Daugherty reverts to *Dragnet* mode. "Sir, this is not about you. We're interested in a Jessica Aldridge, though she may be using an alias. Mid-twenties. Heavily tattooed. Severely underweight. Traveling with a German shepherd. Sound familiar?"

"And what's she guilty of?" Clayton asks a little too quickly.

This stumps Daugherty because Jessica is not actually wanted for any crime. "You should know that among other things, she's a car thief." Technically this is true—the truck Aldridge abandoned is registered to one Brian Newton, deceased.

A silence over the phone gives Daugherty seconds to consider the invasion of privacy suit Clayton might file against the FBI . . . and the possibility of losing his pension. Then a barking breaks from the receiver and another dog starts up in syncopation.

"Sorry, Daugherty," Clayton says through the hubbub. "I'm going to have to call you back."

"Don't hang up," Daugherty shouts. "Sir!" There is dead air. After he redials and gets Clayton's voicemail he tosses Pyle's BlackBerry into his lap. "Keep trying till you get an answer." Fleeing dusk, Daugherty drives them out of Cairo.

Finally, after forty minutes, during which Pyle has been pressing his phone's redial key, Daugherty sees him cup the BlackBerry to speak through the road noise. With the speedometer hovering at 110, the Taurus is vibrating in Daugherty's clenched hands like the space shuttle during reentry. He can't hear a damn thing his partner is saying. "That Clayton?" Daugherty mouths.

Pyle uncups the phone. "His dumb bitch wife! I got through on the home number!"

Daugherty slows the car to eighty and angrily gestures for Pyle's Black-Berry, wondering how he'll explain his partner's crack to Mrs. Clayton.

"Don't sweat it. She's getting T. Everett," Pyle says as Daugherty puts the phone to his ear. "Plus it's on mute."

Fumbling with the device Daugherty nearly drives off the highway. He can hear Clayton helloing as he tries to unmute the call. "Fuck this fucker!"

"Pardon?" T. Everett says.

"Nothing, sir. Just talking to my partner. Agent Daugherty here."

"Ah, yes. About that dropped call. There aren't many cell towers out on 90."

Steadying the Taurus Daugherty cuts to the chase, "Regarding Jessica Aldridge."

"Oh, right. Jessica. Yes. We gave her a ride. Sweet girl. You said she stole a truck. But she says a friend bequeathed the vehicle to her. There seems to be a misunderstanding, probably on your part."

"Mr. Clayton, I didn't want to panic you when I called earlier, but this young woman, I'm afraid, has killed several people. In cold blood." Daugherty doesn't elaborate that this was when Aldridge flew drones. He's learning from Pyle how plastic facts can be.

"Jesus," Clayton whispers, his self-satisfaction dissolving.

Daugherty hears a woman's voice, Mrs. Clayton no doubt, "What's wrong, Teddy?"

"That girl," says Clayton. "She's wanted for multiple murders."

"Oh my God!" says Mrs. Clayton. "She knows our address."

Daugherty lets the couple's anxiety rise before refocusing them. "I'm assuming you dropped her off since we spoke."

"Not five minutes away."

The wife's voice becomes shrill. "I hear someone outside. We have to call 911—"

"Dammit, let go of my arm," Mr. Clayton says. "I'm helping them get her!"

So much for the Claytons' empathy. Jessica is no longer Jessica to them. She's a *she* and a *her*. She's no longer the unjustly accused car thief but a transient killer ready to serve them up with fava beans and Chianti. Something bangs, perhaps a door. Daugherty can no longer hear the wife's screeching.

"Agent Daugherty . . ."

"Yes, sir."

"My disconnect earlier. I didn't know the seriousness of this woman's offenses." Clearly T. Everett's lawyerly brain has taken over. He has grasped that his earlier silence could make him guilty of aiding a fugitive, of obstructing a federal officer on a capital case.

Daugherty gives him his out. "Like I said, I hadn't told you anything, sir."

"When you called she wanted me to drop her off right away, at Castroville. But I shut off my phone. She's here in San Antonio. The Motel 6 in Market Square. It's pet friendly. That's how she met us. Because of Skittles."

"Skittles?"

"Her shepherd. She was stuck in Cairo because none of the bus lines allowed dogs. She said there was no way she was going to leave Skittles behind. Of course we would give a ride to a person like that, an animal lover."

"Of course."

"I was a defense attorney once. I know liars when I hear them. But maybe I've gotten rusty. To me, this girl did not read at all like a criminal."

"Don't feel bad, Mr. Clayton. She's clever. She's been eluding us for a while."

"In hindsight I can see she's a drifter. How many people did she kill?"

"I can't go into the specifics. We'll take care of things from here."

"I understand, but . . . she's still out there. And I mean, is she like that Wuornos woman, that Florida highway killer?"

"Sir, I can almost guarantee that she won't bother you. Just keep your doors locked tonight. Also, Mr. Clayton, you do own a gun, don't you?"

SOON AFTER DAUGHERTY disconnects from T. Everett, Pyle crashes—probably his Red Bull overdose is on the wane. He's like a dead man, mouth open, flopped in the passenger's seat. Beside him, under a lulling half-moon, Daugherty is barely keeping the Taurus on the blacktop, even through flatland. And then he either long blinks or dozes and finds himself gliding over an even flatter blackness. They are crossing a lake on a low bridge and ahead the sky glows like a giant tunnel of light.

"Del Rio coming up, Pyle. Your shift."

The slower Daugherty goes the more conscious Pyle gets. When their car is crawling at the in-town speed limit, Pyle opens his mouth. "Burger King," he yawns at a sign and Daugherty pulls up. Pyle goes for coffee and Whoppers while Daugherty switches to the passenger's seat, warm with Pyle's imprint. Pyle returns carrying a fast-food sack in one hand and a coffee he's sipping in the other. Inside the car he shakes his head and grins at Daugherty. "'You do have a gun, don't you, Mr. Clayton?'" Pyle is fully awake now, recaffeinating.

"T. Everett earned a sleepless night," Daugherty says.

Pyle points his fist at Daugherty, who takes a moment to comprehend that his partner wants a fist bump. Daugherty bumps. It's a brave new world and one that Daugherty is less adapted to every day. But after Pyle puts the car in gear and they've passed the outskirts of Del Rio east—doing ninety in a thirty-five zone—Daugherty thinks about Jessica Aldridge. It's one thing to give headaches to people like T. Everett who deserve it, another to slander the person you're charged with bringing in. Aldridge is no murderer. Her file describes her as an ex-serviceperson with posttraumatic stress and a knowledge of military secrets. In other words, she qualifies as a low-level national security risk. Last November she had disappeared from a VA hospital in Loma Linda and Daugherty's job at the time was to return her there. But his former partner and he may as well have been sifting for a body vaporized by an H-bomb. Aldridge was that gone. Then, with the new year approaching and pressed by other duties, he finalized an interim report on the missing woman.

The rest of winter, spring, and half the summer passed before the higher-ups reprioritized the Aldridge case. The waiting worked, for like a psychic's trick, an electronics records search reconstituted her ghost out of the void. She hadn't started using ATMs or credit cards but had reactivated her military savings account. Unfortunately the information she gave the bank led him and Pyle, his new partner at winter's end, to a nonexistent address. A day later they traced her largest account debit to a bank draft written to a nursing home. The home's accounting department stonewalled them with claims of patient confidentiality. But on their way out Pyle took aside a nurse's aide with a prison teardrop tattoo. According to the ex-con, whom Pyle coerced by asking the name of his parole officer, only one young woman about Jessica Aldridge's age visited regularly—visited, in fact, almost every day. She came to see a dying woman whom the aide called Miss Shelly. At this point, an RN asked Daugherty and Pyle to return to the premises with a warrant.

He and Pyle set up a stake out in front of the facility and by midafternoon had followed the most likely suspect to a cinderblock one-story in a rough San Bernardino neighborhood. Then came the over-the-fence confrontation with the dog they now know as Skittles and the suspect.

To Daugherty, the skinny, tattooed girl looked at best to be a dissolute cousin to the uniformed Aldridge he knew from photos. And so he stopped Pyle from taking her down. Big mistake. Overnight Aldridge submerged again. But at least they'd taken her truck's plate numbers. Those have gotten the agents this far, so far.

Pyle has driven them beyond Del Rio's halo of light and now Daugherty is able to stare at the million stars piercing the southerly night over Mexico. There, over the border, is where Jessica Aldridge would be right now if she were really guilty of something.

"So what's her crime?" Daugherty asks himself, realizing too late that he's mumbled this aloud.

"You still awake?" Pyle says. Then, after two mile markers pass, Pyle responds to the question. "She probably emailed secrets to WikiLeaks."

Despite all the trouble she's caused them, Pyle's crack irritates Daugherty. "I doubt that. She got an honorable discharge."

"She's still a skank, boss. You going sentimental on me?"

"*Yeah*," Daugherty says, dissembling.

"So, shall we just let her go?"

"Sure. But let's catch her first. If she's too small, we'll throw her back." Pyle's badass attitude is infectious. And maybe anyway he doesn't trust the sympathy he's beginning to feel for their fugitive.

Pyle starts in again, talking over the tires' hum. "I'll give her that she conned a dumbass lawyer into giving her a ride. The bitch is clever."

In the windshield a distance sign appears. Daugherty calculates they'll reach San Antonio in forty minutes, if their engine doesn't blow or a tire burst. "More than clever. Smart enough, according to her file, to make drone pilot," he says.

"And that's why she's in for a world of hurt after we catch her," Pyle says.

"How do you figure?"

"First of all, the case file DC gave us is Swiss cheese redacted, so we know that whatever she's wanted for is big."

"You mean, over-our-security-level big?"

"I mean, congressional-hearing big."

Again, Daugherty finds himself defending Jessica. "If it was that serious, DC would have told us."

"Not if the CIA's behind it. Think about it. We know that Langley directs the Air Force's drone ops. And we know it can't run all the ops it wants because there's a pilot shortage. My guess is they're trying to develop a program to put more drones in the air. That's where ex–Technical Sergeant Aldridge comes in."

"How?"

"Maybe she fucked up a mission she was pilot on, which if word got out would put the drone program under scrutiny. Or maybe I'm wrong. Maybe she *is* Julian Assange's latest pen pal."

Daugherty doesn't buy the latter scenario. "If she sent secrets to WikiLeaks, it would be news already."

"I'll give you that," Pyle says.

Groggy from their twenty-hour chase, they are speculating like conspiracy-minded bloggers. But all they factually know is that somebody up the food chain wants, wants badly, Jessica Aldridge brought in.

"Could be she's not guilty of a damn thing," Daugherty says, ready to end the conversation.

"Right," Pyle says as they overtake a livestock trailer. "I'm sure she's a *real* innocent."

A POSTER OUTSIDE the McDonald's in San Antonio's Market Square offers Daugherty a McRib—which sounds like how he feels, double punched in the kidneys. He tells Pyle to pull up by the sign so he can use the restroom. Inside, gray faced, he cups his palm under the running faucet and slurps down a Cardioquin for his arrhythmia.

He'd been a healthy subject until his divorce six years ago. At least he'd had no major complaints. Now, at forty-seven, he also takes pills for his prostate and blood pressure. And once a year something new blows up on him. If his knees keep aching the way they do, he'll probably be due for replacements before the next national election.

"Get over yourself," Daugherty says to his pale, self-pitying scowl.

"Sir?" a young woman's voice calls through the bathroom door. "The restaurant is closing now."

"LOOKS LIKE YOU just woke up in a morgue freezer," Pyle says, arms folded, leaning against the Taurus.

They take a short walk across the parking lot to the Motel 6, where they catch the night clerk surfing porn on a laptop. He's so voyeuristically entertained by the agents' tale of a young woman and her dog that without asking he magnetizes a key card with Aldridge's room number. Though she'd paid in cash, he'd insisted on seeing her ID.

"Company policy," he explains. "Also, I should go with you when you take her."

"You'll cool your fat ass right here," Pyle says.

"Your cooperation is appreciated, sir," Daugherty adds with a smile he does not attempt to make real.

Taking the long way to room 211, around the back parking lot, he and Pyle find no escape routes. A perimeter walkway provides access to the rooms, which must abut a common inside wall. Some may have adjoining interior doors. But 211's will be locked since Aldridge only paid for one room.

When they reach her wing, Pyle mounts the stairs first and Daugherty follows. Daugherty sees that Pyle has taken along pepper spray. "In case the bitch gets jumpy," he explains.

"Her dog, you mean," Daugherty says, imagining he's still in charge.

"No," Pyle replies. "I mean the fucking bitch we're hunting."

Aldridge, Daugherty sees, is probably still awake in her room—light is bleeding from the edges of 211's curtained window. Since he's not expecting a shotgun blast greeting, he stands in front of the door and knocks. It's not a policeman's knock, but it is firm. This shouldn't be a hard arrest, not physically. "Jessica," Daugherty calls more softly than intended.

There is no response. Pyle moves in and starts pounding the door, making its frame rattle. "Aldridge! Jessica Aldridge! We know you're in there!" Bang, bang, bang.

"Great. Let's invite the neighbors," Daugherty tells him, envisioning an assortment of red-blooded gun owners peeved by their noisemaking. Dragging off a young woman in the middle of the night is a surefire way of turning a citizenry's ire into stupidity. Daugherty can already foresee the bullet holes in their car.

Pyle stops banging. "Come on. The goddamn key card," he says as though Daugherty has gone senile. They have been in each other's unbroken company for too many hours and the rush of the imminent arrest is compounding their irritation. Daugherty swipes the key and, with the toe of his shoe, pushes open the motel room door. It swings in all the way, unchained. Pyle lowers the pepper canister and shoves past. Daugherty almost doesn't follow; he can tell that no one's home.

While Pyle checks the bathroom Daugherty realizes that his heart is racing—fluttering but not pumping blood. He deflates onto the bed—

into an indent that Aldridge or her dog must have made. He puts up his feet and lies back.

Pyle comes out of the bathroom with a trashcan. "She was here," he says, rummaging, pulling out a McDonald's bag. Then he sees his partner lying on the bed. "What the hell you doing, Daugherty?"

"The trail is cold," Daugherty says and shuts his eyes. "The room is paid for." He is trying to sound worldly and nonchalant, coolly above any disappointment over losing their target again. "May as well get some rest." In truth, though, Daugherty wouldn't be able to move if the bed were on fire.

CHAPTER 35

New York City

"Juliette, damn it, I should be there for Ethan. For Zoe," Alex says, his eyes masked by the low-battery warning on Juliette's iPad. They have been video arguing for far too long.

"And miss the deadline for Sergei's mural? Right now he is very important to us." Juliette is again being the schoolmistress, reminding her difficult student of his error.

"Yeah," Alex says, "but Russians appreciate tragedy. Sergei will give me a few days off for a funeral."

"Alex, you are an artist. Stay there and put your feelings into paint. Besides, you did not even like this Zoe, not after all she did to your Ethan."

"You mean forget the dead and collect my paycheck. What's the Bible say? 'Gain the world and lose your soul.'"

"Now you are religious? And a million rubles is hardly the world. Thirty thousand dollars. Your work is what counts. That is your soul." Juliette clicks away another battery warning. She cannot recharge because this Starbucks has blocked its power outlets.

"My *work*. You talk like I'm Picasso. It's scary how you hype me."

"I only see what others see. What your *ami* Ethan saw before anyone. That's why I respect him. *Oui*, I do. You see, part of him says he wants you home to say goodbye to Zoe. But his other half wants you to succeed. Don't forget, he has two dozen of your paintings, your best early work. They are worth a lot by now."

"What the hell are you talking about?"

"I did not want to distract you but your show has all red dots. There is a buying frenzy. I have even just heard that Dean Cato resold *Money Shot*."

"But it's still hanging in the gallery."

"His hedge fund manager bought it for twice what he paid us. People are betting on you to be big. Basquiat big."

"Basquiat is dead."

"Basquiat is what they are saying. Some very influential people. Financiers. Bankers."

"What do those people know about art? It's just an investment to them."

"They are the new Medicis," Juliette says, "and they can make you great."

"You mean *rich*. You know what? I should have kept the original title on Cato's painting—*Blood Money*. That would have scared away the speculators."

"When you want people to see, you don't throw acid in their eyes. And *Blood Money* wasn't your title anyway."

"Just because it came from Ethan—"

"*Écoute-moi*, Alex." When Juliette gets heated she slips into her French Canadian. "Listen, your Ethan is bitter because he has lost his job, his apartment, all his money. He is going down while you are coming up. I do not even think he will take Sergei's job, after all my work. Don't let misplaced guilt hold you back. You are not responsible for his failure."

"Ethan is my friend. And *Blood Money* came from his anger."

"But your art is not about the words. It's about the *painting*. Ethan will understand."

"The *painting*. Jesus. I can't believe Cato resold *Money* before he even took it home."

As Alex says this Juliette senses him relenting, finally if just barely, to pride. He is, as he should be, not displeased with his success. *Their* success.

"This is your moment. Your chance to be famous." Ideas pounce through Juliette's head. "You know, maybe you *should* come back for a few days. The *Wall Street Journal* is asking for images. Perhaps I can get the *Times* interested in a profile. Then Sergei wouldn't mind your coming home. It would give his mural more prestige."

"Christ," Alex says, sighing, "you're always minding the store. We should be talking about my coming home to help Ethan, to say goodbye to Zoe, not to leverage this . . . whatever this madness is that's going on."

"*Je comprends, mon chéri.* I know. It's sad about Zoe. But you can do nothing for her. Truly you cannot. In fact, you are *upset.* So maybe it is better you stay at work on the mural. We must be very careful about your image."

"And what about Ethan? He needs me."

"*Chéri,* I will see to Ethan. Didn't I introduce him to Sergei, find him his new apartment? So let me help him again. You have only been crippling your friend, letting him hang around in the studio. He has lost his independence, his pride. Did you see what he wore to your opening? Dean Cato thought he was *homeless.*"

"So you're going to turn Ethan back into a presentable friend for me, *the great artiste.*"

"Come, Alex. You know you can't help him."

"Where do you get this great confidence?"

"I have helped you, no? And it is not confidence I have. I do what is realistic. That is all anyone who is responsible can do. I will help Ethan for *you.*"

As Alex pauses to consider her promise, Juliette's iPad warns again of her diminishing power. She will lose Alex soon. But she is almost finished.

"All right. I'll stay here. Who knows if I could get there in time anyway. But I won't make excuses to Ethan about missing the funeral."

"I will take care of him. Now, what have you done today?"

Alex sighs out of Juliette's screen. "Not much. I'm not really into it yet."

"Point your phone. Let me see," Juliette says, inflecting her voice with energy as if their twenty-minute quarrel has not drained her.

"I've had some ideas," Alex says defensively.

"Remember, it is Sergei's fiftieth in two weeks. He is planning a grand unveiling. There is a deadline and—"

"Christ, I'll do what I can. But stop it. Stop being the fucking shopkeeper!"

And then, with no further warning, her iPad goes dark.

"I WILL TRY to be not so much the shopkeeper," Juliette tells Alex through her recharging iPad. She has migrated two blocks to Astor Place, to a Starbucks that is freer with their power receptacles. She is not looking at Alex but is observing the wall on which he is to complete Sergei's mural. The area, prepared with a coat of plaster, sits between the room's grandiose curved staircases. Juliette sees that after his third day at work Alex has very little paint on the ten-by-twenty-foot space. He is not progressing as he normally does, in bold swaths. He has only put down a jumble of unsure slashes.

"I'm just not getting any traction yet," Alex says. "And it's not looking anything like the sketches we gave Sergei."

"Alex, you are the most talented artist I know," Juliette says.

She tells him this because she also needs to believe it. She needs to justify the last ten months of her emotional life, the monthly rent on his Chelsea studio, the social IOUs she'd called in to make his Medusa opening succeed, the professional promise she'd given Sergei that Alex Carr would produce for him a brilliant mural. Has she pushed Alex beyond his abilities? "Paint anything. Sergei will be pleased with whatever you do," Juliette says. But this is a fib, for unlike most of her clients Sergei *has* an eye. There will be no convincing him to accept anything mediocre.

"Whatever you say," Alex replies.

"And I will take care of Ethan tomorrow at the funeral."

"All right. Thanks."

"Really, you don't need to worry about a thing," she tells Alex. As the shopkeeper, *she* will keep up the accounts.

THE NEXT AFTERNOON, beneath a sidewalk canopy, Juliette meets Ethan with what she imagines are mutual looks of disregard. Juliette's has to do with Ethan's appearance—the beltless pants, the scuffed loafers, the nest of hand-combed hair, the business jacket grimy from being used as a smock in Alex's studio. Ethan seems in the final stages of unmaking what he once was, a currency trader entrusted with millions of dollars, according to Alex. Yet even in the wreck that stands before her, Juliette can sense his former competence.

And what does Ethan see as he looks at Juliette? She can guess—that *petite salope* who prevented Alex from being here to say goodbye to their former lover.

"*Bonjour,* Ethan," Juliette says with all the sympathy she can feign.

Attempting to peck his cheek she smells alcohol seeping from his pores. "*Ça va?*" she asks nervously. "You are okay?"

Ethan's breath is toxic. "Supposed to be my funeral. Didn't invite *him*. He's already inside."

Juliette can partly decipher this gibberish only because, following her promise to Alex yesterday, she began to burrow into this Zoe business. After locating a helpful detective in the Seventh Precinct, Juliette learned that, lacking next of kin, Zoe's remains were released to the first person willing to cover the burial costs. A friend of Zoe's from Washington had balked at getting more deeply involved and so Detective Chen had called Ethan. *So*, it is *his* funeral, in that he is paying for it. Who the uninvited party already inside might be, however, Juliette does not know.

Up the block a church bell chimes the hour. It is time but Ethan stays rooted to the sidewalk. "Are you ready, Ethan?" Juliette says. She enlaces his arm and turns him about. He is leaden and they weave through the funeral home's entrance.

A mournful-appearing man directs them into a chapel the size of a living room. It is set up with rows of chairs, all unoccupied. When Juliette lifts her eyes to the bier she understands Ethan's reluctance to enter. Half the coffin lid yawns open.

"You asked for a viewing?" Juliette says, diminishing her surprise.

"I . . . I have to see her again."

Almost ceremoniously, arm in arm, Juliette and Ethan pass up the aisle. A Bach arioso infiltrates their ears. Aside from another couple, an older man and a youngish woman standing not far from the bier, the room is empty.

"Did you not send out an announcement?" Juliette asks Ethan, perhaps sounding critical.

He doesn't respond.

"I could have helped," Juliette says, but she is talking to herself.

They are close enough now to look into the coffin, into the overly made-up, unevenly puffy face of the young woman. Laid out as she is, like a collapsed puppet, it is difficult to imagine this Zoe alive.

Ethan pulls away from Juliette's arm. "What's this?" he asks as if the corpse would tell him. Juliette can only stare as Ethan reaches into the coffin and lifts Zoe's wrist. He pulls at something attached to her hand.

"Ethan," Juliette whispers.

"Pardon me?" says the older man. "Pardon me! Stop that!"

He is dressed with the bland authority of a Washington politico—navy jacket, diagonally striped tie, light blue shirt. With his intellectually long-ish hair, he also radiates the pompous self-seriousness common to the capital. Having stepped back politely when Ethan approached the bier, he now takes a threatening step forward.

His companion tries to hold him. "No, Dr. Coombs. He is suffering," the woman, who has a scar on her face, says. Her voice is pleasantly ca-denced despite its alarm.

"This engagement ring," Ethan says loudly. "How did it get on her finger?"

"Please stop. It belongs to her," says Coombs. "It was from me."

"But she didn't accept it. Did she? Not when she was alive," Ethan shouts. No, not shouts, screams. He wrenches at Zoe's finger. "Why would you think she wants it now?" Ethan is pulling so hard at the ring that Juliette fears some morbid accident.

She grasps Ethan's shoulder to suggest restraint. But with a frenzy of elbows Ethan shrugs her away and Juliette topples backward off her platform shoes. Folding chairs spring like mousetraps as she crashes into them.

Juliette lifts her head from the wreckage and flips down her upturned skirt to cover her thighs. She raises a hand toward Ethan. On her feet, she accepts a tissue from Coombs' companion.

"Your temple. It is bleeding," the woman says, her brow knit.

CROSSING FIRST AVENUE, a block from the funeral home, Juliette pur-sues Ethan—who has set a smart pace as if he suspects what she intends: an intervention. Platforms are not running shoes; however, she has made a vow to Alex and tries to catch up. "Ethan!" she calls, then she is along-side. She is uncomfortable about being the shopkeeper on this day of mourning. But she may not have another chance to speak with him. "You have not worked for a long time, no?"

Speed walking even faster, Ethan retorts violently, "Don't I work in Alex's studio almost every day?"

"But this is not your real work." Jogging in his wake, Juliette thinks that they must make a curious sidewalk pair—the woman in black Helmut Lang chasing the disheveled homeless maniac. Fortunately no one cares. This is not Quebec.

At Second Avenue, a light corners Ethan. Juliette catches up again. "Ethan, please listen."

"No! You just want me to stop coming to his studio."

"I only think—"

"You think I'm Bartleby?"

"Who?"

"A man who wouldn't go away. And I won't. Not unless Alex tells me to go."

"But you know he would never do that."

"I'm not holding him hostage."

Though tempted, Juliette does not reply with the truth—that it is Ethan who is hostage. Ever since college he has been living through Alex—first by buying his friend's paintings and then by stretching his canvases and cleaning his brushes.

"I'll explain it simply," Ethan says. "I've lost Zoe and now you're taking Alex away."

"What? Ethan, no."

"You want me to work for Sergei a hundred miles away. Maybe . . . if Zoe were . . ." Ethan has stopped walking. "I can't breathe," he says.

Juliette takes his arm. "I did not know that you and Zoe had gotten back together."

"We were . . . I mean, there was a chance."

"Here," she says, leading Ethan to a door. "Let's get off the street."

JULIETTE ORDERS A chamomile tea for herself and insists that Ethan have a sandwich. He picks at it, takes a bite. "I am not trying to get rid of you," she says, realizing that she *had* been competing with him for Alex. But not now. Not really. Nevertheless, what will help Ethan will help both Alex and Ethan. Alex needs to separate himself a bit from Ethan in order to grow up. And Ethan needs a focus—work. "Sergei likes you. He's offered you a great opportunity."

"To rip people off."

"But that's not really what he's asking you to do."

"Isn't it? At least it's not as bad as what I did for UIB. But what's the point anyway."

"Ah," Juliette sighs. "You mean, without Zoe?"

"Without anybody."

"*Oui*, it's terrifying. Being alone," Juliette says. "Terrifying." She reaches across the table and touches Ethan's hand. "But you are not alone. You can help Alex a little, if you'd like."

Ethan looks up. "How?"

"We should not talk business today. But you understand currency exchange. And Alex will soon have a million rubles stuck in a Crimean bank. It was the deal I made with Sergei."

CHAPTER 36

Nevada

Voigt has an airman in trouble. Sanders is a good drone operator, reliable, superior at his tasks. But he has an issue with stress.

The passivity of UAV duty has likely caused part of the strain showing on Sanders. But also, many in the force disrespect the job. People join up for the romance of actual flight, for a chance to pilot incredible machines at unimaginable speeds. What glamour is to be had sitting at a stationary console . . . even though this is the future. Soon the newest fighters and bombers will no longer carry flesh and blood pilots—the g-forces of tomorrow's aerial combat would turn the human brain to mush. Remote operators, Voigt knows, represent not just progress but the end of a marvelous era. Being harbingers of this loss, his people take a lot of flak from the manned aircraft squadrons.

For Sanders, the stress has manifested in a lack of self discipline. He eats too much, doesn't exercise enough, has been warned and written up and demoted and warned again that he must lose double digits in pounds. There is nothing more left to do with him.

"Have a seat," Voigt says when Sanders enters. It's hard to look at the man. Pressed and tucked in though his uniform is, the flesh beneath it is unruly. Sander's neck, which merges with his chin, is ready to pop off the top button of his shirt.

"So your separation is going forward."

"Yes, sir."

"I'll be contacting that company we talked about with your letter of introduction. They need a man of your experience."

"Yes, sir."

"Now, do you have somewhere to stay down there in Arizona while you get your new employment straightened out?"

"I'll find a place, sir."

Voigt studies Sanders one last time. "Good man. Dismissed."

ANOTHER GOOD AIRMAN lost due to issues beyond pure job performance. *How many have there been?* Voigt thinks. "Hell," he whispers. He
is standing in the commissary checkout.

"Would you like to go ahead, sir?" asks the second lieutenant in line
before him.

"I'm good, son," the colonel says firmly. He could use his rank to jump
the line, and he probably should in order to maintain that necessary aura
of military authority. But Voigt is chilling for a minute, enjoying the break
and the air-conditioning before crossing the various sun-blasted tarmacs
between here and his office. His wife likes the organics here, the tomatoes
and squash. It's the kind of food, Voigt thinks, that Sanders ought to have
been eating. But an airman will handle the stress of drone duty in his
or her own way—most commonly through junk food or nicotine. Voigt
would ban the vending machines dispensing edible garbage if this wasn't
likely to incite insurrection. He'd certainly crack down on the open-air
smoking. Now, out under the hot sun, he remembers once scolding Jessica Aldridge, despite her taking her cigarette in a designated area. Wasn't
she Sanders' drone partner? She had been the smartest candidate in his
program to convert enlisted personnel into drone pilots. *Dammit*, she
must have known that writing her father could lead to a security breach,
that his mail would be opened.

Not long after Jessica went off the grid, Sloan from DHS told Voigt
about Donald Alan Aldridge, who was serving a twenty-year sentence
in a South Florida prison. Over the ten months since he's been reading
the man's correspondence, Jessica has colonized a part of the colonel's
mind—so much so that a few months ago he'd contacted the warden at
the prison. Aldridge kept sending letters to his daughter even though all
till then had been returned undelivered. *Why?*

"Is the man crazy?" Voigt had asked Warden Wagner.

"Probably. But he's not stupid," said Wagner.

"Tell me about him."

"Repeat offender. First got into trouble selling drugs in the eighties. His cellmate, Ramirez, says it had to do with some runaway he'd holed up with. Apparently when Aldridge got out of prison he tracked her down up north. Turns out she'd had a kid by him, a daughter."

"You mean, *Jessica*," Voigt said.

"No, no," said the warden. "These lowlifes can have complicated family histories. Anyway, this young girlfriend of his died in a car crash. Aldridge blamed himself for it. Meanwhile his actual wife was bringing up Jessica in Pompano Beach, that is, before she dumped the kid on her sister."

No surprises there; Voigt had seen that a lot of enlistees came from unstable backgrounds, looking for a solid place to land. "You seem to have a lot of good intel on your prisoner," Voigt said.

"I do," replied Wagner, acknowledging the compliment. "I swapped out Aldridge's cellmate for a body I can work with." Wagner told Voigt about Hector Ramirez, a Mariel boatlift refugee who had worked his way into a position teaching Shakespeare at a Miami university before committing a murder himself. "I haven't completely converted this Ramirez to the cause yet. But so far he's given up a few details on Aldridge that aren't in the record."

"Tell me more about the murder," Voigt said. "Aldridge's, I mean."

"Aldridge was an addict. To pay for it he dealt in oxycodone prescriptions that a doctor wrote for him. One morning the doc was found floating in his pool up in Fort Lauderdale. He'd been strangled not drowned. All the DNA pointed to Aldridge."

"DNA usually doesn't lie," Voigt said, yet he'd been thinking not about Don Aldridge but al-Yarisi. They were just getting back the first intelligence that al-Yarisi might be playing dead, that a bag of his blood carried by his double had provided false DNA proof of death.

LATER THAT NIGHT, after writing a job recommendation for Sanders, Voigt goes to the Florida prisons website and looks at Don's picture on the inmate database. He is big, this Don Aldridge, a little sloppy looking but with large, penitent eyes. Nevertheless, he is not a man to gamble your secrets with.

CHAPTER 37

New York City

Detective Chen is wrapping up the paperwork on the Leston drowning. With the coroner's report open ended, she is leaning her assessment toward the accidental rather than the deliberate. But an unrelated factor is also weighing in. The stories her grandmother told her as a child: Chinese ghosts can be very vengeful to the living who have betrayed them. And though Chen believes in spirits as little as she expects Martians to land in Central Park, her rationality does not block twinges of childhood sentiment. Because of her grandmother's stories, Chen carries an aversion to maligning the dead. If Zoe Leston's death was an accident and she deemed it a suicide, this would haunt her more than the opposite error.

"Crap, Eddie. Make some noise," she says as Banco appears behind her.

"Finishing up the Leston suicide," he says.

"How is it a suicide?" she asks.

"The ritual of the candles."

Ethan Winter had made the same observation. "A woman doesn't need a special occasion to light candles for a bath," Chen says.

Eddie hardly lets her finish. "I saw only enough melted wax in the room to account for the candles lit that night. The candles were a onetime occasion, like killing herself was."

"DO YOU KNOW much about Ms. Leston's family history?" Chen asks Winter. She has called him to the station again.

Knotted in her guest chair, Ethan's hair is askew, his clothing slept in. A man letting himself go. Chen, perching on the corner of her desk, tries to appear sympathetic. If Zoe Leston's ex-fiancé was not in Washington, she would have called him in instead of Winter. Chen's goal is simple—to clear her desk and her conscience. She wants to put this ghost to rest, or at least send it to haunt someone else.

Winter's eyes display the bloodshot sclera of a hangover. Perhaps he's coming off a binge.

"What do you mean by family history?" Winter finally says, reminding Chen of his tendency to answer questions with questions. But this is not an interrogation, not really, so she allows his quirk.

"Did you know, for instance, that her grandparents adopted Zoe after her mother died?"

Chen watches Winter debate with himself about how much he should admit. "I knew it before Zoe did," he confesses.

Which means, Chen realizes, that Zoe Leston must have been ignorant about her background until adulthood. For her to have learned in her twenties that she was not who she thought she was . . . this fact weighs toward her being a suicide. Such a revelation would shake anyone's sense of self. "How did you learn about Ms. Leston's background?" Chen asks.

"Zoe's grandfather gave me some documents before he . . . died."

"But that was almost a year ago," Chen says, assuming these must be the documents that she found near Zoe's body and are now in the evidence room. "Wasn't Ms. Leston living in Washington by then?"

"Yes."

"So you were having a long-distance relationship?"

"No."

"No? Then why did her grandfather give these private papers to you and not to his granddaughter?"

Ethan stares at Detective Chen, then grudgingly responds. "The man was dying. He had a fantasy that Zoe and I would get back together. That I could help her deal with . . . everything."

"By *everything*, you mean not just the news about her adoption but what her grandfather was planning to do to himself and his wife?"

"I suppose," Winter says, looking down again.

"So Dr. Leston *trusted* you."

Winter grimaces at the floor. "Only I didn't want his trust. Zoe had left me that summer. I didn't even look at the documents for weeks. Then Zoe called me about . . . the deaths."

"I see," Chen says, pondering what Winter must be thinking: if he had immediately contacted Zoe about the documents she would have spoken with her grandfather before he acted. Possibly, then, the fatal sequence of events might have been averted—including Zoe Leston's final bath.

Winter's eyes well. "Exactly," he says.

Chen has opened doors that should have stayed shut. But now she knows—in part from Dr. Leston's trust in Ethan, in part from the emotions he's displaying—that he has a right to know what she knows about Zoe Leston. "I'm sorry, Mr. Winter. I didn't call you in to ask questions but to provide you with answers about Ms. Leston's background—"

Ethan rises. "May I go?" Chen opens her mouth but Ethan cuts her off. "I know that Walter Leston and his wife were her grandparents. I know that their daughter, Zoe's mother, was a runaway who died in a car crash. I know they never told Zoe. And I know that Zoe died alone. That's *enough* knowledge." He looks down at Detective Chen as she stands up from her desk.

"Do you know *why* Dr. Leston never spoke to Zoe about her mother?" Chen asks.

"Why else? To bury the tragedy."

Chen considers. "Your answer tells me you don't know. That the papers Dr. Leston gave you contained only half the story."

"Does it make a difference? They're all dead. The whole twisted family is dead and buried. Or cremated."

Winter turns and walks away, but like a predator Chen follows him through the maze of desks in the station house. Does he suspect what she wishes to do—free herself of a burden by putting it on him?

"*No*, Mr. Winter. They are not all dead. There is Zoe's father."

This stops Ethan. "What?" he says.

"I've located Zoe's biological father. I've even spoken with him."

Ethan massages his neck. "The family had a lot of secrets."

"They can be dangerous," Chen says.

"What do you mean?"

It's too complicated for Chen to explain that if Zoe knew of her father, had through his example been aware of her own weaknesses, that she might not have taken those pills and stepped into a bath. "I mean nothing. What's important is that Zoe Leston's drowning was an accident."

Ethan's reddened eyes meet hers. "You're certain of that, detective?"

But there is no certainty here. Chen knows that with very little diffi-
culty she could bend her evidence toward suicide. No one but Zoe can
know what she did.

"Yes, I'm certain," she says. And with this half lie, she exorcises her
grandmother's stories and, for her at least, the ghost of Zoe Leston. But
Winter's tormented expression shows that he remains haunted.

She cannot absolve Winter of his pain or his guilt, but perhaps she can
make him feel less alone in his misery. She takes a leather-bound notepad
from her back pocket and tears from it a scrap with writing—*Donald Alan
Aldridge, Inmate 82747L, Seminole City Correctional Institution.* "Zoe's father," she says, pressing the scrap into Winter's hand.

CHAPTER 38

Florida

Descending into Miami the change in altitude causes Daugherty's heart to race, to ineffectually flutter. The agent closes his eyes and visualizes a lake, the gentle lapping of waves against a floating dock from which he has cast a fishing line. He visualizes a striped perch underwater as it eyes a baited hook. This exercise usually slows Daugherty's pulse, allows his mitral valve to close sufficiently to pump blood and feed his limbs with oxygen.

"Boss, you're looking pale," Pyle tells him. Pyle has been keeping an eye on his partner since he passed out on their fugitive's hotel bed three days ago.

"Fear of flying."

"*Right,*" Pyle says.

In the meantime Daugherty tells himself that a desk job would kill him faster than the heart attack he's headed for as he chases Jessica Aldridge around the country. That he's kept his official health record clean is due to his choice of doctor—a sympathetic smoker who runs him through his EKG until it has flicked out a satisfactory length of graph paper. With luck, though, he'll be able to maintain this charade of health for three more years and attain the two decades allotted to a field agent before forced retirement. In Daugherty's fantasies, he receives a gold service award key from the director and keels over.

But for now Daugherty's heart is pumping happily again. So much so that he almost leaps up to grab the heavy case in the overhead bin. Giddy is how Daugherty gets whenever he manages to return his pulse to a viable rate—giddy with a sense of defeated mortality.

"I can carry that," Pyle says.

"Do I look like your grandmother?" Daugherty says. Besides, Daugherty is the one who insisted on bringing the *box*—the polygraph kit.

He and Pyle don't speak again to each other until they're examining their rental in the Hertz lot. It's an Impala, anonymous except for the color. Candy apple red. They're out of black, white, and silver.

"It's a goddamn fire truck," Pyle says.

"In Miami red is as invisible as gray," Daugherty tells him. "Anyway, we're not tailing anyone. Just paying a visit."

"Want me to take it?" Pyle asks, moving toward the driver's door.

But Daugherty keeps the keys. "I've been to where we're going."

This is Daugherty's biggest advantage over young agents like Pyle—he has covered more territory. Unfortunately his memories don't snap back like they once did. He almost misses the exit ramp for the Palmetto Expressway. "Gonna pull a little Mario Andretti here," he warns Pyle before gunning the engine and cutting the wheel.

The Impala swerves between a pair of cement trucks and dives onto the Palmetto. Peripherally, Daugherty senses Pyle's eyes burning holes through his face. "Smooth," Pyle says, sarcastic. "And who the hell is Mario Andretti?"

For the next forty minutes, Daugherty concentrates on not making any wrong turns. And he doesn't. But the effort of keeping his senior moments at bay turns the trip into less than the laid-back jaunt he'd planned. Despite the frigid air-conditioning, he's sweating through his shirt and jacket, his underwear and pants. Meanwhile, Pyle, partly reclined in the passenger's seat, looks as relaxed as a sunning panther.

"You've done seventeen years as a field agent, right?" Pyle asks.

"Three more until they boot me," Daugherty replies because that is the drift of his thoughts. But Pyle is going somewhere else.

"So how many times has the head office left you out to dry like this?"

"You're talking about the need-to-know status of field agents?"

"I'm talking about DC not giving us the father-daughter connection until yesterday. You and your ex-partner might have nailed Aldridge ten months ago with that intel."

"Knowledge is power. People in Washington don't share power," Daugherty says.

"Makes us look bad. I mean this is not intra-agency cooperation with the CIA or DHS we're talking about. For our own people to hold back information from us, that blows."

Pyle's federal expectations seem drawn from old G-man movies in which the Bureau functions like a single-purpose machine for apprehending criminals. In actuality, an agent's primary job is the same as any bureaucrat's—to protect his or her turf. Daugherty takes the opportunity to instruct Pyle. "Field agents like us are errand boys. You either get used to being a tool or you get a desk in Washington and pull strings."

A one-lane ramp funnels them off the turnpike. They pass below a sign with a cruciform indicator that points to Key West straight ahead and to Biscayne Park and the Everglades to the left and right, respectively. They're going to none of those places. At the first traffic light instinct tugs Daugherty's steering hand right and a mile later, after they've left behind the palmy medians of Seminole City and are passing fields recently stripped of some summer crop, Daugherty gets his next directional clue—an old fireworks stand. He's a detective tracing his own past, though just barely, and he hesitates making the turn.

"Forget the way?" Pyle asks and before Daugherty can say "nah," Pyle is studying a map on his phone. "We're good," Pyle says, sounding disappointed.

Soon his memory is vindicated. A roadside field cordoned by rings of fencing appears. Inside the innermost fence, which is frothed with barbwire, white-and-gray barracks shimmer in the heat. Daugherty pulls in by the compound's only decorative flourish—a section of wall outlined in aqua blue that announces DEPARTMENT OF CORRECTIONS.

WARDEN ELI WAGNER, a man with a prickly military haircut and bearing, is either not happy to see them or wears a naturally pinched expression. Matching the institution he runs, Wagner's coloration is white and gray—white hair, gray eyes, gray suit—except for his complexion, which is unhealthily tan. Surgical tape hides the end of the warden's nose—evidence perhaps of freshly removed skin cancer.

"Agent Daugherty, a call would have saved you a trip," Wagner tells him with an almost-erased Virginia drawl. "The prisoner is currently in solitary."

"Solitary? For what?" Daugherty asks, because clearly national security will trump some local rules violation. Wagner will have to allow a visit.

The warden, studying the agent, modulates his frown into a mild sneer, as if he has established Daugherty's place in the pecking order and concluded that it is not as high as Daugherty imagines. They are sitting with Wagner's immaculate desk between them. The warden unlocks a drawer and removes some sheets of paper that he slides over the polished surface.

Putting on his glasses, Daugherty silently reads. "Dear Jessica . . ." blah blah blah. And then the letter gets interesting, especially the second page. "To Whom It May Concern. To YOU Who Are Hunting My Daughter . . ."

"Your bosses never showed you that?" Wagner says, not displeased by Daugherty's ignorance. "I passed along a copy ten days ago."

Now he understands why Washington reactivated the search for Jessica, with Don Aldridge's threat to widen the al-Yarisi drone scandal.

"I don't so much care what that letter means to the outside world," Warden Wagner tells him. "But Aldridge has violated prison rule number one. You don't disrespect authority. A prisoner needs to remember who's on top."

"Amen to that," says Pyle, his first words since they sat down in the warden's office.

"That's right," Wagner says, nodding at Pyle. "I won't be returning the man to the general population for a couple more days," he says to Daugherty, "not till he's had his full two weeks in isolation. Come back then and I'll give him to you for an hour."

Wagner stands. Annoyingly to Daugherty, because he is not yet done here, Pyle too stands. Then he steps away to peruse a wall littered with the memorabilia career bureaucrats like to display—diplomas, photographs, framed newspaper clippings. Stubbornly Daugherty remains seated.

The antagonism in the room is palpable, and natural—the standard conflict between national and state bureaucracies. Wagner wants to make sure that Daugherty knows who's boss here. As this is not a federal prison Daugherty has no authority to order an interview with Aldridge.

Daugherty could make a call to Washington, but that would reflect badly on his own competence. Instead he smiles. "I'd hate to waste three days of taxpayer money waiting," he says to Wagner.

"That's why you make a phone call in advance," Wagner says. "Saves everybody time."

"If I could have made the call I would have. My partner and I have been on the chase. First from California to Texas to New Orleans, then back to California and down here to Florida. As the prisoner's letter shows"—Daugherty is folding up the pages Wagner had given him; he intends to put it in his pocket—"we're dealing with issues of national security."

"Not exactly." Wagner says. "I spoke to Aldridge's lawyer and he gave nothing to the press. That letter there is just an inmate rattling his cage. *And* it's prison property." The warden comes around his desk, which makes Daugherty reflexively stand.

Daugherty gives back the letter. "Let's go," he tells Pyle, who is diddling with his government-issue BlackBerry like some bored teenager. Pyle looks up and grins, not at Daugherty but at Wagner.

"My stepfather was a CO at James River. Lee Benkowsky," Pyle says, relevant to nothing Daugherty can conceive. Not only that, Pyle is lengthening his vowels slightly in a convincing accent.

Wagner stops and studies Pyle.

"Your award," Pyle explains.

On the wall by which Pyle has stationed himself Daugherty sees a commendation plaque bold with Wagner's name.

"Lee's your old man?" Wagner says. "So how is he these days?"

"I'm told cancer took him five years ago," Pyle says.

"Sorry to hear it."

"No one's loss. He was a drunk SOB."

Wagner makes a grunt as if humored. "True enough."

"I called him my stepfather, but he never married my mother. We moved back to Richmond after living with him about six months. Six months in hell." Pyle comes forward and sticks out his hand. "Nice meeting you, Warden."

Wagner takes Pyle's grip but doesn't reply. He lets a grin lift his mouth.

Daugherty's the first to exit Wagner's inner office to the foyer. There a secretary, a fortyish woman behind a gunmetal desk, is busy typing.

"Ann," Wagner says. "Let's get Donald Aldridge over to the visitation center. Then instruct these gentleman on how to get there."

Slack jawed, Daugherty turns. The warden has a hand on Pyle's shoulder just like he's the son of an old friend.

"Right away, Warden," says Ann.

"You'll have privacy in the VC today," Wagner tells Pyle. "No public hours." He turns back to Ann as if chasing an afterthought. "Remind me who that woman detective was that called down from New York."

Ann takes a second to recall the answer. "Sarah Chen. Manhattan Seventh Precinct."

"She might know something the Bureau can use." The warden aims a squint at Daugherty as if he and Detective Chen are equally annoying types. "This Chen is the one who put Aldridge in solitary. Got him upset over his daughter."

"Pardon?" Daugherty says.

"No, not Jessica Aldridge," Wagner replies. "Some other daughter in trouble. Her drowning in a bathtub must have set off his paternal instincts. After hearing the news, Aldridge wrote his letter." Wagner shakes the copy of the damning letter at Daugherty but doesn't hand it over.

"NICE WORK," DAUGHERTY tells Pyle after marching through a maze of windowless corridors toward Aldridge. His partner's success with the warden irks, but there's no gain in getting pissy. Besides, now Daugherty's curious about Pyle's stepfather. "Fill me in on this Lee Bunkhouse."

"Benkowsky," Pyle corrects. "He was an eyewitness to the prison riot Wagner put down at James River."

"Your stepfather worked with Wagner? That's one damn lucky coincidence."

"No, chief. Benkowsky is mentioned in the article hanging next to Wagner's heroism plaque. I found his obituary online and got all the facts I needed for my stepfather story."

"You made that up? Then how do you know this Benkowsky was such a son of a bitch? They don't put that in obits."

"Not many prison guards lean toward sainthood."

"And I suppose you also guessed he was an alcoholic?"

"Benkowsky died of cancer waiting for a liver transplant. I bet on cirrhosis as the cause."

Pyle has an answer for everything. "What counts," Daugherty says, "is that Wagner bought it."

Pyle guffaws. "The warden didn't believe a word I said."

Daugherty's stride slows. He is a literal two steps behind Pyle and a figurative ten. "If Wagner knew you were lying, why didn't he call you out?" Daugherty asks, not loudly. But Pyle, well ahead now, has already turned a corner.

Whatever mind game went on between Pyle and Wagner, all Daugherty grasps of it is that he will never play at that level. Pyle's acuity, once he puts in his field service minimums, will lift him to positions in the Bureau Daugherty has only fantasized about attaining. Rarely does Daugherty so clearly see his limits—the fact that *he* is the mark, the straightforward kind of guy who in a poker game will not only lose his shirt but have it dry-cleaned before handing it over. It's a good thing for his career that most criminals are idiots.

At a door with a mesh window, Pyle awaits him. "Ready, boss?"

Daugherty appreciates Pyle's acknowledgment that his seniority still counts, even if just for meaningless courtesies like waiting. It's clear, though, that Pyle should be in charge. Because Daugherty's supposed to be, he puts away his scuffed ego and goes to work.

"We'll need the box," Daugherty says—a suggestion for Pyle to get the polygraph, which Daugherty deliberately left in the car before meeting with Wagner. Best not to let the warden in on his plans.

Pyle pushes into the visitation room and stops. "That may be a problem," he says, not unhappily.

"Hell," Daugherty replies while examining the room.

Long and narrow, it contains a row of stalls with bolted stools and glass partitions. This is not going to be a contact visit.

Going back to Wagner to request an interrogation room is a nonstarter. So Daugherty makes an executive decision. One of the things that had impressed him about Pyle was the man's military record; he had done interrogations for army intelligence in Afghanistan.

"You be the lie detector. You ask the questions," Daugherty says, while telling himself that this is *his* idea, that he's not an old man capitulating to the next generation, that he's not Pyle's sock puppet.

THE CONVICT IS a big man with receding hair slicked straight back. His complexion shines and his green jumpsuit radiates sweat halos from the armpits due to his time in solitary. Peering through the security glass, past Pyle and Daugherty, Donald Alan Aldridge seems to be searching for someone else. When he realizes that only the agents are visiting, he bares his teeth. They are remarkably even and white, probably state provided.

Pyle signals the prisoner to pick up the handset. Fortunately, this is not a public visitation day. Nobody is around to overhear state secrets.

Aldridge lifts his handset, and his mouth starts moving before it nears his face. The glass muffles his shouts, but Daugherty makes out "feds," preceded possibly by "goddamn." After Aldridge gets off this rant he settles onto his stool and talks calmly into the phone. "Sure am glad to see you boys." Daugherty can hear Aldridge speak because Pyle is holding his handset at an angle. Pyle absorbs the convict's mood swing in silence.

Daugherty is beginning to think that Aldridge's comment has confused his partner, as it has him. Then Pyle responds. "And why would you be glad?" It's that same nastily sardonic tone Pyle has recently used with a stubborn waitress and a reluctant motel clerk.

"Simple, ace," Aldridge says. "You guys being here means you haven't nailed my little girl. Why else would you visit?"

"Mr. Aldridge," Pyle says shaking his head, his tone turned grim, "I wish that were so. We're here to tell you that your daughter has been in an accident."

Aldridge retracts his cock-of-the-walk grin. A twitch settles into one side of his mouth. "You must be talking about my kid in New York. I know about it. She drowned. I know about it."

"No," Pyle says. "I mean your other daughter. Jessica. Jessica's been severely injured."

As this untruth seems of little value other than for sadistic purposes, Daugherty wonders if Pyle's lying, in general, might simply be sociopathic.

"Bullcrap," Aldridge says. "What are you talking about?"

"She was hitchhiking in Texas. It was the middle of the night. A driver with one headlight sideswiped her. She's in intensive care," Pyle says.

Aldridge doesn't look convinced. But perhaps to support his crumbling confidence, he leans one of his big shoulders against his stall's side partition. "So you guys came all the way down here just to tell a convict about his hurt daughter. Ain't you humanitarian. Like I said, bullcrap."

"We think she was on her way here, to visit you. There are a few details we need to clear up. Thought you might help. If you do, maybe we'll fly you to Dallas for a mercy visit. Does that interest you? By the way, I'm Agent Pyle and this is my boss, Agent Daugherty." Pyle, seated on a bolted stool, winks at Daugherty with the eye hidden from Aldridge.

The prisoner scratches his chin stubble. "You're going to get me out of here for a trip?"

"Like you mentioned, we're feds. We can make special arrangements for cooperative witnesses."

"Yeah. Witnesses to what?"

"To what your daughter might have told you. At this point we just want to undo any accidental harm she did to national security. Any information would help."

Aldridge's expression reverts to a sneer. "You expect me to rat on my girl? There're two words for that." But with his boldness deflating, Aldridge doesn't say them. "Anyway, you already have everything she wrote me."

"But you have phone privileges. You don't mean to tell me that in all the time you've been inside you've never spoken with your daughter?"

"Spoke to her? Not since she was a kid. She just started writing to me a couple of years ago. I'm lucky to get letters, let alone a call."

"Mr. Aldridge. You'll have to try harder for us." Pyle's tone is calm, absent of emotion. Somehow this sounds crueler than if he were shouting. "You have a few more days in solitary. Search your memory. Maybe we'll try again."

"Come on, man, be straight with me. If you really have Jessica in the hospital, why aren't you asking her your questions?"

"If she were conscious, we would," Pyle says crisply and hangs up the handset.

"Hey!" Aldridge shouts, his voice muffled by the glass barrier. "How bad off is she?"

Pyle turns away as if ignoring a chained, barking dog.

"Hey!" Aldridge shouts.

And now Daugherty, too, is leaving. But he glances back when the pounding starts. Aldridge is beating the glass with his handset.

"Tell me about Jessica, you lousy fucks!"

At the obscenity Aldridge's face plunges forward into the barrier between prison and freedom. For the second or two that Daugherty watches, the prisoner's eyes display their whites and his lips smear blood against the glass. A guard, Daugherty sees before turning away, is pressing a stun gun into the man's neck.

OUTDOORS IN THE prison parking lot, Daugherty is too angry to talk.

"Well, that went well," Pyle says without sarcasm.

"Did it?" Daugherty says, just able to contain his fury. "Aldridge told us nothing and we got him zapped." Daugherty has said *we* because *he* took Pyle off his leash. "You can take to the bank we'll be called out on this one."

"I doubt it. Wagner was looking to punish Aldridge beyond solitary. We did the warden a favor. He won't complain."

"Maybe so, but the prisoner didn't deserve a stun. You set him off with the lie about Jessica."

"It was a good tactic considering he's just lost his other daughter."

"No. It was just sadism."

Coming to the red Impala, the agents separate. This time Pyle is not interested in driving and grimly goes straight to the passenger's side. Daugherty's downer attitude is getting to him.

"I appreciate your being old school. But the world has changed." Pyle is speaking patiently. He might be a caregiver spooning oatmeal into the mouth of an invalid. "These days, boss, you've got to push hard or get pushed over."

"The voice of experience," Daugherty says.

"Just of five years in Talibanistan."

"Pissing on the bodies of your enemies?"

"Screw you, Daugherty."

Daugherty gets in the car and it's a pizza oven. After cranking the engine, he elevates the air conditioner to gale force. But the vents blast humidity for a good minute and he's sopping before they clear out.

Pyle remains standing outside the car—waiting, Daugherty realizes, for its interior to cool. Daugherty is beginning to sense in this minor thing, as in possibly all their interactions, that Pyle is manipulating him. This realization, that he no longer trusts his partner, that he in fact *hates* Pyle, takes Daugherty like a sucker punch.

"I guess it's out of this swamp and back to California," Pyle says after buckling up beside him.

Daugherty, behind the wheel, reads Pyle's comment as a test of suggestibility. Maybe Pyle expects, now that Daugherty's been cued, that he will chauffeur them to the airport and book them on a return flight home to LA. But this is not how it will go. Daugherty still has authority. "We're not going home empty handed," he says.

"I'll bet you're thinking about hooking Aldridge up to your lie detector."

In fact, Daugherty is considering this. But he can't let Pyle know he's floundering for ideas. "After what just happened I doubt Wagner will grant us another interview. But if he did, I'd use the polygraph on Aldridge. Why not?"

"Because it would make no difference. Aldridge could turn Boy Scout and not tell us anything we don't know. Look, chief, I've done enough military interrogations to read a man like him. We broke him today. We took all he has."

"Fine. Forget the old man." Daugherty is burning to show that he, too, can think two moves ahead. "We'll pick up his daughter when she pays him a visit. Did you see how he looked when we walked in? He was expecting to see his daughter, not us. I think she's planning a visit."

Pyle stays quiet while Daugherty backs from the parking space. When Pyle's sure his partner can manage driving and thinking simultaneously, he points out a flaw in Daugherty's thinking. "If our person of interest is bright enough to elude you for a year, she's not likely to visit a prison where she'll have to show ID."

"Why else would she come to Florida if not to see her father?" Daugherty snaps.

"Maybe she's coming back because this is where she started out."

"So she's a salmon?"

Pyle isn't baited by the mockery. "I'm saying that there's other people she'll be more likely to visit. Her mother for one."

"And you have that address?"

"I'm working on it."

Of course Pyle is, since he always seems to be two steps ahead of Daugherty's two steps. And Pyle's logic has possibilities. But this case is no longer about locating ex–Technical Sergeant Aldridge. It's about Daugherty and Pyle.

"We're not chasing shadows up and down Florida," Daugherty tells him. "We're coming back here to stake out this parking lot. Let's assume Jessica Aldridge doesn't know she has to sign in to visit a prisoner. Or maybe she's going to try a false ID. In any case, I'm not letting a correctional officer take the credit for collaring her."

"All right," Pyle says. "That's not unreasonable."

"Why thank you," Daugherty tells him. "If she doesn't surface we'll look into the mother and follow up on the New York side. I hope you took down that detective's information."

Pyle doesn't need to flip open his notebook. "Chen. Seventh Precinct."

"Maybe she can tell us if the sisters were in touch."

"I doubt they were," Pyle says. "But you're the boss."

And though Daugherty is, his heart is fibrillating again, a bird beating its wings against a cage of bone.

CHAPTER 39

New York City

"*Bonjour*, Ethan," Juliette says. It is a pleasant September afternoon and she has arrived at the Jamba Juice on Houston and Mercer, where he had texted her to meet him. "This is a little out of our way, no?"

"I first met Zoe there," he says, nodding across the street to a corner. "Almost exactly two years ago."

"Ah," says Juliette. She busses Ethan on both cheeks, noticing that his face is closely shaved, his hair cut, his shirt fresh. It is as if he's going on a date. Or perhaps he is just a man intent on his own rehabilitation—he *is* carrying a gym bag. It's as if Juliette's proposal to engage Ethan as Alex's financial adviser has snapped him out of his depression.

Inside they order flatbreads, Juliette to be amenable, and they sit to discuss Alex, still at work on Sergei's mural five thousand miles away. "He is very happy you've decided to help," Juliette says, putting away the documents Ethan had brought for her to send to Alex—papers he must sign to cede Ethan control of the rubles Sergei has deposited for him in a Sevastopol bank.

"He's always been bad with money, with planning for his future."

And what about your future? she wishes to say. *Sergei will not wait forever for you to take up his job offer.* But it is not her place to be the shopkeeper with Ethan. "Yes, artists are impractical," she says. "But what you do, isn't it also a work of art?" Ethan frowns and she corrects her overstatement. "At the least it is magic."

"No, just a bit of timing," Ethan replies. "Maximizing an exchange of rubles."

"Surely it is more than this," Juliette says.

"Not really."

Now Juliette frowns. "But I'm sure you know what you're doing."

When later they rise to leave, with Juliette disposing of her flatbread, she sees that Ethan is standing straighter than he normally does. He is looking more in control of himself and this eases her concern about Alex's rubles. "You are going to a gym now?" she asks, seeing him holding the duffel from which he'd removed the banking documents. The bag has a large Nike swoosh.

"Oh, this?" he says of the duffel. Then he unzips it and shows her the metal urn inside.

Juliette takes a breath. "Is that . . . ?" she says.

"Zoe," Ethan says. "I've been taking her back to all of our spots. Here. Washington Square. Battery Park. I've even shown her some new places. I don't think she'd ever been to Liberty Island before."

"That's . . . very romantic."

"I was a homebody. But Zoe always liked going out. I hate thinking of her cooped up. Now we're going on a trip. Florida."

Juliette smiles tightly. She is thinking of how to tell Alex that his friend has gone just a little mad.

PART FIVE

HOMECOMING

September 2013

CHAPTER 40

Pompano Beach

The waves roll in, lick Jessica's heels, soak the butt of her jeans. Rolling out, they siphon sand through her toes. To the north, beneath a light-house, a sport fisher breaks from an inlet that is pointing a diagonal path in front of her toward the Bahamas. Already the boat has raised outriggers so it won't be traveling that far, 150 miles. Jessica has never been to the islands and doesn't precisely recall how she knows the distance and tri-angulation. Having grown up nearby, she must have absorbed a local nau-tical chart. One of the reasons she did well in the drone program is her memory for spatial data. She had been proud of this ability until it had been misused. Now she wishes she never had it.

Skittles behaves as if it's her first time before an endless expanse of water. Jessica can believe this since Newt and Shelly were definitely not beachgoers. Their dog chases sea foam and barks at hovering gulls.

"Quiet, girl," Jessica says, though there's no one else around to com-plain about the yelps. Jessica retracts her legs and wraps her arms around her shins. She tracks the fishing boat against the haze on the horizon. It is a humid, airless morning and the sun is a disappointing smear, a wet lozenge instead of the orange fireball she had hoped to watch rise.

The familiarity of the area behind her—the flat expanse of the land-scape, the wind-bent palms, the canals and quarry lakes, the low concrete houses, the midrise hotels and condo developments, even the grungy strip malls—makes her nostalgic. She shouldn't feel so at home here in her hometown. She's been in exile too long.

By age twelve she was long fatherless but unprepared to be completely orphaned. That was her age when her mother explained to her how lucky Jessica was to be alive, that six months before she was born, on the day her mother was scheduled for a D&C, her father convinced her to marry him. The biggest mistake of her life, her mother added cutting a lime for her second gimlet of the morning.

Only later did Jessica grasp why her mother had told her these things. Joanne wanted her to understand the inconstancy of her mothering—the disappearances, the empty refrigerator, the infrequently washed clothing. Despite this neglect, through Jessica's unconditional love, Joanne remained a goddess. Until, to keep a boyfriend who disliked children, she abandoned Jessica at her sister's. ———

Jessica's aunt lived in central Florida and was raising as devout Christians a quartet of boys. She took in her sister's girl to save that "lost child's soul." But Jessica thought her soul was fine and, not a month after she moved in, vowed that she would get away from her aunt and her aunt's church— Martyrs of the Lamb—as soon as she could. Five long years later, after graduating from high school, it was the Air Force that saved her—at least from her family.

Cawing gulls draw Jessica's attention down the beach, to where a lifeguard is striding toward her. With his rescue buoy he fends away Skittles' curious approach.

"She's friendly," Jessica shouts, not wanting the guard to hit Skittles.

"No dogs on the beach," he says.

"Sorry. I didn't know."

"Read the signs."

The guard is typical—young, tan, ripe with muscular health, hair bleached to a white-sand blond. In comparison Jessica feels like a carcass washed ashore. Especially given her weariness, the journey from California, the breakdown in the desert, the resurfacing of her pursuers and her flight from them.

After the Claytons had dropped her in San Antonio, Jessica met a night-shift trucker at the McD by the motel where'd she'd taken a room. She'd gotten worried about staying the night—the call Mr. Clayton had taken kept replaying in her head. The trucker brought her and Skittles to New Orleans, where a trio of broke coeds, or so they claimed, let her hitch to Gainesville for gas money. Jessica risked a withdrawal from an ATM and that leg of her trip took two days while the women tanned on the beach in Panama City. After this she had less luck on the road; her inked arms attracted loners whose stares demanded more for a ride than she was willing to spend. The tattoos, no doubt, also discouraged regular folks from picking her up. She was closing in on her aunt's country—the wary Koran-burning Christian heart of Florida.

Traveling on foot, Jessica was more concerned about being detained than happy to see any police cruisers. Those that did track her must have discounted her ability to violate any criminal statutes with a dog in tow. Or maybe the authorities just didn't want to confront Skittles, who, like Jessica, was starting to look feral. On the eastern edge of Gainesville she came upon a campground amenable to pets.

After a brushing for Skittles, a shower for herself, and a night under a lean-to, a retired couple with an RV gave the young woman and her dog a lift to Daytona. They said goodbye at a gas stop near the speedway, and at a Dunkin' Donuts Jessica tied up Skittles in the shade. When Jessica returned with her coffee and a cup of water for Skittles, a lean, tough-looking woman was kneeling there stroking the dog.

"You from Oregon?" the woman asked.

"No."

"Kids with tats traveling with dogs remind me of Portland. Great city," said the woman.

Jessica didn't balk at being called a kid. She figured she must have lost years along with her weight. "I'm from California," Jessica told the woman. "The Inland Empire."

"Yeah," she said. "And where ya going?"

The woman, Nell, drove a pickup with a kennel in the bed. She was heading to Miami after her dog's evening races. That night, after Flying Pumpkin earned only participation fees, Jessica chipped in for gas, handing over her last twenty, and they were traveling. Two hours later, near Fort Pierce, Nell pulled in at a rest area and Jessica thought, *Uh-oh*. But all Nell wanted was sleep. The downside was her snoring. So Jessica kept company with Skittles and Pumpkin in the pickup bed.

Before dawn they were rolling again and soon Jessica's exit drew near. She mentioned a desire to see an ocean sunrise and Nell drove to the beach, where she wished Jessica and Skittles luck.

And now Jessica is back to where she started—this time facing an un-friendly Adonis.

"Cops see your dog out here you'll get a fine," says the lifeguard.

Jessica pushes herself up from the sand. "C'mon, Skittles," she says, and they start off.

"Your pack!" the guard calls, angry as if Jessica were purposely trying to trash his beach.

Jessica walks back to get her worldly belongings.

On the path to the road there's a shower tap. Jessica waters Skittles and checks to see if the guard is going to yell again. But he's already forgotten them. He's striding in the sand toward his little tower.

THE MULTISTORY BEIGE-AND-OCHRE buildings on this barrier island seem unchanged from when Jessica was last here, a dozen years ago. The structures were old then, dating from the sixties. It's hard to believe, after a decade of foul coastal storm seasons, that so much of the past remains unmolested.

On the road to the mainland drawbridge stands a newer struc-ture—low, slablike, windowless, a United Imperial Bank. There's a flag-pole planted there, too, but no American flag is flying from it yet. Too early. Gathering courage, Jessica locates the bank's cash machine and feels her heart thump as she thinks about her pursuers—Daugherty and that other younger, meaner agent. Pyle. Though it's not really them she fears. It's their bosses who can put her away. Maybe for good. There's no parole for souls imprisoned in psych wards. That her skinny, tattered spirit is so obviously wrecked gives them a perfect excuse to commit her, to lock away whatever secrets they fear she might reveal.

Looking into the ATM mirror, Jessica considers the hidden camera taking her picture. Some day such monitoring will be tied to a network that instantly sends ID and facial data to whatever authority might want it—much the way she once transmitted coordinates and imagery from circling drones to ground troops on missions.

But already she knows that she can't completely hide. Without friends like Newt and Shelly, she is going to have to surface a little. She dips her bank card.

As usual, Jessica doesn't know if it is good or bad news when out come fifteen twenties. Maybe her trackers don't really want her that desperately, not desperately enough to lock her account. Maybe they're not using un-limited resources to hunt her. Maybe she's *not* public enemy number one. Jessica decides to go with all these maybes.

Then, as if the future of ATM surveillance has already arrived, a po-lice cruiser pulls up. Jessica is stuffing the money in her knapsack when the officer approaches. He's not smiling. With his mirrored sunglasses he resembles an emotionless movie cyborg.

"Morning," he says to Jessica and passes on to the cash machine.

"Morning," Jessica says, and then, "C'mon, Skittles." They start walk-ing toward the drawbridge, a block away.

Coming over it, a pack of Harleys growl and fart. The riders acknowl-edge Jessica with whoops as if she's some kindred spirit, probably due to her tattoos. After the last bike passes, the drawbridge rises, stopping Jessica on the sidewalk. And the police cruiser pulls alongside her. They wait. As Jessica watches a sailboat motor by, she can feel the heat of the officer's lenses. Then the bridge lowers and the officer drives off.

HOMECOMING NOSTALGIA, OR something opposite—that human impulse to pick a scab—guides Jessica's steps over the sticky tarmac to her old neighborhood. It is less than a mile from the drawbridge but over twelve years back in time. When she comes to the sandstone build-ing where Joanne and she lived, her pulse quickens. This is not because Jessica fears that *she* will be there, sipping her gimlet and peering through the slats of a jalousie window. Joanne, or so wrote her berating aunt two summers ago, is still unrepentantly drinking. But she has long since de-parted Pompano, has been migrating between West Palm Beach and Port Saint Lucie—between her two Medicare-eligible boyfriends.

The news left Jessica colder than usual. For by then she had not spoken with Joanne in six years. And before that she could count her mother's combined visits and phone calls to her on fingers and toes. The piety of her aunt was partly to blame. She called Joanne a sinner, said it was her duty to enlist Jessica into the army of God. Thus, in the eyes of Jessica's legal guardian, the less often Joanne phoned Jessica or came to see her, the better. And so, trying to ignore the sisters' dispute, Jessica became numb toward the women in her family, which eventually rekindled her desire to know her father. Jessica was in the Air Force by then. No longer a child, her reality could not so easily be upended by family, or so she thought. She would be the one in charge now. That the relationship would be conducted through letters to a person who couldn't visit didn't hurt either.

Joanne's old building recedes, and so do Jessica's memories of her. What remains is Jessica's responsibility to Don: she's the one who started communicating with him. If she abandons him altogether, or even if she doesn't write to him soon, won't she be doing what her mother did to her?

"YOUR PUP LOOKS overheated," calls out a shirtless, big-bellied man in a straw hat. He is holding a watering hose over a hibiscus hedge and Skittles, tongue hanging, pulls toward him. As the man seems more comic than dodgy Jessica also steps off the tarmac and onto the healthy lawn.

Skittles laps at the water the man is running into his cupped palm. "You're a good girl, aren't you? Aren't you?" the man says to her.

In the meantime Jessica studies the property—a pink two-story apartment building. She counts maybe a half-dozen units and has already noted the FOR RENT sign in the yard.

"They allow pets here?" Jessica asks.

"We're pretty flexible, me and the wife. Got a furnished efficiency upstairs just vacated. Wife's cleaning it now. Care for a look?"

CHAPTER 41

LaGuardia, Richmond, Miami

"Is this a cremation urn, sir?" the screener asks Ethan.

"Yes."

"They're not allowed as carry-on, not if our scanner can't see into them."

"You mean . . . you want me to open it?"

"No, sir. That's against the rules, too. Just let me see the paperwork."

"The paperwork?"

"For transporting ashes." The screener is trying to do his job, but the line of bodies waiting for their scan or pat-down is growing.

"This is ridiculous," Ethan says.

"They're the rules."

"They don't make sense. It's not like this is filled with explosives."

"I understand, sir," the screener says calmly. "Would you step this way, please."

"Not if you don't give me back my urn."

The screener, who is shorter than Ethan but bulkier, someone who might have been a high school football tackle, considers his screenee's defiance. Ethan can see the man's eyes mirroring the algorithms of his thought process: *Should I use handcuffs or the taser? Nah. Neither. Bad PR.*

"Here," the screener says, giving back Zoe's urn to Ethan. "Now will you come this way?"

Ethan is led behind a partition with a few chairs. Left alone, but not having his ID or bag, he can't walk away. Twenty minutes later a uniformed official comes by with Ethan's things.

"Sorry for the delay. But you check out."

"You mean I'm not Al Qaeda on a mission?"

The man's relaxed attitude changes. "We never thought you were, sir. And I'd be careful about that kind of talk in an airport."

"I've missed my plane."

"We notified your airline that you would. This way, sir."

"Where are you taking me?"

The man doesn't say. He leads Ethan to an unmarked door. As if he's been sent back two squares in a board game, Ethan finds himself locked out of LaGuardia's postsecurity concourse.

AFTER A 3 a.m. bus transfer in Virginia, an old man with scarred hands sits down beside Ethan. The man keeps glancing at the urn in Ethan's lap. Eight hours before, when Ethan boarded the Greyhound upon missing the last Miami-bound Amtrak from Penn Station, he went to stow the urn in the overhead bin. But he couldn't. Coming out of a year of destructive behavior—filing fruitless lawsuits against his old company, mismanaging his finances, losing his condo—this clinging seems a comparatively benign whim.

"If you want, I'll hold it careful for you," says the old man an hour later. He's awakened by Ethan's struggle to leave his window seat while cradling the urn. "Take my word, you're gonna need both hands in the john. It's bouncy back there," the old man says.

"Thank you," Ethan says. His voice, unused since he bought his bus ticket, is a croak.

"Your mama?" the old man asks, respectfully taking the urn.

Ethan shakes his head.

"Not your wife?" the old man asks dolefully.

This time Ethan doesn't respond.

After the lavatory, when he's back in his seat with the urn, "Fiancée," he says to simplify things.

The old man nods then shuts his eyes.

"I'm taking her to her father," Ethan says.

The man opens his eyes. "Oh? That's hard. Real hard."

"Yeah . . . but . . . he never knew her."

"What? Never knew his own daughter?"

"And she never knew about him. Her grandparents kept it a secret."

"Well, isn't that something." The man closes his eyes again.

This makes it easier for Ethan to talk. "Now her dad's the only family she has left."

" 'Cept for you." Ethan's companion keeps his eyes shut.

"To be honest, she wasn't my fiancée."

"Terrible thing when a young person passes."

"But I have to do this for her."

"Hmm," says the man, a sleepy therapist.

"She was the one."

The old man begins to breathe deeply through his open mouth. Ethan turns away to the window and watches the shadows of swaying trees. After popping a Xanax, Ethan dozes through the storm.

SUNLIGHT PIERCES ETHAN'S pupils. The old man is gone. A metal bar in the seat back gnaws his vertebrae. Ethan skims the *Times* on his laptop then closes the machine. He takes more Xanax and lets the road unroll. A nuclear sunset inaugurates another night. In Orlando he swallows an Ambien and the twilight embraces him.

The next thing he knows he's being shaken.

"End of the line," the bus driver says.

"What? . . . What time is it?" It's dark out.

"One in the morning."

Ethan fumbles between his thighs for Zoe's canister and finds the brass eerily warm, as if there's something alive inside. But the heat is only from his own body. Reaching his free hand to the overhead rack he takes down his duffel. Clutching the bag and Zoe's urn, he steps down into the humid night.

"South Beach," he tells a cabbie.

CHAPTER 42

Seminole City

Dear Jessica,

I am glad beyond tears to read your words. Glad to know that you are okay and free. Glad to learn about your journey from California and hear of your adventures with the brokedown truck and your good dog. But it was dangerous of you to send your new address in a letter to a prisoner. Even if that prisoner was not me.

Dont get me wrong. I am not worried that Hector is going to rat us out. As my cellmate he has plenty of reasons to keep his mouth shut. The problem with you writing to me through him is that all mail to prisoners is looked at. You have taken a big chance.

But you knew this. Our writing each other was what started all your troubles.

Even before this last letter of yours I figured you must be on the run. So there is no need for you to apologize for your long silence. Why else would you have stopped writing to me unless you could not? Why else would you send me a present of music but not dare even a hello?

Well. I guess there could have been other reasons for you to skip writing. But I believed the worst. That somebody was after you. And not a week ago two FBI men paid me a visit and finally confirmed my bad thoughts.

If these men are why you left California I can tell you that you made a wise decision. This pair will do anything to grab you and I have stun gun marks and a split nose to prove it. They are why I cant risk giving you away by sending THIS letter. Not even under Hectors name. Not even though you expect me to write.

It eats my soul that you might think I have turned my back on you.

Yet what can I do but hide this letter away with all my other unsent and returned letters. Unless maybe Hector has some advice on the matter. He is a much smarter man than me and I trust him as much as you can another man in prison.

Be safe and stay free.

Your loving father,
Don

CHAPTER 43

Fort Lauderdale

"These are so you don't end up seeing stars the rest of the day," the electrologist says.

The wraparound sunglasses the technician offers Jessica are the functional kind favored by seniors. Their tint turns everything into shades of black and the tattoos on her arms become less visible, as if in anticipation of what she is having done.

"Wow!" the technician says. "Your phoenix here has a lot of ink."

"It's a sphinx," Jessica says to the woman, who is cleaning Jessica's shoulder with something cool and astringent.

"So the sphinx is a cover-up?"

"Uh-huh."

"What's underneath?"

"Is it important?"

"No, not really. Sorry," says the technician. "I guess that's why you had it covered up in the first place. So you could forget it. Or him."

"It used to be an eagle," Jessica says, hoping to close the matter.

"Oh," says the technician. "You had an ex in the service or something?"

"Or something," Jessica says.

"I hear ya," says the tech emphatically, commiserating with Jessica over the nonexistent military lover of Jessica that she's imagining.

At first the pulsing laser feels merely interesting, like a rubber band snapping her scapula really quickly. Then the sensation gets warmer and the heat congeals into a burning. The odor, of Jessica's own flesh roasting, is sickly sweet. She licks sweat from her upper lip.

The electrologist pauses her zapping. "Shall we keep going?"

"I'm fine."

"Holler if you're not."

The laser pulses are so rapid they sound like clacking plastic teeth. About an hour of Jessica's time passes, though it turns out to be only thirty minutes on the clock, before the plastic teeth go quiet.

"You did good," says the technician as she helps Jessica up from the table. With her lab coat, green-tinted goggles and cabled laser gun, the woman could be playing a nuclear physicist in an old sci-fi movie. "If you're up for it, I have time to do an arm today."

After twenty, forty and then sixty actual minutes pass, the plastic teeth have nibbled up and down Jessica's right biceps and forearm. She hears a final clackety-clack and then silence. "That does it for now," her tormentor says.

Jessica removes the protective glasses and studies the blasted arm. A crusty blister of dying skin covers the Maori spirals.

"It'll be seven more sessions or so to finish this one. The ink is deep," says the electrologist sympathetically. "We can do the next treatment after you heal. Eight weeks say."

"And what about this arm?" Jessica asks, offering up her uncooked limb, the one with the fantastic green and purple foliage. She has saved it for last.

"Maybe you should rest a day or two. This whole process will take about a year, so there's no hurry."

"I need to get it all started now," Jessica says.

It's not the anticipated pain that Jessica fears will change her mind but remorse: at betraying Miss Shelly, and even herself. Her tats are part of her. But the temptation to be anonymous and plain and safe pulls her on.

"Put on your glasses," says the electrologist, who lowers her own sci-fi goggles and then raises her laser. Swallowing, Jessica watches darkly as the device bites at Shelly's canvas.

CHAPTER 44

South Beach

"Jesus, you look like something Lucas Samaras smeared across a canvas," Alex says. Ethan has called him in Sevastopol and their video link has momentarily turned them into pixilated blurs. The strange tone in Alex's voice, though, is probably just microphone feedback—Ethan is sitting poolside and, nearby, tween girls are screaming and plunging into the chlorinated water like continuously reanimated virgin sacrifices.

"I'm in Miami," Ethan says, as if to excuse their crappy connection.

"Juliette said you've been acting strange, dude. She thinks you've lost it. You know, she put a lot of work getting you this opportunity with Sergei. You're blowing it man," Alex says. He sounds agitated.

Ethan figures he's just interrupted the artist at work, "Did you get the FedEx from her?" he asks.

Alex's response lags. "It came. Thanks."

"Okay. Good. Now all you have to do is sign the power of attorney and set up a joint account under our names at Sergei's bank. After that I can start moving your money. I checked the ruble this morning and it's trending favorably against the yen. So that's the direction we'll likely go. And then—"

"Hey," Alex says. "Let's stay on the subject. You're fucking up your future. You need to get up to Long Island right now. Sergei's starting to have doubts about you."

"But . . . I don't want to work on the island," Ethan says, not wanting to go into all his reasons.

Alex looks away from Ethan's screen . . . and then back at it. "You *need* to wake up."

Patiently, Ethan absorbs his friend's irritation. "Okay," he says.

"You *need* to get over this Zoe obsession. Come on! Don't ruin your life over her."

What's this? Tough love? Ethan thinks, but he keeps his surface calm. "I'm honoring her, Alex. Zoe and I could have built something together."

"No, man, that was never going to happen. Not with you and Zoe. And Eth, it wasn't just what she felt about you. It was you as well. And now you're dreaming about what never was, carrying her ashes around the country. *You* didn't invest that much in the chick when she was alive! Snap out of it!"

Snap out of it, Ethan thinks. *Snap out of it?* "You," Ethan says, actually, physically, seeing red, "snap the fuck out of it." He leans toward Alex's image and with both hands smashes down the laptop's lid.

"OMG! Did you see that?" one of the tweens shouts.

"*That* was totally awesome!" says another.

The young girls are smirking as though Ethan is more loser than lunatic, like he's one of those sad types their parents discuss over dinner— jobless Uncle Frank the pothead, or the neighbor whose wife ran off with the lawn man, or the crazy guy who totaled his two-thousand-dollar laptop by the hotel pool.

CHAPTER 45

Pompano Beach

"Sorry, sir. . . . Sorry for bothering you," Jessica says and hangs up on the babbling stranger. The readout on her prepaid phone, just bought at a Walgreens, is correct. The number she has dialed is, or was, for Shelly's room. It's been ten days since Jessica left Shelly, a lifetime for a terminal patient. Now Jessica takes a breath and rings the hospice's main line.

"Wait, I see what's wrong," the receptionist says over her clicking keyboard. "The patient went home last week."

Went home—is this hospice-speak for *died*? A moan comes out of Jessica.

"Everything okay back there?" asks the bus driver. Jessica's in the seat behind him and he brings her back to where she physically is. Riding home up to Pompano Beach. "You need a stop, just say."

"No, no," the receptionist says, bringing Jessica back to California. "Sorry. It's not that."

"I don't understand," says Jessica.

"She was *discharged* last week," the receptionist says. "Hold a sec. Here's someone who knows about it."

"Miss Jessie? Is that you? I heard you went away. I am so sorry if it was because of me. Those men came and—"

"Reggie," Jessica says, recognizing him finally. "Don't worry about any of that. Tell me about Miss Shelly?"

"She decided to live," Reggie says. "She went back on dialysis."

"Thank you. Thank you," Jessica tells him as if it was his doing. And then she's tapping Shelly's home number into the phone. But Jessica doesn't press dial. She closes the flip phone and gets off at her stop. For now, it's enough to know that Shelly's alive.

Kelso, her landlord as of four days ago, is as usual watering his yard. She thanks him for watching Skittles.

"*No problemo,*" Kelso says. "Dogs is good security. Hey, how'd you get burned?"

The salve on her lasered skin makes the blistering appear nastier than it is.

"Just getting some tattoos removed."

"*Some?*" Kelso asks, inspecting the breadth of her treatment.

"All of them," she corrects.

Jessica is supposed to avoid the sun and so she takes Skittles up to their efficiency instead of out for an afternoon walk. "Tonight, girl," Jessica promises. Having bought a *Sun Sentinel* for the want ads, she spreads the paper on the carpet and begins her job search. She's digging in. She won't be running away anymore.

CHAPTER 46

South Beach

It is the witching hour, 2 a.m., the time of night most murders occur. Outside Ethan's door a crowd in the hall plays musical chairs with their hotel rooms. He pulls a pillow over his head but can't escape the voices . . . until, finally, the revelers disperse. But he's goggle eyed—overrested from the depressive daytime nap he'd initiated with a dose of Ambien after his fight with Alex. So there will be no return to unconsciousness for him.

Ethan sits up and browses the internet on his phone. He learns that the driving time from South Beach to Seminole City Correctional is fifty-six minutes. He also learns that he does not meet the requirements for a prisoner visit since he hasn't sent in the advance paperwork.

But there are exceptions. And what is transporting cremains to an inmate if not an exception?

After he maps the location of a car rental, Ethan's phone goes dark, its battery dead. He's hoping his brain will shut down, too. But he starts thinking of Alex.

Ethan's anger toward his friend slackens. Clearly, Zoe *had been* searching for something she couldn't find in him. Clearly, he *had* failed to give her the attention she needed. He'd made her secondary to his job, and not even a close second. What an idiot he'd been. What a fucked-up idiot!

He ought to call Alex, ought to charge his phone. Maybe Alex is trying to reach him right now. But drugged and emotionally wiped, Ethan turns his head on his pillow and gazes at the outline of Zoe's urn. These are his last hours with her. Alex will have to wait.

CHAPTER 47

Pompano Beach

Having waitressed at a Cracker Barrel while in high school, Jessica knows how to memorize daily specials, roll up silverware inside paper napkins and balance multiple dinner plates on one arm. Jeans and tees aren't quite the best interview clothes, so on the bus to her interview Jessica stops at a JCPenney for slacks and a long-sleeve blouse—and to ask a cosmetician for help with eye shadow. They settle on a color called Eternal Sunshine. Changing into her new clothes in the store bathroom, Jessica smiles at the mirror.

"Pleased to meet you. I'm Jessica Aldridge," she practices. It's a good thing she can come out with her name because with her tattoos covered and her eye sockets high-beam bright, Jessica barely recognizes her reflection.

Down Airpark Road, Phantom Diner is a brick-and-clapboard building with a blue-tiled roof and quaint bay windows. It looks okay, and then Jessica is inside asking about the job.

"The boss isn't in yet," says the day hostess. "We're not a chain and we don't have medical," she adds discouragingly.

"That's fine," Jessica says, smiling as though she'd be happy to work here for free. And truthfully, any lack of probing corporate benefit paperwork is all right by her. In a quiet corner Jessica fills out the one-page application.

When she turns in the sheet the hostess, glancing it over, doesn't inquire about her yearlong employment blank but merely says, "So long." If this hard young woman has anything to say about it, Jessica will not be getting the job.

CHAPTER 48

Seminole City

Stubbornness with the guard at the prison gate gets Ethan into the warden's antechamber, a room as institutional as a principal's office. Likewise, a woman assailing an ancient keyboard attached to a boxy monitor incites further déjà vu. When her dot matrix printer begins to rattle out a sheet, Ethan is a sophomore again, in need of a hall pass. In this case his *pass* is the visitation request paperwork to see prisoner 82747L, Donald Alan Aldridge.

"That's all we can do till the warden gets back," the efficient woman says when Ethan turns in the completed form. "He shouldn't be ten minutes now. You're quite welcome to wait here, Mr. Winter."

"Thank you," says Ethan and settles onto a bench near the outer door. An overhead vent blows pleasantly cool air down his collar.

Forty minutes later, a tall man in a gray suit bursts in and hurries across the anteroom. "Hold my calls, Ann," he says without noticing Ethan. With a second bang the man disappears into the inner office.

"The *warden*," Ann whispers unnecessarily. Her newly creased brow confirms that her boss is in a bad mood. At a double ring she snatches up her handset.

"Yes, sir. I'll get him on the line right away." Ann signals for Ethan to be patient, then she dials a number. "Agent Daugherty," she says to her caller. "Warden Eli Wagner at Seminole City Correctional would like a word. Hold on, please."

Ethan is shivering now. The blowing air vent is chilling him and he gets out from under it. Standing, he can see that the line-busy indicator on Ann's phone is lit—Wagner's call. After a minute, Wagner is still talking and Ethan is still hovering. Ann looks up from her keyboard though her fingers keep typing. "It shouldn't be long. He does know you're out here. You can have a seat."

Ethan gives Ann a resigned smile while thinking of his ex-supervisor, Dwayne Hoke. One of Dwayne's power plays was to make his subordinates wait. "I'll just stand a while. Unless you mind."

"Suit yourself," Ann says, assailing her keyboard. She must type 120 words per minute, like a computer coder on amphetamines.

Ethan puts down Zoe's cremation urn and leans left and right to loosen his spine. His vertebrae crack and he stays standing to burn off his anxiety. By the time the light blinks out on Ann's phone, his back is stiffening again. Wagner and whoever Daugherty is have had a lengthy talk—most likely, Ethan thinks irritably, so Wagner could demonstrate how irrelevant Ethan's time was compared to someone of importance.

Ann's intercom buzzes.

"Yes, sir," Ann tells the handset, her manner militarily precise. Upon hanging up she offers Ethan an apologetic expression. "Warden Wagner says he can't authorize an inmate visit on an hour's notice. You'll have to come back tomorrow."

"*Tomorrow?*"

Ann's face tightens. "Mr. Winter, the rules say you need to apply for a prisoner visit a month in advance."

"The problem is"—Ethan leans over her desk—"I'm here about a death in the inmate's family that took place *three* weeks ago. So how could I have applied for a visit *four* weeks ago?" While Ann absorbs Ethan's logic he realizes that he's being a Hoke, an unnecessarily aggressive asshole.

"You know," Ann says, "the warden is already giving you VIP treatment. Usually special visits like yours have to take place on visiting days—on a Saturday or Sunday. The warden is allowing you to come on a Friday."

"All right," Ethan says, capitulating to her reasonableness. "I'll be back tomorrow."

"Nine on the dot," Ann says. Then she studies the ash urn that Ethan has placed on the corner of her desk. "That's not for Donald Aldridge, is it?"

"Is that a problem?"

"The only items you're allowed to give prisoners are food from our vending machines or nonpicture books. You know, like Bibles."

"Oh," Ethan says. "But—"

"No, sir. There's no way you can leave behind anything like that." Ann begins to square the papers on her desk. "And about tomorrow," she says, looking uncomfortable. "We have your New York address, but the warden wants to know where you're staying in Florida. I mean, you know, just in case."

"In case? Of what?"

"In case of ... gosh, I don't know. I mean, the warden ... he's in charge of three hundred staff and sixteen hundred prisoners. That's a lot of responsibility."

Ann would make a lousy poker player. "I still don't understand," Ethan says.

"Warden Wagner," she says, eyes averted, "has his ways is all."

"I guess I'll find out what they are tomorrow." Ethan gives her his hotel and goes to the door.

"Mr. Winter!" Ann says.

Turning back to Ann's desk Ethan sees that, somehow, he's forgotten Zoe's urn.

CHAPTER 49

Pompano Beach

By midafternoon Jessica has been called back to Phantom Diner for an interview with the boss. One eyed, crop haired, and ramrod straight, Wilton Sheeler admits to having piloted Phantom jets in Vietnam, hence the name of his restaurant. Then he asks Jessica what it's like to drive a bird remotely—irrelevant though it was, she had included her drone flight experience on the job application.

"Sometimes you feel like you're right up there," Jessica answers. "But not usually. Mostly you're sitting in a chilly trailer watching nothing happen on the monitors."

"Even so," Sheeler says, his good eye squinted, "don't you think waiting tables is going to be too much of a come down for you, Sergeant?"

"More likely it'll be a comeback," Jessica says.

Sheeler seems sympathetic. "I'm not even going to ask you what you've been doing the past year. We're short handed. How about can you start tomorrow night?"

"I can, sir," Jessica says, just managing to restrain a salute.

On the bus ride home, she finally reaches Miss Shelly.

"Seems like the reaper works both ways," Shelly says. "When your time is up he's going to take you out no matter what. But try to hurry him along before then and you'll just grow old waiting. What the hell. I'm even going to put myself back on the kidney wait list. Might as well try to live all I can."

"Me, too," Jessica says.

"You have a home here if you ever come back."

"Thanks. Thanks for everything you gave me."

"You kidding me? More like thank you for all you gave us. Newt, he really loved you."

"Oh, Shelly . . . ," Jessica says, wondering if Newt might have tried harder to live if he knew that Shelly would end up alone. That Jessica wouldn't be there for her.

"I'm still here," Shelly says into Jessica's long pause.

"I'm glad you are."

CHAPTER 50

South Beach

After returning from Seminole City and settling Zoe by the window in his hotel room so that she could look out over Collins Avenue, Ethan fully reconnects with his phone.

"Dude. Let's talk," reads his latest email alert. It's from Alex.

Alex's *dude* takes him back to their college days. The term was anachronistic even then, so, of course, Alex used it ironically. These days, though, Alex employs his *dudes* mostly when he wishes to remind Ethan of their long friendship.

Abandoning Zoe by her window, Ethan finds his way to a beachside restaurant. The hostess seats him under an umbrella on the sidewalk, and after the waiter takes his order, Ethan looks at his email. Saving but not reading Alex's messages, he begins deleting the dating, diet, and Cialis spam when he stops at a curious subject line—"Yo! Homie!" It's John Guan.

His food arrives and Ethan puts his phone face up on the table. He takes a bite of the burger, and then uses a clean pinky to tap open the email.

Buddy,

Sergei's putting on the pressure. Wants you to sign ASAP. Told me to get you hard. So let me tell you what we just got in. Fucking quantum mainframes. Bitches come out of Canada. I don't know if these boxes are really doing quantum whatever at the atomic level, but they scream like thousand-dollar whores. Combined, we are talking a hypothetical twenty petaflops at six gig, you hear. Give me a break. Get your ass out here and let's have some fun.

Smell ya later,
The Guanman

Ethan deletes the message and scrolls to Alex's email. Alex is sorry for talking shit. He respects Ethan more than anyone he knows. He feels guilty about not coming home for the funeral. He says that Ethan should take Sergei's job offer. That Sergei is okay. Except that he might have slept with Juliette. Though this was before he and Juliette met. He thinks. He doesn't know. "Skype me, dude," he closes. "Anytime, day or night."

Alex's operatic, egocentric life is too much for Ethan right now. There are things to finish here in Florida before he can refocus on his old life. Or does he mean his new life? Will it be Sagaponack after all? Ethan taps Reply and thumbs an excuse. "Dude, trashed my laptop. Back in city soon. Talk then."

Ethan takes another bite of his burger and watches a cruise ship depart from the Port of Miami. He thinks of Walter and Elizabeth Leston traveling the world one last time on such a vessel. And this brings him back to Zoe's father, a convicted murderer, Don Aldridge stuck in a cell and going nowhere. What good can it do for Ethan to visit such a man?

CHAPTER 51

Pompano Beach

"Don't you look nice," Kelso says as Jessica walks up. Kelso is giving his yard its usual late-afternoon watering.

"Job interview," Jessica explains.

"Did you get it?"

"I did."

"Congrats," Kelso says. Then he takes something from his back pocket. An unopened letter. "This just came. It's got your apartment number. Ain't anyone you know, is it?"

The handwriting on the envelope is unfamiliar, almost a printed calligraphy. It *does* contain her apartment number. But it's addressed to an Arturo Ramirez in care of Kathleen Baker. Jessica doesn't know an Arturo Ramirez; Kathleen Baker, however, is her aunt in Ocala. The return address says Hector Ramirez, Seminole City Correctional Institution.

The letter is what Jessica has been waiting for. She had sent a "Wish You Were Here" postcard to her father's cellmate, writing on it only "Don't worry" and a nameless return address, *her* current address. Hector, the professor, had figured it out, or shown it to Don, who recognized her handwriting. A line of secret communication to her father is open.

"It's mine," Jessica admits.

Kelso gives her a look. "You know, I never did a tenant screening to make sure you were who you said you were. You're not going to disappoint me, Miss Aldridge? Or is it Miss Baker?"

Jessica holds Kelso's gaze. She is not a good liar, but the fib she invents is close to the truth. "Baker is my aunt's name. My dad isn't supposed to write to me from prison so we send letters through his cellmate and disguise things."

"Uh-huh," Kelso says a little skeptically. "And what did your dad do?"

Jessica doesn't speak for a few seconds. "He's jailed for murder."

That the offense is extreme seems to relax Kelso's suspicions, as if a liar would have downgraded the crime to a lesser felony. "Shame about that."

"Yes. He's all I have now."

"What about your aunt?"

"She's too religious for me," Jessica says, easing herself toward the staircase to her efficiency.

"I hear you on that," Kelso says. "Your aunt and my wife's family, both."

"Yeah," says Jessica, pausing on the stairs as though she's not trying to escape further interrogation. Then she starts climbing again. "Sorry, Skittles must be dying for a walk by now."

When she reaches her landing, Kelso calls up. "That reminds me, there's one more thing I was thinking."

"Oh?" Jessica says. Putting her key into the door lock, she is just able to stop herself from rushing inside to peace.

Kelso, large bellied in his cabana shirt, is smiling up at her. "Oh, it's just about Skittles. Why don't you leave her with me when you go to work?"

"I'll be doing a night shift."

"That's no problem. Me and the wife can use the company."

Closing the door behind her, Jessica is too tense to read the letter right away. She peeks from a window to make sure that Kelso is no longer outside and then escapes with Skittles for a walk. They go all the way to the public pier, the old fishing pier she liked visiting as a girl. But it's a dollar for sightseers now and no pets are allowed. So she and Skittles stick to the sidewalk, which is separated from the beach by a coral-embedded knee wall and a barrier of sea grape. When the trees' twisted trunks thin and Jessica can see down to the surf, she steps over the wall and has Skittles jump it, too. Settling themselves on the sand, the dog props her head on her paws and Jessica leans back against the wall. In the late-afternoon light, breakers shimmer a hundred feet offshore and Jessica watches the ocean. Then she takes out Hector's letter and reads.

Dear Nephew,

Your father tells me that you have a new love in your life and no longer stay at home. Thus I take it upon myself to write directly to your new abode in care of your girlfriend. Hello, Miss Kathleen Baker. I hope you do not mind my contacting my nephew through you. I'm afraid that you are the only trustworthy means of reaching him that I can think of, if you take my meaning.

Nephew, we have much to discuss. Yet I feel as though I can best sum up my thoughts by recounting a tragic event in the life of another. A man whom I shall refer to as don Malagueña—thus to honor a gift of music given to him by his deeply loved daughter, a child for whom his heart, like King Lear's, aches, so many tribulations has he caused her.

One moment, please. This don Malagueña, standing here by my shoulder, is complaining that this letter sounds convoluted. Gobbledygook is what he calls my sentences!—a criticism heard by many professors. But the don should know that I cannot communicate in a mode less baroque. If I did, then some unwanted eye, that panoptic reviewer of our prison missives perhaps, might suspect these words to be not my own. For the sake of a necessary obfuscation, please bear with the lingo.

As I was saying, Nephew of mine, before my amigo don Malagueña interrupted, he has experienced much upheaval of late. Principally, he has received a visit from an unexpected pair, a Mutt and Jeff wearing serious black suits and badges, who roughly interviewed the don in connection with an absent person—the very daughter for whom he pines.

Thus unfolds the tragedy, Nephew. The tragedy of an enforced separation. For despite our Lear's despair, despite "his wish to pray, and sing, and tell old tales, and laugh at gilded butterflies with his lost Cordelia," despite all this, if our don Malagueña could utter direct words to his child, he would ask her to harden her will. He would advise her against any closer approach. He would warn that she cannot visit him without consequence. He would counsel a retreat into the shadows. He would assert a desire that she remain aloof from the cavaliers known here as Mutt and Jeff, dangerous men who would take her from her life to destinations unknown, to a cell perhaps akin to his own. Such a tragedy, the don declares, would be far more lethal to his spirits than even the miserable lacuna of his Cordelia's absence.

In brief, "follow him not, stay yourself" are the sad words he would paraphrase to her.

Now, in humble fashion, dear Nephew, I end my letter. I trust that there is in don Malagueña's circumstance a lesson for you. What this may be, I cannot judge. I am merely a presenter of particulars. I leave their unraveling to others. And so, from our cell, we send out a wish for your well-being—the don and I.

Your adopted uncle,
Hector Cabrera Domingo Ramirez

CHAPTER 52

Seminole City

"The rules are simple," Ann says. "Though this is a special visit, you're to have no direct contact with the inmate. You'll be talking through a glass barrier on a phone. Keep in mind that everything you say will be monitored, so no jokes about saws in cakes or anything."

It is 9 a.m. on this Friday morning. Ethan Winter has returned to Seminole City Correctional despite a brief reconsideration yesterday. If he doesn't owe it to himself, he owes it to Zoe to finish what he's started here—whatever this may be.

"If you've no questions, we'll be on our way," Ann says.

"No questions," Ethan says.

Ann picks up her phone and presses one of its function buttons. "I'm taking Mr. Winter over now, Warden." Ann listens for a second and then hangs up.

"I'm really getting the VIP treatment," Ethan says.

Ann gets up from her desk but is not looking at him when she replies. "We try to be sensitive when an inmate's suffered a death in the family." Then she leads Ethan into the corridor.

Watching her slightly ahead of him, Ethan fixates on the woman's rust-colored hair—he can smell its fresh dye. Other random details imprint on his senses. A dent in the exterior exit door. The swelter of the outside heat. The raucous buzz of cicadas. They follow a concrete sidewalk and go completely around the building until they reach a door marked VISITATION CENTER. There must be a direct route through the building, Ethan notes, and why they didn't take it seems strange—maybe this has to do with the inscrutable methods of Warden Wagner. Ann leads him into a steamy entry hall that smells of sour laundry.

"Hi, Todd," Ann says to the sweating, cannonball-shaped guard who's intercepted them.

"Ma'am," Todd replies. Then he turns to Ethan. "Assume the position," he says in a bored voice.

"Pardon?" Ethan says.

"Pat-downs are standard procedure," Ann says. "Just like at the airport."

Ethan spreads his feet modestly and puts out his arms. The guard frisks his upper torso then goes down on one knee and slides his hands up and down a pants leg, which makes Ethan feel like he's crossing a divide. What's next—a strip search, a delousing shower, incarceration in a cell? The thought of being stuck in here makes his bladder go weak and he must count out the seconds until the guard is done with his other leg. Fortunately there's a men's room a step away.

"Okay," says Todd. As the guard backs off, he eyes Ethan critically.

"Excuse me," says Ethan and steps toward the lavatory.

"Hold up, pal," says the guard.

But Ethan is already pushing into the restroom . . . where a linebacker-size man in a black suit blocks his rush to the urinal. The man's small eyes pretend not to see Ethan as they maneuver around each other. *Oh, hello,* Ethan is about to say, thinking he might have seen him before—wait, was it last night in the hotel lobby? But the man is out the door.

"Sorry," Ethan tells Ann upon exiting the bathroom. "It was an emergency."

"Inside this institution," Ann interrupts, not happy at all, "you will need to pay attention to the rules. When somebody orders you to halt, *you* halt."

"Oh. Okay," Ethan says.

"Let's go."

Ann brings Ethan into what could be a college seminar room set up with tables and chairs. There's even a blackboard, though Ethan imagines that it's for announcements not lessons. The only classroom anomaly is the steel mesh shielding the windows on the *inside.*

"Our waiting area," Ann explains. "Have a seat. The PA will announce when Don Aldridge is brought up."

"Thanks," Ethan tells her.

"Thank the warden. Don wasn't going to take your visit, but the warden convinced him."

This strikes Ethan. "Why would the warden do that?"

Ann frowns like Ethan's examining the teeth of a gift horse.

"I know, he has his ways," says Ethan.

Ann's expression softens. She considers one of the meshed windows. "Just don't let Don get you involved in anything," she whispers. "Prisoners can do that." In an even quieter voice she adds, "And mind what I said about your conversation being monitored."

"Sure," Ethan says. Now he's feeling even more anxious about meeting Zoe's father. What, if he ever knew, did he hope to accomplish by coming here? Ah, yes. Closure. Or was it something more. *Transcendence?* Whatever it is seems beyond quantification.

Ann touches Ethan's arm. "No ashes today?"

"Pardon?"

"You didn't bring the urn."

"There didn't seem to be any point."

"You might could have shown it to Don through the glass. Maybe that would have helped."

CHAPTER 53

Pompano Beach

"Down!" Jessica shouts and yanks Skittles' leash, too hard. The dog yelps.

Turning from the cash machine, Jessica sees Skittles topple backward. She sees, above the dog on a palm trunk, a lizard with an orange wattle— Skittles' new obsession. She had only been treeing it.

"Crap," Jessica says and kneels to smooth her fur. "Sorry, girl."

But Skittles won't look at her. Skittles is a rescue dog with an unknown history of traumas and Jessica has never been mean to her before.

Jessica returns to the cash machine. She needs to calm herself but can't. She's been careless: this is her seventh withdrawal from her account in as many days. At least she's used multiple ATMs. Folding the bills into her jeans she scans the street, not for pickpockets but for the two men Hector Ramirez warned her about. Any moment Mutt and Jeff might cruise up behind her in their black SUV. If the agents went so far as to interrogate Don in prison, then they'll surely be tracing her bank activity, which may be why they haven't locked her account yet. To them, she *is* public enemy number one and they'll be mapping her cash stops—standard procedure for tracking terrorists, Jessica remembers from drone school. Investigators follow the money like a bread-crumb trail.

A few blocks of fast walking calms Jessica a little, and brings her to their next destination—a Winn-Dixie, where Jessica leashes Skittles to a bumper post near the automatic doors. "Stay," she tells Skittles, who looks up at her as though punished.

Inside the store Jessica cruises the aisles for generic Wheaties and Alpo. But she's distracted. Since deciphering Hector's letter, she's been stumbling toward a realization. It's that Daugherty and Pyle are on a case that has grown bigger than just trying to return a shaky ex–drone driver to the security of a VA hospital. A cross-country FBI chase means she *is* on someone's most-wanted list. And she can begin to guess why—public approval is the toughest part of maintaining the war on terror. When the news came out that al-Yarisi was alive, Jessica became a bigger loose end than ever—a potential whistleblower.

And, in truth, Jessica is tempted to talk to someone again about the strike, about the young women she killed, the ghosts of her dreams— the collateral damage as everyone else would call them if their deaths were disclosed. Yet to have told her father in prison is one thing, but to be the source of a report on *Sixty Minutes* or in the *New York Times*—Jessica doesn't think so. She has, despite everything, her loyalties still: to the Air Force, to Voigt, to the ideal of what she thought she'd become when she enlisted—a person keeping the world safe. Even if she had been mistaken, she can't fight back in that way. The only ears that will ever hear this story belong to Skittles.

In the freezer aisle Jessica examines a quart of Ben & Jerry's ice cream, but it costs too much. She needs to be frugal. She needs to make no new ATM blips on Daugherty and Pyle's radar. Maybe she'll be able to fly under it by stretching out her waitressing tips. Maybe her new boss will let her cash her paychecks at the restaurant and she can avoid the banks.

Outside the store, blinking in the day's glare, she goes to where she tied up Skittles and drops her bags. Jessica is imagining how, jumping for a lizard, the dog unhooked herself. "Hell," Jessica tells the parking lot as she scans it for her loose companion. "Skittles!" she shouts. "Here, girl!"

Her stomach becomes a knot. She runs between the parked cars, looking beneath them with her stomach pressing the burning pavement, hoping to spot Skittles' legs skittering past. But nothing. Jessica gets up and, brushing herself, slowly turns around. "Skittles!" she calls in a commanding tone. A white SUV pulls up alongside her.

"You aren't looking for the dog that was tied up out front?" the woman asks. "I saw some boys teasing her. But they're gone. *Teenagers*," she says sympathetically and drives on.

There's a commotion on Route 1, the six-lane highway next to the Winn-Dixie, and Jessica finds herself sprinting through the parking lot.

A car almost hits her as she crosses to the blocked left lane, where a man is dragging something golden onto the landscaped median. Jessica pushes the man hard and he trips backward onto the grass.

"What the hell are you doing!" he yells.

Jessica kneels beside Skittles. The dog's eyes are open and she doesn't seem to have a scratch. Jessica smoothes her fur but feels only a stillness.

"I was doing the speed limit," the man says. "Your damn dog ran right out in front of me."

Jessica's eyes are level with his vehicle's dented plastic bumper.

"She didn't suffer. She was already dead when I tried to move her."

Jessica is breathing so quickly she sees stars. "No. You *can't* be dead," Jessica says. Or has she shouted?

CHAPTER 54

Seminole City

Finally the PA crackles out an announcement. It's in Sufi or Mandarin or some indecipherable version of English, but because Ethan is the only visitor in the waiting area, he can guess at what's been said. "Donald Alan Aldridge up" maybe.

It's been forty minutes since Ann deposited him here and sitting on a flat-bottomed chair has deadened his legs. He stands and shuffles his prickling feet toward the check-in desk. Behind it, Todd puts down a paperback of Grisham's *A Time to Kill* and reviews some papers on a clipboard.

"Ethan Winter?" he asks, and Ethan nods. "ID," he says, as though Ethan might have changed persona since his frisking. Ethan digs out his driver's license. After barely a glance, Todd flicks his chin at a corridor. "Booth six," he says.

Ethan's feet move sluggishly but soon he finds that what he's entered is not a corridor. It's a room, narrow and deep, that contains on one of its long flanks a row of adjoining booths. These, he observes as he walks by the first, abut windows that look into a parallel universe. What comes to his mind are the glassed-in exhibits of a zoo house—an inhuman comparison that sickens him slightly. Lowering his eyes Ethan counts his way past the carrels until, at the sixth, he finds himself staring at a one-legged stool bolted there to the floor. Then Ethan lifts his gaze.

The first impression Don Aldridge gives Ethan comes from his wrestler's body, from the big arms folded atop the belly of his collarless prison shirt. Uneasily Ethan's gaze rises to the man's wide, textured face, his crooked nose, his eyes' broken blood vessels. His presence, even separated as they are, makes Ethan feel insubstantial—an impression not helped by

Ethan's reflection in the partition glass. It is ghostly, gangly, thin necked. A nothing in a logoed polo shirt.

"Mr. Aldridge?" Ethan says, not sure he has the right man, for he sees nothing of Zoe in the prisoner. "I hope you don't mind me coming?" he says, very quietly.

Aldridge gestures for his visitor to pick up the phone. But Ethan's situational incompetence has emptied his brain. He is wordless.

"So, you knew my little Zozo," Aldridge eventually says.

Ethan nods, surprised that Aldridge has heard why he has come. But then he recalls that Aldridge had at first refused his visit. The warden must have convinced the prisoner by mentioning what it would be about. Ethan considers for a moment why such an effort was put into making this meeting happen. Is it supposed to have a rehabilitative influence? In any event, Ethan is relieved of the need to explain himself.

"Zoe and I were close," Ethan says.

Aldridge, narrowing his eyes, becomes a TV father giving his daughter's date the once-over. But his institutional shirt, his slicked-back hair, his unevenly shaven cheeks quickly destroy the impression. Aldridge is the kind of man Ethan would be more likely to observe panhandling around Zuccotti Park. "Weren't you her fiancé?" Aldridge asks, pronouncing *fiancé*'s last syllable as *see*.

Ethan could simply answer with a yes. And he would, if not for Zoe's invisible presence. "No. We just lived together awhile."

Aldridge nods. "That's good. I'm glad she had someone."

Ethan would like to be equally consoling but the void of Zoe's immeasurable absence reopens. If he's come here to regain a sense of being with Zoe by being with her father, it is not working.

Aldridge takes up the slack. "The last time I saw Zo she wasn't five months old. So of course she don't remember me."

For a heartbeat Aldridge's relaxed grammar brings Zoe back to Ethan. He must force himself to remember that she is not in the present tense. "She knew about you toward the end," he says, imagining that Aldridge might find it comforting to know that he was not an absolute unknown.

"She knew her father was a con? I'd have liked her to imagine me something better."

"No, I only meant that she found out recently . . ." And here come the complications. "She found out only last year that her grandparents weren't her biological parents. That they adopted her. So she knew she had a father somewhere. That's all I meant."

Aldridge, holding the handset in the crook of his beefy neck, leans his forearms on the counter before him. His canted face comes closer to the glass separating them. "What do you mean 'found out recent'? You telling me Leston never spoke to her about her real parents? About me and Suzie?"

It is Ethan's arrogance to forget that people who might never have heard of algorithms can use them to make leaps of reasoning. Now he must explain what Aldridge has deduced. "Just before he died, Dr. Leston gave me documents and newspaper clippings that told some of the story."

"Uh-huh," says Aldridge, measuring Ethan with a squint. "Kind of sounds like you were scheming with old Leston behind Zoe's back."

Ethan tries to explain himself. "Zoe and I were living apart by then."

"Wait. Now let me get this right. You had broke up with Zozo, and Doc Leston *still* gave you these secret papers. You really were his bitch, weren't you?" Aldridge's tone is more descriptive than insulting.

"*No,*" Ethan says. "I just don't think he had anyone else to give them to. I guess he expected me to help Zoe through all the stuff she might learn about."

"Yeah," says Aldridge. "Doc was always trying to keep me out of the picture. Did it to his dying day, did he? So how'd the old bastard kick anyway?"

"Cancer," Ethan says. But he worries that Aldridge might catch him being evasive again. "He had cancer but opted out."

"Opted out? You mean, like, he ate a bullet?"

"He took pills."

"Right," Aldridge says. "And his old lady? She still breathing?"

"Dementia," Ethan says, considering how much truth to reveal.

"Too bad. Met her a couple of times. I don't think she hated me. Bottom line on her was she always followed her husband. Except about getting Suzie an abortion."

"He gave his wife the same pills he took."

Aldridge doesn't look surprised. "He did that kind of crap. Make life and death decisions for everyone. It's probably why I'm in here now. If he'd of let me be with Suzie and Zozo that might have kept me straight."

Ethan can't imagine that Aldridge believes this to be anything more than a comforting myth. But how many of those would Ethan create if he were locked up? How many has he already created . . . about himself and Zoe?

"I have your daughter's ashes," Ethan says, coming to the crux of why he is here. "What would you like me to do with them?"

Aldridge doesn't give the matter any thought. His eyebrows knit into a horizontal line. "That's up to you, Winter. I didn't know her. And you're a decent guy, right?"

Ethan shrugs.

"Well, you're not a drug dealer or murderer, are you?"

"I work in banking," Ethan says.

"That's almost as bad," Aldridge says, and Ethan can't tell if he's joking. "I'll bet that's what must have impressed old Doc Leston."

"I suppose."

"What did he expect . . . that after he suicided himself you would take care of his little girl?"

"Maybe," Ethan says.

"So what went wrong? I heard how Zozo died. Drowned in a bathtub. Well, I guarantee nobody drowns by accident in a tub unless they're high. And nobody gets that high in a bathtub unless they're trying to drown."

"I don't know," Ethan says. Aldridge is arriving at a conclusion Ethan has already made: he wasn't there for Zoe when she needed him the most.

"Want to know how Zozo's mother died?" Aldridge asks, almost barks. His face is reddening like he's working up a rage.

"Car crash," Ethan answers tersely, trying to put some distance between himself and Aldridge's emotions.

"Ain't half the story." Aldridge looks away. When he faces Ethan again his eyes are bleary, not enraged but damp. "Maybe we got more in common than you think. But I can't talk anymore now."

"All right."

Aldridge stands but doesn't yet hang up his phone. "I'm glad you came," he says, and his lips tick to form both a smile and a frown. The familiarity of the expression troubles Ethan. He is seeing, finally, a little of Zoe in her dad. "You have her mouth," he says. "Zo's."

"Think so?" Don Aldridge's, *Zoe's*, grin deepens.

"When she was upset, she smiled like you do."

"*Christ.*" Aldridge exhales like he's been stomach punched. "Winter, you got to do something for me. Come see me again. I got stuff to tell you. But not now," he says, hanging up the phone.

CHAPTER 55

Seminole City

Dear Jessica,

Was it wrong for Hector to write you? Did you even understand the letter we sent? I hardly did because as you can guess this Hector is smart but a character. In fact it was his idea for me to reply to your letter the cockeyed way we did. I figured it low risk since Hector dont take chances. And neither will I anymore. Not when it comes to your freedom. So from here on I will be writing you only through unsent letters like this one. At least I get to write my OWN words.

If you could not figure out Hectors lingo then let me tell you about the feds who came asking where you were. A lot of good it did them. And me. Like I said in my last unsent letter I got my battery charged from it with a stun gun is all. Now those boys want a do-over. Hector says this is good news since it means you are still free. He also told me that getting zapped is torture and a legit excuse to pass up on their invite.

The feds have not been my only callers. Just now a man called Winter came. He is all right except that he has stirred up memories. What I must tell you Jessica is that you had a half sister. I only knew her as a baby. As Zozo. After her mother died and her grandparents adopted her I never got to see her again. And now this Ethan Winter filled me in that Zozo grew up knowing nothing about her blood parents.

Well. The grandfolks keeping quiet about me I get. Denying your granddaughter knowledge of her true mother I dont. You can imagine what kind of household your sister grew up in. But who am I to talk? Anyway two weeks ago a lady detective from New York called to say that Zo died and that except for a confused aunt I am her last living relative. But what could I have done about that in here?

Winter took care of the funeral. Though he would not last a day behind bars he is a man who I think knows how to operate on the outside. If he ever comes back to see me I might tell him about you. Maybe he can help.

Stay safe child and forgive me for keeping your sister a secret.

Your loving father,
Don

CHAPTER 56

Pompano Beach

Jessica is leaving for work when Kelso, watering his hibiscus, intercepts her. "Me and your pup have a date tonight?"

It takes her a second to recall her landlord's offer to sit Skittles. "No," Jessica says soundlessly.

"Pardon?" Kelso says. "Are you all right?"

"I have to go," Jessica says and hurries off.

Hitching a ride on Federal Highway she makes up some time, but she still arrives at the diner a half hour late for her training shift. She should have called.

"Didn't think you were going to show," says the night manager. His eyes are icy and unwavering.

"It won't happen again, sir," Jessica says, not lowering her gaze from his.

"Next time will be the last," the man says casually. "Now let's see what you can do."

The man takes Jessica to her instructor, Beth, a woman in her forties who smells of menthol gum. Beth tells her the names of the cook and busboy and has her write her own on a badge that Jessica pins to her blouse. She then tags along after Beth like a little sister, but because the job is not flight mechanics Jessica quickly masters the register and credit card machines, and, by the time the early-bird diners arrive, she's waiting tables solo . . . and feeling a numb déjà vu. It's as if she'd never left Florida or done any but this kind of work. It's as if her five-year escape into the Air Force was a dream.

The night crawls forward and every so often Jessica reawakens to the sting of her new reality. Although she feels hollow inside, she tries to smile at the customers. But the tipping remains miserable. By her nine-thirty break she's collected only enough to pay for one of the early-bird specials.

A half hour later the night manager takes Jessica aside. "Your smirk is giving me indigestion. The customers, too. There's a Denny's down the road. People can as easily eat there."

"I'm not smirking," Jessica says. In fact, the night manager is the one with the smirk.

"The boss will shorten the night shift if we don't make our numbers. That what you want? Or maybe you think you're too good for this job?"

"No."

"I'm going to keep my eye on you."

Midnight, closing time, arrives. After wiping down the tables Jessica stops in the washroom to study herself in the gray light. Her face appears to her drawn, ratlike. Has she lost even more weight? She brushes at her bangs and unlooses her hair, which she had gathered into a tortoiseshell claw. She tries to smile at the streaked mirror, but the mirror grimaces back. Here is someone who has let down her family, her country, everything and everyone who relied on her. Even strangers. Jessica thinks of those two girls in burkas, their momentary images ever present to her.

"You aren't a person," she tells the reflection. "You're nothing."

CHAPTER 57

South Beach, Seminole City, Pompano Beach

Just before nine, when the car rental around the corner opens, Ethan goes downstairs to check out of his room.

"Sorry," the desk agent says, returning his rejected MasterCard. He gives her a Visa.

"Great," she replies, too brightly.

Great, Ethan's brain echoes—not in the agent's peppy voice but in his father's ironic one. A decade ago, when Ethan had told him that he was switching majors at Columbia, Robert Winter had commented, "For God's sake, go seek your fortune in Silicon Valley. Do anything with your ability but banking." His father was worried then about Ethan's moral insolvency, not his financial bankruptcy. Yet now Ethan is near to achieving both.

He has no one but himself to blame. A happy childhood and successful siblings further incriminate him—a brother working as a civil engineer, a brilliant sister who's writing a textbook on non-Euclidean geometry. That his father teaches physics and astronomy at Rutgers and his mother raises money for the arts means that, except for Ethan, his family uses their facility with numbers to good purpose.

But just wait, Ethan had thought back then, as a callow student, after his mother had called him out for choosing a "shell game" profession. *Wait, Mom. Wait five or six years and I will endow your museum with a wing.*

"Your receipt," the desk agent says. He passes through the hotel's fern-filled lobby.

Around the block, the rent-a-car will accept his credit-challenged Visa if he downgrades to a Hyundai and insures it against flood, famine, and theft. Too bad he's lost his Zipcar membership. He'd always heard that the poor pay more, but experiencing it is new.

Hunched behind the wheel of his Korean subcompact, Ethan pulls onto Collins Avenue and a Ferrari dodges his fender. Driving west, attempting to summit the bridge leaving South Beach, he stomps the gas and the little car groans. As he accelerates on the downhill, a Lexus hybrid silently zips past.

TODAY AT SEMINOLE City Correctional the guest lot is all but full. It is Saturday, a regular visitation day. But Ethan's visit is unscheduled and so once more he must go to the main office. Ann—after reaching Warden Wagner at home, making a few calls, and then finally getting a callback from Wagner—prepares the paperwork Ethan will need to see Don today. The effort seems like bureaucratic overkill, but it's certainly not Ann's fault.

"Looks like the warden wouldn't be able to run this place without you," Ethan says, signing one of her forms. "Thanks for getting me in today."

"It's no problem."

"Next time," Ethan tells her, though he doubts there will be a next time, "I'll plan my visit in advance."

Ann stops her paper sorting to give Ethan a concerned look. "Don Aldridge is not getting you involved in anything, is he, Mr. Winter?"

"Not that I know of. Why?"

Ann averts her gaze. "No reason. Can you find your way to the visitation center?"

The waiting area is filled today, with people Ethan would normally only rub shoulders with while renewing his driver's license. What seemed, yesterday, while empty, a good-size space has become close quarters. Ethan stations himself by a pillar in the middle of the room. A small boy with a shaved head crawls up to him.

"Barack Hussein!" a woman calls. "You don't know that man!"

Then the public address squawks what sounds like a warning. Ethan studies the box speaker and determines, after a few more crackles, that it is announcing the inmate being brought up and that his visitors are to proceed either to the room of booths or out to the yard. Through a caged window Ethan can see family contact visits happening among picnic benches.

The indecipherable announcements come every ten or so minutes. And when a person or party goes to the check-in desk, Ethan can deduce that a name other than Aldridge has been called.

After an hour the PA blurts, "Kalkrich, konald kalan. Kindor kisit." Since no one else in the room budges Ethan chances a trip to the guard and shows him his documents.

"Booth six," the guard says, a man other than yesterday's Todd.

"Funny, that's the same booth Todd gave me yesterday," Ethan says.

"Saved it special for you," the guard says indifferently.

At his booth, Aldridge sits behind the glass wall with his arms folded onto his belly as if Ethan has been keeping him waiting. Aldridge nods and then picks up his handset. Ethan does the same.

"Decent of you to come back, Winter," Aldridge says.

"You have something to tell me?" Ethan says, already anxious to leave.

Aldridge smiles. "Have a seat, amigo."

This is for Zoe, Ethan tells himself, and sits. "Well?"

Aldridge leans forward. "Hold on. Before we talk I got a mystery to put to you. First off, and don't take this wrong, but you're just a nobody citizen, right? You're not my lawyer. You ain't law enforcement. So the riddle is, how are you able to get same-day prisoner visits? Visits like this have to be set up weeks beforehand."

"I assume the warden's letting me see you because of Zoe," Ethan says.

"Wrong," Aldridge says. "They don't hold your hand around here. You get your bad news and you deal with it. That means these visits of yours don't add up. There's a reason you're here that you don't even know about, Mr. Ethan Winter."

"Oh?" Ethan says. The hairs on his arms stiffen. What was it that Ann mentioned about Aldridge getting him caught up in something? Ethan can feel it happening now. It's like a slow-motion crash.

"What's going on is," says Aldridge, "they're letting you see me because they think I might tell you where to find someone."

"Look," Ethan says, "why would you even tell me anything like that in the first place?"

"Because you're a decent guy. And because you might be interested that Zozo had a sister."

This news does strike Ethan. "A sister . . . Look, Mr. Aldridge . . . Don"—where Ethan got the confidence to call this man by his first name he doesn't know—"if you *did* tell me something in confidence, I wouldn't repeat it. But this is none of my business."

"You wouldn't have to repeat it," Aldridge says. "There's ears on us right now."

Ethan nods because they are talking through wires. "So there's not much that we can do here."

"But that ain't good enough. She's in trouble," Aldridge says. "Zozo's sister. Half sister. Still, I bet if Zozo was alive and knew about Jessica *she'd* try to help her."

Ethan's desire to avoid involvement grows weaker. "What kind of trouble?" he asks before growing wary again. This Jessica probably has money problems or a meth addiction.

Don Aldridge studies Ethan for a long second. "Ah, forget it," the prisoner says.

This may just be a tactic to pull him in. But it works. "Listen, Don. If there's something I can do before I head north," Ethan says, marking out the limits of his cooperation. *This is for Zoe*, he tells himself again. It's a half lie because his curiosity about this sister is growing. Does she have Zoe's eyes, her nose, her smile?

"What I need is for someone I trust to make sure she's okay. Only thing is, I can't tell you where she's at."

Ethan feels himself nodding, confirmed in his prejudice that anyone close to Don must have major issues with reality. "That'll make it hard for me to check up on her, won't it?"

Don's chin sandpapers against his handset's mouthpiece. "Yeah. Anyway, let me ask you something crazy. You're a banker, right. How's your memory for numbers? Address numbers say?"

"I imagine it's pretty good."

"Better than average?"

"Probably."

"Me. Sometimes I lose a person's name ten seconds after I hear it. And phone numbers, no way they stick."

"Maybe you aren't paying attention."

Don's eyes become slits. "That's the key, man. You got to pay attention."

Don raises his left fist and leans closer to the glass dividing them like he's going to punch through it. Ethan then realizes that Don had been clenching that fist throughout their meeting. But now the fist is opening, like a blooming flower caught by time-lapse photography. A line of scrawl unfolds on the palm and it presses the glass.

An instant later Don withdraws the palm and spits into it. Rubbing both hands furiously together until they are ink smeared, the prisoner obliterates the address Ethan had glimpsed. When Don looks up again, his eyes question Ethan's.

Ethan blinks an affirmation. He's got it. Apparently he's a faster study in this prison visitation business than he would have guessed. He feels a little proud of himself.

"I knew you were okay," Don Aldridge says. "You find out anything, write me. And remember, there could be eyes on you. Jessica flew drones for the Air Force. She was in on some big operation that went south. This ain't no game, Ethan."

A guard appears behind Don and hangs up his phone. The visit is over.

BECAUSE THE ADDRESS scribbled on Don's palm was not one of the Florida Keys, Ethan heads north out of Seminole City, the very bottom of landlocked America. To the east is the ocean. To the west, the Everglades. Logically, then, north it must be. A map on his phone tells him the Pompano Beach exit is seventy miles away.

The drive is mostly through suburban housing developments and an occasional remnant of grassland. There is nothing to fend off highway hypnosis, not even a billboard, and when Ethan's phone snaps him awake, by sounding its mystery-caller ringtone, Ethan sees that he's drifting, crowding a black pickup passing in the center lane. Its driver, through the open window, takes aim at him with a hand—or is he actually pointing a small pistol? Ethan jams the brakes, swerves behind a flatbed carrying port-a-potties, and takes his call.

"Yes?" he asks, breathing hard.

"Mr. Winter? Are you okay?" The voice is whispery, southern, female. He can almost identify it.

"Who's this?"

"It's Ann. You know, from the warden's office at Seminole City."

"Ann? Hi. Was I supposed to sign out or something?"

"No, Mr. Winter, it's nothing like that, no. And I am not supposed to be talking to you either, but you seem like good people." Ann is talking quickly. "I just had to tell you there might be folks following you because of Don Aldridge."

"What?" Ethan says.

"FBI men. I've got to go now. Watch out for yourself."

"Ann? Hello?"

Ethan tosses the phone onto the passenger's seat and speeds around the porta-potty truck. Then he slows down until the truck catches up and shields Ethan's vehicle from the cars directly behind him. After a few minutes the only thing Ethan notices in the rearview is a persistent red dot far back in the center lane. But even he knows that FBI don't drive red cars. And here's his exit. He merges with the easterly-bound traffic.

Yet, heeding Ann, he plays a little trick on his potential pursuers. He slips into the left lane and doubles back through a break in the median. Then he pulls into a Taco Bell's parking lot. He takes his time parking the Hyundai and watches as a car, a red car, makes the same U-turn he did. Driving toward Ethan, into the afternoon sun, the vehicle glints blindingly. Only when it passes can Ethan see who's inside—two men. They stare straight ahead and the car keeps going.

"BURRITO, CHIPS, STRAWBERRY Frutista Freeze," Ethan tells the cashier while drying his washroom-damp hands inside his pockets.

When Ethan's number is called he hustles his tray to a booth and tears into his burrito like a jackal into a wildebeest carcass. He chases the mash with a gulp of freeze . . . but the paste stops at his windpipe and he hardly notices the man sitting down opposite him, not until the mouthful in his throat starts down again and he can inhale.

"Now *there's* a diet that will kill you," says the man. "I should know. I've eaten this kind of junk almost every day for twenty years. Name's Daugherty. Federal Bureau of Investigation." He offers Ethan his hand across the table.

Daugherty's grip, though firm, is clammy. His eyes, weary and circled with shadows, match the tint of dark coffee. Silently Ethan retracts his hand.

"And this is my partner, Agent Pyle." Daugherty nods toward the man sliding in next to Ethan in the booth. He's blocking Ethan's exit.

Ethan remembers this man. "You were in my hotel lobby the other night. And . . . in the men's room at the prison."

Pyle studies Ethan the way a scientist might regard a microbe on a specimen slide.

"Then I guess you know why we're here," says Daugherty.

Ethan shakes his head, plays dumb, for all the good he knows this will do.

"Jessica Aldridge," Daugherty says.

Pyle breaks in. "We listened in on your talk with her father today. And yesterday, too, pal."

Though Ann had warned him there might be eavesdropping, the fact of being monitored still rankles Ethan—it's like completing an internet search and then discovering ads in your browser for everything you looked up. "Did you put the transcript on your blog?" Ethan says to Pyle.

"Don't be a smartass," Pyle says. He is a big man with deep, close-set eyes and a block jaw. Pyle is probably fit enough to rip the table off its floor bolts. "Convicts have no privacy rights. And neither do you when you talk to one," Pyle adds.

"Guilt by association?" Ethan says.

"We haven't accused you of anything yet, mother fu—"

"Stand down," Daugherty, leaning forward, intervenes, "both of you." The older agent sits back, his eyes radiating their coffee warmth. Though Ethan knows this man is playing him, he doesn't dislike Daugherty, the good cop. Ethan, in fact, does believe in Daugherty's implicit message— that only he can save Ethan from his partner. "Sorry for the hassle, Mr. Winter," Daugherty says. "We're just doing our job."

"Which is to follow me? To threaten me?" Ethan says, resisting the agent's pleasantness, testing how far he can push the rights of his citizenship.

"We're asking for your help," Daugherty says. "However, we really do need to locate Ms. Aldridge soon." Daugherty is speaking with a quiet urgency, as if Jessica is being held by a dastard about to tie her to a sawmill log. "And *you*, Mr. Winter, are our best hope."

That Ethan has never met Jessica makes no difference. He has an interest in protecting Zoe's sister. "If you were listening to my conversation with Don Aldridge," he tells Daugherty, "then you know he never mentioned his daughter's whereabouts." This is not an outright lie—Don had *shown* not *told* him.

"True." Daugherty folds his hands together atop the table. He gives Pyle a glance before returning his eyes to Ethan's. Moments pass in silence.

"I mean, look," Ethan says, feeling the need to explain his logic—there's a Monte Carlo simulation of possibilities running through his head. "If you've been monitoring him, then you know what he knows. What I'm saying is, if Don did know where his daughter is, so would you."

"Uh-huh," says Daugherty. Beads of moisture have collected on the agent's upper lip. Ethan also notices that Daugherty's face seems mildly bloated—perhaps the symptom of a fast food diet. "Do you mind?" Daugherty asks him and reaches for a clean napkin on Ethan's food tray. Daugherty mops his mouth and folds the napkin in quarters. "Don't you work for a bank?" he asks.

The agent's question chills Ethan. "Are you investigating *me* now?"

"No more than anybody might, using the internet. Your name showed up in a couple of places."

"I worked for UIB. They terminated me."

"That's not really surprising, is it?"

Ethan takes the insult silently.

Daugherty continues, "What I mean is, bankers add up numbers on paper and expect to get the same sums in the real world. But it never works out, does it?"

"What's this got to do with anything?"

Daugherty napkins his lip. "I think you're applying banker's logic to

Don Aldridge's situation. You're only taking into account the *known* knowns, not the *unknown* unknowns. A prison can hold bodies, but it's a sieve when it comes to information. Another inmate could have told Mr. Aldridge the location of his daughter. Or a coded letter. Or a contraband cell phone. We have no way of knowing. Just as we have no way of knowing if he told *you* where she is. That makes you our *unknown* known, Mr. Winter." Daugherty looks at his partner. "Or is he our *known* unknown?"

Pyle, adjusting his position on Ethan's bench, eliminates the air gap between them. Ethan feels a beefy right biceps pressing into his narrower left one.

"But there are some things we are sure about," says Daugherty, recapturing Ethan's attention. "For example, we know you rented a car on Miami Beach today. We know that Don Aldridge talked to you about Jessica today. We know that just after you two talked you did not return your car to Miami Beach but drove forty miles north out of your way. Can you explain the trip?"

"Am I obligated to?"

"Not unless you want an obstruction of justice charge," Pyle tells Ethan's left ear.

Turning from Daugherty to Pyle, Ethan releases his irritation. "Don't think you're intimidating me, asshole."

Pyle's eyes go flat. A millisecond later Ethan sees, peripherally, the big agent's far hand arc over the tabletop. But Daugherty, with a smack, stops the open-handed slap before it reaches Ethan's face. "That's enough," the older man says, and Pyle withdraws the hand. Ethan momentarily considers whether this is all just part of their good cop, bad cop game. "I'm sorry, Ethan," Daugherty says. "You will have to come with us."

"What's the charge?" Ethan says. He has his rights . . . he thinks.

Daugherty gives Ethan a questioning look. "There's no charge. Oh, that's right. You probably don't know that we can hold you without charges for forty-eight hours."

Before Ethan can reply Pyle yanks him out of the booth—Pyle must outweigh him by forty pounds of muscle—and slams Ethan facedown onto the tabletop. Ethan's mouth cracks the edge of the serving tray, and behind his back he feels metal cut tightly into his wrists. When Ethan realizes that he's handcuffed and being frisked, he remembers Don Aldridge's last words to him—*This ain't no game.*

"It's okay, people. We're FBI," Daugherty says generally. From the corner of an eye Ethan can see the frightened onlookers. "Let's move it," he tells Pyle.

Propelling Ethan into the parking lot, Pyle manhandles him the way UIB security did on the day Ethan was fired. Ethan stumbles but the big man's grip keeps him upright, until he shoves Ethan headfirst into the backseat of an overheated car, a red car. Agent Pyle slams the door, locking him in the swelter.

Ethan pushes himself upright and twists around to look out the car's back window. The two agents are heatedly but quietly talking behind the trunk. Daugherty is wearing a sour look and after a minute Pyle gets in on the driver's side.

"Where are you taking me?" Ethan asks—and tastes metal. Wiping his mouth on the shoulder of his shirt, he smears it with blood. "I'm hurt," he says.

"Quiet," Pyle says, then starts the engine.

Minutes pass. The car's climate control exhausts the swelter. Then Daugherty joins them. He rests an elbow on the front seat back and half turns to Ethan. His face, in profile, is gray. "You could have made things easier on yourself."

Aware that he will spout gibberish if he replies, Ethan bites his tongue. But his hands are tingling from lack of blood and his desire to be unhandcuffed is immense. Already his decision to be silent about Jessica has weakened. What, after all, does he know about her situation . . . about any situation? Less and less it seems. Jessica might be a threat to herself. It might be wrong of him not to help these men.

Pyle twists the car out of its parking space and Ethan topples onto the floor between the front and rear seats.

"Because if you think," Daugherty says, looking down at him and apparently continuing a thought Ethan has missed, "that I've spent the last year in pursuit of this woman for no good reason"—the agent reaches over the seat back and presses an index finger against a vein in Ethan's neck—"then, my friend, you are dangerously mistaken." Daugherty is breathing hard.

"You okay?" Pyle asks his partner.

"Drive," Daugherty says, releasing his finger. "Someplace secluded."

"The Everglades?"

"Gator land it is."

"This is bullshit," Ethan mumbles.

"*Bullshit?*" Daugherty says. "I'll show you bullshit." He turns to Pyle. "Bring up that picture on your phone. Let's show our guest some of the enhanced interrogation you applied in Afghanistan, just so he knows where his noncooperation is taking him."

"You're the boss," Pyle says.

What Ethan sees on the BlackBerry, looking up at it from the car's rear floor, is not an image he can easily absorb. Daugherty is showing him a naked, bearded man with his arms bound behind his back. The man is standing crouched and has a bit of a belly. Beneath the belly, a penis, a rather small penis but one that is quite erect, pokes from a matted nest of pubic hair.

"So here's how this will go," Pyle, at the wheel, says. "We work on a person's weak spots. Muslims, for example, are particularly attuned to personal shame. If, say, you have a Haji in custody who is not well endowed, you offer him some green tea laced with Viagra, strip him bare ass, and then get a female interrogator with a superb Afghani accent to comment on his shortcomings in Pashto. It's a process."

"Bullshit," Ethan manages to whisper.

"What's *your* weak spot, Winter?" Pyle asks him. "That dead girlfriend of yours. Oh, yeah, we know all about her. But don't worry, I doubt she killed herself because of you. I mean she was a real babe, and man, did you ever *look* at yourself in a mirror?"

"That's enough," Daugherty says. Pyle's BlackBerry is buzzing and Daugherty studies its screen.

"Like hell that's enough," says Pyle. "We're finishing this today."

"Have you been communicating with Wagner behind my back?" Daugherty asks his partner unhappily.

"Yeah. So what? He likes me," Pyle says. "More than you."

"He sent you an address. Aldridge's cellmate just gave it up." Daugherty looks over his seat back and down at Ethan. "Your lucky day, isn't it?"

"Fuckin' A," says Pyle hitting the brakes. The car skids a little and then Pyle bounces it over the landscaped median. The vehicle stops sideways in the oncoming lane. Fortunately there's a break in traffic.

"That was dramatic," Daugherty says.

"End of the line, shithead," Pyle says exiting the car. Then he is pulling Ethan off the backseat floor. The cuffs come off and blood rushes like nettles into Ethan's hands.

Pyle gets back in the car without shutting either side door. When he hits the gas the doors slam by themselves. Ethan, standing in the road, wonders how much he could have taken before telling the agents Jessica's address. He hopes it would have been a lot.

A BUS, LIKE a trained elephant, kneels to take him aboard. Seated by a window Ethan gazes at the gated communities and sun-bleached strip malls, the plots of land cleared for storm drainage or imminent development. The bus passes over the Florida Turnpike and glides down below the tree line. Ethan presses a yellow strip bordering his window and makes his ride pull over. It can't be twenty minutes since Daugherty and Pyle released him. There might still be time. He crosses the street and gets into his leased Hyundai.

His phone's GPS steers him into a neighborhood of cinderblock homes with tar-paper roofs. Ahead, above in the treetops, a red glow hiccoughs off palm fronds.

You don't have to do this, he tells himself. You can just turn around.

But he doesn't. Ethan pulls up a few houses from where the emergency vehicles flicker. A senior in a quilt robe glares as he crosses her gravel. Then the flashing fire truck, leaving, eases through the spectators. Ethan goes into the small crowd, which stands back from a stationary ambulance that silently winks its various lights.

"What's up?" asks a shirtless twenty-something in Bermudas. The man's not talking to Ethan but to his companion.

"There were these guys looked like detectives." The companion, barefoot and in jeans, points his chin toward a pink, two-story apartment building with an exterior staircase.

"They come for that chick?" asks Bermudas.

"What chick?"

"Lives upstairs. Lotta tats. Seen her walking a dog."

"Never saw any chick."

"Skinny. But doable."

Ethan looks up at the staircase landing. A man in a blue shirt is slowly backing out of an open door there. He's supporting one end of a stretcher.

You are part of this, Ethan's conscience says. She's Zoe's sister.

Straps hold a draped body as the paramedic angles the stretcher to get it onto the narrow staircase. Then the other lifting paramedic appears—but Ethan cannot see the victim's face, only the breathing mask that hides it. Pyle appears at the landing's door and follows the stretcher bearers downstairs.

Ethan feels, then, what he felt when he first saw Zoe, crossing in front of that cab—a longing, a desire to save her. He *can* save Jessica. He will. This time and from now on, he will do the right thing.

But as the stretcher comes closer he sees that the hair and eyes of the victim are not female. It's a man lying on the stretcher. *Daugherty*. Ethan is standing only two feet away as the paramedics pass with their burden. But Daugherty's dark coffee eyes don't see him. They are staring up at the sky without blinking.

"What happened?" Ethan asks Pyle, who is still following the stretcher.

"Back off."

"Where's Jessica?" Ethan steps in front of Pyle, and Pyle shoulders him out of the way.

Seconds later a siren blip warns the bystanders and chunks of lawn fly as the ambulance spins onto the tarmac. Pyle follows fast behind in the red car. Ethan looks back to the second-floor landing, at the open door there, and heads for the staircase.

"You looking for Jessica?' someone says.

Ethan turns around. It's a heavyset man in a guayabera.

"THANKS," ETHAN SAYS. He takes the iced tea from Kelso's wife. She is slender and wearing a blue dress that exposes her tanned knees. Ethan is in her kitchen seated at a table covered by a plastic cloth.

"Have you known Jessica a long time?" the woman asks.

"I was a friend of her sister's."

"*Was* a friend?"

"She passed away."

"Oh, that's terrible," says the woman.

The sound of a toilet flush comes through the drywall. Kelso, who had introduced himself to Ethan as Jessica's landlord, rejoins them.

"So you think they were real FBI?" Kelso asks. "They showed me ID, but you can fake documents at Kinko's. I know that much from renting apartments."

"Does that mean you didn't tell them where to find Jessica?" Ethan asks.

"I made out like she was home and brought them to her door."

"Even though you knew she'd left?"

"Once you start lying there's no turning back. I pretended a little surprise when I knocked and got no answer. That's when the big one kicked in the door. I don't know what he was trying to prove since I had my key out. Well, once we were inside anyone could see no one's living there anymore—there's no personal stuff, no dishes in the sink. Jessica left it neat as a pin. That was when the other guy . . ."

"Daugherty."

"He kind of drifts over to a wall, gets real close to it. His back's to me and I can't figure out what he's looking at. But then his partner helps him lie down on the floor. The man's face had turned blue." Kelso shakes his head. "Paramedics when they came called in a cardiac."

"Teddy," Kelso's wife says. "Show him the note."

Kelso studies her before reaching into his back pocket. "Found this under our door earlier. I'm going to burn it."

"But suppose it's evidence?" asks Kelso's wife. "You could get in trouble."

He hands Ethan the sheet. It's torn from a restaurant pad. The handwriting on it is cursive, precise.

Mr. and Mrs. Kelso,

I am afraid I have two pieces of bad news. One is about Skittles. She got hit by a car yesterday. It was my fault since I tied her up outside of a grocery store so I could shop. She got free somehow. You know she was a good dog. You don't know how much I'm going to miss her.

My second news is about betraying your trust. Though I did sign a lease I cannot uphold my end of our agreement. I must give up your nice apartment. Knowing your generosity I expect you will want to return my deposit. But please do not worry about the money. I am moving on to another phase in my life and will not need it.

> *Best wishes,*
> *Jessica Aldridge*

"So tell me. Who doesn't need money wherever they're going?" Kelso asks. "She must be in a lot of trouble."

"I think her note sounds depressed," says Mrs. Kelso. "Maybe we *should* tell the police."

Kelso slips Jessica's note from Ethan's fingers. "I don't know," he says, staring at it.

After a moment, "Burn it," Ethan says. He is channeling Don Aldridge. "Let her stay free."

Getting a nod from his wife Kelso takes the letter to the sink and strikes a match. Ethan watches as Jessica's words, the only thing of hers he's touched, become ash.

CHAPTER 58

Homestead Air Force Base, Reeger Air Force Base

There is no clock on the wall and an officer has taken Jessica's phone so she doesn't know how long she's been in here. The room has a conference table surrounded by plush high-backed chairs. On the walls hang framed photographs of aircraft. It's a windowless room, but Jessica is not exactly a prisoner. The door is unlocked and she is free to roam to the restroom, water fountain, and vending machines in the corridor. Whenever she does, a lieutenant, stationed at a pass desk farther up the hallway, looks up from his *Airman* magazine. But since Jessica keeps to her end of the building he's not too interested in her activities, perhaps because she's come in on her own volition.

Surprisingly, sirens did not go off when Jessica presented herself at the airbase's gatehouse. The airman on duty, after Jessica told him of being chased across the country by the FBI and of wanting to turn herself in to her own people, looked her up and down and figured her for a nutcase. Jessica told him how she had piloted the UAV on the botched al-Yarisi strike.

"Yeah," he'd said. "Tell me about the aircraft."

"A Reaper. A 950-horsepower turboprop. Flies like a hawk compared to the Predator. Goes twice as fast, twice as high, and almost twice as far."

Her knowledge had little effect on the airman, even after she described the Reaper's Hellfire payload—missiles they'd called angels, as in angels of God and all the wrath that suggests. Finally, though, the guard made a call that brought a staff sergeant, Briggs, in a long blue pickup bearing the Air Force security forces logo. "Climb aboard, Sergeant," he'd said.

Briggs drove her past a baseball diamond and a parking lot filled with RVs and small boats on trailers, amusements of off-duty airmen.

"There's my Whaler," Briggs said, indicating a fifteen footer with a Merc outboard.

"Nice," said Jessica.

A longing grabbed her, a homesickness for the life she had built in the Air Force and then lost. By the time she swallowed the ache, Briggs had pulled up to a building next to an airstrip. Here he handed Jessica off to the lieutenant, who has been her uncommunicative monitor for the past hours.

Clearly there have been orders to quarantine her. So Jessica waits patiently. She will not hurry whatever decisions are being made about her future. She will live quietly on vending machine food—three Milky Ways so far—for as long as the powers that be want to keep her here. Her only problem is that she's crashing from the sugar and has an urge to rest her lolling head in her arms on the conference table—will it end up being her interrogator's interview table? she wonders. She lays her head down and shuts her eyes, planning to do so for only a few seconds.

In her dreams, Skittles runs away from her into the ocean. When she goes in to rescue her, a lifeguard pushes her under the waves, where she discovers she can breathe. This bit of illogic makes Jessica aware that she is dreaming.

"Sergeant Aldridge," a soft dream voice says. And then again, "Sergeant Aldridge." The voice is real.

Groggy, Jessica blinks coming out of her nap and quickly stands and snaps a salute—a reflex that's apparently still in place when she's addressed by a superior to her former rank. "Yes, ma'am," Jessica says to a young blonde woman with pulled-back hair and a sun-reddened face. Her uniform carries captain's bars.

"At ease."

Jessica relaxes, or tries to. But her salute has hiked her sleeve and now the scabbed tats on her wrist show—seven more laserings until they're gone. Even if she's no longer an airman, being on base with nonregulation ink feels wrong.

"Someone wants to speak with you," the captain says. She has brought in a landline phone and finds a place to plug it in. "Sir," she says to the receiver, "Sergeant Aldridge is available now. . . . Yes, sir."

The captain gives Jessica the receiver. "Hello," she speaks into the electronic void.

"Jessica," a familiar voice comes back. Its owner, however, has never before called her by her first name.

"Colonel Voigt?"

"I've been thinking about you, Sergeant. Glad you're back with us."

"Yes, sir. I . . . I'm sorry for any trouble I've caused you."

"Trouble? Well, you did blow a hole in the noncom UAV pilot program. But you haven't caused *me* any trouble, not on a personal level."

"Sir?"

"That's enough of the *sirs*."

"Yes—" Jessica says, though she continues to stand at attention.

"Are you alone yet?"

Jessica looks around and sees that the captain has slipped from the room. "I'm alone."

"You're in a wing conference room with encrypted phone lines. Not even the NSA can unscramble what we're saying. We can talk freely, so let's. I hear you've been on the run."

"Yes. From the FBI. At least that's who they said they were."

"Fill me in."

"That's all I know. I didn't wait around to ask what they wanted."

"Did you ever think they just needed to know what *I'd* like to know—what happened to you after that little hiking mishap of yours? You duck out of a VA hospital and then disappear. Why?"

"I . . ." Jessica hesitates.

"An expert on classified Air Force programs cannot go off the radar, not immediately after her discharge."

"I didn't plan it, sir," Jessica says. But how does she explain that when the Air Force discharged her it erased Jessica Aldridge? If she went off the radar, it was because that part of her didn't exist, not for all those months. This truth, though, is not a good answer to give a commanding officer like Voigt. "I left . . . ," Jessica says, gazing at one of the photograph-decorated walls. A quartet of F-16s caught in tight formation takes her focus. "I left because I had no wingman to watch my six."

Voigt stays silent for seconds. "You've done well flying solo. Eluding the FBI all this time."

"Wasn't too hard."

Voigt gives a short laugh. "You've got a talent," he says. Then he gets serious. "I want you to know that I did not put those people after you."

"I wouldn't think so."

"But with all this business I *have* had the opportunity to think about your situation these months. I'm working on a proposition that might solve all this trouble for us, if you're up for it."

Jessica responds like a recruit in boot camp. Raising her chin in the empty conference room, she states loudly and clearly, perhaps to convince herself, "I am one hundred percent, sir."

"Glad to hear it. There's a C17 making a hop from Homestead to Reeger at zero six thirty. Can you be onboard?"

"I can."

"Then I'll see you tomorrow, Ms. Aldridge."

"Colonel," Jessica says and leans forward as if she is standing before his desk back in Nevada—it's the way she last saw him. "Before you go . . . can I ask you why?"

"*Why?*"

"Why, really, are you going to all this trouble for me?"

VOIGT, TURNING TO the window behind his desk, watches a Reaper—an ugly buglike machine truth be told—touch down on the airstrip two hundred yards away. His jaw pops as he considers Jessica's "*Why?*" And then he decides to be forthright. "It's because I'm wearing silver eagles on my shoulders. I got my promotion after we took out Yarisi."

"But—" he hears Jessica distantly protest.

"I know. He turned up in Yemen two months ago. For a year, though, everybody was patting themselves on the back for the kill. The UAV program got A-plus marks. The CIA got expanded powers or God knows what. I got my eagles. And then . . . we fools discover our dead terrorist is breathing, plotting to take down airliners. Pardon my French, but what followed was a world-class shitstorm about how to inform the public. Some congressional security committee ordered an inquiry to cover their rears. And that's why we're talking now. Your actions that night cleared our strike team. And they cleared me as squadron commander."

"I don't understand. We missed."

"It's how we missed that counts. You delayed firing on the initial targets because you suspected something. That something turned out to be what central intel thought was Yarisi's convoy."

"But it wasn't. And we blew it up."

"True. But that isn't the bottom line. You're aware of the cameras in our operations center—that it's not just the terrorists who get monitored. The video that day shows you, and then me, reacting negatively to the Agency recommendation to fire on those vehicles. Anyone who watches it can see that we would have aborted the strike if given the choice." Voigt's eyes are on the airfield. He's watching the bug taxi toward a ground crew. "Well, so far that *anyone* includes a congressman who's not too happy about the . . . collateral damage."

"It was all collateral damage," Jessica says quietly, giving Voigt pause.

"I owe you this one, Sergeant, though I doubt it'll put your mind to rest. The convoy we took out was bait. Yarisi was sending a look-alike on little trips around the countryside. The girls in the convoy weren't his wives. They were kids from a nearby village. Hell, goddammit, we'll always be at a disadvantage fighting people like Yarisi. Psychopaths. Men without morals."

Voigt hears no response. He worries that he has revealed too much. It is his job never to waiver in his conviction to his duty. But deep down, he trusts Jessica. Is it that they are, at bottom, kindred? But this is getting too sentimental.

"Are you there, Sergeant?" Voigt asks.

"I'm here."

"It was not my idea to separate you from the Air Force. There was pressure from some deputy in Homeland Security who'd got wind of those letters to your dad. You know, there's little Washington hates more than a leak. My recommendation had been a psych eval and then disciplinary action. That would have slowed your career but kept you with us. And I'd still have an ace UAV driver on the team. Believe me, we don't have a quarter of the personnel we need for the missions Washington wants."

There is another pause in the conversation. Then Jessica speaks. "I wanted to be a good airman for you, sir."

"You were. Remember that." And then Voigt is ready to terminate this call, which has gone deeper into his emotions than he likes.

"Colonel," Jessica says just as Voigt readies to take back control of the situation. "What were their names?"

He doesn't speak for a full five seconds. "Whose?"

"Those girls. The kids I killed."

"That's war," Voigt says. He hears his voice rising. "You didn't kill them. The war did! Yarisi did!"

"But you know their names?" Jessica says back to him quietly. "You know who died in the strike."

"I don't keep that information in my head." Voigt, though no longer shouting, feels offended.

"Can you get them for me, the names? I mean, the dead aren't classified, are they?"

"Damn it. As a matter of fact, they are." Voigt considers pulling rank, but then he remembers that Jessica is not under his command. She is beyond that now and she is due respect. And knowledge. Some knowledge, anyway. "That's why the feds chased you across the country. Your dad threatened to go public about your letters."

"What?"

"He thought he was helping you. But he didn't consider that you're the only person who could confirm his stories. Washington decided to make sure you never got the chance to talk to the press, not that you would."

"I wouldn't."

"Anyway, I'm glad the bastards didn't catch you. I'd hate to see one of my old team chemically lobotomized to keep her quiet."

"I know how to keep quiet now."

"No more letters to papa."

"No."

"No more questions about the dead and buried."

Voigt waits for Jessica's reply and then takes silence as agreement.

"Good. And you'll be on that transport tomorrow?"

"Yes, sir. I'll be on board," says Jessica.

"We're going to put you back to work at what you do best."

CHAPTER 59

Seminole City

Dear Winter,

You may think a week is no time at all to a jailbird with a twenty year sentence. But doing time waiting to hear from someone when you are already doing time multiplies each day into a month. Which makes it seven months in my world since we spoke.

First of all I expect you want to know how I got your New York address. That was easy. I asked the warden's office. I guess they must like reading what I send out. But their spying on me makes no difference anymore. I have no secrets now. Not since I learned that my cellmate ratted out where Jessica was living. I wrote directly there in care of the landlord and this nice fellow Kelso wrote back right away with good news. He says that the FBI did not catch my little girl. He also says that a man of your description stopped by. Anyway I want to find out what has happened to Jessica since and am writing for your help. As I know not to expect favors from anyone maybe we can do a trade. I have a story to tell you. One that might set you free.

You already know I am not much of a man. Just a two-time loser who has got what he deserves. When I was young I was the kind of punk to abandon his wife and three-month-old daughter. To shack up in a Miami Beach motel with an underage runaway. And when the bucks ran out I was dumb enough to sell an ounce of baby powder to an undercover cop. Only there was enough cocaine in the Johnsons for a ten month sentence. So adios me. Six months later though I get a letter from my runaway begging me to come get her. She is going to have my kid she says. And that is how your Zoe came into the world. Soon as I got free I headed north for her and Suzie.

Well Suzie by then is seventeen and bored. She starts sneaking out to see me behind her parents backs. The old man caught us once. Gave me a lookover and put me down for a dirtbag. Held off calling the cops though. Probably afraid of the scandal. Just told me to get lost. Like I would. And Susie kept coming to me. Sometimes she brings Zozo. Biggest eyes on a kid you ever saw. Eyes that have me making plans for our little family. We are going to run off to Canada. To Mexico. To Australia even. All dreams. All lies. And Suzie is no dunce. She is figuring out that the best honest job I will ever get is minimum wage. That I will never have the money she needs to escape her life. Three weeks into our reunion and all we do is scrap.

Then one night Suzie sneaks out to the Trumbull roadhouse where I told her I got a waiter job. Only she catches me in the kitchen elbow deep in soapy pots. Fuck you she starts yelling. Fuck you fuck you fuck you fuck you until the manager drags her out the back door. Of course I am right there. Right until she locks herself in her dad's Land Rover. I jump into my Florida junker and block the lot exit. But Suzie drives out over the sidewalk and then torches the pavement. My mistake was to go after her. Chased her in my old wreck onto the parkway. Thats when she really took off. Her taillights disappeared around a bend and the next thing I know. Oh hell. I see the overpass and the fire.

Every night I ask myself why I went after her. And every morning I crawl out of the sack asking for forgiveness and knowing I'll never get it. After that what kept me going was thinking of Zozo out there living her life. Now I dont have that. So what I am telling you Ethan is something you got to believe. What happened between you and your Zoe was not what happened between me and Suzie. I aint no priest and I dont have rights so all I can do is tell you that you are not guilty. That you got to let go of your ghost. Put our little girl down into her grave before she owns you the way my ghost owns me.

Don Aldridge

CHAPTER 60

- -

Sagaponack

"This place is *sick*," Alex says, enthusiastic as a teenager, of Sergei's mansion. After Sergei's fiftieth, Alex had hitched a ride on his patron's jet, which set down in East Hampton an hour before. Ethan has just arrived by jitney from the city, where he'd been holed up in his apartment since his return from Florida—until Don's letter awoke him. Ethan and Alex have texted sporadically, but this is their first face-to-face since before Zoe's funeral.

Alex looks puffier than he had. He seems a little worn. This is odd to Ethan since Alex had always gotten energy from doing his art. But then Ethan had never known his friend to take a commission before. He had always painted what he'd wanted. Maybe it was the flight home. Then Ethan notices that Alex is in a windbreaker. It's not something he would normally wear, and this jacket especially not since it is logoed. There's an SAS over the heart.

They are leaning on the rail of a high deck that overlooks a field and then a dune and then the ocean—Sergei has bought the land to keep the view. Ethan is facing the ocean. Alex has his elbows on the railing and is admiring the house, a small distance away and accessed by a raised walkway.

"Truly sick," Ethan says. "In college I wanted to be this rich."

"In college I wanted to be the next Jackson Pollock," Alex says.

Ethan turns to lean back against the railing. From the rear Sergei's house has an Escher-like appearance. External staircases lead to dead-end cupolas as if in homage to the widow's watches used by sailors' wives.

"The thing is," Ethan says, "you still have a chance to be a Pollock."

"You mean, because of those reviews." A *Times* critic had favorably

mentioned Alex's show at Medusa and *New York* magazine listed it in its
Approval Matrix. "I can thank Sergei's PR team for those."

"He must think highly of your work."

"He thinks more highly of his ability to spot talent."

Ethan cannot really say whether Alex's paintings are good or not—not
any more than Alex could determine if one of Ethan's predictive algorithms was viable. After all, what's really big in art seems to be giant pup-
pies made of flowers or great white sharks embalmed in vitrines, and these
don't appeal to Ethan.

The two men, hearing screeches, turn back to the ocean. Just off the
beach a mass of seagulls is harassing an underwater shadow. Gleaming
fish begin to leap and the birds swoop to feed.

And then someone else comes onto the deck.

"My man, 'bout time you got here! How is *it* hanging. Not too droopy,
I hope."

"John Guan. Alex Carr," Ethan says, introducing his two worlds.

"Artiste par excellence, I hear," says Guan.

"Thanks, I think," says Alex.

"It's all good," says Guan. Then he turns to Ethan. "How cool is this?
We going to be working together again, bro." Guan, wearing his gangsta sneakers and sagging pants, is still cultivating his own style, has even
added a goatee—facial hair that employment at UIB had disallowed. And
this grooming actually almost works.

Ethan looks at Guan's outstretched hand. "I just came out to give
Sergei some respect. Tell him no to his face."

Guan, for a second, resembles a confused robot—*This does not com-
pute.* "Fuck me," he says. "You got another job. *Nyet, nyet, nyet.* The Russian won't be digging that."

Ethan looks at Alex, who starts to nod. *I get it now, dude. Run for your life.*

"It's not another job," Ethan says.

"Then why, homie? *Why?*" Guan asks.

"Excuse us," Ethan says to Alex and pulls Guan to the far side of the
deck. "John," Ethan's face is stone now. "This isn't the only reason, but
that decimal point. Did you move it?" Ethan knows that Hoke couldn't
have done the work on his own.

Guan takes a step back. "*Homie.* I mean, get real. Screw you over like that? I mean . . . *shiiit.* It wasn't like that. I mean, like . . . *wait.* Remember that morning you called my voicemail, said you were taking a personal day?"

How could Ethan forget? He was calling from the hospital in Ulster County while Zoe was getting her stomach pumped.

"I was slammed that morning, bro. Eventually got to what you asked—dry-ran those patches you installed the night before. Something was buggy and I was doing a trace when Hoke pulled me in to block a hacker breach. I warned him there was shit in your code, but he blew it off. Said, 'Fuck Winter's bonus.' Anyway, later, after the Islamabad car bomb and your algo got jiggy, the Hokemeister had to punk you to cover his ass."

"Hold up," Ethan says. "*I* programmed the error? That's not what Sergei told me." He is getting that sick feeling in his gut again.

Guan, grinning, leans close to Ethan's ear. "What I told Sergei was"— Guan's voice is barely louder than the waves breaking on the beach— "that the bad code was not *your* bad, that it was Hoke's. Get me?" Ethan listens to Guan breathing in his ear. It is as if they are little boys sharing secrets. "Homie, I didn't give Sergei the detailed why—which was because El Duce put me on another task. But yeah, bottom line, you did code that blip. Can't help that Sergei thinks otherwise." Guan pulls back and looks at Ethan as if he expects thanks.

But Ethan is feeling paler now. His coding confidence is shaken. His desire to code, leaking away. Ruined as much by his error as by the betrayals behind it, as by the uses his talent had been put to and would still be put to. "John, you could have told someone that Hoke didn't let you find the error. That it wasn't all mine." He is grasping.

Guan squeezes his eyes shut and then opens them in a disbelieving blink. "Come on, my man. Get real. Then UIB would have put you, me, and Hoke out on our asses. Besides, you knows I was that bitch's bitch. Anyway, so what I be saying is, today, me and you, in the here and now, we are cool, brutha. That old stuff was UIB biz. A completely diff situation, *stitch*uation, son-of-a-*bitch*uation. Not anything I would do on my own. Like I said it was all *achtung, Sieg heil, jawohl mein Herr Hoke!* But that's done now. World War III's over. Armistice's declared. Prisoners are released. I vouched for you to Sergei, didn't I? So you can't hold anything against me. Right? Right, Ethan? Yo, bro. We are cool, *right?*"

Ethan is walking away. Passing Alex, he grabs his duffel and descends from the deck onto a staircase that leads toward a dune.

"Dude, where you headed?" Alex calls after him.

"Gotta go, dude," Ethan calls back.

"Where? *Where* are you going?" Alex shouts.

ETHAN IS NOT an outdoors type, a reveler in nature and life, a man like Thoreau to whom "the sun is but a morning star." He sees only a fearsome nuclear sphere descending toward the western horizon, a ball that would incinerate this planet if it orbited any closer. The few others sharing the beach with him on this late September afternoon—a fisherman, an older couple with hiking poles, a twenty-something running her greyhound—seem less wary of this precariousness. Of Ethan's, they certainly take no notice. He walks past the seaweed line and collapses by a sand castle, battered from the last tide but still possessing a turret. From his bag, he removes Zoe's urn and pushes it into the beach between his sunken heels.

The day is passing. The sun is sinking lower, growing smaller and less intimidating. Along the water's edge travel infrequent passersby who don't look Ethan's way. And then the incoming tide begins a new siege of the castle. A breaker topples its turret and sends Ethan crab-scampering backward to stay dry. When the wave recedes he retrieves the abandoned urn and, gathering courage, tries to pull off the lid. After a minute he figures out that it's threaded.

Inside the urn Ethan discovers a tied bag. The plastic packaging, being just that, seems disrespectful, unnatural, and he undoes the tie and tilts the urn until the ash, fine and gray, begins to pour. She runs silvery through his fingers. Zoe.

EPILOGUE

January 2014
Florida, New Jersey, Arizona

Dear Ethan,

Glad to hear from you again and a happy New Year to you too. Your last letter adds up to three each we have exchanged over the past months. That probably makes us regular correspondents by now. Funny what brings people together. What I mean is you know me because you knew a daughter I never did. And now we are corresponding about another daughter I have lost and whom you never met.

First off I appreciate you still trying to find out what happened to Jessica. Your offer to hire a detective on your own dime is solid generous since I doubt you are making buckets of money. But if doing your old work was making you sick what else could you have done but got out of the biz. I dont know much about banking except those people in it long as they make money dont care if they put families on the street. So I bet your gut was telling you something important that your head had not caught up with yet. Your old man by the way sounds like a great guy finding you that teaching gig even if you did have to move out of the big city. After you figure things out maybe being a teacher permanent will be the course you choose. But like I always say. What do I know.

One thing I DO know though is that gutshot feeling. If I had ever paid attention to it I might have built a different life for myself. Starting back by sticking with Jessica's mother. And that would have changed history. Ours anyway. There would have been no Zoe and you and me would have never met. The big question is where would we be today. Me not in prison maybe. But you probably still at your bank and not sick over what you do. So here is a fact I do know. For whatever reason you have a chance at something I missed out on. I never grew into anything better than what I was. Is that what Zoe's death was about? Making you a more decent man? It got to have some meaning.

Anyway about Jessica. I been thinking over what Zoe's mother taught me. That it aint no good to chase after people who do not want to be chased. So my friend. No detective.

And besides I have big news. A picture postcard came.

Except for my prison address there is no handwriting on it. But the postmark is Tucson and the picture shows a big cactus that seems to be waving. I might be reading more into it than there is but I believe that Jessica is out there saying she is OK. That she will reach out to me when she is ready. That I should just be patient. And so this I will be. Our search for Jessica is over.

But I do hope this dont mean that you and me are done writing. I expect those middle school kids of yours will be giving you plenty of war stories I will want to hear. And not to go soft on myself but sometimes I think a good teacher could have helped me way back when not become the man I turned out. What I mean is that if you save one kid well that is worth something. Its about more than teaching them math.

Ha Ha! Hearing all this from a con. Just keep writing me Ethan and I will be keeping you on the straight and narrow like a preacher. But to go back to serious. When I do get word from Jessica again I will let you know. Maybe you will be lucky enough to meet her someday. On an Arizona vacation maybe. And maybe then you can tell her a little about what her sister was like. Anyway. A man can dream.

Your amigo,
Don

Dear Don,
I'm writing you during school hours—after school actually since as a rookie instructor one of my assigned duties twice a week is to monitor the afternoon detention class. I'm beginning to see that many of these kids actually try for detention just to stay off the

streets. It's safer in here from the drugs, the bullying, the God knows what. So even if I'm no great shakes as a teacher, at least I'm doing this much for them.

About your Jessica. It's curious how much I think of her, someone I only know through you and your letters. Of course this must have to do with Zoe, whom I think of every day, though not every minute of every day as I used to. Sometimes I come out of my daydreams not believing she's gone forever. It must be a little like how you feel about Jessica—in mourning for her absence, her absent letters. If you ever want me to take up our search again just give me the word. Knowing she could be in Tucson would narrow things down for us.

As to my moving out of New York, I guess there are some regrets. But those years I spent in the city I was pretty much a zombie, trudging the streets between work and home. I could have been living anywhere. It helps that my best friend has moved away also, up the Hudson to where life is saner for an artist than in the Manhattan hustle. We've become suburban boys, just like we were to begin with. He tells me he likes the quiet, the mountainscapes. I tell him I'm getting used to the chalk under my nails and how the decibel level in my classroom picks up whenever I turn to the blackboard. I certainly am collecting those war stories you wrote wanting to hear about.

One is happening now. A young man just asked me what I was working on so hard. He said I looked funny, hunched over, like I was taking some kind of exam I hadn't studied for. This made my other detainees laugh. I explained to him that I was writing to a friend who was a prisoner. My student nodded. Then he took out a sheet of paper and started writing. He's asked me a couple of times how to spell words. 'Arrested.' 'Penitentiary.' Maybe he's hustling me for sympathy. Or maybe I motivated him to write to someone he knows in prison. His dad, an uncle, an older brother. That more than a few of my students might have a relative in prison wouldn't be unlikely. Anyway, Don, I don't know if I could even save one of these kids. That's a large request you've laid on my plate. How does one learn how to really help another person? Or even yourself? There's no twelve-step program for that. All I seem to know is that it's going to take me a lot of steps to get to where

*I need to be. And maybe a trip west as you suggested, to the land of the
waving cactus, will be one of them.*

*Okay. My class is getting rowdy. Detention hour is nearly over. It's
back to work for me, dismissing the kids in one piece. I'll stay strong if
you will. Till later.*

Your friend,
Ethan

"Go west. Go to the arroyo!" Jessica whispers.

She is frustrated. The figures on the monitor have started moving
again. But they're headed northeast, the wrong way. They're going deeper
into the desert.

"No," Jessica says, though of course the couple can't hear her. And then
she worries about who can. There's a camera in the corner of the ceiling,
but it's merely there to document who enters and exits. Jessica doesn't
think it's an employee spy cam so it probably doesn't have a microphone.
But who knows.

Turn back, Jessica silently pleads. The couple, now climbing a hillock,
are going to force her hand. *You don't want me to call the* federales. But she
may have to, to save them.

The phone rings and Jessica answers it through her headset. A digital
voice says, "Count backward . . . from one hundred . . . by sixes." It's another random check to make sure she's not snoozing on the job.

Jessica responds, "Ninety-four, eighty-eight, eighty-two, seventy—"

"Thank you." The robotic call disconnects.

Though Colonel Voigt recommended her for this position, he would
hardly approve of the corporate efficiency. At least two people were responsible for flying any single Air Force drone, but here, in a windowless
Tucson warehouse, Jessica is left alone for hours at a stretch monitoring a
retrofitted Predator while it tracks the Sonoran Desert. True, the vehicle
is smart enough to pilot itself home if she drops dead at the stick. The
thing's image-deciphering algorithms will even tell her when there's suspect activity on the ground. So mostly Jessica babysits. She suspects the

main reason Defense of America, Inc., hired someone with her experience was because its government contract required it.

Atop the hillock the couple stops to scan the horizon. They are in a basin surrounded by distant ridges and their options are nil. Just from being where they are tells Jessica a little about them. They are poorer or more hurried or more inexperienced than the usual illegal. She knows this because they did not hire a good *coyote*, if there is such a thing. Theirs didn't even escort them to within sight of a road, wasn't going to risk patrolled land, had merely got them past a remote part of the border fence and dumped them in the desert. They probably hired the first border rat they met in Nogales.

The woman, shading her eyes with a hand, begins to turn slowly around. Jessica targets her with the drone's camera and zooms. Through heat waves rippling off the sand she sees why the woman could not wait another day to immigrate. Her stomach is bulging; she's trying to get into the States to give birth to an American citizen. But if the Border Patrol catches her before this happens, they likely will expedite her deportation.

"For the kid's sake, turn around," Jessica whispers at the man, who has started to slog down the desert side of the rise.

Yet he has just resolved Jessica's conflict. Now she has no choice but to have the two immigrants picked up. She will execute her job to the letter—as Voigt guaranteed she would four months ago.

"Bar none, Aldridge here is one of the best UAV operators around," he had told the group from DoA, Inc. They were the reason he had flown her back to Reeger on that transport. And a day after that Jessica was traveling down to Phoenix to see about their job offer. She was nearly sidelined by her interviewer's first question.

"Why did you leave the Air Force?"

"Family matter," she'd said.

"That has to do with letters to your father in prison."

"Yes."

"Much of your job will be to watch for Mexican cartel activity. As such, you're prohibited from associating, communicating, with anyone who has a record of drug offenses. Your father, for example. Can you agree to this?"

Jessica took a moment. Then she nodded.

Later she would worry less about being fired than about disappointing Voigt. Would the colonel consider her disloyal if he knew about her word-less cactus postcard to Don?

Back in the now, Jessica is circling her drone a mile above the couple. The man waves at the pregnant woman to follow him deeper into the desert and Jessica opens a pop-up window on her screen to copy their coordinates into an email to the Border Patrol in Tucson. They will for-ward the location and coded explanation—probably a 10-60 and a 10-11, meaning "sensor hit" and "investigate subject"—down to their Border Patrol's Ajo station. DoA has yet to work out a better system. Never-theless, if Jessica hits Send, a mobile border agent will likely contact her and she'll assist him with real-time coordinates the way she did ground troops in Kandahar. With luck she will get a military vet who knows his nine o'clock from his three o'clock and the intercept will be clean. Or maybe the CBP won't have the resources to send anyone out today, or even tomorrow, and the couple will end up as bones in the desert.

Jessica enacts in her mind a best-case scenario: the couple's future capture—their hearing an engine, their taking cover in the scrub, their slumped posture after Jessica leads the border agent's vehicle to the cou-ple's hiding place—and she hesitates. She always hesitates now before pulling any such life-changing trigger. She no longer even pretends to be a dispassionate operator executing orders. And then, from her eye in the sky, Jessica watches the woman stubbornly refuse to follow her partner's disastrous course into the wasteland.

Jessica is transfixed. She does not believe in telepathy, yet the woman—unlike the men she had targeted in Somalia—seems to have heard her thoughts. At her insistence, the couple has turned west and after ten minutes has come upon and are now following an animal path through a shaded arroyo. The gulch leads to an old jacal—a mud shelter that, over the past months, Jessica has seen used as an end point by desert hikers. She hopes the couple will find there some bottled water and, possibly, dehydrated food.

And then, behind her, the warehouse door swings open. Dry heat presses in and Jessica turns to see, early for his shift, Bob Sanders. Pasty and sweating through his dress shirt, he shakes his head at Jessica and his chins follow. "Hellhole hot out there, Sergeant," Sanders says and shuts the door.

"Airman," Jessica replies. Using their old titles seems to keep Bob's spirits up, though for Jessica the nostalgia is tolerable perhaps once a day. She turns from Sanders to refocus on the UAV's controls.

"Action on the ground?" he asks.

By now her couple is off the monitor. Jessica is banking the Predator toward where it's supposed to be, forty miles southeast, between Organ Pipe and the border. "I spotted a couple near the jacal . . . hiking."

"Friggin' socialist yuppie sport," Bob says.

As well for old times' sake, to show her old friend solidarity, she doubles down on his hiking crack. "Right. If it was a real sport they'd show it on TV."

"Amen the NFL," Sanders says, putting his hand over his heart. Then, hovering by Jessica's shoulder, he scans the UAV display. "You sure those hikers aren't smugglers?"

"They weren't backpacking marijuana bales as far as I could tell. Might have been illegals though. Maybe I should do another flyby?"

Sanders stretches his chins toward the instrument readouts. "For two strawberry pickers? Nah. Save the fuel."

Sanders goes off to raid the coffee cake in the fridge, not asking if Jessica wants any because they are prohibited from snacking at the controls. But ten minutes later, after slapping the crumbs from his hands, Bob sidles up again close to Jessica's shoulder and looks at the monotonous yellow-brown expanse of desert discoloring the monitor. "Ready when you are," he says.

Jessica unhooks the headset and stands away from the driver's seat.

When Bob's settled in, she asks, "Mind if I borrow your jeep?"

SAHIRA. AZHAAR. THE names of the village girls, fourteen and fifteen, vaporized in a heat blur twenty seconds after she obeyed Voigt's order. What she believed then, what she *needed* to believe, was that the colonel was carrying the burden of conscience for their deaths. But the burden was hers . . . and it still is even if she no longer pilots vehicles that can

launch missiles. When Voigt finally gave her their names he must have
been hoping Jessica would be able to forget them. Sahira. Azhaar. But she
hasn't. She won't.

Sanders' GPS turns her off El Camino del Diablo, the Devil's Road,
which is less a road than a worn groove in the desert. Jessica is traveling
over open country as the crow flies, or trying to. The ancient jeep doesn't
have power steering, and the soft sand and sagebrush are giving her arms
a workout. Ahead the sun is dipping toward the horizon and—according
to her coordinates—she is not a mile from the jacal. Her immigrants will
be there. They *must* be there. For if not, she knows what will happen next.
She will drive circles through the night until she finds her couple. And
find them, she will.

ACKNOWLEDGMENTS

Thank you: Barbara Kingsolver, Kathy Pories,
Terry McMillan, Nancy Pearl, Sam Stoloff, everyone
at PEN American Center, Algonquin Books,
and Workman Publishing.

And also: Sondra Arkin, who never wavers in her support
of my writing and always gives me the space in which to do it.

- - - - - - - - - -